Last Star of the Morning

Claire L. Wilkinson

Claire L. Wilkinson

Last Star of the Morning

Independently Published 2021

Amazon Publishing

Copyright © Claire L. Wilkinson 2021

The right of Claire L. Wilkinson to be identified as the author of this work has been asserted by her in accordance with the Copyright, Designs and Patents Act 1988

All rights reserved. No part of this publication may be reproduced, stored in or introduced into a retrieval system, or transmitted, in any form, or by any means (electronic, mechanical, photocopying, recording or otherwise) without prior written permission of the publisher.

Any person who does any unauthorised act in relation to this publication may be liable to criminal prosecution and civil claims for damage.

Chapter One

A long long time ago, just over 2000 years to be exact, a baby was born under the northern star. It was a beautiful night, the world was at peace and everyone celebrated the glory of his birth. They walked for miles to bring him gifts, the angels sang about him, people came from all around just to have a first glimpse at the future saviour of the world and the Holy son of God... Of course, everyone forgets that he wasn't the only baby born that night. I bet there were thousands of babies born all around the world that exact same day. It was just my bastard bad luck that I had to be one of them. That good old little baby Jesus stole my thunder, took away my shine and no one even realised that I had come into the world... not surprising really considering how the rest of my life turned out.

My father was not the Almighty God, so at least I can be thankful of that, I did not have to go and get myself killed or crucified just to prove to the human world that faith existed. What kind of father would let their child die just to make themselves look good to the human race? Although, my sweet daddy dearest was not all that perfect himself, far from it, in fact.

My father is the Devil. No, I am not exaggerating by saying he is evil, I mean the actual real life big guy with horns, kind of Devil. The exact same one that started out life as one of God's angels then fell from grace and landed in the fiery depths of Hell where he was made to spend his exile from Heaven for the rest of eternity, or so the stories say. There are a lot of variations on that so I learned pretty quickly to take everything I heard with a pinch of salt, especially when it comes from a demon's mouth. Anyway, he became the ruler of Hell and when he eventually had children of his own they became what people aptly named as the Sins, all seven of the Sins are feared, worshipped, and sought after... However, I was born unlucky number eight so I didn't get a snazzy job title or a cool Sin to call my own, I was more of the runt or black sheep of that very dysfunctional family. Sure, growing up in Hell sounds like it would be nothing but fun and everlasting parties, but I didn't really have any friends, so it was quite lame to throw a party just for one. It is not like there is a Devil child school to go to or anything, no little Anti-Christ play dates for me, just lots of free time, hanging around with demons and shit. Although some of them do have some pretty cool stories to tell, the majority of the higher level demons around Hell started out life as angels just like my father and most of them have egos bigger than a small country. They all went against Gods rules when they followed my father then forfeited their wings, and fell from grace, whatever the fuck grace means. I just think it's fluffy clouds and people in white dresses playing the harp... totally boring, so boring in fact that I have no idea why anyone would voluntarily want to go up to that heavenly place and spend the rest of existence trying to please an invisible old man in sandals.

My brothers and sisters are all sociable, well-liked lazy pieces of shit. No wonder they are the Sins incarnate, they live up to their names on a daily basis because they suck big time. They just got handed lives where they could do fuck all and still tempt human souls enough for them to end up in Hell. Father loved them for it, they brought him new souls to torture for all eternity and they didn't even have to lift a finger to do it. In my experience, I have found humans are too easy to tempt anyway, they lack willpower and dedication, are weak and easily led. No wonder Earth is going to shit all around them, one day very soon they might be faced with imminent death and every one of them will deserve it all.

Growing up as an outsider, I felt like an embarrassment to the family, I was a no-one compared to all of them, I couldn't make my father happy, they were handed fame and followers from the day they were born. I was handed nothing but a name and was forgotten about. I didn't even have a mother to look up to or care for me as we were all raised by my father's minions in Hell. All of my father's children were born to different mothers, each one a mortal in the human world who personified the Sins that they created. So even if I did know my mother, she would be long dead now anyway and she was clearly not even worthy enough to give me a title like my siblings.

I couldn't make anyone happy in Hell, even myself, so I kept my head down and worked hard instead. I wanted to prove to myself that I could do more with my life than my siblings ever could, so I left my home and my shitty little bedroom, the family that acted like I did not even exist and the castle where my father's throne sat, I kept my identity secret from everyone outside of the family, and started from the very bottom.

I wanted to better myself, to do something for me for a change so I started small and worked down in the pit, gaining experience and knowledge, mostly about torturing techniques, but I have to admit it was quite interesting, so many fucked up human brains to play with, and the screaming... oh, I did enjoy it, I would be lying if I said I did not, all be it had very long hours... hundreds of years in fact, until one day I worked my way up the ranks high enough to became one of the most powerful soul reapers that ever existed. Then, as if things could not get any better for me, I was handed the honour of Keeper of the Veil, watcher of the night. Protector of the last unseen shroud between our world and the human world, and I guarded the Veil for centuries... I slaughtered all who dared to challenge me, just my name brought fear in to the very hearts of my enemies before I ripped them out, which I have done on several occasions with my bare hands, there was not a single person who could get the better of me and for that I knew the Veil was secure, I was the single most important being in the universe at the time because I knew that there were no better hands for it to be in than my own... I was utterly amazing. If my stupid Sin siblings could have seen how powerful I had become they would shit themselves. But after a while, I realised that no matter how much I worked or what I did, no one would ever give me any sort of recognition as they didn't even know who I truly was. I never told anyone my true name and my family eventually forgot I had even been born. It's been many years since I saw any of the Sins or my father, so as time passed I found myself wanting more from my life, wanting more for me, eventually, I decided to take a break, no one would miss me after all. I had worked my ass off from the day I was born, and I wanted a change, to experience the mortal world for once. I stepped down from my position that guarded the Veil and disappeared, my aim to blend in with the humans so that anyone I ever knew could forget about me.

That was 157 years ago and life has been good ever since...

"Do you ever just sit and wish a new plague would come along and wipe all of the arseholes off the planet?" Lily says, surprisingly deadly serious as she leans on the counter top. She has been staring daggers at the group of young men who are sat over the far side, by the window for the past few minutes. It is the kind of look that could kill if only she had the power to do it.

The coffee shop has been quite quiet today, not that I minded much. Unlike most other small businesses I don't really rely on the income generated by having actual real life customers that spend their hard earned cash on my offerings. I am already extremely wealthy and could easily disappear then live on a tropical island somewhere if I so desired, but I like my little coffee shop, it makes me feel like a valued part of the human world.

There is nothing better some days than people watching. Seeing them come in to take a break and grab a drink, makes me wonder what kind of lives they lead and what brought them to my counter that day. But today there has not been too many of them to watch. It has been snowing for a while, not heavy enough to make everyone stay in their own homes but enough to slow the street down. They are only still passing at this time of night because of the late shopping hours in the complex near by on the run up to Christmas. It got dark hours ago but we are always open way after everyone else has left the area, and the regulars like to stop by when everyone else has gone. I like working here, I could just pay my staff to do it for me, hire a manager and fuck off, but when you find something you love, you don't want to leave... even if the customers are arseholes.

"What kind of thing are you thinking about? The plague would have to be quite specific, but I guess with the right preparation it is doable... then again how would you define which ones are arseholes and totally worthy of such a plague?" I reply quite casually. "Is there a arsholeness scale? Kind of like, the higher you score the more painful the death?" Lily glances across at me then laughs at my very dry statement before picking up her empty tray.

"For now, just that table will do," she smiles. "Christmas always brings out the idiots around here." She puts on her best fake smile then goes to head over to the table with the young men sat around it to collect their empty coffee cups, but I stop her, after all, it is nearly Christmas and I suppose being nice to my staff brings a little Christmas cheer.

"Let me," I say quickly and take the tray off her. I do feel a little sorry for her sometimes, she is a very attractive young woman and seems to get a lot of unwanted attention, especially from the men. Her large breasts and fondness for tight skirts do not help the matter, but as I keep telling her, it is her body, she can dress how she wants as long as she is in uniform and has good customer service when she is at work then I don't care. However, if anyone over steps the line, I immediately bring out my boss lady voice, which I do several times a week when horny scummy teenagers spot a busty blond as they walk past. Not that Lily cannot handle herself, her quick comebacks are one of the things that made me hire her, her lack of experience was not an issue when I felt drawn to the feisty attitude that lay inside. "Are you guys all done?" I ask them casually as I start to collect the several empty cups and cake wrappers from the table. There are four of them, all dressed in what I can only describe as a terrible fashion sense for the youth of today, baggy sportswear that hangs off their arse, with so many stripes and ticks that you get a migraine just from looking at it... Oh, late Victorian fashion, now there was a look. I was a bit partial to a bustle skirt and corset, although I was also quite fond of the 1920s, the look of a real gangster, someone who oozed charisma, people used to know how to dress to impress back then, now most of them just look like fools.

"Do the carpets match the drapes?" One of the young guys laughs at his own question as his friends giggle along. Over the years I must have been asked that question a thousand times, one of these days I might actually hear something new that would surprise me. They all look early 20's, clearly very immature for their ages, I do not even remember being only 20, but I am sure I was not a complete waste of space like these guys.

"Unfortunately, that is not something that someone like you will ever have the privilege to find out," I smile back as I pick up the few empty sugar packets they have left on the table that have annoyingly been ripped up in to tiny little squares and scattered all over.

"Is it true that your kind don't have souls?" another says. I can't help but smile more at that one, his question is quite amusing to me. If only he truly knew who he was talking to right now, but to him it is all just a silly joke because of the colour of my hair.

"Ha ha, very funny," I reply sarcastically. "Maybe it is time you guys... leave," my words are firm, giving emphasis to the word "leave" and for a moment all four of them just stare blankly at me, taking in what I have said, processing the command I have given them in silence. After a short pause they all nod as one, and get up to leave. "Oh, and it is nearly Christmas. Don't forget to leave a tip, a very sizeable one for the inconvenience you caused to my staff with your unwanted adolescent attitudes." Again they pause, then simultaneously take out their wallets and place several notes down in front of me before leaving without saying another word. Taking a moment to wipe the table over with a cloth, I try to hide my feelings of power before composing myself, to the outside world, I am just another human, inside though, I am probably the furthest you could ever get. "It is getting late," I say calmly to Lily as I head back over to the counter with the empty cups and rubbish. "Why don't you get off home, I can lock up fine by myself."

"It is OK, to be perfectly honest I could really do with the extra cash, so I would rather stay and work my full shift," she replies. There is no one else in at the moment, those young guys were the only customers we had in over the last 90 minutes and I do not fancy standing around for the next couple of hours until I close, trying to make small talk with her when there are no customers to focus on. It is not that I dislike her, it is more to do with having nothing in common and there is only so many times I can listen to her talk about reality TV's celebrity gossip and pretend to be interested in the lives of rich people who get handed wealth without any real talent. I don't particularly like pushing people to do things against their will, especially not in the open like this, but sometimes it is just the easier option, plus some humans can be so clingy, they create bonds with each other and the majority of them have a distinct smell of failure that lingers on their essence, that always gives me a headache after a while. I place the money that the men left as I tip, down on the counter and Lily's eyes widen. The cash they left is more than she is paid for her full shift, so I just smile and push it towards her before speaking again.

"Lily... go home," my voice is gentle as I use my persuasion on her. It comes in very handy against humans and because of who I used to be, it works quite well on most other lesser beings as well. Lily stands silent for a moment as she takes in my words, letting them go deep, then just like the young men did when I did this to them, the words hit her and she smiles.

"You know what, maybe I will go home, if that is alright with you?" she asks. "The place is dead and I hate to leave you by yourself, but I could do with an early night, plus this tip they left will come in really handy."

"Sure, I will manage fine by myself. I am only expecting Fred and the gang to stop by as they pop in for their free coffee and cake," I reply casually as I move the tray then start putting the cups in the under counter dishwasher to clean up.

"Awesome, thank you. I promise I will make up my hours some other day," Lily takes off her apron and places it on the hook on the back wall before grabbing her coat from the rack and swiftly leaving me alone to enjoy the silence.

My shop is cosy, small enough that it doesn't take much upkeep, and a lot of the time people walk straight past as they do not even notice it anyway, but to me it is my home. The entire back wall is covered with different coffee beans from all over the world, most of them I hand picked whilst travelling, I have pretty much seen all the wonders that this world has to offer now, but I will never get bored of its beauty. The counter top is made from reclaimed wood that is hundreds of years old and the seating area is only big enough for around 30 people to sit in at any one time, large comfy chairs and sofas are dotted around, it is nice, and it is my happy place.

I potter on for a bit, rearrange some of the shelves to pass an hour or so then glance at the time, it has just gone 9pm and I am a little bored, this is usually as eventful as my days now get. Not that I mind too much any more, it is nice to have a relaxing retirement, right? Pretty soon the local homeless men will come by for their free stuff, I have been giving out coffee and cake, blankets and clothing for the last few years. I do what I can, they are nice gentlemen and do not deserve the harsher side that the human world has to offer sometimes. The small bell above the door chimes and I instinctively glance over and smile, thinking it is my usual late night visitors, but I end up giving my best customer service appearance for a young guy, possibly late 20's as he hovers by the entrance whilst looking around, slightly uncertain of himself.

"I'm sorry, I didn't realise that you might be closed," he says to me as I stand behind the counter and put some cups away. "I just saw the light was on and I was getting freezing cold standing outside across the way there, I have been debating about coming over to get warm for ages but I guess I left it a little late... I will go, sorry to disturb you," he laughs at himself then turns to leave.

"It's alright," I call after him, stopping him in his tracks. "I am still open for another hour. The damn snow is keeping everyone away so it has been a bit quieter than usual today. Why don't you take a seat and I'll sort something out to warm you up." The young guy smiles gratefully and closes the door behind him before wandering over to a small table to the side wall. Even though I can see him shivering with the cold, he takes off his bulky winter coat and drapes it over the back of his chair, before he sits down near a radiator and looks around at the old fashioned décor, then to the wall of coffee behind me.

"Are you always open so late?" he asks me casually, trying to make polite conversation as I head over to him.

"Most nights, yes," I reply. "Although when it gets to this time of year things start to get a little slower." He picks up the menu off the table as I speak so he can look at it, browsing the information on the different drink selections and snacks. I wait patiently for him to read as I watch him, he has cute eyes, sort of icy blue in colour and he wears a very plain black shirt over his dark jeans. He looks like the athletic type, probably works out quite a lot from the way the jeans hug his thighs... no wedding ring that I can see. I wonder what brings him here tonight, and why he said he was stood outside for so long. Maybe meeting someone? A date that has not shown up possibly.

"What do you recommend?" he asks then looks up at me and smiles kindly. I can't help but smile back, he is actually alright looking, and I don't think I have seen him around here before, I am usually quite good at remembering faces.

"All depends on what you are in the mood for," I reply with an unintentional hint of flirting, but he smiles at the comment as he notices the playful tone. I clear my throat slightly and continue in a more professional manner. "But the Sulawesi Toraja beans from Indonesia are a particular favourite of mine at the minute." He thinks for a moment before nodding his head.

"Sounds good. I guess anyone who works in a shop with that many varieties of coffee on display must know their beans," he forces a smile this time then takes his phone from his pocket to check the time. He seems distracted by his own thoughts so I leave him be whilst I go and brew his coffee. The snow is starting to fall a little heavier outside and as he sits silently waiting for his drink I notice he has no shopping bags or anything, usually the only ones still out and about this late are getting Christmas presents, and it is not the kind of area you just go for a stroll around at night. The bell above the door chimes again making me refocus and I smile as Fred comes in with a couple of his friends.

"Good evening, Rosa," he beams as they head over towards the counter. "You are looking lovely this evening."

"You are such a sweet talker," I laugh in response. Him and his friends must be at least in their 50's, due to various circumstances they do not have full time homes, mostly living on the streets. I have tried in the past to get Fred in to a flat or rented accommodation but he is too proud to accept that sort of help, it breaks my heart sometimes to see such good men in such difficult positions... And then sometimes I wonder if I am going soft in my old age by being surrounded by humans all the time. A couple of hundred years ago, I wouldn't have given a shit at all, probably would have enjoyed torturing them if they ended up in my corner of the pit, I didn't chose which souls went to Hell, I just dealt with them according to my job title once they arrived. "Give me one minute whilst I serve this young gentleman his coffee and I will be right with you." I pick up the fresh brew and take it over to the table, the young guy is still checking his phone and seems a little uneasy as his eyes keep watching the door.

"Thank you," he smiles up at me as soon as I place it down. I just nod then head back over to the counter to sort Fred and his friends some warm drinks to take away.

"It looks like you guys have hit the jackpot today," I say as I start taking some of the sweet pastries and cakes out of the display cabinet on the counter and put them in to bags. "With it not being too busy I have a load of stuff left over so you guys may as well make use of it. A nice little sugary feast for you."

"Rosa, you are an angel," Fred smiles. I am a lot of things, but an angel is not one of them, not even close. And from what I have heard about angels, I don't think I would want to be one of them at all. I spend a little time making up a few takeaway hot drinks before the men say their thanks and leave me to close up, which I usually start to do when they have been as it signals the end of my day. The young guy is still here and he has not even touched his coffee to have a sip which has me intrigued, there is more to him than meets the eye, I can feel it deep in my bones.

"Hey," I say cautiously as I walk over to see if everything is OK. "Is there something wrong with the coffee, I know it may not be to everyone's taste, it is quite a strong blend so if I can get you something else instead..."

"No, sorry," he laughs at himself then picks up the cup and takes a sip. "I am totally in a world of my own... Oh, that is really good actually," he smiles then takes another drink. I do debate about just leaving him to enjoy it and starting my close down but he is slightly intriguing to me, I just don't know what it is about him, but I am drawn to him.

"You are not from around here, are you?" I inquire but he forces a smile then continues to sip the coffee, avoiding having to answer my question. He has peeked my interest, so I give him a little push instead. "What brings you along this way?"

"I was sent to meet someone in this area a little while ago, then I came in here out of the cold. They didn't turn up or maybe I was in the wrong place, it's stupid really, I don't know what I am doing here, or even who I am supposed to meet, he never gave me all of the details, just said I needed to..." he stops himself from speaking as though he is not sure why he told me all of that. "Sorry, you didn't need to know that," he shakes his head and rubs his face in frustration, clearly confused as to why he let slip what he was doing in this area to a random stranger that he has never met before. "It has been a long day, I should get out of your hair and let you close up... Thank you for the coffee," he says then places some money down on the table before standing and picking up his coat. He seems a little uncomfortable by telling me that so I do not push him further, my curiosity will have to be left wanting. The bell above the door chimes again as I pick the money up from the table then head over to place it in the till. Standing by the door this time are three men, I can't help but notice that they look a little shady as they glance around the coffee shop, not heading to the counter or to sit down, but instead they watch the young guy put on his coat with great interest and check to

10

see who else is here, but there is only me, an innocent looking woman in a coffee apron.

"Can I help you guys?" I ask loudly in my most friendliest of voices as I stare at them, but they do not even look over to me, almost as though I do not exist in their little world right now. Cautiously, I head out from behind the counter and start to walk towards them, I am getting a pretty bad vibe from their little group, almost like a dark echo from their aura, not the kind of thing I would normally feel from people in this area, which is one of the many reasons I chose to settle here and make this city my home. "I am so sorry, I am just closing up so I am going to have to ask you to leave." Again they ignore me completely. The young guy stands still for a moment as though he is debating what to do, he looks between the men and the door then cautiously glances towards me as though he knows that danger is imminent, does he know these people? Because they really do not look like his friends. I casually wander over and purposefully stop in front of the three men, so that I am currently standing between them and the young guy, they are pretty big, kind of brutish looking, they do not look friendly in the slightest. Not the usual late night customers that I am now used to. "Hi," I wave my hand in front of their faces slightly and smile, trying to draw their attention or at the very least make it seem like I actually do exist to them. "I said I am closing up the shop now so unfortunately you will have to leave. I am open again first thing in the morning, at which time I will be more than happy to offer you a coffee on the house for the inconvenience of turning you away tonight." The largest of the three men turns his head and stares at me, the kind of stare that says "who the fuck does she think she is speaking to" then slowly looks me up and down before he smirks. I truly do detest that look. The look that someone gives me when they just see what is on the outside and has no idea who I actually am. I am average height, possibly a little more well toned than most of the pretty girls around here, as I used to work out quite a lot back in the day so I wouldn't exactly say I was petite, but the way he is looking at me, as though I am a small insignificant woman to him just makes me want to smile. My long multi-toned auburn hair is tied up in a high pony tail and finished with a black ribbon and bow, quite smart though to go with the casual uniform of black fitted t-shirt and figure hugging denim jeans that I am wearing, plus the cute blue and white coffee house apron that I wear around my waist really makes me look like nothing that could be even considered as threatening... especially not when I am compared to the size of them. To the outside world, I probably look in my mid to late 20's, I have gray-blue eyes and a pretty nice figure, curves in all the right places if you know what I mean, and I am very appealing when I dress more sexy or make a bit of an effort.

"I don't think we will be going anywhere just yet, Princess," the big brute smirks down at me then looks over to the young guy again. I fucking hate when people call me Princess, the word is associated with some innocent damsel who gets constantly saved by her Prince Charming, and I sure as Hell do not need a Prince Charming in my life at all, nor do I need my cute ass saving. I can see fear and uncertainty on the young guys face just by having these men in front of him, this all stinks of trouble and that is one thing I have successfully managed to avoid for many years now. A coffee shop is not the place that attracts trouble, but I am not going to stand by and let things get out of hand if anything was to happen, especially in here, this is my happy place. "We have been following you for a while. The boss thinks you are getting too close and he sent us to warn you to back the fuck off before you get yourself in to some deep shit that you have no idea about." I now have no clue what is going on but I do not move from my position that is right in front of him, if they start anything in my shop and break as much as a cup, I swear I will end them.

"Then if your boss thinks that I am getting too close, there is no way I am stopping now," the young guy replies with a surprising strength in his voice. "It just lets me know I am heading in the right direction and that he definitely has answers that I want." The brute laughs at his words before glancing to the two men with him.

"Does it look like we are just going to let you walk out of here. You only get one warning and that was it, Smokey. If you don't back off now and leave the city tonight then you might find yourself dead in a ditch somewhere by sunrise tomorrow," the brute smiles at the young guy as he waits for a reply. The entire shop falls silent whilst the tension grows, and I categorically know that I am not having them cause issues in my shop. Whatever is going on, I am bringing a stop to it right now.

"So..." I say loudly to cut through the uncomfortable feeling as I know I need to get them to leave, a little persuasion might do the trick. "You guys should all leave now. Whatever you were hoping to achieve here tonight... it was a bust. Go home, fuck your wife if you have one and then forget you were ever here." I know I said it loudly enough for them all to hear but they stand watching me for slightly too long that it makes me feel a little awkward for a moment before the two smaller guys nod their heads simultaneously and start to head for the door, doing as I told them to do. Quickly, the big brute in the middle grabs one of their arms stopping them from walking away and snapping them out of my commands.

"Where do you think you are going?" he asks them confused as to why they have just turned around to leave after being told to do so by a worthless woman. "We have a job to do and we are not going anywhere without getting answers, either that or we make him disappear." I take a long deep breath and process what has just happened. My usual persuasion works on pretty much every human, or at least all of those who are lacking unending faith in the Almighty God, but it didn't work on the brute, not even a slight flicker. He certainly does not look as though he is the bible reading type.

"Who do you work for?" the young guy asks, trying to show his confidence. "If your boss wants me dead for trying to find out the truth then I would very much like to know who he is and exactly where I can find him." The brute laughs again then casually pulls a gun out from the back of his jeans and takes off the safety as the other two guys ready their stance for a fight. The one on the left is the smallest of the three, looks a little unsure of himself in the current situation but holds firm. The one of the right looks shady as shit, tattoos across the side of his head and seems like he knows what the inside of a jail cell looks like from personal experience. All of this tells me that I should just walk away, slip out the back door and let them all kill each other whilst I ring the police... but there is something about the young guy that makes me what to know more, and I am not sure what it is just yet. It is a strange feeling, like I need to learn everything I can about him, who he is, where he comes from, what his favourite type of dog is, why the fuck he ended up in my coffee shop, but I don't know why.

"Everyone needs to calm down," I try to diffuse the situation. "Please take your disagreement outside and..." my words stop abruptly as the big brute lifts the gun he is holding in his hand and points it directly at the centre of my face without any emotion or thought about his actions.

"Let the big boys talk, Princess," he glares at me with a look of pure evil in his eye. "This has nothing to do with you, so I suggest you shut your pretty little mouth and do exactly what we say. Because right now, the only thing standing between you and a bullet in your brain is this kid, and if he doesn't cooperate either then I will kill you just for the fun of it... And I do very much love to have fun." I have to really force myself not to laugh at him so I bite the inside of my cheek to keep from smiling, I need to be serious, act mortal and scared so they don't find out who I am. The world right now is not a safe place for those people who are different. But I can't remember the last time I was in a sort of life or death situation, and honestly, the thrill of it is quite amusing.

"You don't have to involve the girl," the young guy says quickly then goes to step forward to try to help me but the brute moves and pushes the barrel of the gun firm against the skin on my forehead, forcing my head back slightly as I stand frozen on the spot, making the kid instantly stop in his tracks. I stand as still as possible, my arms up at the sides sightly to show that I am no threat to him, because obviously getting shot in the head would not be an ideal outcome for anyone right now, especially not me, as I really do not want to have to scrub my own brain mush out of the carpets in here, they were only deep cleaned a couple of month ago and blood can sometimes be a bastard to bleach out. It stains like a bitch.

"How about we start with something simple, and you tell us who you were meeting this evening then maybe I won't kill this innocent bystander," the brute says as he stares at the young guy. From the way I am standing I cannot see much else apart from the gun in front of my face, but I do notice the other two men also pull out weapons now, following the actions of the brute who is clearly their leader. This is quite the predicament that I have found myself in tonight. I have a very good life, I enjoy what I do, I love my little coffee shop more than anything and the peace is glorious. Yes, I did used to be a bit of a rebel, even when I first came to the human world I mixed with the wrong crowd and got a little bit of a reputation. But now the current look I have going on was done intentionally to blend in, go under everyone's radar and look like just another normal human woman, especially with all the shit that has been going on in the rest of the world over the last few years, rumours of vampires and those other evil monsters that lurk in the shadows have been slipping out, and the humans are starting to believe that they are actually real. I am glad I don't live in the types of shitty countries where not being 100% human can get you killed in a heartbeat, there are too many extremist groups and militia around that incite witch hunts for the smallest of things. So that is why I like to go totally unnoticed and pretend I have no idea about anything, ignorance is bliss... I really do not want to jeopardise the life I now have so I make sure I keep away from all kinds of drama. But if these guys wreck anything in here, I will kill them all without any hesitation.

"I swear to you that I don't know," the young guy replies quickly. "I wasn't told who I was meeting, I don't know who he is at all or anything about him. I just know that they were important, I wasn't told specific details, just to be in this area tonight and I would find what I am looking for."

"Sounds like bull shit to me," the smallest of the three men snaps at the kids statement as he points his gun at him.

"Do you want us to kill this girl?" the brute asks seriously. "See, I didn't think you would be so heartless as to want to watch me murder someone for my own pleasure. Especially not this innocent little girl. Her death would be on your conscience forever, is that what you really want to happen? You will have to live with the fact that you were responsible for her losing her life... or at least until we kill you also."

"I swear that I am telling you the truth," the young guy's voice shakes now, clearly starting to realise that he has very few options left. "I just met this weird guy, it took me months to even find him. He spoke a load of bollocks I swear, kept talking about demons and that the rising was coming, but I don't know what that is, that is all he said... please, just let the girl go, she is innocent and does not deserve to get hurt, you said it yourself, she has nothing to do with this. I told you what you wanted." The brute watches him with great interest for a moment as I just stand silent and come to terms with the fact that they are discussing demons very openly in my coffee shop... Fucking demons? Most of them are the plight of existence, they have Napoleon complexes where they all think that they are the best thing since sliced bread. Fucking arseholes, the lot of them. Yes, I know, technically I grew up and worked with them and sort of am one, but I am still allowed to have my own opinions, why do you think I left Hell and got away from it all? And the fact he just mentioned the rising?... I remember being told stories about that by my father when I was a child, but that is all it was, just stories told to scare me because that bollocks isn't real. It is the Hell equivalent of a fairy story.

"You humans are all the same, you just don't know when to walk away with your mortal lives," the brute smirks, and I sigh very deeply at his last statement. Fuck sake, he isn't human, that is why I couldn't push him to leave. I was only using a small fraction of my power, over the years I got used to just using it on humans and never even considered the possibility that they were anything but. Fuck! I should have pushed him harder. I should have known by the unnaturally strong smell coming off him, almost as though his true self has been tainted by the mortal world and it covers his aura. This is stupid though, demons do not get involved with the human realm like this, especially since evidence of the existence of supernatural beings started to hit some other parts of the world. Thankfully where I live, people are smart and laid back, they keep their heads down and go unnoticed. They do not start wars, they do not admit to being a none human on live TV and they especially do not go around threatening to kill humans in front of other people for no reason. As much as demons are all massive cunts, they know categorically how to keep a low profile. You won't find a demon making headlines. There is something more going on here, and as much as I would like to know what it is, I really can't get involved. I have been very good at hiding and keeping who I really am a secret, I am retired for fuck sake. I am way to old for any of this shit.

"You are one of them, aren't you?" the young guy asks which makes the brute smile more as though answering his question. "I won't stop until I find out the truth. I made a promise that I would never back down, so you are not going to intimidate me, I will not let your kind walk all over me again. Whatever is happening with the world, I swear I will stop it. I must have gotten this far already for a reason."

"Too bad that you will be dead before you can go any further," the brute replies then swiftly aims his gun at the young guy instead of me, ready to shoot him. "You have no place meddling about in our world, you may think you are doing a service to your country whilst trying to keep us in line, but you are just a pest that will quickly be exterminated. I will send my boss your regards."

I know that this is totally none of my business at all, this human kid clearly has some sort of issues going on and found himself having a run in with a demon. That is what you get when you play with things that you have no real life knowledge about, some humans still don't even believe in anything other than themselves, they are deeply in denial, so I am surprised to see one now who is trying to not be intimidated when faced with something supernatural that could probably kill him quite easily even without the gun... I am so confused though, I really feel the need to not have the young guy die in my coffee shop right now, almost as though my entire body and soul is needing to protect him on a much higher level than I currently can understand, but he is no one to me, I have never met him before. As soon as the brute moves the gun away from my head and takes his focus off me, I grab his wrist, push it away, and force it off target, the gunshot rings out, missing the young guy's head by mere inches, then the bullet smashing through a picture on the wall behind him. My face drops in disbelief as I stare at it for a second, the antique frame crashes to the ground and the glass covers the table below where it was, then I slowly turn back to the brute, clearly not amused by his actions at all.

"That picture... That picture was taken in Paris, and has been on that wall for 40 years," I snap then in a split second, punch the brute in the gut before he has a chance to react to my comment, he instantly doubles up in pain from the blow and drops to the ground, gasping for breath. For a demon who thinks he is a big boss man, he isn't very resilient, I didn't even hit him that hard, fucking soft piece of shit that he is. After all, I am still trying to maintain the facade that I am a normal woman who just runs a coffee shop and knows nothing at all about demons or fighting, the total opposite of who I actually am which is why I tried my best to hit him lightly, I held back a little. Both of the other men turn their guns on to me instantly after they see what I did to their leader, but I can also tell by the looks on their faces that they have no clue what to do without his instructions, just two mindless thugs accompanying this douche bag for backup, lost little puppies when not being given orders.

"Don't move," the smallest man says quickly as the brute slowly tries to push himself to his knees so he can get back to his feet.

"You will not shoot anyone here tonight," I say firmly, making them do as I say, and they both stare blankly at me as they take in my persuasion. "Tell me why you are trying to scare away the kid?"

"He is getting too close to the truth," the tattooed thug says instantly without even thinking about it. I sigh with frustration and roll my eyes at his response, that was not what I was hoping for.

"Yeah, I got that bit," I reply sarcastically as the brute groans whilst pushing himself up, he will only get in my way of the questions I want answered so I grab his collar and knee him in the face, sending him back to the ground and keeping him at bay for the moment so I don't have to deal with him as well as his two minions. "The truth to what?" I push for an answer as the young guy cautiously takes a few steps towards us as he realises that they will not attack him and picks up the gun that the brute has dropped, so that he can arm himself and take a few seconds to process what is happening.

"To everything," thug guy replies tome. "The kid has been digging around where he is not wanted, we were told that he was trying to find information on the Veil. We have been following him for weeks and until a few days ago he had no leads on where he needed to go, then he met with someone known as Lucious Monroe and we knew then that he had to be stopped before he got any closer." I pause for a moment and glance around to the young man who is just stood, now aiming the gun back at the two guys, his hands firm but even from here I can see slight fear in his eyes, which is strange because he seems surprisingly strong willed when faced with the prospect of death, almost as though he has already seen it and the end of his own life is not the thing he actually fears. He looks human to me, smells like any other normal human does, he responded very easily to my persuasion and if he was anything but normal then he would not be so uncertain of his actions right now as his eyes keep checking the exit for a way to escape. But then again, why would a human be talking to the very illusive man that I once knew as Monroe or more to the point, why would Monroe be talking to an average basic human?

"You should leave, kid," I say to him and nod towards the door to encourage him to go but he doesn't move. He swallows hard and stands his ground instead, quickly thinking of what to do.

"My name is not kid," he replies abruptly. "It's Jake, and I can't leave, I have been searching for months, this is the closest I have gotten and..."

"Leave!" I push him firmly. "You need to go." He stares at me blankly, then after a moment of silence he nods his head and moves towards the door. As soon as he does my soul seems to relax, as though his safety was my main priority and with him gone everything will be right. Thinking about that is strange, there are some really strong gut feelings about him but I am unsure why, I have never felt that kind of protective connection before and especially never with a human. I am so lost in my own thoughts, contemplating what to do... I haven't heard the name Lucious Monroe for many years, and never has it been uttered in the mortal world that I know of. "Wait," I call out, stopping Jake from leaving. "Why were you talking to Monroe?" He opens his mouth to speak, but quickly stops when the door opens again, causing the little bell to ring and fill the silence. Everyone turns to look as another man who is large, very well built with pure muscle, skin like caramel and sporting a leather biker jacket, just stands in the doorway looking around the room and taking in the clearly tense situation.

"I told you, I didn't need backup," Jake says to the new stranger whilst shaking his head in defiance as the brute finally starts to get back to his feet properly in front of me now that he is no longer dazed.

"Then care to explain what is going on? Because to me it looks like you might need help," the biker guy replies with an accent that could melt butter, he is very easy on the eye and I really wouldn't mind getting to know more about him. I get attracted to people way too easy these days, after living so long, there are some pleasures I will never get board of, and the company of a very attractive soul is extremely appealing... and if he comes as a double package with the kid then that is even better, I am not too fussy... a girl has needs. And this girls needs are never ending.

I was kind of too preoccupied with starring at the hot leather biker guy and thinking of all the nasty things I could do with him, to realise the brute was up on his feet fully and very pissed off with me, and before I know it, I catch the back of his hand right across my face. The force sends me flying across the room, over the counter and crashing in to the wall full of coffee beans, which I then kind of slide down until I am sat a little dazed on the ground behind the till. Multiple glass jars full of beans are smashed around me on the floor, I have broken wood off the shelves sticking uncomfortably in my back and the smell of coffee fills the air, not to mention that I now seem to be covered in a lot of blood. The exposed skin on my arms and chest are cut off the glass, and I can feel it freely flowing out of my now broken nose and down over my chin from a bust lip. I am so fucking angry with myself for getting distracted like that, I knew he was a demon, I know how strong they are compared to humans and I let my guard down. What just happened was my own stupid fault. I moan a bit as I force myself up on to my knees and look over the counter top, I feel like I have broken a few ribs when I hit the shelves behind me, not that it will bother me for long, the cuts on my arms are already healing, and the pain in my face from the blow is down to a dull ache so in a few minutes I will be as right as rain. Although, I haven't been injured in quite a while, I know that a few little cuts and scrapes are pretty much nothing for me to deal with.

Taking in the unfolding scene in my coffee shop, I see that all of the men are now fighting, throwing punches, and smashing my tables. With every piece of furniture that breaks I get more furious with them all. This is not my fight and I do not care who wins or what is going on any more. It is all just a load of testosterone fuelled dickheads that do not give a shit that it is currently my property that they are destroying... Fuck it! I lower myself back down on the floor behind the counter, get comfortable, grab a few bags of crisps from the bottom shelf next to me then sit and eat them whilst I mind my own business.

It is a good 5 minutes before the noise becomes deafening, lots of shouting and screaming then several gun shots ring out... everything falls silent except the sound of me munching on savoy snacks whilst I keep out of the way. My back doesn't even hurt any more, sometimes I wonder how humans manage to live so long with their fragile bodies and bad decisions. A little bit of the sniffles puts a man on his back for a week. Maybe the brute and his two cronies killed the kid and the hot guy, that would be a shame really, but that is what happens when you square up to demons and get yourself involved with things that you have no idea about. Whatever happened though, I am going to guess that I have some serious cleaning up to do, there goes my insurance premiums.

"Hey, are you hurt?" Jake says with panic in his voice as he rushes around the back of the counter, his face is a bloody mess, he looks like he has narrowly escaped a gun shot wound in his arm with a hole through his coat sleeve, but his eyes roam my face with kindness as he crouches down next to me as though his injuries do not matter because he needs to make sure that I am alive. He grabs a cloth from the counter and gently dabs my face to remove some of the blood whilst I casually stuff more crisps in my mouth, not realising that the blood is all that is left as my wounds went away ages ago, I just need a good shower and possibly a drink... something stronger than coffee.

"We need to go," the biker guy says as he looks over the counter towards us. "The last thing we need is your special buddies getting involved, if we leave now then we can be clear of all of this shit without anyone knowing we were even here." I place the now empty bag of crisps down on the floor next to me as Jake shakes his head, thinking quickly of what to do.

"I can't just run, my blood is all over this place, it would be easy to match my DNA and know I was here, and those guys will draw a lot of unwanted attention when people start asking questions, you know that the specialist unit will be involved," he pauses from cleaning my face before taking his phone out of his pocket.

"This is a very bad idea," biker guy sighs then heads back to what I assume to be three dead men. "We need a cover story and fast. This is not going to look good for you at all." Jake takes a long drawn out breath as he thinks about what to do. Just hearing that slight exchange between them both has me intrigued all over again. Who the fuck are they, and what the fuck is going on? I need to know.

"Who were you really meant to meet tonight?" I ask Jake with a little push, and he stops to look at me before he dials his phone. "Monroe is not someone who concerns himself with this world. Who did he send you to find?"

"Monroe didn't tell me, just that I needed to find someone who was very important," he says truthfully, unable to hold back from speaking to me. "They were the Keeper, some sort of a Guardian and he said that they were the only one who could help me get answers." I have no words to respond, my mind is actually blank. There are not many times that I can't think of anything to say, but running through a lot of the key words that have been said tonight, Keeper, Guardian, the Veil, the rising... "Are you OK, Miss?" He asks me extremely concerned. I can't speak or even blink, I just stare at him. Why would Monroe send a human to meet with the Keeper? I left that world over 150 years ago, I wanted to retire and spend my days just chilling out, having wild sex and drinking coffee... How did Monroe even know where to find me?

"I... I erm, I am fine," I force out as I sit trying to figure out what is going on.

"You are not fine, you are bleeding and I need to get you some medical help," Jake says, looking down at the blood where all of the cuts and gashes were, then dials a number on his phone. What is so important about this human that he has demons wanting him dead? And why does any of this have to involve me? If Monroe sent him my way then there is something very bad about to happen, and I seriously do not want to get sucked back into that world. "This is Detective Jake Parker," he says as the call is answered then smiles sweetly at me as I try not to panic. "There has been another incident, it is the same as before, it is not... normal."

Chapter Two

It didn't take long for my shop to be swarming with police, once they were on site, I tried to stay out of the way whilst they dealt with the fact that I had three dead men in the coffee house, and one of them was bleeding thick black blood. A total giveaway sign that he was a upper level demon, I should have noticed sooner when he was being such a dick, I thought I sensed something that was off with him. I did not fancy having to explain that one to the police, so I casually hovered around the till whilst Jake and the hot biker guy handled the situation. I have no idea what they said in regards to the black blood, or in fact why the people who came to investigate the incident did not question it at all, but they all seemed to just get on with the job in hand as though it was a normal every day occurrence to them. Which was strange to say the least, possibly they are part of one of those new special task forces of some kind that deal with supernatural beings, human police that try to act like they understand the hidden world around them.

"Can I ask you some questions, Miss?" a middle aged gentleman in a police uniform asks me. I guess I can not avoid them forever so I just nod in reply.

"You don't need to ask her anything," Jake comes straight over upon hearing the Officer talk to me and tries to interrupt him, clearly concerned by what I may say. "I told the Sargent that I would sort everything out, she didn't see much, I am..."

"Parker!" a stern and very intimidating voice calls over, stopping Jake from saying any more. "I will be taking your statement personally when we clean this mess up, let the Officer do his job and interview the young lady. Unless you have something to hide?" He stares over at us for a few moments before Jake reluctantly shakes his head and glances around to me. I can see it in his eyes that he is afraid of what I will give away, that if I tell them what really happened, it will get him in to a lot of trouble. What is he hiding?

"What would you like to ask me?" I smile at the Officer as Jake nervously stands behind him so that he can hear everything that I say.

"Can you tell me what happened here tonight?" the Officer asks, and I nod in compliance.

"Of course," I begin. "I was close to closing the shop down, the snow has kept a lot of customers away today, when three men came in the front doors. I just thought they were wanting to grab a late night coffee or come in from the cold but they came straight over to the counter and pulled a gun on me, demanding that I open the till and give them all of the money that I had." Jake's face drops when I give the Officer my statement then the biker guy stands next to him with his arms crossed, just silently listening and staring at me, kind of in a judging way as though they can not believe the bullshit that is coming out of my mouth. "I was terrified that they were going to kill me, the biggest one, I think he was the one who was in charge, he told me that he was going to... going to erm... put a bullet in my brain and he didn't care if I lived or died," my voice shakes as I speak, I have amazing acting skills and I pause for a moment as tears fill my eyes just to add to the effect.

"It's alright, Miss, please just take your time," the Officer says gently which makes me smile a little.

"Thank you. The next thing I know one of the smaller men comes running around the counter and tries to push me out of the way. I guess I was taking to long to open the till so he wanted access to it himself, he shoved me and I smashed in to the shelves... I was so scared... I thought I was going to die," I wipe away the tears that are falling down my cheeks, and try so hard to keep my laugh in as I tell a load of lies.

"Do you need medical assistance?" the Officer asks me as he looks over all of the blood up my arms and on my face. My nose pissed with blood, and I know it is still all over my skin off where it just gushed over me.

"No," I say quickly. "I am not hurt. I know I look covered in blood but I assure you it is not what you think it is. It is... red velvet coffee syrup. When I hit the shelf, it smashed a bottle of it and I covered myself in it... See?" I lick my finger and rub the blood off the skin on my arm so that the Officer can see that there are no wounds underneath. Nothing to indicate that I had been injured or bleeding at all, and nothing to give any signs that I am not human. "I am fine, honestly, I am actually very lucky in the fact that these two amazingly fearless gentlemen were passing in the street," I smirk at Jake and biker guy. I catch the mystery man's eye for a moment and he just scowls at me with disapproval. "They must have seen the commotion and came running in to help me without a thought for their own safety. They could have been killed, I am so grateful to them both, they are true heroes."

"Parker? A hero?" the Sargent scoffs. He must have been listening as well, probably very interested to get an account of this evenings activities from an innocent third party. "That is the last thing I would call one of my detectives that had been on extended leave due to an incident whilst on suspension. The special task force was formed to eradicate incidents like this, we need to keep the peace and prove that we are better than that kind of scum, but yet they just keep following you around. This mess has you written all over it, Parker. In fact, just knowing you were here will finally give me a reason to take your badge for good. You will not work a day in your life again, after this. This kind of thing seems to be attracted to you like flies on shit." I turn to look at him and smile slightly. He seems like he could cause more trouble if they do not believe my story so I need to give him a nudge, humans are far too easy to manipulate, kind of makes me feel sorry for them sometimes. Plus, Jake mentioned Monroe and that has to mean something, especially when the Keeper was talked about in the same sentence.

"Yes," I say as I stare at the Sargent. The Officer who had been interviewing me steps away leaving the four of us alone so I take my chance and say what I need to whilst the rest of the men in the shop do not over hear. "That man is a hero. I do not know what he has been involved with in the past but he saved my life tonight, and after hearing my statement you don't need to question him further. He is not of your concern any more. He is to be praised, not punished, and you will back the fuck off and leave him alone." There is an extended silence whilst I pray he takes to my persuasion before he nods his head.

"It looks like you were in the right place at the right time, Parker," the Sargent smiles then slaps Jake on the back to congratulate him before waving the Officer that just took my statement back over. "Probably a good thing that this happened, one less of those evil bastards on the streets. I am going to head back to the station, I don't need any follow up from Detective Parker so make sure this ladies details are recorded." The Officer nods and smiles towards me as the Sargent turns back to Jake. "You did good. Enjoy your time off, and for the excellent work today, I will make sure your pay is fully reinstated. We can not have a hero like you being punished any longer, can we." Jake and the biker guy stand in disbelief as the Sargent walks away happily then leaves my store as the coroner starts to bag up the bodies of the dead men.

"Is there anything else you need to know at the moment, Officer, or am I able to go and get some fresh air?" I ask. "As you can imagine it has been a rough night and I need some time to adjust... to things." He quickly nods his head so I walk through the shop and out in to the freezing cold night air to grab a few minutes of silence. I stand leaning up against the front window as I take a deep breath and relax. Everything about this tells me that I should not have lied in there, getting involved with human situations is not what I should be using my time for, but I cannot ignore the fact that the kid was sent to find me, he just doesn't know it is me that Monroe sent him after yet.

"Mind if I join you?" I look around to see the biker guy come outside. He pauses for a moment and watches me closely as he waits for my response, staring at me as though he already hates me without even knowing who I am. Eventually I shake my head at him so he walks over and stands directly in front of me... far too close

22

in front of me in fact, but I just stare back at him, showing him how unintimidated I am by his presence as he looks me up and down with great interest. "What did you say your name was?"

"I didn't," I reply with a hint of sarcasm. "But it is Rosa Moon, and you are?" He just smirks at me and doesn't answer my question, so I take my time to look at him. He is fairly large in size, easily a foot taller than me, pure muscle, his hair is dark and his eyes are the colour of chocolate. "Tell me your name," I give him a little push to get the answers that I want from him but he just smiles more.

"No," he replies bluntly, and I instantly know that he is not human, which is intriguing me even more... The plot thickens. "How about you answer my questions instead. Why don't you tell me why you lied in there and how you were able to make the Sargent believe your bull shit story?" He steps forward as he speaks and places his hand on the window beside my head then leans in close, probably trying to intimidate me, thinking he is better than me, but the closer he gets the more I can't help but take in his scent, it is so appealing, he smells different from any one I have met in this world before, almost intoxicatingly sweet and I haven't had someone like him in my bed in such a long time. That dominating nature of a big hunk of a man... Mmm there is nothing better. I could really have fun riding him.

"I don't know what you are talking about. I spoke the truth," I try again to use my persuasion, giving it a little more effort to push harder so that he believes my words but after a few seconds he just shakes his head.

"You are not human, are you?" he says quietly, making sure no one can hear him.

"Are you?" I retort with a smirk on my face but he doesn't answer.

"Your blood is not black so I know you are not a demon," he says to himself as he looks down across my body again, taking in the multiple splatterings of crimson blood. "I saw you get injured, I heard your bones break when you were thrown in to those shelves. But yet you stand before me as though nothing even happened... What are you?" He stares in to my eyes as I unintentionally lick my lips, I could get lost in his arms, they are massive. I bet he could rag me all over with pure strength and I would happily let him spank me till I screamed.

"I can be anything you want me to be," I smile playfully. He is really good looking, possibly too good looking as I haven't felt this drawn to someone in a very long time. I don't quite know what it is. He oozes power maybe, possibly sheer dominating strength but I don't know where it is coming from, just being close to him is making me feel so turned on. Humans do not give off this type of aura but yet he doesn't smell like he comes from the pits. "But I assure you, what you think you saw or heard, wasn't real. I am perfectly normal in every sense of the word." He watches me for a second then moves closer, his breath cascades across my cheek as I stand pinned up against the window then he teasingly leans in and slowly licks the now dry blood off my chin before backing off slightly to look me in the eye.

"Hmm, that really does not taste like coffee syrup," he almost whispers, and I can't do anything but smile wildly as I get a flutter in the pit of my stomach and my breathing quivers with desire.

"Oh fuck, that is so hot," I giggle. "Do it again." I bite my bottom lip as he scoffs at me then gives me a look that says he thinks that I am absolutely crazy, but at the same time I know he wants to know more about me, just as I do with him.

"I will find out who you are. I will make sure of it," he says, and I just smile. "I will not let you get out of my sight."

"I look forward to it," I reply cheekily. "I have so many sights that might thrill you." He pauses for a moment as though trying to think of a come-back before he just walks away, leaving me standing in the cold as he heads back inside.

It is another couple of hours before everyone leaves, and my coffee shop is cordoned off completely. I am not allowed back in there for a few days as the police still want to do some further investigations but it doesn't really bother me, it just gives me an excuse to be closed for once over Christmas, although I suppose I will have to inform my staff and make sure that they are well compensated with a hefty Christmas bonus. The biker guy left with Jake a little while ago and I handed the keys to the shop over to the officers before I went home. I say that I went home, I literally have a small flat over the coffee shop so I went in the side door and upstairs. The apartment is nothing flash, a little two bedroomed place, it is quite sparse with the decoration as I don't usually spend much time here, it is just one of my many properties. This one is just convenient right now as I do not plan to sleep any time soon, I feel surprisingly wired and have an abundance of energy to burn.

I spend a little time getting changed, applying some make up and making myself feel good. I throw on a low cut, strappy top with one of my favourite tartan pleat mini skirts and my knee high heeled boots, grab my leather jacket then head back out in to the cold. I don't mind the cold so much, spending so much time in Hell growing up you would expect me to favour the warmer climate but Hell is not all fire and brimstone. The majority of the place is cold and void of life, barren with endless cells where the worst of the worst souls are kept just for fun under the earth... But enough about that right now, I have much more important things on my mind like the fact that I have been walking for the past 15 minutes and there is someone following me.

My destination is just around the corner, so I ignore my new stalker and head up the steps in to the Bunny Hole strip club. It is not sleazy like some of the other ones in the rough area and it is most defiantly not my first visit here, or even my 100th. The club itself is large, very open plan with a massive triple pole stage that includes a main walk way down the middle. It is about 3am and the place is still busy, it always is, as they have cheap drinks and quality girls but still maintain very high standards. I head straight over to the bar and sit on an empty stool, the barman is serving a man in his late 50's at the other end so I wait patiently to be seen. He smiles over when I catch his eye and as soon as he is finished, he grabs a bottle of tequila off the back shelf then comes over and pours me three shots of the neat spirit.

"You are late in tonight, I was starting to think that we would not be graced by your wonderful presence," Gary smiles as I pick up my first shot and down it whilst he leans on the counter casually.

"It was a bit of a weird night. Some guys got in to a killing fight in front of me and it looks like the coffee shop won't be open for a while because of it," I reply then down my second shot.

"That is shit. I know how much you like the place," he says as he refills the first two shot glasses for me without me having to ask then places the bottle down next to them.

"Can I ask you for a favour?" he instantly nods at the request. "Without making it too obvious, is there someone watching me right now?" Gary takes a deep breath and stretches, standing up fully so he can quickly scan the area before leaning over again.

"Yes," he nods discretely. "Some big dude, I've never seen him in here before. Why? Is he an issue? Do I need to inform security?" I shake my head straight away and smile to myself.

"Does he have a leather biker jacket on?" Gary nods in response. "No, it is alright then. I can handle him myself." He smiles then goes to serve a different customer as I down another shot and contemplate my next move.

"Miss Moon, it is nice to see you this evening," Scarlet smiles as she perches herself on the stool next to me. She is the manageress here and knows me very... intimately, I could say. She still works the floor and dances for a price, her current outfit is very appealing, fishnet stockings with leather skirt and black corset. She has fucking amazing legs and the platform heels she is wearing shows them off very nicely.

"Such formalities, Scarlet. Miss Moon makes me sound so old," she laughs as I take another shot then turn on my stool so that I am leaning back against the bar counter, finally looking over to the hot biker guy who is sat on an armchair, alone by the side of the stage. Even though there are scantily clad girls dancing up there trying to draw the attention of the paying crowd, he is not watching them at all.

"Will you be using the VIP room this evening?" Scarlet asks me as I pick up the bottle of tequila that Gary left on the bar for me.

"Most defiantly, yes. I need to take my mind off other things, so let me know when it is ready," I say as I get up from the stool.

"Do you have a particular preference tonight?" I pause as Scarlet asks and I think about a reply as she waits patiently.

"Surprise me," I smile. "You know what I like." I flash her a cheeky wink then grab two empty shot glasses from the bar counter and make my way over to the biker guy. He shifts uncomfortably in his seat when he notices me coming towards him but doesn't move, it is not like he can hide anyway and he knows I can see him clear as day. When I approach, I stand in front of him and place the two glasses down on the small circular table to the side, and pour them before handing one to him to drink. I pick up the other and wait politely, eventually after a few seconds he nods reluctantly and downs it with me.

"Is Rosa Moon your real name?" he asks me but I just smile at his question then refill our glasses.

"Of course it is," I lie. "Why would it not be my real name?" He watches me closely as I drink another shot.

"I have never heard the name Rosa before, I have been in a lot of circles and know a lot of people, but not you... and I know you are not human so you do not originally come from this world," he ponders to himself. "But yet you own a coffee shop, blend in with the humans, act like one of them in public and..." he pauses as he thinks, clearly confused by trying to work out who I am. "Do you work here as well?" He asks as he looks at what I am wearing, granted the skirt is a little short so I do not blame him for being mistaken, but I like it.

"Why would you ask a lady such a question as that? Are you after a dance?" I smirk then put the bottle down on the table and playfully move towards him, straddling his lap and placing my hands on his shoulders as he grips the arms on the chair he is sitting in, now disparately trying to avoid making eye contact with me. His entire body goes ridged with having me so close and it just makes me smile so I lean in and whisper to him. "What is wrong? You are the one who asked the question." Then I playfully nibble his ear lobe as he remains like a statue beneath me. He inhales sharply and tries to ignore me, which makes me more intrigued, his dominance outside the coffee shop with me is certainly failing him now that I seem to have the better position. I can't help but pause for a moment and deeply inhale his scent, the sweet smell making me go slightly light headed as my chest heaves with excitement, but this so strange to me. Yes, I get attracted to people I find good looking, but he is something else and it is like nothing I have been close to before. I force myself to snap out of my daze then lean over to grab another drink. "Are you going to tell me your name yet?" I ask him whilst trying to calm myself down, my core feels like it is already on fire for him and I don't even know who he is yet. He shakes his head to avoid having to tell me then changes the subject.

"Why did you lie about what happened tonight?" he asks.

"Why did your human friend meet with Monroe?" I ask straight back.

"That is none of your concern," he scoffs. "What happened tonight was a fluke, he was just in the wrong place, things are complicated."

"Indeed they will be complicated if you guys are looking for the Keeper... and then talking about the rising as though that is a real thing," I smile as I teasingly rock my hips in his lap, as much as he is trying to ignore me, he can't deny the fact that his bulge is currently growing with the friction I am causing against his jeans... and it is very much turning me on. His aura is amazing, almost like pure magic. I have met my fair share of beings throughout my lifetime but he is like nothing I have felt before.

"How do you know about..." he stops himself and sighs deeply. "Did Jake tell you? This power that you have, you can make humans tell you the truth with it?"

"Not the truth as such, more just that they are easily persuaded to talk to me sometimes, comes in handy when humans ask too many questions whilst I am trying to keep a low profile," I reply honestly, he thinks for a moment then goes to ask another question but we are interrupted.

"Miss Moon?" I turn my head as Scarlet comes over and stands smiling at me. "Your private room is ready for you when you are." I see her eyes flash between me and the mystery man, wondering who he is or what is happening between us, but she stays professional and does not say anything.

"Thank you, I will be there in two minutes," I nod. "And Scarlet, as I may be a little preoccupied and will not be able to keep my new friend here company, can you sort him out a dance, on my tab of course." She smiles and nods before walking away. "I think that is my cue to leave you alone." I smile as I look back down at him.

"Private room? What for? Drugs? Prostitution? Are you involved with those people in the coffee shop? I know there is something bad about you, I can feel it within you, I just can't put my finger on what it is," he asks me seriously.

"Relax," I whisper in his ear. "So many questions will make all those pumped up muscles of yours go all tense, you need to let go of all that negative energy you are feeling and enjoy life more. Maybe a dance will cheer you up a bit, you are so fucking serious." He goes to protest but I quickly place my hand on his shoulder again and lean in to kiss his lips to stop him from speaking. As I do he freezes, I trial my tongue along the opening of his mouth as I tease him, savouring the sweetness that I can taste on his lips and making it wet before gently biting his bottom one. His mouth opens to mine so I take the opportunity to kiss him deeply, slipping my tongue inside and playing with his own as he reciprocates. His touch is intoxicating, and the more I kiss him the more my body wants to surrender to his. My mind seems to get lost in a blur but after a few moments and him not moving his hands off the arms of the chair, which he is currently gripping for dear life, I lean back and smile down at him. Trying to regain control of my breathing after feeling like a cat on heat, I need to focus on the task at hand. "I have a prior engagement, but this was fun," I smile as I feel so fucking horny just looking at him. "All these questions, the back and forth... it feels like really intense foreplay, do you think it feels like foreplay?" He swallows hard and scoffs at me, trying to remain unaffected and not showing any indication that he is feeling the same things I am.

"Foreplay would require a certain level of attraction, but there is none between us," he says but it just makes me smile more.

"Then perhaps you should tell that to your cock," I reply, and I wiggle slightly in his lap causing him to try to stifle his groan of pleasure as I rub across his rock hard erection. I tap him on the chest playfully then get up as a young, very beautiful dark haired woman in bright red matching thong and bra comes over. "Give him the works," I say to her then give him a cheeky wink. She smiles as I walk away, leaving the biker guy stunned in the chair trying to hide how turned on he is already.

The VIP area is literally just a small curtained off section at the far side of the room. Heavy thick purple drapes ensure privacy and the only thing in the area is a large, very comfortable sofa. I head over to it, take my leather jacket off and throw it over the arm as I sit down in the middle and wait. I have spent many fun times in here and just thinking about them makes me smile. After only a couple of minutes, Scarlet appears alongside another girl, one who I have never seen before so that instantly peeks my interest as I have met everyone who works here previously.

"Miss Moon, before we get started I thought you may like to know that your gentleman friend refused his dance from Lorna and moved seats. I am assuming so that he can keep a closer eye on you, possibly wanting to know exactly what it is you are doing in here," she says as I glance to the small gap in the curtain, leaning back on the sofa slightly, I can just make out the biker guy sitting not too far away, positioned so that he can see me, which makes me smile.

"Maybe we should give him a show then," I reply, biting my bottom lip slightly at the thought of it. Holy shit! That thought of being watched by him is so fucking hot. Scarlet nods then goes over to the curtain to fake closing it so that she can readjust it instead, the angle now means that he can see me clearly without giving anything away. I don't quite understand his fascination with me right now but I am far too laid back to ignore the possibility of fun when it is now also standing right in front of me.

"This is Ruby," Scarlet introduces the new girl to me. She is tall, slim, with long blond hair. She is currently wearing a white lace baby-doll dress and thigh high boots. "I thought you may enjoy someone a little different tonight. Ruby has only been with us for a few weeks, but I have told her all about you and what kind of things you like. She is willing to give things a try, if you want her." I look her up and down, her slightly tanned skin is toned and even from here I can see she looks after her body, clearly prides herself on her very stunning appearance.

"Turn around," I order Ruby and she slowly turns on the spot, briefly pausing with her back to me so that I can admire her amazing tight arse then she bends over to tease me, I bite my bottom lip more and smile. "She is perfect." Scarlet nods then sits on the end of the sofa as Ruby turns back to face me. Her eyes are sapphire blue and I just stare at her as she slowly steps towards me then reaches out and runs her fingers across my cheek as her other hand strokes up my thigh. The music in the club is loud so I relax back on the sofa and let Ruby do her stuff, solely giving her my full focus.

She sways on the spot, making sure I am captivated with her before she effortlessly straddles my lap as she dances for me, grinding her hips in time with the music, her skin so soft that I just want to reach out and touch it, but I resist, allowing her to get lost in the song. She runs her hands up her own thighs, takes hold of the hem of her baby-doll then lifts the white dress up and over her head, discarding it on the floor, so that she is left in only her white lace thong and boots. Her breasts are at eye level with me, the gyrating of her hips forcing her to leans in closer, her supple assents so close to my face that I am already getting very turned on as she moves. I was already feeling all sorts of frisky after kissing the mystery man who I believe is still watching me, so having Ruby now so close is driving me wild with desire. Ruby runs her hand through my hair as it hangs lose around my shoulders then pulls my head forward, my mouth being forced to connect with her left nipple as she smiles down at me, so I take it in my mouth and suck on it gently to tease her, twirling my tongue around it, making it get bullet hard before she pulls back and runs her free hand down the front of my top. Her palm slips in to my bra and squeezes my breast playfully as she continues to writhe in my lap, my nipple getting so hard and sensitive with being caressed, and I can already feel myself getting very wet.

"How old are you?" I ask her as she watches me.

"19," she replies sweetly, and I smirk. Oh, to be 19 again, she is so young and innocent, the whole world is ahead of her. She has so much to experience and I love that I can feel the life dripping from her skin. She playfully stands up from my lap and turns around, swaying to the music, letting me admire her curves before spreading her legs slightly and bending forward, running her fingers teasingly down her thighs as I watch her dance, I want to know everything about her, I want to touch her all over. I can't take my eyes off her as she shakes her ass in my face, the string of the thong hardly skims between her cheeks and leads towards her pussy, barely covering it fully, making my mind race as I think about what she might tastes like.

Ruby steps back without turning to face me and sits in my lap before lounging against me then she grabs my hands and places them on her breasts. I can't stop myself from gently kissing her neck as she lies across me, my fingers teasing her nipples as I play with her, feeling how soft her skin is under my palms. She is so beautiful and she smells like flowers, perfectly perfumed to the point I can almost smell the life in her soul. After another minute of grinding she moves again, standing up to face me. She pauses for a moment and just stares in to my eyes and I don't quite know what she is doing until she places her hands on my knees and slowly parts them, allowing her space to stand between my legs before leaning over and playfully licking my bottom lip. I reach up and place my hand on her hip, my fingers playing with the fabric of her panties, twirling it around, thinking about what I would do to her after I ripped them off, then sliding around to touch her bum, but she stops dancing when I do this, moves back and slaps me hard across the face. I sit stunned for a moment as I look up at her, the slight sting on my cheek only lasting a second.

"No touching without me saying so... you very naughty girl," Ruby smiles playfully, and I am quickly overcome with lust for her.

"I am a very naughty girl," I smirk back as I bite my lip again, harder this time as I groan, I am already soaking wet because of her actions. Holy fuck, she is so fucking hot and feisty, no wonder Scarlett thought I might like her.

"You are so naughty that maybe you need to be taught a lesson," she replies, and I just sit still and watch as she slips her hand up under my skirt, teasingly moves the fabric of my underwear to one side then slides her fingers straight towards my clit. I inhale sharply as she connect with it, it is already throbbing and begging to be touched, so she wastes no time before she starts swirling around it, making me squirm in my seat as I try to contain my slight moans of pleasure then she leans down to kiss me passionately. My mouth is consumed with hers, she kisses me slowly, teasing my tongue as she continues to play with me, making me groan more as my loins begin to burn. After a minute and me swiftly growing in pleasure, Ruby steps back, places her hands behind each of my knees and pulls my legs forward forcefully until my arse is right on the edge of the seat, leaving me half slumped, just watching her, fascinated with her actions. She spreads my legs slowly and sways to the music as she kneels in front of me then trails her finger tips up and down my thighs. I can't take my gaze off her, she knows that she has my full attention and it shows in her eyes when she smiles before kissing my inner thigh seductively then licking my skin all the way up towards my mound. Her tongue quickly finds my clit and my head falls back, I close my eyes as her lips envelop me and she gently sucks, making me so aroused that I can feel my own juices drip from between my legs.

"Oh, shit," I moan loudly as my breathing quivers. Ruby teases my hot hole as her mouth dominates my bud, then slowly penetrates me, adding a welcome sensation as she fucks my pussy slowly with her fingers. I look back down so that I can watch her, her face between my thighs, her licking and sucking my juices is driving me absolutely wild.

Scarlet, who has been silently watching what has been going on, moves closer towards me and kneels by my side on the large sofa, she places her hand on my cheek and turns my face to her then starts to kiss me slowly whilst Ruby plays between my thighs. I am totally lost in the moment, handing myself over to the feelings that these two women are giving me. The kissing muffles my moans as I hurtle towards orgasm, Ruby's fingers now fucking me roughly as her tongue laps and swirls at my clit, then Scarlet begins to play with my breasts, pulling down the fabric of my top and bra together so that she can squeeze my nipples, making sure they are rock hard and sending little pangs of pain through me which just make me moan louder. My chest is heaving as I struggle to breath normally, my back arches off the sofa and I cry out with passion, Scarlet moves from my mouth and playfully nibbles on my neck as I cum hard. My entire body shakes as Ruby continues to play through it, prolonging my orgasm and intensifying the feeling as it consumes me. That pure feeling of pleasure just explodes within me and washes over every single inch as I close my eyes and ride the wave.

Eventually, my explosive orgasm starts to subside. Ruby sits back as Scarlet carefully straightens out my top allowing me to regain my modestly and I just sit, breathing deeply as my heart races and the blissful feeling of that epic release relaxes me completely. Ruby stands up slowly, places her hands on my knees then leans over to kiss me gently, I can taste my own juices on her tongue... and I love it so much. I don't know where Scarlet found this girl but I think I have a new favourite.

"Was that alright for you?" Ruby asks me gently as she looks in to my eyes, and I smirk.

"More than alright," I reply. "You have definitely done that before, haven't you?" she nods and smiles before leaning down. She grabs her dress off the floor then pulls it back on over her head, taking a moment to straighten out the lace.

"We will give you a few minutes," Scarlet says as she stands up from the sofa then heads for the curtain.

"Scarlet?" she stops and tuns back to me. "The gentleman that is outside, tell him I will meet him at the bar and that it is his round. If he is still here then he obviously must want more from me than he is letting on and I greatly would like to find out exactly what that is." She nods then leaves with Ruby so I slump back on the sofa and take a deep breath. I needed that, there is nothing better than a good orgasm to sort out my head, especially when it follows all the shit that has happened already tonight in my coffee shop. When I have regained my composure, I grab my jacket and head back out in to the club, the biker guy is perched at the bar with his back to me, and I smile as I approach as he sits with two pint glasses of beer in front of him. I casually wander over, drape my jacket over an empty stool and sit next to him before picking up the glass nearest to me and taking a drink. We both sit in silence for a few moments, I am not quite sure where to start with my next line of questioning for him, so I will let him make the first move.

"Not drugs then," he says to himself without looking at me, almost disappointed that I was not up to anything massively illegal in the private room. I stifle my smirk at his statement as Gary heads towards me and places a black leather wallet and a pen on the bar counter which I open then start to fill in.

"Were you watching me?" I act surprised and he goes bright red with embarrassment as he continues to stare at his glass. We both sit in silence again for a full minute whilst he thinks of something else to say, and I write down my tip totals for the girls so that I am ready to pay when Gary returns.

"So... are you a lesbian?" he blurts out, and I have to force myself not to laugh. He seems a little nervous now, probably knowing that he watched something he should not have. Either that or he found it kinky as fuck and it turned him on, so he is trying to hide it.

"If I was a man," I say very matter-of-factly as I continue to drink. "And I had just had a bit of fun in there with that girl, then come out here... would you ask me if I was straight? Because personally I don't really like labels and that sort of question is very inappropriate to ask a lady such as me."

"I'm sorry," he apologises quickly. "It was a stupid thing to ask, I just..."

"Forget about it," I interrupt him and continue drinking my pint as Gary comes back over to collect my credit card and the leather wallet. "And the answer is no, by the way. I am not a lesbian, in fact I am not really anything, or possibly I am everything... I just enjoy sex, in all of its many forms and I get attracted to all kinds of people, men, women... anything and everything in between," I smile then watch him as he finally turns his head to look at me, my god, he is gorgeous, I really wouldn't mind jumping on him at some point. I lick my lips as I think about it, I know I just had fun with Ruby but nothing beats a good rough fuck. I am a very old demon and as such, I enjoy the simple things that life has to offer, and there is nothing simpler and more natural than sex. My eyes trail down his body as I imagine what he would be like, his skin, his cock... "So what is your deal?" I ask. "Why is little old me so interesting to you all of a sudden?" He sighs heavily and thinks before replying, debating in his mind what to actually say and I am intrigued to know whether or not I am going to get the truth, or another diversion tactic.

"Jake wasn't the only one who spoke to Monroe," he says as I listen to him carefully. "A few years ago, Jake's little brother went missing. The more leads he followed the more it took him on a path that led outside of the mortal world. He had no information to fully go on, but the deeper he got the more he knew that there was something bigger going on that no one knew about. He put a few pieces together when the world learned of the existence of supernatural beings and that only spurred him on more in his quest for answers... That is when he found me, I am a private investigator and he used some of my more unusual contacts so he could investigate without being flagged by his Sergeant, but after a while it became harder to hide the world full of demons and shit from him when it was becoming common knowledge of other things, more every day. He learned of the existence of things much more powerful and dark than any human should know about, at one point I thought it would drive him crazy, but he just took it all in his stride and kept his focus on finding his brother... Now there are rumours of movement, people who are testing the limits of the Veil between this world and the other. The only problem is that no one has noticed yet and no one who actually matters at all will listen. We don't know what is truly going on." Gary comes back over and stands waiting for me to acknowledge him so I nod at him to speak as the mystery guy pauses.

"Sorry, Miss Moon. There seems to be a mistake with your tip for Ruby," he says cautiously. "It looks like you wrote two too many zeros on the total or you missed out the decimal place, maybe." I take the wallet off him then check it before smiling and handing it back.

"No, there is no mistake," I say. "Scarlet knows I tip very well when I am happy, and Ruby made me very happy tonight." Gary nods and goes a little shy, he knows what I get up to when I come in here, as do all of the staff.

"I will let Ruby know that she pleased you," he says then leaves to process my payment. I sigh then turn back to the biker guy.

"So, what does any of this have to do with me?" I ask him and he pauses to think.

"A couple of weeks before Jake spoke to Monroe, I saw him myself," he begins. "I was working on another lead and this guy who called himself Monroe approached me. He kept his face hidden but I could tell that there was something unusual about him. He told me that he knew who I was and what Jake was looking for, but wouldn't tell me how he knew that much. He just said once the kid was in the right place, when he was where he needed to be, then I would find a woman, one who could lead me to someone that could tell us what we needed to stop... whatever is happening, from happening."

"Well, that is vague as fuck," I say to myself then take another drink.

"I am not going to pretend that I know or understand what is going on around us, but the kid notices stuff. He senses unrest and he feels it within himself, maybe... I don't know," he sighs. "Something bad feels like it is going to happen and I would rather be on the side that doesn't die because this whole thing points to the end of the world," I spend a moment digesting his words then shrug at him before standing up from my stool.

"Listen, you sound like a really nice mental person, talking about the end of the fucking world and shit... but I have got to leave, to do anything else but this," I grab my jacket, put it on then take my card back of Gary and shove it in my pocket.

"I know that I am not making any sense, and that I haven't actually told you anything but I think you can help us," he says quickly as I ignore him and start to leave. "Monroe told me a woman who has abilities, not human or like a demon, but someone who was extremely powerful would lead me to the Oracle." I stop and think for a moment about his words. "You are different, you are capable of things I have not seen in a long time, especially not in the human world and I strongly believe that you are the one I am meant to find." I shake my head and start to walk away. I left that life behind, I disappeared from all of that years ago and up until tonight I was perfectly content with sleeping my way through everyone in the city, plus filling my life with fun and coffee. But then again, if Monroe is telling them these kind of things, sending people to find me then something must be more serious, something that could possibly jeopardise the mortal world. It must have him worried as well if he is trying to involve me, nothing could effect him, he was always like ice when it came to life or death kind of situations. I just don't understand why he would speak to a human about all of this. "Mitch," the biker guy calls out after me. "My name is Mitch... please, tell me that I am not wrong? Tell me that you are the one I was sent to find?" I take a long drawn out breath and turn back to face him, he is now stood up, desperately watching me, his eyes pleading with me to help. I know exactly who the Oracle is and where she is, but I still don't understand why I have to get involved in the kid trying to find his brother or rumours about the Veil... But I am far too inquisitive though and I like to know what is going on, so I do something truly idiotic.

"Meet me outside the coffee shop tomorrow at 11am," I say reluctantly as he stares at me. "You and the kid, but I am telling you now, the Oracle talks a load of shit so you will be very lucky to get anything of use out of her." He smiles at me, a genuine smile that I have not seen from him before and it melts my cold stone heart. "But don't get too attached to me, I can tell that you like me and shit... after I take you to her, you and the kid can fuck off out of my life, and save the world without me."

Chapter Three

Last night was an absolute barrel of shit. As soon as I tried to sleep, my mind relived the entirety of my life and I thought about every tiny fucking thing I ever did or said throughout my existence. The first hundred or so years that I was alive, was spent living in my siblings shadow. Constantly being reminded how amazing they were because they were the Sins incarnate and I was nothing more than the forgettable runt. The black sheep who no one noticed was even gone when I finally got so sick and tired of my stupid family that I left. I saw them all occasionally, there was one time I walked straight past my father and a couple of the Sins, and they didn't even recognise me, almost as though I was a ghost. I was nothing to them, a stain on their perfect reputations as being the ultimate bad guys. The human population didn't even have to see them to fear their name, just the stories that surrounded their lives was enough to drive people insane or push them in to the arms of God. Even after all these years, I guess I still have some deep rooted daddy issues that I have yet to fully deal with.

He was the whole reason I left. I suppose I couldn't really expect big family dinners and loving conversations with then, but just a little recognition might have been nice from time to time. I remember watching from the side lines as my brothers and sisters laughed with him, made him proud... I was nothing compared to them. When I first left I wanted to prove to them that I could be something more, but the longer I was away from them, the more I started to realise that I was better off being by myself. I did not need their approval to be who I wanted to be any more. I grew in strength, I found my voice and I gained powers that my siblings could only dream of. They had everything handed to them and that is their downfall because they took it for granted. I worked my arse to the bone and when I couldn't do any more, when I was finally satisfied that I had done everything possible to be the best version of me, that is when I stopped and took a break. I wanted to actually really live, to experience everything that life had to offer because I was finally in a position where I was happy.

Then boom! I was just minding my own business, chilling in my little coffee shop when fucking demons rock up and piss all over my rainbow. Out of all the places in the entire world, why did it have to be in my shop? I can't get what they said about Monroe out of my head either. He was never one for showing emotion, he had never even set foot in the human world unless it was for a job before so why and how has he been talking to Jake. How did Jake even find him, unless he didn't and Monroe found Jake instead, but then how did Monroe even know who Mitch and Jake were? I used to work alongside Monroe when I was a soul reaper, he taught me to control the power I had found unexpectedly and he was always very cut and dry about things. Even when he first met me and disregarded everything I was because I was not from a reaper bloodline, he still never showed anything but being content, but I won him over, and his abilities made me strive for more. If a human was meant to die then it was our job to collect the soul from the body after death, occasionally we did a couple of soul bounties together... there were more than a few slippery buggers who escaped Hell and went on a rampage but we were always quick to take them down and put them back where they belonged. Outside of that, he just didn't get involved with the politics of this world. It has been a good few hundred years since I even last saw him, I changed roles and left him to work alone, I became the Keeper and guarded the Veil. Now I have a human and whatever Mitch is, sent to find me and I have no idea what is actually going on. To the normal world, I shouldn't exist. Not even my own fucking family know who I am, so why am I so important now?

I glance across to the clock and see that it is almost 11am, so I drag my arse out of bed and get dressed. I just throw on a pair of jeans, a warm white fluffy jumper and boots then grab my jacket before heading downstairs. When I get outside it is still freezing cold. Snow is settled on the ground but the sun is shining above, and across the alley, stood right outside of the front of the shop is Jake and Mitch. I do pause for a moment and contemplate if I have actually done the right thing in telling Mitch I would take them to see the Oracle but just as I work through all of the plus points and negatives of my actions in my head, Jake glances over and I catch his eye.

"Hi, we didn't get a chance to properly speak at all last night," Jake says as soon as he sees me, then comes straight over and holds out his hand for me to shake. I stand and look at it for a few seconds, unsure what to do with it before just nodding at him to at least acknowledge that he spoke to me. Just being close to him makes the hair on the back of my neck stand on end and I get such an unusual vibe about him all over again. He looks a little awkward but ignores the gesture and continues speaking. "Thank you, for what you said last night to my Sargent, he can be a real ball buster and..."

"So you are not a vampire then?" Mitch interrupts Jake mid sentence as he stands leaning up against the wall with his arms crossed, and stares at me. The same quizzical look he gave me last night when he was trying to work out who I was. Jake seems a bit thrown by the statement being said so off handedly so he just falls silent between us. "The sun," Mitch elaborates and points slightly towards the sky above. "You are not affected by it, so it rules that out." I take a deep breath and sigh, I am already getting bored of him and his human companion, I wish I had stayed in bed.

"Again with all the questions?" I ask. "Listen, I had a really shit nights sleep, I am cranky and can not arsed with any of this, so why don't you just stop interrogating me so I can take you to see the stupid Oracle and then I can come home and sleep."

"So what Mitch said about you is true?" Jake says cautiously. "You are one of them? Not a human, that is." I yawn and totally ignore his statement before turning around on the spot and just walking away. I don't really get too involved with the lives of humans, they are mostly all the same and once you have met one, you have pretty much met them all. You do get the occasional one that shines, and I have made a couple of friends out of them over my time in the mortal world, but I tend to not get too attached, they die too easy and their lives are very short. So whoever this kid is and whatever reason they have to visit the Oracle is none of my business at all, the humans can do what they want as long as it does not affect my life. Eventually the guys realise that they should be following me, so they hurry to catch up. "Sorry, I just haven't met too many of your kind yet. I am still getting my head around the whole none humans thing, you know, because of all that crap that happened abroad, I'm glad it is not like that here, people getting killed and going missing. Although it did mean I got a pretty cool job and I get to investigate crimes committed by supernatural beings here in this city, they need to follow the law as well I guess, although the few beings that I have met so far usually end up trying to kill me."

"And why is that?" I ask Jake as he waffles on and walks alongside me. "I heard your brother went missing, then you did some digging around to find him but I don't understand how it got from that to having a demon trying to kill you in my coffee shop."

"Well, my brother didn't go missing exactly," he tells me as we all walk. "It was a few years ago now, before the existence of other things was even rumoured. I was woke up in the early hours of the morning by the sounds of our upstairs window being smashed then I heard him scream. He was only 14 at the time... I rushed out of my bedroom and when I got on to the landing I froze. I just couldn't understand what my eyes were seeing. It was like nothing I had seen before, definitely no human, with features that I can only describe as being charred, like burned flesh and it had massive wings, so big it could hardly fit in the space that it occupied," he pauses as he tries to explain what he saw, seeing the image clearly in his mind as though forever branded in there. But I don't need him to tell me any more, I know exactly what he is describing already so I stop walking and think. I take my time to look between Mitch and Jake, running through so many possible scenarios in my head and trying to talk myself out of what I am concluding. I get the extremely strong feeling that they know much more than they have told me so far, but they are still holding back. "It looked like a demon of some kind," Jake continues. "But it had a snake wrapped around its wrist, I think, it was dark so I could be mistaken, I don't know what it was or why it took my brother that night. I just..."

"Astaroth?" I scoff to myself as I cannot contain what I am thinking any longer. "You have got to be fucking kidding me." Mitch stares at me and I can tell by the look on his face that he recognises the name instantly but Jake has no clue what I am on about, the name has no meaning to him. "What is going on? You guys are not telling me something and I can see it all over your face." I stare back at Mitch but he doesn't say anything, almost as though he doesn't want Jake to find out what he is clearly hiding.

"You know who that demon could be?" Jake asks me hopefully. "Please, if you can help me in any way to get my brother back..."

"You won't get him back," I say bluntly, knowing that he will more than likely be long dead. "It is a waste of time even looking, he will be long gone. The demon that took your brother is not..." I pause as I see the devastated look on Jakes face at my statement and for a second my heart hurts for him. "What I mean is, you won't get him back right away," I lie. "Let's see what the Oracle has to say and you can take it from there." Jake nods and forces a smile as I silently debate whether to say more, before I swiftly turn and walk in the opposite direction instead.

"I thought the Oracle was this way?" Mitch calls after me.

"She is, but after this new revelation about the involvement of Astaroth, she will need a steep payment for the things you want to know." They both follow me in silence, even if they did ask a question I am too much in my own head to answer so it is a quiet pleasant walk, then I eventually get to a small herbalist and speak to the owner whilst they both hang back by the door. There is nothing really in here to look at but I do know that they stock some very rare species of seeds and shrubs, some of which are extremely expensive. Good thing I brought my credit card. After only a few minutes I pay for a small plant then leave the shop before heading back in the opposite direction again and towards where I need to go.

"What is that?" Mitch asks as he starts to walk along by my side. "It looked expensive, how did you get the money to pay for it?" I just sigh and ignore the never ending questions. "How old are you? I mean you look mid 20's maybe but you seem like you have knowledge that only a much older person would know and if you do heal, which I am pretty certain you do, then you may be way older than I could even guess." He can clearly see that he is starting to get under my skin with all the questions but it just makes him smile. "You know, it would be easier if you just told me who you were, then I wouldn't have to keep asking." He is cocky as fuck as well. Any other time I would probably laugh and have a witty come back, but I am too lost in my own thoughts to play along. "There are not many species with healing properties like yours. I know you will deny it, but I did see you get injured last night. Is it a form of magic, like witchcraft? Where you gifted it or were you born like that?" I remain silent as he watches me to see if I give anything away. "Just give me your hand, we can do a little experiment. I will make a tiny cut on your palm and then I can prove myself right and you wrong. We will all watch the wound heal then I can smugly smile in your face." I continue to ignore him as we walk down the high street. Jake walks behind us, not wanting to get involved as he doesn't have too much knowledge about our world and I think my attitude is slightly intimidating now that he knows I am not human. "Come on, give me something... You were not this quiet last night."

"Will you just shut the fuck up!" I snap then stop in the middle of the street and hand Jake the small plant before I am tempted to smash it in to Mitch's face. "Who or what I am is nothing to do with you. I don't have to talk to you, I am not coming along to make friends. As soon as I have taken you to the Oracle you guys can leave me the fuck alone. I don't want to be involved."

"OK, calm down," Mitch scoffs at me as he hides his smile. "I am only trying to get to know more about you."

"You don't need to know more about me," I say seriously. "You guys are involved in something that I do not want any part of... just wait around the corner, two minutes because I seriously need a coffee and if I don't get caffeine soon, the next question you ask me will be your last because I will kill you." Mitch smirks at me which just pisses me off more so I turn on my heels and head into the coffee shop next to us. It is a little busy in the shop but I don't mind, it gives me time to try to calm down. There is a lot more going on with those two than it looks on the surface, although I suspect Mitch knows a hell of a lot more than Jake does.

The mention of Astaroth has me intrigued but at the same time, I know that just his name means serious trouble. He is an extremely powerful demon, one who commands legions of warriors and forms one third part of the Trinity as the Duke of Hell... my father being his direct commander. Why the fuck would he be entering the human world to kidnap a 14-year-old boy from his bed? I am consumed by my own thoughts and before I know it, I have been served, bought the biggest fucking coffee on the menu and headed back outside to meet up with those two fuckwits who are playing a very dangerous game. I notice them standing just around the corner of the alleyway a few shops along where I told them to go, then start to walk towards them. I swear to Lucifer, if Mitch asks me another pointless question, I am going to snap.

I just manage to get to the alleyway opening when Mitch steps towards me quickly, opens a flick knife then goes to grab my hand, pulling me away from the street. I was just about to take a much needed sip of coffee and don't quite see what is happening until it is too late. My free hand instinctively wraps around his wrist to try to stop him and I go to step away but my back hits the stone wall of the alley behind me and Mitch is pulled forward towards me by my grip... It all happened so fast that for a moment I am not sure what he was trying to do but then he freezes on the spot as we both just stare at each other.

"Oh, fuck," he says quickly as I go to take a breath in, but seem to struggle, my lungs instantly feel like they are filling with liquid and I can't stop it. "I am so fucking sorry, I just wanted to see that I was right, that you healed your cuts, it was only meant to be a tiny thing..." his voice shakes as his eyes go wide, staring at me in utter shock. I still have hold of his wrist with my left hand, the wrist that was holding the flick-knife and whose blade is now firmly deep into my chest, and the way that my eyes are already starting to lose focus, I assume it has penetrated my heart. I don't know what happened. I went to move his hand away but because of the wall behind me, I had nowhere to move it to except straight in to my flesh.

"Holy shit, what have you done?" Jake shouts as I drop the coffee cup I am holding, the hot liquid bursts from the paper container and splashes all over the ground. I manage to look down to the knife in my chest as Mitch leaves go of the hilt and steps back, my whole body shakes then my legs collapse beneath me and I slide down the wall until I am sat slumped on the cold ground. With all my remaining energy I reach up and pull the knife from my flesh then toss it to the floor, it clatters as it hits the concrete and blood instantly covers my white jumper as it freely flows from the wound, the blood now unable to pump around my body to keep me alive.

"I am so sorry," Mitch says, stunned at his own actions, remorse very recognisable all over his face. I can see it in his eyes that he knows it is bad and that I will more than likely be dead within one minute, that is if I even last that long. If the blade did in fact penetrate my heart, which is how it feels as immense pain rips through my chest, then it can no longer supply oxygen rich blood to my brain which is why I am fighting against passing out.

"Mitch, call an ambulance," Jake shouts as he kneels by my side and quickly applies pressure to the wound to try to stop the bleeding. "Rosa, it is going to be OK," he says with sheer panic in his voice as my head rolls back against the bricks, my body not strong enough to hold it up any more, and I feel my own blood start to fall from the corner of my mouth then drip down my chin as it works its way up my windpipe. The wound is severe enough that I know it is going to kill me, my healing abilities are good, but not that quick, and not with a knife through the heart... Fuck!

"W... what have... have you... done?" I force out through gargled breaths, the liquid now filling my mouth and restricting all attempts to get air in to my lungs. Mitch takes his phone from his pocket, his hands are shaking uncontrollably as he dials the number then waits for the operator to speak but I don't see much else as my eyes get heavy and they close against my will... and at this point I know I need to act fast as my brain is now shutting down as I bleed out. If I die right now, my power will automatically kick in and take the life force I need to survive from the nearest possible human being. In this case, if I live, I will kill Jake, which, as much as I am not too fond of them right now, I can't let happen because for some bastard reason, I think he is important somehow.

I block everything else out and try to focus on my surroundings, feeling the natural energy of the earth vibrate around me and the souls of all the living people as they go about their daily lives. This is not a great impression to make on a cop that is currently trying to save my life and on whatever the fuck Mitch is, but this is who I am and what happens next is totally on the shoulders of Mitch, he caused this to go this way. One last bolt of excruciating pain and I know my heartbeat has fully stopped, everything falls silent as my body goes still and with my remaining essence I focus on not killing Jake. I haven't had to do this is a very long time but it still comes quite naturally to me, and it doesn't take me long to choose and do what I need to do... In the distance I can hear a scream, the sounds of commotion coming from across the street opposite to where we are in the alleyway, then an intense burning radiates through my chest where the knife wound is.

"Please, someone call an ambulance," a woman screams and it echoes around in the cold air. "He just collapsed, please, he is not breathing, we need help."

It's a good thing I learned a long time ago how to control my powers so that I would target someone else, it is quite easy to feel a humans soul, know how much life they have left in them. I know that I am the daughter of Lucifer and I should be evil and hate all human life, but I do not like killing for no reason, so I tried to choose a life that was near its end but unfortunately there will be no peace for his soul after he leaves the mortal realm, no pearly gates for him to look forward to... it is purely being used to give me life. And to a reaper that gets injured or dies, that is all a human soul is good for.

I take a deep gasp of air to fill my lungs, my eyes shoot open and sit up fully. Jake falls backwards in shock, scrambles away slightly then sits on the ground staring at me as Mitch slowly hangs up the phone without saying a word, the voice on it now being ignored. I concentrate on regulating my breathing as he looks between me and the dead man now lying across the street where all of the commotion is as Jake finally speaks.

"What... what just happened?" he asks as his voice shakes and he stares at me in a state of complete shock. "You were dead, for a minute anyway. You had no pulse, you bled out."

"That arsehole just killed me, that is what happened," I groan as I push myself up from the ground, throwing Mitch the dirtiest look ever then sigh at the state of my white jumper that is now saturated in blood. My chest still hurts slightly and my ribs ache as I stretch, but another minute or so and I will be completely fine. I am already fully heeled, so the blood that now adorns my front is all that remains of the injury, the energy I gain from taking a soul is almost instant. Angrily, I wipe the blood from my chin then pick up the very expensive plant that Jake put down when he tried to help me. There is still a lot of noise in the street as several people try to revive the old man but he won't come back, his heart will never beat again. I know that for a fact. We are lucky that the ally gave us partial cover so no one noticed what just happened to me, I do not feel like having to explain that one to the humans.

"That man... did he collapsed because of you?" Mitch says nervously, I know that I should not admit it, any other time I would just slip away and ignore the situation, but instead I nod in reply. I am so furious with him that I can't even look him in the eye right now. All of this just to prove a stupid point, how fucking childish could he be.

"You killed that man?" Jake asks confused, but before I have a chance to answer or explain, Mitch speaks again.

"No, it was me, I killed that man," he says with sadness in his voice. "He died because I wouldn't take no for an answer. His innocent death is on my conscience."

"I don't understand," Jake looks to Mitch to try to get more from him but he doesn't take his eyes off me. I can see that he can't believe he just did that, that he just stabbed me in the chest and potentially killed me just to try to prove that what he think he saw was an actual fact.

"You... you are a soul reaper?" he asks and I reluctantly nod in response. "I am sorry, I am so sorry that I forced your hand. It was not my intention to... I just wanted to see if... that man, he died because I was being a dick... I am truly sorry." I sigh deeply then finally look up at him, his remorse is making me soften to him even though he is still doing my head in.

"Be sorry to his family, not to me," I say calmly. "I only did what I had to do to survive. I had to make a choice before..."

"I know," Mitch interrupts me. "I know exactly what happens when a reaper is killed. What they need to do or what their power does unintentionally around humans." I nod my head as he glances to Jake who still has no clue what is going on. He has no idea how close he came to losing his soul.

"The Oracle is just around the corner," I inform them then take a deep breath to try to relieve some of the tension that is currently building inside of me and threatening to explode. "If you can try to not be complete dick heads for the next half hour until you have seen her, I will then happily fuck off and let you both continue your little death wish game." I am clearly not in the best of moods as we walk the rest of the way in silence, I don't even care that I am getting some really strange looks from people passing by because of the amount of blood I am covered in. I just care that very soon, this slight interruption to my life will be gone and I can get back to my lazy retirement. Away from the talk of demons, the rising and all the shit that seems to be surrounding this human and Mitch. All I have to do is get them here, that is what Monroe told them they needed me for. "It is in there," I stop outside a store front and Mitch instantly chuckles.

"You are having a laugh, aren't you?" he says looking around. It is a run down, old fortune telling shop, just off the high street. From the outside it seems like no self respecting person would ever go inside and I don't think any normal person would really want to as people would think whoever was inside, didn't know their elbow from their arsehole, never mind be able to tell anyone their fortune.

"Jake, head inside and do what you need to do," I say to him and he just nods, still probably a little shocked off watching me die, so he doesn't argue as he opens the door. Bells Jingle as he does and Mitch just laughs more. We both stand outside in silence for a minute, me avoiding having to speak or even look at Mitch, before Jake comes back out within only a minute.

"Wow, was it that bad?" He chuckles as Jake comes over to me. "Quick in and out job, could have probably done better myself."

"The receptionist said that there is no one in there called an Oracle and that Madam Fictus is on vacation so cannot see anyone until the end of next week," Jake informs me, but Mitch laughs louder.

"Madam Fictus? The word Fictus means fake in Latin. Could that be more obvious that all this is a con," he shakes his head and I force myself not to smile. I hadn't realised she had changed her cover name and the new one she chose is quite farcical. I take the small plant off Jake and head inside the shop myself, encouraging him to follow me. Once inside I head straight for the small table at the back of the little entrance room. The decoration is old, dark fabric drapes across the ceiling and walls, crystals hang from the windows and behind the desk is a young woman with long dark hair, adorned with plaits and feathers. She is casually sitting reading a book, her outfit of harem pants in bright psychedelic colours and gypsie type top that scoops her shoulders is unusual but fits in perfect with the theme of the place. She doesn't look up as I approach, just silently acting like we do not exist, Mitch and Jake hang back slightly behind me then I just wait for her to acknowledge me first.

"As I said to the boy, Madam Fictus is on vacation," she eventually says without looking away from the book. "She will be back next week, appointment book is closed for now." I hear Jake sigh behind me at the fact she has just told me the same thing, then I casually place the plant on the desk in front of her and wait. Mitch goes to speak but I put my hand up to stop him from talking and everything falls silent. After the longest couple of minutes, she glances to the desk top and quickly looks at the shrub before speaking again. "If you want to make an appointment, then I may be able to make an exception on this occasion."

"The boy wants to speak to the Oracle," I say calmly as she smiles at the mention of that name then concentrates on her book again instead.

"As I told the boy, there is no one here by that name," she replies and goes back to ignoring me. I can tell that Mitch and Jake are getting restless behind me, but I don't care, they need to have more patience if they want to get answers.

"I understand. We are sorry for bothering you today. I guess I will take this perfect specimen of a Viola Cryana with me and leave you to enjoy your book," I say casually then go to pick up the plant but she quickly grabs my wrist to stop me touching it again.

"A Viola Cryana?" she asks and I nod as she finally looks up at me. "That particular plant species has been extinct for over 70 years." I smirk slightly at her, I knew she would not be able to resist.

"If you don't want it then I can take our business elsewhere. I am sure I can find someone else who..."

"I didn't say I didn't want it," she puts her book down and sighs deeply. "Damn you Rosa, you always did know exactly how to make me break character." I smile down at her as she looks over to Mitch and Jake to see who I am accompanied by. "Who are your friends?"

"Well, you should know that already, seen as though you are a great and powerful fortune teller," I smirk and she just shakes her head then stands up from her chair, smiling at me. "Alysia, this is Jake and Mitch. Guys this is Alysia, or you can call her the Oracle." Jake instantly steps forward and holds out his hand for her to shake but she just smiles more then walks around the back of the desk to give him a hug instead. Jake just stands motionless as Alysia hugs him tightly, a prolonged embrace which many people would find a little awkward.

"Any friend of Rosa is a friend of mine," she says then steps back before looking Jake up and down. She takes a long drawn out breath and shakes her head, looking sad all of a sudden. "Oh, I am sorry. You are still so consumed with pain over your brother." He nods his head as he listens to her. "Even now you have not given up hope... come, we should have privacy to talk." I flash her a smile before she takes hold of Jakes hand then leads him in the back. At this I take my chance to head back outside and get some air but Mitch follows me out and stands by the door as I debate whether to just leave now or wait first to see what Jake has to say, although I don't give a shit what Alysia says to him. Maybe I am just a little inquisitive of the reasons why he was sent to me, and why when I first met him I felt an overwhelming need to protect him... Or maybe I just have not had enough sleep and my mind is taking the piss out of me.

"I'm sorry again," Mitch sighs as I avoid having to look at him. "I truly didn't know... and I honestly didn't intend for that to happen at all." I cross my arms and lean up against the window as he hangs back, giving me space, but he watches me closely to see what I do.

"Do you stab everyone you try to get to know or was I just lucky?" I ask sarcastically.

"Do you give lap dances to every random guy who follows you into a club, or did I get lucky?" I laugh at his come back which relieves some of the tension between us. "It has been a very long time since I last met a soul reaper, and never one who owned a coffee shop in the human world."

"Yeah, well, I haven't been a soul reaper for a while. I am enjoying being retired," I sigh. "Are you going to tell me what is so special about Jake?" Mitch looks at me as though he has no idea what I am asking. "Oh, drop the act. I can tell that you know a lot more than you are letting on. Astaroth was a dead giveaway with that." Mitch sighs then comes to stand next to me.

"I am only trying to protect him," he says. "The less he knows, the safer he will be."

"Hmm," I grunt as I am still no further forward. We go back to that uncomfortable silence whilst we wait for Jake to return. There is so much I want to know but my suspicion tells me that Mitch will not give me the answers I seek, no matter how much I push him.

"Hey," Jake calls over as he comes outside.

"What did the Oracle say?" Mitch asks straight away.

"A lot, actually," Jake replies. "The rising is real, what I felt was right all along, I knew there was something big happening, but she told me that if no one acts soon then it could rip through this world and..."

"Jake?" Alysia says as she comes to the shop door. "Remember, the most important thing right now is to find the weapon. Without it, we will all be doomed... nice meeting you, have a great day," she smiles then heads back inside. Now that is over with I can leave, I did what Monroe wanted me to do. I start to walk away and leave the guys behind so I can resume my nice uneventful life as Mitch and Jake discuss what was said by the Oracle.

"What weapon is she on about?" Mitch asks as I go to cross the street.

"I am not sure, she called it the star of the morning, or something," Jake replies and I stop dead in my tracks, my heart skips a beat and I momentarily forget to breathe.

"The star of the morning? I have never heard of such a weapon. Are you sure that is what she called it?" I assume Jake nods in response but my back is still to them. "Rosa?" Mitch calls after me then runs over to where I am stood. "Have you heard of a weapon called the star of the morning?" I quickly shake my head and put my hands in my jacket pockets.

"Nope, sounds made up to me, I warned you that she speaks a load of bullshit and that just proved my point," I blatantly lie to him and quickly change the subject. "Anyway, I've done my part. Brought you to the Oracle, so now I am just

45

going to leave, I have a coffee shop to clean up."

"You can't leave now," Mitch says quickly as he grabs my arm to stop me walking away. "I know you are lying to me, Rosa. If the rising is already in the process then we need to find that weapon. The rising is..."

"The rising is a fairy tale!" I cut in as my hands shake unnaturally so I keep them in my pockets so that no one else sees them. "It is not real, if it were then I would know, there would be signs but..." I stop myself in case I say too much and give something else away. "Just keep me out of it, go home, focus on something else. I am sorry but you are wasting your time trying to fight against something that doesn't exist."

"Please, I know it sounds far fetched but it is real. We can not ignore it, we..."

"No, take your stupid little stories and leave me alone," I say harshly. "You and Jake will be much better off if you keep your distance from me and..." I pause and look around as something feels strange, like energy that had been surrounding me has suddenly been drained. "Where is Jake?" Mitch turns on the spot as we hear loud bangs and screeching tires before I see, what I assume to be Jake with a black sack over his head and his hands in cuffs, being bundled in to the back of a black van. Mitch goes to run after them but they quickly close the van doors and drive away with Jake inside.

"No!.. Fuck!" Mitch shouts and I walk over towards him as he now stands in the middle of the street just staring at the spot where the van had been.

"That is not a normal thing to happen," I state the obvious then Mitch turns and punches a parked car at the side of the road in frustration. His fist goes straight through the window, shattering the pane but he doesn't seem injured, the glass not breaking the skin on his hand at all. "So... care to tell me what is going on now?"

"I thought you said that you didn't want to get involved?" Mitch snaps at me.

"I don't, but I get the strong feeling that Jake is extremely important in all of this somehow and you refuse to tell me anything," I calmly reply. I know I should walk away, I know that bad things happen when I get sucked in to crappy situations but they mentioned the star of the morning and combined with everything else I have heard in the last 24 hours, it now has me very worried. Not that I am going to tell Mitch that, I will not admit anything to him. He takes a deep breath and debates what to say next so I give him a little encouragement. "I could tell you where he has been taken," I say and Mitch instantly turns to look at me. "I recognise one of the guys who bundled Jake in to that van. My guess is he will be taken to head office, to see his boss. Why? I don't know or understand but I get the very strong feeling that you do." I stand patiently and wait for Mitch to speak, eventually, he sighs and nods his head.

"I will make you a deal," he finally speaks and looks at me. "Help me get Jake back, make sure he is kept safe and alive... and I will tell you everything. I will tell you it all."

Chapter Four

"If you want to get Jake back alive then you will follow my rules and do exactly as I say," I inform Mitch as he follows me down the street. "If you do not follow the rules I set, Jake and both of us, will get ourselves killed."

"I understand," Mitch agrees. "Is there a plan of attack? How many hostiles are we looking at?" I smirk at him as I enter a clothing shop and he stays close by. "If we get in to trouble, do you have weapons?" I casually walk up to a very well dress gentleman at the back of the shop and he gives me a discerning look as he sees the state of my top. "What is it that I need to arm myself with?"

"You need a suit," I smile. He finally looks around, we are stood inside the most extravagant tailors around here and I know by the look on his face that he is thoroughly confused.

"No, we need to leave and save..."

"No, you need to follow my rules and we survive," I stare at him firmly. "The place we are going is not somewhere you just barge in, all guns blazing." He deliberates about saying something else but the staff member approaches us before he does.

"May I help you?" he asks, looking between us, I just turn to him and smile.

"Yes, please," I beam. "My friend here would like a suit," I reply as Mitch wanders over to have a look at the price tags on the shop display items. He turns one over in his hand, it is on a very plain looking shirt and his eyes almost bulge at the amount it costs which makes me smirk.

"Rosa, I can't afford this," he says very quietly to me when he comes back over and tries to avoid the assistant hearing him as a young woman hovers by the till watching us as well. "That shirt alone is two grand. I hate to think what a entire outfit would cost.

"Maybe you would be more comfortable at a department store," the assistant says off handedly. "Their prices may be more in line with your clearly limited budget." He looks Mitch up and down, he is currently dressed in jeans, a plain t-shirt and his biker jacket, nothing flash or remotely designer. I casually remove my wallet from my pocket and skim through the several cards that I have on me before sighing.

"I assume you take credit cards?" I ask the assistant and he just smirks as if to say he knows the lowest range suit in here would max most peoples cards out.

"Of course we do, unfortunately for you though, our range is rather exclusive and..."

"Would you prefer my JP Morgan Chase Palladium card, my Stratus Rewards visa or my American Express Centurion Card?" I force myself not to laugh as his face drops and absorbs what I have just said. I have a very high net worth and it is not really safe to just carry around large sums of cash all of the time. My plastic is not what the average person would hold.

"Erm..." the assistant seems a little uneasy by my question as I wait for an answer. "The erm... American Express will be fine." The young woman approaches me and I hand over my card so that she can go to charge it. "What kind of suit are you looking for?" he asks me as he carefully removes Mitch's jacket and takes out a tape measure to start fitting him. "Double breasted? Dinner suit? Tuxedo?"

"He needs trousers, jacket, shirt and shoes, I am not too fussed with a tie. As for fit... again I don't really care," I say as the young woman hands me back my card. "As long as it is the most expensive one you have in the shop and it looks good, then that is fine with me. He needs to make an impression." The assistant smiles and nods to show his understanding then I place my wallet back in my pocket and go to leave.

"Where are you going?" Mitch calls after me.

"To get ready," I reply. "What? You don't think I am going looking like this, do you? Meet me outside the coffee shop and 8pm. Don't be late," I say then leave him standing whilst the assistant kneels in front of him and takes his inside leg measurement. The sudden change in position startles Mitch which makes me giggle slightly.

One very important thing that I have learned since being in the human world, is that money speaks extremely loudly. And it is certainly a very hot topic when it comes to the people who now currently have Jake. There is always an option for the hard hitting approach, to fight our way in, kill everyone who stands in our way and take back what we want, but I didn't create a good life for myself here by making enemies. I need to play this right and hopefully Mitch does his part and does not fuck up my current plan of action.

49

It is almost 8 pm when I slip my shoes on and stand admiring myself in the mirror in my bedroom. I don't get too many opportunities these days to dress to impress so it has literally been years since I last wore this dress but I do have to admit, I look fucking hot in it. It is a very figure hugging, bright red dress. The neckline scoops the top of my cleavage, with very thin straps across my shoulders then the back plunges, exposing all of my skin till the line of the dress stops about an inch from the top of my arse crack. The material then skims lightly over my bum and falls loosely to the floor with a very high cut slit up the side. There is a lot of flesh on display and it doesn't leave much to the imagination, but that is the perfect look for tonight. My shoes are accented with diamonds, the straps fitting perfectly around my feet and the heel is tall. I wore my hair up, neatly placed with pins and curls so that it didn't cover my neck and my make up is striking, with the smoky eye and the blood red lipstick. It is a far cry for my coffee shop plain Jane uniform.

"You scrub up well," I say to Mitch as I see him standing outside. The cut the store assistant chose shows his muscles very nice in the black suit, he wears a crisp white shirt underneath with the top few buttons undone and I have to admit, he is very pleasing on the eye. Mitch looks up as I speak, he still seems a little unsure of things and has no idea what he is about to let himself in for or what I have in mind for tonight.

"I should do, you have no idea how much this get up cost and..." he stops mid sentence as he finally sees me fully. I just stand for a moment, trying not to smile as he takes it all in, then I see him swallow hard and go to say something else to me but no words come out of his mouth which makes me smirk.

"Thank you for your kind words," I say sarcastically. "Oh, this old thing, it was just something I had in the back of the wardrobe," I joke and he is still lost for words. "Are you going to stand gawking all night or would you like to see if Jake is still alive?" Mitch nods his head then coughs to clear his throat as I approach him.

"Yes," he says quickly. "Yes, Jake, of course... You erm... that dress is... wow." I laugh at his statement. "Sorry, Rosa. You look stunning."

"Thank you," I blush and I don't quite know why. I know I look good. I don't need anyone to tell me that but sometimes it is nice to get the compliment. "You do not look too bad yourself."

"Thank you back, am I to presume you do not have a weapon hidden under that... very tight dress," he asks and I smile more.

"Now that would be telling," just as I say that, a black Mercedes pulls up next to us and the driver gets straight out then comes around the car to open the back door. He nods at me when I look at him and smiles.

"Miss Moon?" he gestures for me to get in and I smile more.

50

"Shall we?" I say to Mitch and he looks stunned by everything but goes around the other side of the car and gets in with no objections. We both sit in silence in the back seat for a good 20 minutes before Mitch finally speaks again.

"Who are you?" he blurts out and I smirk. "There is so much more to you than you are letting on and it has me extremely intrigued. You cannot possibly just be a reaper, the money thing alone is..."

"In about 40 minutes we will arrive outside a very exclusive club," I reply, totally ignoring his question. "Once inside, all eyes will be on us so I need you to follow the rules I am about to set and do not deviate from them one tiny bit. If you do, we will be rumbled and Jake will be killed." He goes to speak but I cut in before he has a chance. "You will refer to me only by the names Miss Moon or as your Mistress, never call me Rosa. From the moment we enter you will be in constant physical contact with me at all times unless I say so. This includes, but is not limited to, holding my hand, placing your hand on my hip, stroking my arm, touching my back, you may kiss my neck, touch my cheek... you get the point. You need to act as my escort, my servant, my bodyguard and my..." I pause briefly and try to hide my smile. "And my sex slave."

"What?" he says confused. I force myself to not look at Mitch or I will laugh. "Where the fuck are we going?"

"If someone approaches us, you will speak on my behalf," I continue to ignore him. "You need to be aware that as soon as we go in, I will be asked to join the company of the manager. He will try to get me alone, it is your job to ensure that never happens. He will try to control your actions, again play along but never leave my side. He thinks he is more powerful than he actually is and even after all these years he still knows less about who I actually am than you now do. Most importantly of all, never let slip what you know about me, where I live, where I work or what you have seen of my power."

"How does any of this help us find Jake?" Mitch finally asks a relevant question.

"Because, once I get in a position where the manager is under my thumb, I will make him give Jake to us willingly," I say. "Back to the rules. When you look at me, you will act like you worship the ground I walk on but you will not get jealous if I interact with another person." Mitch sighs in frustration and sits back in his seat as I continue to talk for the rest of the journey until we finally pull up in a very quiet street filled with empty buildings. We both get out of the car and I inform the driver to wait outside for as long as is needed before I start to walk towards a break in the path, with steps that lead to a door that looks like a basement to nothing. "Any questions before we head inside?" I ask Mitch as I pause from opening the door.

"Just one. You said I was a sex slave?" Mitch says and I laugh at him. "I do not have a clue what is happening but I cannot follow these stupid rules of yours. If I see Jake, regardless of how many enemies are inside, I will take my chance to get him out. I am not going to play silly games."

"Then you will get us all killed," I say bluntly. "If you don't follow what I have advised then you will fuck this up and Jakes death will be on your head, just like the poor old man that died this morning because you wouldn't listen to me." We both stand staring at each other, waiting for the other to back down. "I don't care if you are not used to listening to the advice of someone else or if you think you are one of those people who has to be the fucking hero and do everything alone. For once, try to think of the big picture. Jake is currently probably being tortured for information about shit I don't know anything about. I could have easily walked away and left you to get on with things because you guys mean nothing to me, but against my better judgement, I am now stood here trying to save your life, and jeopardising mine. Just give me something, anything, to help me save Jake." Mitch inhales deeply and reluctantly nods at my words. "Good, try not to fuck this all up," I say through gritted teeth then head inside, the night has not even started yet and already Mitch is testing my patience. There is a long straight corridor that only leads to one place and that is to an open lobby with one door to a lift and a table with a very pretty young blond woman sat behind it. She is dressed very smart in a navy suit and she smiles brightly when she sees us approach.

"Good evening," she greats us. "If you could have your membership cards ready for me to scan then I can get you straight in, pending ID verification." In front of her on the desk is a small laptop, to the side is a card reader and in the centre, directly in front of where I am now standing is a small black box with a white circle on the top. I did think that there would be a bit more security, but I guess if no one really knows that this place exists, then they will not need it, or at least think that they don't.

"We do not have membership cards," I reply polity and she seems a little taken aback, not expecting any one to come here who is not a member.

"Oh, well we do have a waiting list but I can give you the forms to fill in if you would like to apply for one," she says as she opens the desk draw and takes out several papers. "It can take up to 48 hours to process your application, at which time..."

"No," I hold my hand up to stop her talking. "You seem to be misunderstanding what I am saying. I do not need a membership card."

"Have you received a personal invitation from a platinum member? If so then you will be on my list, I will just check that for you," she says happily then turns to her computer to load up the database.

"I am not on that list," I inform her and she stops again then looks back up at me, slightly confused. "In fact I won't be on any of the member lists that you hold." She goes to speak again but I cut in before her. "Try looking under the name for owner." She falls silent for a moment and thinks about my words as she glances between myself and Mitch.

"I am sorry, what did you say your name was?" she asks cautiously. Clearly she has never been told to look there before.

"Moon, Rosa Moon," I smile, and her face drops, letting me know that the name is recognised.

"Erm... Apologies Miss Moon, I was not..." she bumbles now that she is a little flustered. "Please, if you would not mind, just for security purposes... I hope you understand..."

"Of course," I reply and place my thumb on the little white circle, on top of the black box. She goes back to the laptop and after a few seconds of her typing, I feel a sharp pain as the tip of a needle pierces the skin on my thumb and the box below analyses my blood. Instantly the little white circle turns green and I remove my hand.

"My sincerest apologies, Miss Moon. We were not anticipating your arrival and you..."

"It is fine," I interrupt her again. "I trust that it will not happen again." She quickly shakes her head before pressing a button that opens the lift doors.

"No, it will not. I will make sure everyone else is made aware of your arrival," she nods nervously and I turn to head for the lift, followed swiftly by Mitch who thankfully remained silent through all of that.

"Owner?" Mitch asks as soon as the lift doors close.

"I have had a very diverse life," I say as he stands at the opposite side of the small space watching me. "And you are already letting me down with the rules I gave you. You have approximately 10 seconds till the lift doors open, and you are not in physical contact with me." He swallows hard then steps forward and places his hand on my shoulder, I look at it and roll my eyes, then sigh deeply before the door opens, that is not exactly the type of physical contact I was meaning but it will have to do right now. The lift sits at the top of a sweeping staircase that leads down in to a dimly lit, open plan bar. The bar counter is a circle that sits at the centre of a large dance floor and around the edge of the room are large booths with comfortable sofas and tables, each one adding a touch of privacy to its guests as it is surrounded by high walls and drapes. The music being played is at a suitable level to enable conversations between groups to remain private without being too loud to make you shout, and is also valuable when private groups get a little more intimate in the main member area. The walls are painted a deep red with large black satin coverings that hang between expensive artwork, and dotted around the high ceiling are several crystal chandeliers. As we step out of the lift I can see that nearly every single person in the club is looking towards us, taking in the sight of the woman in the immensely expensive red dress with a hunk of a man next to her. It is not particularly busy right now but there are enough people staring for me to know that we are about to make a scene. I casually reach up and take Mitch's hand off my shoulder and hook it around my arm so that he can escort me down the stairs.

"What now?" Mitch leans in close and whispers to me as we get to the bottom.

"Now, we get a drink," I reply and head to the bar where there is already a young and very good looking barman waiting eagerly to serve us.

"Good evening, Miss Moon," he says nervously as I approach. "Can I get you something to drink?" He asks me but looks at Mitch and waits for him to reply on my behalf. After a few very uncomfortable seconds I side glance at him but he doesn't speak so I sigh again to try to hide my growing frustration and speak for myself.

"I will have the house special," I say, and the barman quickly nods before going to get what I requested.

"What?" Mitch asks as he can see that I am annoyed. "How am I supposed to know what you want to drink," he snaps then leaves go of my arm so that he can lean casually on the bar top which makes me more angry with him as I can tell people are watching us. This is a very private club, and to most of the people here right now they will want to now exactly who I am and why the staff are currently all glancing nervously at us. I quietly seethe as the barman returns and places a cocktail glass down in front of me containing a thick dark red liquid. I pick it up, take a sip them quickly spit it back in to the glass and place it down on the counter.

"I am sorry, Miss Moon, is that not to your satisfaction?" the barman asks as he visibly shakes in front of me with fear. I would be lying if I said I had not slightly missed that look, the look of someone so eager to please me because they know of my reputation.

"How old is the bottle you poured from?" I ask him and he inhales sharply indicating the answer. "Bring me something fresh, that already displeases me. The standards here are definitely slipping." Then he walks away again before Mitch leans over to me to speak.

"Please tell me that was not blood," he asks at a whisper but I just glare at him, he is starting to greatly piss me off.

"I expressly told you that you need to follow my rules," I say firmly under my breath so that no one else hears. "People are starting to stare, this club has a reputation to uphold and right now everyone will be thinking why the fuck I would bring someone like you in to a place like this."

"What is that supposed to mean?" he snaps back quietly.

"Constant... physical... contact," I say slowly. "Three words that I assume are very easy to understand, however right now, we look like we have never even had sex before."

"We haven't ever had sex before," he reminds me and I have to take a moment to breathe deeply or I am going to scream at him.

"Do you want to get Jake back?" I ask seriously. "Or are you doing all of this on purpose just to piss me off." He stares at me for a moment, deliberating what kind of sarcastic come back to have, but eventually he sighs.

"Fine," he responds to my frustration. "You want me to play by your stupid rules, then I will play by your stupid rules."

"Thank you," I reply through gritted teeth as the barman comes back and places a second drink down on the counter. He almost holds his breath as I pick it up to inspect it, to the untrained eye the drink I have been given would be identical, but I can smell the very subtle difference in it as I lift it to my lips and take a sip. "That's better," I say and he exhales as I confirm the drink is alright, then he looks at Mitch for further instructions.

"Bring two shot glasses and a bottle of Tequila," he says and I smile slightly as that was my drink of choice in the strip club. As the barman leaves for a third time, Mitch cautiously steps towards me, I can tell he is a little unsure about things but he gently skims his hand across my lower back before letting it settle on my hip, he then moves closer still until his chest is almost pressed up against my shoulder as he stands slightly to the side of me, looking down at me. "Is this better?" he whispers and I just shrug, brushing him off, I bet the majority of women have had more physical contact from a gynaecologist. "Hmm," he grunts at my dissatisfaction as though he is hating the fact I am forcing him to do this before grabbing my waist firmly, turning me to look at him them pulling me in close, his hand flat on the bottom of my back to hold me in place as I am now pressed up against the side of his body. Without leaving go of me he picks up the bottle of Tequila that the barman has placed down on the counter with his free hand and pours two shots before picking one up and handing me it. He picks up the second and smiles down as he can see I was not expecting him to do that, in fact the very sudden burst of dominance makes my breath catch as I have to hide how I truly feel about it from him.

"I suppose this is a little better," I force myself not to smile too much as we both drink the shots then I feel the hand on the bottom of my back move, his fingers trail up and down my spine slowly over the exposed skin. Another sudden feeling catches me off guard, almost a stir of lust, primal attraction to the most annoying man I have met in a long time, but I try ignore it and keep my head in the game.

"So what happens now?" he asks as he discreetly looks around the room to see what is going on then refills the shot glass. "Or do we just drink all night?" I take the glass off him again and down it as I secretly start to enjoy his touch on my skin, it is strange, I can feel his energy flow from him, usually that only happens with extremely powerful beings but I still do not know what he is and it intrigues me more. The strokes of his finger tips get lighter, teasing me and I jerk slightly as it becomes ticklish then he smirks down at me. "What's wrong? People will think I had never touched you before." I can not help but smile wildly at his comment as it shows how quick witted he is, and he spends a moment just looking down at me.

"What?" I ask him as he isn't saying anything now.

"You have a gorgeous smile," he replies gently. "This is the first time I have seen a genuine smile from you." I scoff at his words and try to avoid his gaze.

"Don't get used to it, it wasn't intentional," he laughs at my reply then pauses and looks over my shoulder. I can sense someone is behind me and waiting to speak but I do not look around. "Yes?" Mitch says firmly to whoever is there.

"Apologies for the interruption," a man's voice says very timidly. "But Mr Cuthbert requests Miss Moons presence... he would like her to join him in his study for a private conversation." There is a long pause as Mitch stares at him before answering.

"Tell Mr Cuthbert that Miss Moon has a prior engagement and therefore will go nowhere without me," he says firmly and I try to hide my face in his chest, I am becoming pleasantly surprised with his acting.

"But, Mr Cuthbert said..."

"No, I don't give a shit what Mr Cuthbert said," Mitch cuts him off. "Run along and tell Mr Cuthbert that no is my answer." Eventually the man leaves and Mitch turns his attention back to me. "What kind of club did you say this was? Because I am pretty sure there are people having sex in one of the booths behind me."

"A very exclusive one, and thankfully very secret and hidden from the human world," I smile. "The clientele range from demon billionaires, escorts, blood slaves..."

"Blood slaves?" Mitch interrupts me with disgust in his voice then scoffs to himself as though everything falls in to place. "That means... this Mr Cuthbert guy... is he?"

"Yes," I confirm. "Vampires are scarce around here, even more so as many went in to hiding a few years ago and never resurfaced but this one thinks that he is very powerful. Not many of his men are the same though, he controls large portions of this city's wealth and the crime statistics would be a lot better without him. He is your typical vampire however, in the fact that I have never met a single one who wasn't a narcissist. Him being one of the worst."

"And you think this is the guy who has Jake?" he asks.

"Absolutely," I nod as Mitch keeps up his act and pours us another drink. "Nothing happens within 100 mile of this club that he does not know about and the men who took Jake report directly to him. He has his hands in everything from drugs to human slavery. I wouldn't be surprised if the dick heads that were killed in

56

my coffee shop last night also came from him, they did say that they were sent by their boss, so I assume Cuthbert is it." Mitch nods in understanding as I drink another shot.

"So how do you and this Cuthbert guy know each other?" Mitch enquires.

"We have a very... colourful history," I smirk. "I had money, he wanted it, things happened, I got bored and then I left. Last time I set foot in this place I was still pretending to be madly in love with him." Mitch glances over my shoulder again and I pause from speaking.

"What do you want this time?" he says to the timid man who has returned.

"Apologies for the second interruption to Miss Moon... please don t kill me," he says the second part very quietly as his voice shakes, I may have forgot to explain my reputation here to Mitch. "Mr Cuthbert is entertaining some guests in the private area and would like to invite you both to join him." Mitch looks down to me and I nod slightly before he glances back over to the nervous man.

"Miss Moon gladly accepts his invite," Mitch tells him.

"Excellent. If you would like to follow me," the man replies and Mitch nods before moving his hand from my spine to my waist instead to enable us to walk side by side to the private area. From this point on I won't get a chance to speak privately to Mitch to make sure he is doing everything right, so I just have to trust that things do not go downhill. We are led through a curtained off area in to a secondary bar. This one is much smaller than the main club but is still decorated in the same style with a bar counter to one side and a scattering of sofas. At the side is a pool table and mini dance floor, it is all exactly the same as I remember it. Sat on the sofas are several people I do not recognise, but instantly can tell which of them are here as friends, which are hired muscle and which ones are servants. "May I introduce Miss Moon to the room," the man who led us in here says to the guests as I enter, then everyone turns to look at me and Mitch. I feel his grip on my hip get tighter as he has his arm around me, I am not surprised though, there are about 25 people in here right now, scattered around and to an outsider it can be quite intimidating when you have no idea what is about to happen. After a few moments of silence and me not moving, a gentleman with long dark hair, neatly tied back in a low pony tail stands from his seat between two very beautiful young ladies. He is dressed very old fashioned, the suit jacket is flamboyant with its filigree pattern over his gold waistcoat and black shirt. He always did like to be the centre of attention.

"Hello Darian," I say as he just stares at me. No one else moves or dares to say a word but I can feel the tension, even more so between the several members of staff that are dotted around as they will have heard the stories about my past here.

"I see you are not alone, that you have brought a new toy alone with you," he grimaces as he looks at Mitch. Gazing over his build, taking in his features and the more he sees the more I can tell that he hates him already. "No word from you in almost 67 years then you just waltz through my door and..."

"My door," I stop him abruptly. "Be under no illusion who owns this place. You were always just the manager, nothing more, but after the shit I was served when I first walked in here tonight, I am now starting to believe that you cannot even do that job correctly." There are a few moments of very high tension and awkward silence before he forces a laugh to make his guests believe it was a joke between us and everyone around us relaxes. There are not many people that have ever spoken to Darian like that in his long lifetime, anyone else who did usually ended up dead, but not me, I guess I was special.

"I missed that mouth of yours... my sweet Rosa," he says then walks towards me and holds out his hand for me to take. I do think about shunning him, making him wait but I need to play nice, keep up the act if I want to get Jake back so I take it and he slowly raises my hand to his lips then kisses the back of it gently before smiling up at me. "You are still the most beautiful woman I have ever laid eyes on." I force a smile to keep up the ruse then glance at the two women who he was sat between when we entered, they look like twins, the kind of slim build you would see on a super model and they are stunning to behold. Something about a woman's legs always attracts me and I can not help but lick my lips as I look at them, so young and full of life. I can feel from here that they are human and I bet they can get quite wild. He notices me gazing at them before quickly placing his fingers on my cheek and turning my head back to look at him, making sure he is the only one who holds my attention. He knows from the look on my face that it is not jealousy I am feeling towards him having such beautiful company, he knows I would be more attracted to the stunning ladies sat beside him, than to him himself. "What brings you here tonight, my Rosa?" he asks as the people behind him go back to talking amongst themselves. I always found the elite classes in this world to be a lot more self absorbed so when a conversation did not focus on them, they were not too interested, which is perfect when I am trying to keep a low profile. That question however, has me a little stumped as I did not actually think about what I would tell him when I walked back in here for the first time in 67 years, he probably looked for me when I disappeared but I am very good at covering my tracks and did not want to be found. I go to reply but before I have a chance to speak, a woman, possibly looking mid 30's stands from the sofa on the left and interrupts me in a shrill tone.

"He is a rather nice specimen," she says loudly, her eyes transfixed on Mitch. "Where did you find him?" She is wearing a short black dress that accentuates her curves beautifully, her short blond bob fits her face and overall she looks pretty but I can see from here that the dress is second hand and the shoes are knock off, with Darian's usually high standards, I can't help but wonder how she gained entry here. Possibly new money, possibly invited so she becomes a snack later, or a well presented groupy who is looking for a thrill with a local vampire. Darian steps away to let me speak, going back to sit with his girls, so I take the opportunity to turn towards Mitch and place my hand on his chest as he continues to hold me close.

"I didn't, he found me," I tell her truthfully. "And I am very glad that he did. Easily a top standard, fully compliant and tastes divine... On that thought though, could you get me a drink?" I ask Mitch then nod towards the bar. He leaves go of me and walks away without protesting which I smile slightly at, at least he is now following my rules.

"How much do you want for him?" she asks as she approaches me and I have to force a smile, she is already getting on my nerves and it is the hight of bad manners to interrupt me when I was speaking to Darian.

"He is not for sale," I inform her as I know Mitch will be listening to everything that is being said and I am sure he does not want to become someone else's sex slave tonight, he was less than pleased when I said he had to pretend to be mine.

"One million? Two?" The blond is persistent, I don't really blame her, Mitch is an extremely attractive man. Even I was overcome with temptation when I first met him, then he opened his mouth and he has slowly went down in my opinion ever since, then of course the killing me thing did not help matters. She stands waiting eagerly for me to accept her offer but I casually shake my head. "Well, how about a swap, just for this evening?" She asks desperately then signals to the man who was sat beside her to stand up. When he does I have to force myself not to stare at him. He is tall, ripped and extremely appealing. He is not wearing a shirt. Only tight fitted black pants and I can't help but trail my eyes down across his abbs, his body is chiselled like a Greek God with a slight tan that highlights the pumped muscles of his arms and chest, and for a moment I just let my eyes wander down further to his bulge. Any other time I wouldn't hesitate in saying yes, the Adonis standing before me would instantly spark my interest and I would have no option but to give in to my craving and see exactly what was tucked away in those trousers... but I have a job to do, I have to think about Jake.

"I don't think he will be my type," I lie as the very beautiful man slowly approaches me so that he can try to please his Mistress and entice the swap from me. He smells like pure unadulterated sex, the musty aroma fills my nose as he gets closer and I am really struggling to hold myself back from reaching out and touching his amazing body. I bet he feels like marble, his smooth skin just begging to me licked and bitten. He stops about two foot in from of me and just stares in to my eyes for a moment whilst I unintentionally lick my lips.

"May I touch you, Mistress?" the hunk asks me and I nod, a little too quickly maybe. I have to maintain my cover after all, just because Mitch is here doesn't mean I should ignore who I am and how much I used to like to play. This is why I spent so long in Darian's company, the freedom and sex was always so exciting and intoxicating that I just could not get enough. The hunk reaches out and gently strokes his finger tips across my cheek then steps close to me and places his other hand around my back, his fingers playing under the material of my dress just above my arse, skimming the top but not exploring any further as of yet. I cannot deny that I am incredibly turned on right now, who wouldn't be, his aura seems so dirty in a kinky sort of way. Everyone else in the room continues their conversations, ignoring us completely as this sort of thing happens all the time, it is what the club is known for and it caters for all walks of life and their many taboo needs. Out of the corner of my eye I see Mitch approach with my drink and he just stands, unsure of what to do or how to react to this sight before him as the hunk leans in slightly, his breath cascading across my cheek. "May I taste your lips, Mistress?" Oh now come on, I am trying so hard to be good, I need to ignore my urges but this is just too nice of an opportunity to pass up... fuck! Not what I had in mind when coming in here tonight.

"Yes, you may taste my lips," I reply, trying to hide just how much I would like him to then he slowly leans in to kiss me, my breasts are now pushed up against his chest as he can not possibly get any closer to me. I don't even care any more if Mitch is watching me, I have done much more risky things than just kiss someone whilst here in the past. This club is fuelled by money and sex, so who am I to deny myself a little fun when it is served up to me on a silver platter, I am not sweet or innocent in the slightest, and really, the though of rescuing the kid should not stop me being myself. The hunks touch is gentle as his lips brush my own, teasing me slightly as though knowing the slower he goes the less I will be able to resist him and the more likely I will be to accept the terms of a swap with his Mistress. My mouth opens to his as I start to enjoy him and he slowly lets his tongue explore, caressing my own and giving me feelings that penetrate deep inside, making me want to know everything about him and his body.

"So, do we have a deal?" the hot guy pulls back from me just as I was getting in to the swing of that kiss, as his Mistress eagerly awaits my answer. She is stood to the side of us now, watching us closely to see if her little pet did his job. I let her stew for a moment as I step back, free from his touch and hold my hand out for Mitch to give me my glass so that I can have a drink whilst I ponder my decision. I suppose I could offer her something else instead of Mitch as he would not willingly go with her, something more valuable to allow me time to explore her pet some more without any disruption. I take the glass of Mitch as I gently nibble my lip and think about all the naughty things I want to do to the hunk, then without me even having to prompt him, Mitch moves close behind me and places his hand on my hip before stroking my arm with the other, which makes me smile. At least he remembered the constant physical contact rule that I set in place for him, the more he does this the better he makes me look. I go to reply to the blond, use my power to persuade her to take a new deal, one where I get all of the benefits, but before I do, Mitch moves his fingers to my chin, angles my face up towards him instead of her then kisses me. He kisses my slowly, sensually teasing my lips with his as my mouth instantly opens to him and wants more, my entire body relaxes in his arms as our tongues play, exploring each other, discovering every part and I can't help but moan. His hand on my hip plays with the light fabric of my dress, and my heart skips a beat, almost begging for my dress to be removed so I can feel his touch on my skin. It catches me so much off guard, that I completely forget about the hunk and the blond who will probably be gawking at us right now. My entire focus is on Mitch and the way his lips taste like candy, how much his aura shines, drawing me in as though I want to get lost in him forever.

After a moment Mitch pulls back and just stares in to my eyes, that came out of nowhere and for a second I can't remember the reason we are actually here until I hear the blond exhale sharply beside me, I guess I am not the only one who found that kiss extremely erotic and became completely turned on by it.

"Unfortunately, I do not think we will be staying long enough for me to agree to any terms or swaps you may have to offer tonight," I reply to her without taking my eyes from Mitch then I lift the glass to my lips and take a sip of my drink. Her face drops and she storms back to her seat, quickly followed by the hot guy as though I just ruined her entire week with refusing her access to my escort. I would say I was disappointed to not get to road test the hunk but Mitch has my full attention now and he smiles devilishly at me because he knows it. Who is he? Why is he so different to any being I have met before, his soul sings, I can feel his power and his energy is so electric. The longer I am around him the more I want to know, but I am not sure getting to know more about him is the right thing for me to do. Especially not now that I know him and Jake are in to some deep shit, I said I didn't want to be involved, I told them I was going to walk away. No matter how much I want to ask Mitch more about himself and what is going on, I have more pressing matters as I know I promised to help Jake. He is human after all and who knows what they have already done to him. There are too many people in here to press Darian for answers right now so I need a new plan. "Darian?" I say suddenly as I turn to him to get his attention and alleviate some of the sexual tension that is swiftly growing between me and my mystery man, Mitch. "This party of yours is getting a little boring, nothing like the play sessions I remember us having back in the day, it is a bit of a let down... maybe something a little more intimate will liven things up." I see his eyes light up at my comment, he quickly stands and starts ushering the majority of his guest to leave. Eventually there is just me and Mitch, Darian, the twins and what I assume to be two of his hired muscle. Darian leaves his girls alone on the sofa then wanders over towards me and takes my hand then leads me over to the pool table, away from the bar to speak in private whilst Mitch follows close behind me and both of his hired muscle stay at a safe distance.

"If you like, I can arrange for us to be... completely alone," Darian smiles as I lean against the pool table to relax and he stands directly in front of me, not giving me much room to move and not allowing Mitch to get any closer. He knows that if he has me alone then I will not be so easily distracted.

"You always did like to have me all to yourself," I smile back, playing along.

"Never one to like to share." I believe his muscle are armed, possibly both vampire by the way they carry themselves and the hint of a fresh blood smell I get coming from them. The twins are human, I think, judging by the remnants of the bite marks on their necks and wrists, probably here against their will or more of those groupy types that likes to hang around the darker things in life just for the thrill. I hold out my hand to the side and Mitch steps forward to take it, trailing his fingers gently over my skin as he stands watching me to keep up the act, and I instantly know that has gotten right under Darian's skin as he scowls towards Mitch for daring to touch me.

"But you were never satisfied, my Rosa," Darian replies with a hint of anger in his voice as he steps closer still, trying to assert his dominance over Mitch for claim of me, he always was the jealous type. "You always had someone new to play with, flaunting it in front of me because you knew it drove me wild, thinking about all of the things you would get up to without me. The pleasures you would feel, the experiences you would have." Darian places his hands around my waist and leans in close to smell my scent, his lips lightly brushing over the skin on my shoulder as he does. "The last time I saw you, you were wearing that exact dress," he moans as his hands slide down to touch my ass, squeezing it slightly to feel how ripe it is. "I never stopped wanting you, my sweet Rosa. To taste you, to feel you... Mmm let us be alone, I can show you many things, and make you feel more alive that you have in years," his voice is gentle but commanding. At one point I probably did like it, the thrill of the bite, the ecstasy I felt with the mixture of pleasure and pain, the carefree lifestyle but eventually it just got... old.

"Who said we need to be alone?" I tease him as I pull my hand away from Mitch and instead place them both on the pool table either side of me to enable me to jump up on to it and sit on the edge. Darian instantly moves to stand between my now spread legs, running his hand up my thigh where the split in the dress is so that he can feel me as the other goes up and plays with the skin around my exposed shoulders. "You know I never minded having an audience, adds to the excitement, wouldn't you agree?" He smiles wildly then places his hand around the back of my neck to enable him to roughly pull my head forward to kiss me. Passion bursts between us as our mouths play, experiencing him again after so long and letting him have me. He always was a very generous lover, always made sure I never went without, but he got stale and he was so jealous that I was such a free spirit and enjoyed the variety that this world had to offer. Monogamy is not a word that would ever be associated with me, I wanted to experience every single thing I could, whereas Darian wanted me to be his life partner and tried to contain me, to control me and burden me with the thoughts of only having sex with him for the rest of my days... or for the rest of his days, as I would have getting to the point of being so sick of him and his ego that I would snap and kill him... Hence one of the many reasons I left. I move further on to the table to allow for a little bit of room to move as Darian climbs on top of me and forces me to lie back on the green cloth. His hands roam all over my body, discovering my curves again after so many years as I give in to his desires, letting him dominate me, allowing him to try to take me fully again.

"I wonder if you still taste as sweet as I remember," he moans in my ear when he moves his lips from my mouth to my neck instead. My free hand moves between us, skimming across his hip then swiftly finding the now growing bulge in his pants. He groans more when I unzip his trousers and slide my hand inside, feeling his now semi hard erection through his boxers. "Oh, my sweet Rosa," he whispers then I feel the tip of his fangs graze the skin on my neck, desperate to bite me, to be consumed with my blood. He used to love it, and for a time so did I. He groans loudly with anticipation then readies himself to penetrate my flesh, and at this very moment I know I have him right where I want him. I move my hand down slightly, leaving his cock to grow, then just as he is about to latch on to my neck to quench his thirst, I clamp my hand around his balls and squeeze. Darian freezes whilst on top of me, his eyes bulging out of his head and he lets out a strangled cry of pain. His two muscle men run for us straight away as they can see Darian is in trouble but Mitch pulls a gun from under his suit jacket and stands firm pointing it at them, no one moves as the entire room falls silent. "R... Rosa?" he forces out through the agony as I just smile up at him.

"Apologies for the misleading tactics, Darian," I casually say as he places his hands at either side of my head to try to push himself away from me but my grip holds him in place, stopping him from escaping. I always was much stronger than him, but always held back to make him feel more like a man. "But it seems you have something that I want and I knew you would not be so cooperative to just hand it over without a little persuasion."

"Just go easy there," Mitch says to one of the guys who tries to reach for a weapon. "One move and I swear I will blow your head off." At least Mitch seems like he has control of those two, that is one less thing for me to worry about which means I can give Darian and his balls my full attention.

"You have no idea who you are messing with, Rosa. You will never get out of this club alive, my men will..." I cut off Darian's words as I squeeze his balls harder and I can't help but let slip a giggle at his predicament.

"This morning," I force myself to say without laughing at him. "A few of your men picked up a human man by the name of Jake Parker. I want him back, he belongs to me and if I do not get him, I will kill every single person in this building for revenge."

"I swear, I don't know what you are on about, I do not associate with the trivial affairs of humans," Darian is quick to respond but I do not believe him in the slightest so I dig my nails in firmly and he cries out. "OK!" he shouts. "He is just a pathetic human, he was getting in the way..."

"Where is he?" I ask firmly and squeeze again.

"In the basement!" he yells out his answer as he is clearly in a lot of pain.

"Tell me what you know about him," I say, and then wait for his answer.

"His name is Detective Jake Parker, he is on suspension because I pulled a few strings after he arrested a few of my guys, and started snooping around in things that did not concern him. That new task force shit they set up, they have no laws to bind us, we are above their human rules," he begins. "I thought that would be the end of it but he kept asking too many questions about our world, things that no human should know. Then I warned him to leave the city, back down but he killed three of my men last night so I retaliated. He would not be a nuisance any more to me if he was dead."

"I don't care about all that, it is a cops job to sort the shit you do out, and to be perfectly honest is is about time someone knocked you down and peg or two... tell me what you know about Monroe and Jake's brother, why was he taken?" I squeeze again as Darian looks confused.

"What the fuck?" he cries and I try to hide my smirk. "I don't know what you are on about. Who the fuck is Monroe?" I stop for a second and think.

"Your goons last night mentioned the name Lucious Monroe," I advise him as I watch his expression to see if he gives anything away. "That they knew Jake had been talking to him."

"I had men following him for a while, I thought it would scare him away," he blurts out. "They told me that they saw him meet with a guy, I didn't get the name, I honestly didn't even give a shit who he was, I just wanted Parker out of my way. Humans have no place knowing our business, and I intend to keep it that way."

"You don't know anything about the rising?" I ask, realising that the very limited information he has given me is actually all he truthfully knows.

"What is that? The rising?" he asks and I sigh as all of this effort still gets me no further forward in finding out what the fuck is going on. "I don't know what you expect from me Rosa, asking about names and the worthless humans. They are food to me, occasional fuck company, Parker was just in my way and I wanted him gone so he would not cause any trouble in my business." His expression remains confused, surely there is more to all this than Jake being a cop and doing his job by arresting a few of Darian's minions who got out of line. Even if he did go snooping in to vampire run businesses, that does not explain everything else. "Take the human, see if I care, just please, Rosa, let me up." I pause and look up at Mitch who is still standing firm holding back the two men. He better hold up his end of our deal and tell me what is going on after I did all of this.

"Darian... Tell your men to fetch Jake to us at once, when I have him in my possession, only then will I leave lose of your balls, then I walk out that door. If all goes well it could be another 67 years before you see me again... and I won't even mention that you have some serious work to do as manager here to up your security. That young girl on the desk didn't even ask who my friend here was, letting unknown armed men walk in off the street is really bad for business... So, do we have a deal?" I ask and Darian instantly nods. His men back off cautiously to follow my orders and leave to get Jake. I honestly thought that Jake being taken had something to do with what else is going on, with what the Oracle told him and why his brother was abducted by Astaroth. But it now looks like he was just good at his job and Darian wasn't happy about it. Mitch better confess everything when we get out of here because I will be seriously pissed off if I went though all of this and came out of my coffee shop hiding for nothing.

Chapter Five

"Take Jake straight upstairs and through the door at the top, it is unlocked," I say as we all get out of the car. Mitch nods to acknowledge my instructions as he helps Jake to walk. He wasn't too badly injured when we got him back but he does need some rest. He is a bit battered and bruised, luckily it seems Darian didn't get a chance to do what he wanted with Jake before we got there, so that is good I guess, probably waiting until after his little private gathering before the real fun of torturing and murdering got started. I follow them up and into my small apartment over the coffee shop then into the living-come-kitchen area where Mitch is currently stood propping Jake up. "Jake can take my bed tonight. In the morning you guys can leave me alone at last," I sigh then walk over to the far side where the door is and lead them inside the bedroom. Mitch helps Jake carefully sit down on the side of the bed, he moans and groans a bit, possibly by looking at him he might have a bruised rib and most definitely a black eye tomorrow, but nothing more severe.

"Thank you," Jake forces out through his discomfort as he looks up at me. "The guys who set me free said that you saved my life tonight. Did you get any other information to help us?" Mitch goes to respond to his question but I jump in before him.

"No," I say calmly. "Just get a good nights sleep. As soon as your head hits the pillow, you won't wake up again until breakfast tomorrow," I give him a little push and he nods before lying back in the pillows then falling asleep instantly. It was not nice of me to do that but I have a feeling that Mitch will not talk openly to me if Jake can hear, so I needed us to have a bit of privacy. I stand for a moment in silence, thinking of a good way to bring up the subject but I have never been good at the indirect approach to things. "I think you have some explaining to do now." Mitch reluctantly nods then I follow him back out of my room, he hovers in the middle of the sitting room slightly unsure of what to do or say as I walk over to the kitchen area, open a cupboard then grab a bottle of vodka and a couple of glasses. He watches me nervously as I pour two hefty measures and offer him one which he takes off me before falling quiet. "So, what is so special about the kid?" I ask and Mitch breathes deeply as he goes to stand by the bedroom door, watching him sleep, clearly he cares about him, feels a responsibility for him maybe.

"When we first met, I told you that Jake approached me to help with his search for his brother, that I had some of the more unusual contacts that could lead him to potentially finding him without using police resources," Mitch begins then takes a large gulp of the vodka. "Truthfully, I was sent to find him, to protect him from what is to come." I don't say anything, I just stand and drink, listening to what he has to say and trying to understand it all. "There has been a lot of mention already about the rising and I know that you do not think it is real, I have heard all of the stories as well, I know what it would mean if it did happen in real life. And for a long time I denied it would ever become truth... But I can't deny that things are starting to point to it happening, right now." We both fall quiet for a moment before I speak again.

"From what I remember from the stories," I finally say. "A powerful ancient being, one who was there at the start of human creation will lead an army in pursuit of the throne of Hell. Obviously, the Devil will not just give up his seat, so he must be forced to do so. To do this, they would destroy the Veil, bring Hell on earth and make the humans bow at their feet... There were only a handful of people who were even able to sit in that throne, it is protected and if unworthy, death will be swift for anyone who sits in it. When the throne was made, it was forged in Hell by Lucifer himself, so if anyone else wanted to claim it, their blood would have to be old and they need pretty much a direct link to the creator to sit in it... or that is what the stories say. Plus the Veil is not easily taken down, that in itself is near impossible, many have tried over the years and none have succeeded."

"Yeah, but if that did happen. If the Veil did fall and they brought Hell on earth, then there would be no world left, everything would be destroyed and life as we know it would cease to exist," Mitch pauses to take another drink and sighs deeply. "On the night that Jake's brother was taken, there were also 9 other men taken as well. All between the ages of 13 to 28, all from around the same area where they lived."

"What do you mean?" I ask as I watch him carefully. "Why would Astaroth be taking men?" Mitch looks away when I ask him that, I can tell he doesn't want to reveal the truth but he is going to have to.

"Astaroth is working for someone, I don't know who, or indeed how they managed to persuade him to betray Lucifer, but whoever they are, they are looking for the key to destroy the Veil," he finally says.

"The key?" I say almost in disbelief, I had heard a rumour about that whist protecting the Veil but that is all it was, a rumour. "The key doesn't exist," I scoff but the more Mitch speaks the less certain I am of my own knowledge.

"The key didn't exist... until the night that Jake was born," he pauses and I come to a very surprising realisation that hits me like a ton of bricks.

"He is not human, is he?" I ask and Mitch shakes his head. "Does he know?" Again he shakes his head at my question.

"When he was born, his abilities were bound to ensure that they could not be detected. He grew up in the human world, hidden and as a mortal with a normal family. We did not anticipate that his false parents would die and leave a second child that he thought was his real brother. They grew close and he cared for him until he was taken. If Jake is found then the Veil could fall. The key was said to be a sacrifice, one single being with a heart that was pure but a soul that was black." The more Mitch explains, the more annoyed I am beginning to feel. I guarded the Veil for centuries, I slaughtered thousands who tried to bring it down and now he is telling me that the key to destroying it completely is now lying asleep in my bed. The Veil is what holds all the monsters from Hell back, it stops the nightmares entering the human world. "His real mother was an angel and his father a demon. Astaroth was sent to collect humans who were thought to be the key. The night Astaroth entered the house where Jakes brother was... he took the wrong one. We were close to losing Jake that night, he had been watched over since the day he was born and the powers-that-be thought that the only way to protect him was to hide him amongst the humans." I listen very carefully to what Mitch says as I stare at him in disbelief, each little word falling in to place and making me realise exactly who I am now speaking to. "Usually, the politics that concern demons in their own domain do not affect us, they are free to do as they want in Hell as long as it does not impact the human world. If they enter the human world then they are fair game. But as soon as the rising started to happen, we knew we had to act regardless of where that took us. We cannot let it get out of hand and..."

"Get out," I cut him off as I struggle to remain calm.

"What?" Mitch asks surprised.

"Get out of my home," I say, trying to breath normally. "I can't believe I let you in, this was all a massive mistake."

"Rosa, please, calm down. I don't know what you are one about," Mitch says cautiously as I go to the kitchen counter and pour a very large measure of vodka in my glass then drink it all before turning back to look at him. His eyes meet my gaze, chocolate swirls that keep wanting to tempt me, his skin amazingly clear and his body... but now just looking at him makes me feel sick to my stomach.

"What is your real name?" I ask him as he stands staring at me.

"Mitch is my real name," he says calmly.

"Bullshit!" I snap. "I want nothing to do with this, I want nothing to do with you... I can't be near you, just knowing what you are... it makes my skin crawl." I try not to laugh with frustration, he touched my skin, I kissed him, I feel so fucking dirty.

"Rosa, you are not making any sense," Mitch says firmly, but I just laugh at him and shake my head.

"What is your name?" I ask again, almost pleading with him to tell me the truth, then after the longest of pauses he nods slowly and sighs as though knowing I will not drop it. "Because I have lived long enough to know that there is no such angel called Mitch. Especially one who is of so much importance to be sent by the powers-that-be to protect the key to destroying the Veil... What are you? Normal angel? Archangel?" Mitch looks down at the floor as I speak. "You need to leave. I cannot have a fucking angel in my home."

"I don't understand your issues," he tries to say calmly back to me but I can see he is getting as annoyed as I am with my sudden change of attitude. "Reapers are neutral, they do not take sides. They collect souls, regardless of where that soul ends up. Heaven or Hell it doesn't matter, it shouldn't matter at all to you and..."

"Is Mitch short for Michael?" I cut in and he stops mid sentence. "Are you the fucking Archangel Michael?" My hands are shaking as I stare at him, for thousands of years angels and demons have been at war, secretly fighting over the human world. If he knows who I am, the link I have to Hell then he will try to kill me. It is his duty to his lord, to kill me if I am within the limits of the human world. I have never faced an angel before, but I have heard stories of their power, they could potentially rival my own and I do not want to have to fight for my life tonight. Even just the small amount of power I felt when Mitch touched me has me a little nervous. "Please, I need you to leave."

"I am not going anywhere without Jake," he replies quickly. "And I still believe that you have information that could help us stop the rising. You have knowledge, clearly you are hiding something, and your actions in the real world send major red flags my way. You are in deeper than any being I have met and I have never been one to just back down, so how about you tell me what you know." He stares at me, unmoving whilst I think of something to say but my mind is racing and I need him away from me.

"I don't know anything. It is all just a load of shit and even if I did know then I wouldn't tell a god damn angel anything," I say firmly and I see him smirk at my words.

"As I previously said, reapers don't take sides," he smiles more knowing that I am hiding something. "So what are you?" I don't reply to his question so he continues. "See what I think is that you do know about more than you are letting on. You do know about the weapon that Jake was told to find and in fact, I think you know exactly where to find it so that we can use it. Plus given your aversion to angels, I think you are some form of demon, not one I have come across before but one who has very strong beliefs and who probably is not as powerful as they think they are as most demons all think they are above their own status." Mitch approaches me until he is close enough that I can smell his aftershave, leering over me, trying to intimidate me. If he thinks I am a low level demon who is now afraid of him then he will think he can push me around. "If you know that I am an angel, then you know that you cannot kill me in this realm... so why don't you start talking?" I laugh at his comments and he seems slightly taken aback.

"For a so called private detective you are extremely thick in the head," I smirk. I know he is trying to dominate me, show me he is more powerful than me, but he has no idea who I really am and my mouth has a way of reacting before my brain does when I am in a sticky situation or when I feel like someone underestimates me. "The star of the morning is not a physical weapon. It cannot be wielded like a blade... It is a person."

"The star of the morning is a person?" Mitch asks me to confirm and I just nod in reply, slightly kicking myself for telling him, but at the same time I kind of want to tell him. If the rising is happening like he says it is, which I don't actually believe, then certain things will be found out eventually. He remains silent for a minute pondering my statement then it finally dawns on him. "A morning star? Morningstar as in the name?"

"You think that just because you sit up there on your fluffy white clouds, praying to your creator, that the whole world below is black and white," I smirk knowing that he will not like the path the Oracle has sent Jake down at all. "How does it feel to know that the only way to stop the rising is with a member of Hell's royal family."

"It won't be Lucifer," he says to himself as he walks away and starts to pace around the room, thinking. "Then it has to be one of his children. Let me think... He had seven children, each one became a Sin... they could be anywhere, living in the human world, hidden, scattered... Hmm, that is not ideal. If I get close to one of them in the open then it will cause a war, an angel confronting one of Lucifer's children would... Why the fuck would one of them even entertain the idea of saving the humans, they spent their lives tempting souls to get them to Hell... If we had our way, they would have been killed years ago. Wiped every single one of them off this earth and rid the humans of damnation," he stops and takes a deep breath, a million thoughts running through his head all at the same time then looks back at me. "What do you know of the sins?" There is a question that could have so many different answers.

"I know that they are all spoilt brats and not a single one of them is powerful enough to protect the key. They wouldn't have a clue about the Veil, how to guard it or even how to fight as they are too complacent with their own lives and have never had to work for what they had," I say with clear disgust for them. "But that is all you are getting. I want you and Jake out of my house, and out of my life as soon as possible."

"No, I will not accept that," he says then comes back to stand in front of me. "Tell me how you know about the Veil, how you are so certain that the Sins are not responsible for guarding it. No one else that I have ever met has sounded so certain when speaking of such things and after searching for so long to get answers with Jake, you are the only one who I feel knows everything... Please. Tell me how you know all of this."

"I have never met a proper angel before," I say as I know I need to try a different tactic to get him to leave, or at least change the subject. "No wonder you didn't want to touch me in the club, why you were so reluctant to a lap dance... I heard that all angels were so pure that they went their entire lives free from any kind of Sin. Sex before marriage is wrong where you come from, isn't it? That would make you a virgin, wouldn't it? I bet you wouldn't even know what to do with a woman, how to please her, how to fuck her."

"You know nothing about me," he growls, my words getting straight under his skin and secretly I am enjoying winding him up.

"I know that all you angels think you are God's gift," I reply. "That you are all just good little soldiers for the big man up in Heaven. Doing anything your lord commands you to do because he says that it is righteous, when in reality you are all just a bunch of dick heads with wings."

"Tell me who you are?" Mitch says firmly as he is shaking with anger at my words, but I can't, he has already shown me his dislike for demons and the Sins, if he knows who I am then things will go bad.

"No, I can't tell you who I am... but I will tell you the names of the Sins as they reside in this world if you leave, right now. Find one of them, get them to help you and then forget about me," I say but the way it comes out of my mouth sounds almost like a plea, almost as though I am begging him and he knows it but the way his eyes soften at my words. "Forget you ever saw me. For all anyone knows, I do not exist and I have stayed under everyone's radar for the majority of my life."

"Rosa, who are you?" Mitch asks again, trying to be gentle this time as if he knows that if I tell him the truth, everything will change.

"Please, you need to leave," I say and he just shakes his head in defiance. "Please. If anyone finds out the truth, then I will be hunted, there will be a bounty on my head and... you will want to kill me and I will be forced to defend myself then Jake will be left exposed."

"That's not true, why would I want to kill you?" he asks, confused as to what I am saying.

"Because I am your enemy," I blurt out as my voice wavers. "I have spent my entire life hiding my true identity... and I don't want to tell you, because if I do, then it means you will have a very difficult choice to make. I bet an angel would kill for the chance to get near to Hell's royal family, the ultimate glory would await them if they managed to take down one of the most influential demons in Hell... You would have to chose between protecting Jake and going for glory."

"What does this have to do with you?" he asks me, and I swallow the lump in my throat knowing that he will not leave and that I can not keep my secret much longer.

"I met him once you know, Jesus, that is," I say and Mitch listens. "We were born on the same day and I wanted to know what all the fuss was about with him, why he was so special compared to me. Why all these people worshipped him when he was only a human with a couple of cool party tricks. The people followed his every word but yet my own family didn't even acknowledge me most days. I was jealous of him. After I met him, even more so because he was so accepting and kind... He had love and even after his death, all these years later, people still say his name... yet no one even knows mine." I pause and the room is deadly silent. "I left my home and devoted my life to my work, to show everyone what I was capable of but I never went back and no one even knows what I did... You really want to know who I am?" I ask, and Mitch nods gently. "I am the most powerful soul reaper who ever lived, for centuries I was the watcher of the night, the Keeper of the Veil, the protector and the only one who ever made sure the shroud never fell. I was the Guardian... I killed thousands in the past who tried to take the Veil down, I guarded it with my very being and now you are telling me Jake could undo my life's work... The weapon you now seek to stop the rising, is most definitely a person and I know this because... Because it is me... I am a star of the morning."

"Rosa?" Mitch says in shock as I avoid his gaze. "Rosa, who the fuck are you? You are not a Sin, and Lucifer has no other family, he..."

"He had another child," I cut in and finally look up at him. "One who pretty much no one knew about, and wasn't really important enough for him to take pride in... So, the Archangel Michael is now faced with Lucifer's 8th secret child... What does he do?" I can see his chest heaving as he works through all of the information I have just given him, debating about how to take me down. I was brought up to know that if you ever crossed an angel then you took your opportunity to kill it before it killed you. "Come on then, all powerful angel. Now you truly know what I am, I would love to see you try to kill me. That is what you have to do, isn't it? You find someone like me in the human world and you take them down?" There are a very few tense moments before he lunges at me. I lose my footing on my heals and stumble back, Mitch is right in front of me as he rams me up against the kitchen wall, the plaster cracking behind my back due to the force and his forearm is firmly across my chest to hold me in place as he stares at me. "I know what you are thinking, how much you want to kill me just because you know who my father is. That if you do kill me, you will gain glory for your side, you..."

"You have no idea what I am thinking," he snarls at me as he holds me firmly in place. I go to push back against his hold, testing his strength but he slams me back in to the wall, he is a lot stronger than I anticipated so I will need a different tactic to beat him.

"Really? Then why don't you enlighten me to those thoughts in your head," I say sarcastically as I smirk back and wait for him to answer. He is strong, but I know I could take him down if I needed to, he has no idea what I am truly capable of. He watches me closely, his own eyes almost burning as he decides on his next move.

"Right now, what I am thinking is how much I want to rip that dress off you and fuck you so hard, that you beg me to stop," he says as he stares in to my eyes, focusing solely on me then my mouth falls open slightly. I am readying for a fight with him, running through war plans in my head so that I can survive, so I am not sure I heard him right. "Tonight I watched you play with that vampire, his cock in your hand before you subdued him with ease. Then I watched on as you kissed that topless man, he was literally begging you to have him, to take him and use him how you pleased. I could feel the passion burning within you as I touched your skin, I could sense your powerful energy dripping off every word you said... then without thinking, I kissed you in front of all those people and I couldn't get the thought of it out of my head." I have no response to that as his chest heaves then his eyes trail down across my body, falling down my cleavage and admiring my curves. "I don't often find myself in a position where the urge gets too much, I am usually good at controlling it whilst in the human world, but I have to admit, you intrigue me." He spends a little longer just staring, me not speaking or moving whilst trying to work out if this is some sort of weird plan to get me to drop my guard so that he can take me down quickly, before he suddenly moves closer and goes to kiss me. His lips crash against mine, urgency taking control of him as his mouth dominates me and I just stand pinned to the wall, unsure of what is going on.

Mitch moves his arm from across my chest then swiftly grabs both of my hands as they dangle by my sides and rams them into the wall at either side of my head, restraining me roughly so that I can't get away from him. But I don't want to get away, I don't think I do anyway... I don't even attempt to push back as my mouth opens to his and our tongues play wildly, every inch of my body becomes extremely aroused and I find myself getting lost in the moment, moaning slightly through the deep passion and letting him just take control. His body presses up against mine, the rock hard muscles busting to get out of his shirt, one of his thighs angled so close that I can feel it rub between my thighs... I am already out of breath and nothing has happened yet. He pulls back and stands for a moment just looking at me as I don't move, I don't try to get out of his grip, I just stand, waiting to see what he does next.

"Well this is certainly an unusual way to try to kill me," I joke, trying to cut through the mounting sexual tension then Mitch laughs before releasing my hands. But I do not get a chance to do much else as he grabs my waist and pushes me, forcing my feet to move until I am almost leaning over the breakfast bar in the kitchen area, I inhale sharply as his sudden dominating movements catch me off guard and make my loins beg for more. Holy fuck! I do love it when a man takes control of me. My forearms are flat one the counter top and do not move at all as I wait to see what he does next. He stands behind me, close enough that I can feel his breath on my skin as his fingertips gently stroke down my spine, then just like before, I jerk slightly with the slight ticklish feeling, his power dripping off him, then he slowly trails his fingers down, takes hold of the material of my dress that hugs my ass then rips it off me in one forceful motion. The dress hangs loosely from the thin straps across my shoulders as he spends a moment skimming his palm over my now exposed arse. The only other thing I was wearing apart from my shoes was a very revealing red g-string. He hooks his fingers under the thin strap that runs between my ass cheeks, playing with it, enjoying the sight before him, then his hand slides down between my thighs, stroking me through the thin material that is the only thing standing between him and my already wet pussy. I can't help but let a moan slip out as he touches me intimately, the energy between us almost vibrating and just when I think he going to tease me forever to make me wait, he places his free hand on the middle of my back and forces me down, making me bend over fully until my face is resting on the cold counter. He then quickly moves the fabric of my panties to one side and slips his fingers between my lips, going straight to my sweet spot.

"Oh, fuck," I moan deeply as he connects with my clit, allowing me a moment to feel him then he stops. I hear him chuckle to himself behind me before he speaks again.

"Now, if I was being a good sex slave for my Mistress," he says playfully and it instantly makes me smile. "What exactly would I do next?" I take a moment to steady my breathing as he knows how turned on I am already from his actions. Just from the brief few bits of me he has seen, the interaction I had with Ruby in the club and the offer that I had to turn down the the Adonis, he knows I like sex... a lot, and right now he has me right where he wants me.

"That would be up to my slave, their ultimate aim would be to please me," I reply then wait.

"Hmm," he groans, the sort of groan which tells me that he is getting as turned on as I am. After a moment of him pondering my words, he swiftly kneels behind me, he spends my legs roughly, making them a good couple of feet apart then his hands grab my arse cheeks and almost instantly I feel his tongue delve into my pussy before making one smooth stroke to my ass hole. My legs feel like they go to jelly as his mouth plays, my hands grab on to the counter top to hold myself up and I moan loudly as what he is doing feels incredibly amazing. His touch alone is intoxicating, I knew that I could feel something different about him earlier tonight when he touched me, and now I know that it is pure power, his aura is almost like magic. He slips his hand through my thighs and begins to twirl his fingertips around my clit, his actions have got my pulse racing and I am finding it hard to control myself from gushing all over his hand. "How's that, Mistress?" he teases as my legs shake, knowing full well that I am enjoying it as I can not control the sounds I am currently making, then without waiting for a reply to his question he plunges his fingers in to my pussy and roughly begins to stimulate my G-spot.

"Oh, fuck," I manage to force out as his fingers fuck me hard, my heals make me wobble as I struggle to keep up on my feet, but again I just hear a slight chuckle from behind as Mitch is clearly pleased with himself and with the fact he has all the control right now. His digits delve deeper and their movements become more urgent as I hurtle towards orgasm. My moans fill the little apartment, every inch of my skin is warm and tingles with the sensations then just as I relax into it completely, to let myself give in and cum, he stands, pulls me up from the counter and forces me to kneel in front of him instead. Any other time I would be pissed off that I was so close to cumming and forced to stop, but not with him, I don't know what it is about him but I would literally let him do anything to me. I take the opportunity to remove the straps of my dress down my arms then discard it on the floor whilst he watches me catch my breath then I slowly undo his belt and slide it free of the loops. He never takes his eyes off me as I open the zip then pull down his boxer shorts, freeing his dick from the material before leaning forward and teasingly running my tongue along his shaft, taking my time so that he wants it more, teasing his skin so that the desire intensifies in his eyes. It doesn't take long before he gets rock hard, my lips now wrapped around his cock, making him all wet and he moans more the deeper I take him into my mouth, each time I move my head back and forth.

"Shit," Mitch groans as he puts his hand on my head, his fingers playing through my hair then as I take him fully in my mouth again, he firmly holds it in place, stopping me from pulling back for a moment, his cock deep in my throat and halting my ability to breathe. He stares at me as I glance up and we make eye contact, him doing what he wants with me and me letting him fully, not even resisting a tiny bit. My chest starts to burn and my eyes go glassy with tears as he smiles down at me, revelling in the fact that he has all the power here. Eventually, he leaves go and I pull my head back, inhaling deeply and forcing air in to my lungs as I look up at him, my chest is heaving but it all just turns me on even more. All my life I worked hard and was always in control of everything around me, so the very rare instances where I can relinquish that to someone else, is like a massive weight is lifted off me and it makes me feel more alive than ever before. Mitch grabs my hair and pulls me up to stand in front of him, now just wearing the tiny red g-string and my heals, he just smirks as he looks down across my breasts.

"Do you have another bedroom?" he says casually and I just nod. He has me captivated, his whole persona is appealing and I just can't help myself, I want to know what fucking an angel feels like, I want him to fuck me so hard that I scream or beg or cum so fucking hard I pass out. "Where is it?" His voice is commanding but playful and the slight growl instantly turns me to a big pile of girl jelly. I swallow hard and point to a door over in the corner where my bathroom and spare bedroom are. He smiles at me then leans down to kiss me again. He holds my head in place with one hand through my hair as the other roams over my skin then plays with my breast, kneading it in his palm and lightly pinching my nipple, sending little pangs of pain through me which makes me more aroused than before.

Men who can dominate me in this way are very few and far between, but I am not averse to it, I actually quite like it. I have probably given pretty much every kink and sexual act a try at some point but nothing beats a good rough sex session to get my blood pumping. Domination doesn't even have to come from him being stronger or more powerful than me, mostly it is all the mind, the playing, the teasing, the fun... My chest is already heaving by the time he pulls away from me again, when he does I gently bite my lip and it makes him smile, his face filled with lust and I am holding myself back from just begging him to take me right her on the kitchen floor.

"I think now is a good time to tell you, that what you think you know about angels, might not be exactly accurate," he smirks then forcefully spins me around on the spot and playfully pushes me towards the spare bedroom before I get a chance to reply to him. I walk in front, trying to hide my smile as I enter the room then just stand on the spot with my back to him. It is pretty plain in here, a double bed, wardrobe. I never use this room so there isn't really anything else.

"OK, so I admit it," I say as I hear Mitch close the bedroom door and approach me from behind. "All the information I have been given about angels comes from other demons. Even when I worked with Monroe, he never said otherwise and..." Mitch grabs my arm, making me turn towards him and he pulls me in close, my breasts are pushed up against his chest as his mouth consumes mine again. As we kiss, I unbutton his shirt, he removes that and his jacket then just dumps them on the ground, both of us becoming overcome with urgency as our tongues play. His skin is so soft and warm, and I can't help but run my hands over his bare arms as he wraps them around my back, encasing me and giving me a feeling of being completely safe, whilst both of us swiftly build in passion and enjoy each other. His body is amazing. I know tonight I thought the sex slave guy was attractive, but Mitch is built outstandingly well now that I see him for the first time. His muscles are pumped and well defined, his skin is the softest thing I have ever touched and the sweet scent that is coming from him is almost like candy floss now that I am so close. After a minute of us just touching each others skin and continuing to kiss, he turns me around suddenly and forces me to bend over the bed, his actions are driving me wild with lust. Placing my hands in front of me to support myself, I wait patiently as he removes his shoes and trousers before stepping back towards me. His palms skim over my behind, taking his time and making me wait as he clearly enjoys the view of having my arse in the air for him, before taking hold of my g-string and ripping the small piece of red fabric off me with his bare hands. I am not even mad, right now I wouldn't care if that was the most expensive g-string in the world, that was so fucking hot.

I glance over my shoulder and smile as he steps forward, placing his hands on my hips, the tip of his cock slides between my moist lips but he doesn't go any further, almost just waiting to make me want it more, the slight touch making my breath quiver with anticipation, then he thrusts in deep. One fluid motion as he fills my hole to the brim making me moan loudly as it takes my breath away, then he slowly pulls all the way back out and thrusts in again.

"Tell me how much you want me to fuck you," he growls behind me, the tone of his voice sending pangs of pleasure direct to my core as his cock is still inside of me, not moving. Both of us just feeling that connection, which is sending me dizzy with wanting.

"I want you to fuck me so bad," I tell him. Then I hear him groan to my words. He moves his hands to my hips and starts to move his cock, slowly at first as I close my eyes and enjoy the feeling, then moving more forcefully. It seems like he no longer wants to wait, he doesn't hold back, he swiftly picks up pace and very soon I feel like I can't breathe at all. It doesn't take me long to hurtle towards climax, he rams me hard, showing me his strength, taking me completely. I have had more than my fair share of hard fucks in my time, but his power definitely gives him the upper hand. He knows I am not a weak little kitten so he lets go and gives me everything he has got. My knees buckle beneath me as I struggle to stand with the growing pleasure, so he moves me forward to kneel on the bed instead, continuing to fuck me from behind, his fingers digging in to the flesh on my hips as my moans become louder, echoing around the room the longer he continues.

"Holy, fuck!" I cry as I cum suddenly, so hard that my arms collapse beneath me, unable to hold me up and I gasp in to the sheets. My entire body shakes as the pleasure consumes me and washes over every inch of my body, then being prolonged with the fact that Mitch does not slow down, if anything hearing me cum makes him want to fuck me harder. By the time that explosive orgasm starts to disperse, I can hardly breath and my throat is sore, I didn't realise how loud I must have gotten and I can not help smirking as I think it is a good job I persuaded Jake to sleep all night and not wake up. When I finally feel able to catch my breath, Mitch pulls back to give me a moment to calm my racing heart then carefully removes my shoes as I just stay still, trying to regulate my breathing with my ass still in the air, that was so quick, it came out of nowhere but it felt amazing. My heels thud to the flood behind me then he grabs my arm and pulls me up so I am now standing with my back to him, he briefly pauses whilst holding me still to inhale my scent, moaning to himself as he does. He gently skims his lips across the top of my back, letting the soft brushes linger on my skin before he leaves me standing alone and moves to lie in the middle of the bed, pushing the pillows out of the way so that his head is flat, then holds out his hand for me to take. I smile more as I go towards him, his impressive rock hard cock standing to attention for me, I take hold of his hand and attempt to straddle his lap but he instantly shakes his head at me then pulls me forward, making me move away from his erection.

"Who said I wanted you to ride my cock?" he smirks and I look at him confused for a moment before he grabs my waist and moves me up the bed, positioning me so that I can place my knees either side of his head and allowing me to settle down on his face. He quickly wraps his strong hands around my thighs and pulls my pussy towards his mouth, his tongue instantly finding its way inside, lapping at my juices and exploring me intimately. I reach out in front of me and grab on to the headboard for support as he moves his mouth to my clit and gives it his full attention. It throbs beneath his lips as he gently sucks and licks it in to submission, my body already unintentionally bucking against his movements as I am already so turned on and sensitive. I am so aroused by his behaviour that I know I can't hold back for long as I feel the pleasure swiftly rising inside of me again, my soul begging for him to make me cum for a second time as my head falls back and I can not help but let out my cries of ecstasy. The more I seem to move and squirm, the firmer his grip becomes on my thighs, not allowing me to get away from him and keeping me in a position where he has full access to everything he wants. My breathing gets deeper and my skin becomes flush as my clit throbs for a release, then that feeling inside just explodes as I cry out again as it hits me with force, consuming me completely as I orgasm.

I hold my breath as I do, not being able to even think about forcing air in to my lungs as my mind is filled with the sensations he is giving me, knowing that his only goal is to make me cum. He doesn't stop though, he continues to play, my bud now so sensitive that every flick or twirl is making me buck against him and I find myself trying to push away from the headboard as the feeling becomes so all consuming. Mitch senses that I am extremely receptive to his actions, and the louder I seem to get the more he is enjoying it as I swiftly cum again, harder and more intense than the one before, I almost scream with pleasure as the entirety of my loins feel like they are on fire, so much so that I naturally try to force myself up and away from him again, the sensations now becoming too much to bear. My throat is burning as I gulp in air but he doesn't slow down, he keeps going, making my entire body shake, then eventually, when I feel that I cannot take much more, Mitch leaves loose of my thighs and I collapse to the side of him, lying on my back on the bed just staring up at the ceiling as he props himself up on his elbows so that he can look at me. I breath deeply, trying to regain my composure and calm my now racing heart.

"So... you were not... thinking about... killing me then," I say between deep breaths and he just smiles.

"Nope," he replies with a playful tone.

"And, following that... You were definitely not a virgin," I smile to myself as what he just did was amazing and it takes practice to be that good with his tongue.

He has clearly done that before, many times, probably centuries worth.

"Nope," he tries not to laugh at me as I feel like my limbs don't want to move, every inch of me is perfectly relaxed. "So, you used to work with Monroe?" he asks and I just smile as I almost forgot I mentioned that to him.

"Yeah, for quite a while. I don't understand, though, how he knew to send you and Jake to me," I say thinking about everything that has happened so far but the thoughts are all muddled in my head. "I can't even think straight right now. Fuck me! That was intense." Mitch laughs then sits up on the bed, looking down across my body at me as I lie naked in front of him.

"No, time for rest yet," he smirks. "I never said I was finished with you." He slowly crawls towards me until he is on top of me, kneeling between my legs then he takes hold of my hands and playfully pins them down, either side of my head. His fingers wrapped around my wrists as he looks down on me and I see the spark of pure desire in his eyes. I don't know what it is, everything I know about angels and the war we have with them, is telling me to run, to get as far away from him as I possibly can. But at the same time I want him to touch me all over, I want him to consume me, his aura is dragging me in and I have no way of escaping it. He leans down to kiss me, my mouth opens to his instantly as he positions himself then he slowly enters me again, he just glides in as I am so wet from all of the playing already. I let him take me, lying beneath this pure hunk of an immortal man, his muscles hard as rock and lips sweet like sugar, I don't even care what might happen next, I am far too focused right now on how good his cock feels so deep inside of me. He rolls over and takes me with him, until he is lying on his back again and I am sitting on his lap, I smile down at him as I start to rock my hips back and forth, taking the control for a while and watching him enjoy the fact that I am now giving him pleasure. His finger tips trail across the skin on my thighs as I relax in to my own movements and moan deeply, I know I can make myself cum again, quite quickly if I really wanted to but I think now it is my turn to tease and please Mitch.

"Oh, shit, you feel so good," he groans as he stares up at my body, his eyes captivated by my breasts as they move, bouncing slightly with every thrust of my hips but I just smile, and lean back to add to the friction. Mitch moans deeply as he builds toward a release, watching me closely as though the sight before him arouses him more, then he moves one hand between us and begins to play with my clit with his thumb whilst I grind on his cock. It is still very sensitive off before so as soon as he starts playing again, that intensity hits me and I cry out with every twirl and flick he makes. Having him deep inside of me and then the added sensation on my clit is driving me wild and I am trying so hard to hold back, to wait, to prolong the experience but I can't help it, my body needs me to cum. I clench my jaw as I try to hold back, allowing him time to enjoy being inside of me, but he moans deeply and the sounds he starts to make tip me straight over the edge. I try to stop it but to no avail as my pussy tightens around his shaft and I cum so hard, simultaneously from both my pussy and clit, my entire body shaking as I struggle to keep to my rhythm, and as I do Mitch's free hand grabs tightly on to my thigh as he erupts inside of me, joining me in euphoria. But I don't stop, just like he didn't, I keep to my pace as my body quivers to ensure I drain every last hot drop out of him, then when I am certain that we are both done and satisfied, I finally stop, take a moment to breath deeply as we just gaze in to each others eyes, my hands on his chest to steady me as I still feel his cock inside of me. I am not sure who breaks first but we both start to laugh slightly at the sudden, very sexually explosive situation, then I carefully move from his lap to lie by his side on the bed. We both just stay still, staring at the ceiling as we try to regain control of our breathing, and basking in the glow that we created together.

The way the day started, with Jake being kidnapped, finding out the rising was real and thinking that a shit storm was going to commence, I never thought it would end with me fucking who I thought was a mortal enemy, someone I was led to believe would kill me if given half the chance, and me actually telling someone who my father was. I have never done that before, not even to the people I was closest to and who I trusted the most, so what made Mitch different? Why did I tell him and end up trusting him so much with my secret?

When I decided to leave my fathers home and I left that world behind me, I never had any intention on going back and even now, I don't understand why it would all involve me. Surely, out of everyone that exists, the billions or humans, the armies of demons and the heavens full of angels, all the signs can't just point to me, can they? I haven't fought for the protection of the Veil in so long that I might not even be able to do it any more, when I left and came to the human world I assumed another would take my place, so what happened to them and why are they not the one that should be saving us all. Out of everything, there is only one thing I am certain of though, now I know about Jake, who and what he is, plus where he really comes from, he will be safer if he knows the truth about himself and his potential power. No one should have the right to keep that secret from him, and if I was in his shoes, I would want to know that Astaroth and who knows who else is looking for me as I sleep. He doesn't even know that he is one that everything depends on, the whole human race could end because of him.

Chapter Six

After last night, I slept so deeply that when I finally wake up, I don't know where I am or what day it is. I got extremely confused as to why I was lying naked in a strange room that was not my bedroom and definitely not my bed, until I remembered what actually happened and why I ended up in here. When I sit up in the bed, I am alone, the sheets are tucked in around me to keep me warm as though someone made sure I was comfortable and pillows had been placed under my head. The bedroom door is open slightly, I can tell my apartment is not empty as the TV in the living room is on and I can hear someone opening cupboards and looking for things in the kitchen. Once I regain my senses and realise who is making all of the noise, I get up and rake around the wardrobe in here until I find a t-shirt and a pair of panties, there is not much else in here apart from a few items I forgot I had as the rest of my things are in my main bedroom. I pause for a moment and run through what to say when I go out there, do I act like we did nothing last night? And what if I go out there and he has a bunch of angel buddies swarm on me... no, that is stupid. If he wanted to kill me then he had plenty of opportunity to do so whilst I slept, I guess I just have to face him and see what happens, so I put on my big girl pants then head out of the room.

Mitch is currently playing around with my coffee machine and when he sees me out of the corner of his eye, he gets another cup out of the cupboard to pour me one without saying a word. Jake is sat on the sofa and looks up as I walk out of the bedroom. I smile at him slightly, he looks a lot better than he did last night and the deep sleep I put him in seems to have done him the world of good but I get no response back, just a blank expression which is a bit weird as usually he is the first one to speak. I brush it off, maybe he is still processing his kidnapping from yesterday and has other things on his mind, I don't blame him, being taken by a vampire crime boss would make any human go a little crazy. Another few uncomfortable seconds of him just looking at me makes me force my smile wider in bewilderment before I head over to Mitch and take the cup of coffee that is offered to me. He hands me the cup of fresh brew and I thank him and smile but he hardly even looks at me, the only interaction is a slight nod in response to my appreciation then he turns his back on me and continues to make his own cup of coffee. This is not exactly what I was thinking would happen after last night but I guess people deal with things in their own way, he is an Archangel after all and he did just sleep with Lucifer's daughter, that has to break a dozen sins at least where he comes from. I hover for a moment unsure if I should say anything else to him before deciding to give him some space so I a wander away then stand leaning up against the breakfast bar to have a drink. This is a getting majorly awkward now, I try to concentrate on drinking the surprisingly nice coffee that Mitch has made for me whilst I ignore the fact that Jake has not stopped staring at me or even blinked since I got up and Mitch is silently making coffee without acknowledging the weird tension that is consuming the room at all.

"Your injuries don't look as bad this morning as they did last night, a bit of rest seems to have done you good, you almost look as though nothing even happened," I say to Jake but he doesn't reply. This feels very strange, I wonder if he is being like this because he knows I fucked Mitch last night whilst he was sleeping in the next room or it is due to the fact I am literally just standing here in a tiny pair of panties and an old retro band t-shirt. Mitch walks from behind the breakfast bar then goes to sit next to Jake on the sofa wearing the black suit pants and the white shirt which now has its sleeves rolled up, he hands him a cup then focuses on his own to avoid making eye contact with me. Even though Mitch has sat right next to him, Jake still doesn't stop staring at me. "Erm... did you sleep well last night or..."

"The Devil is your dad?" Jake finally speaks and cuts me off. Mitch casually ignores what is going on as he drinks his coffee and watches the TV as though we do not exist at all. "Like, the real actual Devil? The big red guy with horns?" I force myself not to laugh at his comment as I see Mitch bite his lip to stop from doing the same. I forgot how innocent humans can be sometimes, although I need to remember that he isn't exactly human, he just doesn't know it yet.

"He doesn't actually look like that," I say calmly. "He can change his appearance when appearing to humans to influence them, sometimes in a form that strikes fear, other times he blends in so that to not be seen, but..." I stop myself as Jake's face is a picture of pure disbelief, almost not comprehending that I am so casually speaking about Satan himself. "Yes," I smile slightly. "Lucifer is my father." He nods his head then falls silent again. I can not spend all morning with these two if they are going to be acting like this so I quickly think of some way to change the subject away from me. "But obviously the revelation that I come from Hells royal line, is probably nothing compared to you finding out that Mitch is an Archangel," I say and Mitch's eyes go wide, he finally looks towards me and just stares, almost as though he wants to rewind time and stop me from speaking but I smirk back at him as I know he had not told Jake that part yet.

"You're a what?" Jake asks him, totally shocked, but Mitch doesn't know how to reply, which also tells me that he has not told Jake who he actually is yet, that he is not human. Too many lies and secrets between so called friends are not a good thing... although I am not really one to talk about that, I kept my secret and lied about who I was for over 2000 years.

"Well, I erm..." Mitch shifts uncomfortably in his seat as he tries to think of something to say, but nothing comes to mind as I see him laugh slightly with nerves then change the subject again. "So Rosa says that this weapon that the Oracle told you that you need to find is actually a person, a Morningstar if you will, not a Star of the Morning and that she is it, Rosa is the weapon," he quickly says I smile.

"Not just me, no offence to you both, but the less involved I have to get with you two, the better it will probably be for my health," I reply off handedly. "As I told Mitch last night before we..." I stop and smile to myself, remembering what we got up to whilst Jake was asleep, and the thoughts of him making me cum so hard make my cheeks blush, which is uncommon for me, it was just sex, nothing more so I don't know why I feel embarrassed or shy about it. "I told him that the Star of the Morning could also refer to any of the seven Sins, who are also the children of Lucifer and my older siblings. The name Morningstar was my fathers name and it passed to his children, any one of them could also be this weapon that the Oracle told you to locate."

"But I don't believe that they will be able to help us," Mitch adds persuasively. "Not like the way you can help us, Rosa. You told me yourself how powerful you are, what you have done in the past. I am now under no illusion that we were both sent to find you, the Oracle mentioned the star and I think that is you, no one else." I shake my head and sigh deeply. Maybe if I just tell them who the Sins are they will back off me a little, find them and deal with all of this without me.

"I would love to help you, I really would," I lie. "But things are complicated and like I said before, if the rising was coming then there would be signs pointing to it, a lot of signs in fact and I have not seen a single one. Someone out there would be trying to... to..." I get lost off with what I was saying as an image flashes on to the TV screen, catching my eye and I momentarily can't breathe. My heart almost stops as I just stand in pure shock and stare at the pictures.

"Rosa? Trying to what?" Mitch says to get my attention but I ignore him and grab the remote from the chair to turn the volume up.

"Police reports suggest that this was not a targeted attack and instead a burglary gone wrong," a middle aged woman says over the top of a video showing footage from outside a very expensive mansion. There is police cordon tape stopping the reporters getting closer and emergency services vehicles everywhere. "They believe that the intruders thought the house was empty and tried to target the safe which contained millions of dollars in diamonds and precious stones, but they were interrupted when Mr Smith returned home early from work to find them inside his property. Unfortunately, his body was found this morning by a cleaner who notified the police. Sources at the scene say that whatever happened inside that house last night, was something out of a nightmare and the remains of Mr Smith were found scattered in several rooms throughout his home."

"Do... do you know who that is?" I say quietly, my voice shakes uncontrollably as the picture of a middle aged man comes on to the screen. His dark slicked back hair perfectly styled, an expensive suit and the same grey/blue eyes as myself.

"Yeah, I do," Mitch replies casually. "Scott Smith, multi billionaire oil tycoon, he has been all over the news for years, works all around the world buying and selling land and..."

"How did this happen?" I interrupt him. "How did they kill him?"

"Like the news said, robbery gone wrong," Mitch answers, but that is not the question I meant. He clearly does not know the full truth, who Scott Smith really is.

"No," I say in disbelief. "He shouldn't be able to be killed. That man, Scott, he is Greed, he is a Sin." I slowly sit on the arm of the chair as it sinks in. There is no way a Sin can be killed in a robbery gone bad, no matter what kind of weapons those people had, he is immortal.

"He was your brother?" Jake asks cautiously, trying to understand what is going on.

"This isn't right," I say quickly, then stand back up. "He can't be killed like that, it has to be something more, something they are not saying... well, of course they won't say, the humans won't have a clue, to them it will just look like a massacre but... could it have been one of your lot? Could an angel have confronted him and things went down hill?" I ask Mitch, desperately trying to find the answers that I seek but he shakes his head.

"No, Rosa, I'm sorry," he replies gently, clearly seeing how much distress I am in. "If it was done by one of us, it would have been covered up, it would never have getting any attention, not like this, this was done for show, probably to send a message... Rosa, I know you were not close to him, but I am very sorry for your loss." I didn't realise how something like this would affect me. I grew up hating them, they were always mean to me and treated me badly but, when faced with one of them being killed, they were still my family, I can not ignore that. Tears threaten my eyes and I don't understand why, I don't get emotional, I don't get attached to people, so I don't understand how this now hurts, I have a tightness in my chest and I can't catch my breath at all, this is all new for me and I do not like it. Mitch gets up from the sofa and carefully takes the cup from my hands as they shake uncontrollably, then places it down on the bench and stands watching me as I think about what I need to do.

"I guess this is a sign, but it can't be, it can not happen," I say as my voice shakes. "I need to know everything about the rising, erm... I don't know where to start, you had no other information and I erm... I should see the Oracle, Alysia, see what she can say about... I..." Mitch slowly approaches me and forces a small smile of concern.

"Rosa, we will come with you," he says gently. "Go and get dressed." I can't take this all in, there is too much going through my mind to concentrate on my surroundings. The rising wasn't meant to be real, it is just stories, there was no key, the Sins are immortal... everything I thought I knew is crumbling around me and I am starting to lose control. "Rosa," Mitch says firmly but I an transfix on the TV, still showing the footage of the outside of Greeds home, knowing that his mutilated body still remains inside... I don't know what to do. "Rosa, look at me," he says, placing his palm on my cheek so he can move my face to look at him instead of the TV. "Get dressed, then we will go," he says calmly but firmly, and I just nod.

After a few dazed minutes of getting dressed, I head back in to the living room, both Jake and Mitch are standing patiently waiting for me, both unsure of what to say or do to help me right now. When we leave, we walk most of the way in silence, well, I do at least. I don't understand how Greed could be killed and as much as I want to deny that the rising might actually happen, I can't ignore that this is a massive fucking sign. Mitch and Jake have argued all the way as they walked behind me, Jake is not particularly happy to be finding out that the person who he now sees as a close friend, lied to him for who knows how long and he doesn't yet understand why Mitch is here then if he is an angel. I hate to think about how he is going to take the rest of the news about himself once he learns the truth, and that the people who he thought were his family were all fake just to cover his identity. At least now that I know who he is, what I felt when I first met him makes sense. That need for me to protect him, to have him not die in my coffee shop... it was because deep down my soul knew what he was, and accepted that it was my job to make sure the key was never found and the Veil never fell.

"Hey," Mitch says gently as he places his hand on my shoulder to get my attention. "Are you OK?"

"Yeah, I'm fine. Why wouldn't I be?" I force a smile and continue walking. I learned from a very young age that crying never solved anyone's problems, even when I was so utterly alone and decided to leave my home, I never got upset. It was just a waste of time, being emotional is one thing that has no place in my life. If I was to cry for the loss of my brother, it wouldn't bring him back. It wouldn't change how he died, I didn't even like him much so really I shouldn't even care at all.

"Do you want us to come in with you?" Mitch asks gently, and I just shrug, I don't understand why he is being so nice to me all of a sudden.

85

"Whatever," I reply offhandedly and go into the shop as Mitch and Jake follow behind me. There is no one here in the small entrance space when I first walk in but as soon as the door closes behind us, Alysia swiftly appears at the curtain that leads in to the back and just stares at me.

"You have seen the news, haven't you?" she asks, and for a moment I just freeze, unsure of what to say. "I am sorry for your loss," she smiles sweetly but I am confused as to why people keep saying that. It was not my loss, he wasn't a part of my life so when he died, I didn't lose anything.

"How do you..." I try to ask her how she knows I was related to the man on the news but she cuts me off.

"I have known for quite some time," she says sweetly. "I am the Oracle after all, even if you always did think everything I said was bullshit." Her comment makes me smile slightly before she continues. "I know who you are, that you hide your real name, and where you really come from... But now there are other things you need to know, because his death is not the first." I take a moment to digest those words before I find my breathing shake and I don't want her to say any more to me. If he is not the first then that means others have already been lost, and I didn't even know. "Maybe you should come and sit down," she says carefully then beckons for me to follow her into the back so that she can read me. I am reluctant to let her though, it took so much last night just to tell Mitch who I was, without letting the Oracle get inside my head and foresee my future. But I did come here for a reason thought, I can't ignore this no matter how much I want to, so eventually, I nod and follow her through, Mitch and Jake are right behind me for support. "Take a seat," she instructs as I look around the small, dark room. Lit entirely by candles, a table big enough for 4 sits at the centre with chairs around it and everything is styled in the same way as the entrance area. Jake, Mitch and Alysia all sit down as I stand nervously by the side. I don't even know what I am nervous for, it is not like I am about to run in to battle with little chance of survival, I am not about to walk to my death... but I do know that when I sit in that chair and listen to what she has to say to me, it will change everything and I don't know if I am mentally prepared for that.

"I didn't bring anything to pay you with," I say, suddenly remembering that she needs something of value, but she just smiles and gestures again to the empty chair opposite her.

"Finally getting my chance to read you, will be payment enough," she waits patiently but I do not move. "You still don't fully believe that I can see, do you?"

"I don't know what I believe right now," I reply truthfully. "Yesterday I didn't think the rising was real or that an immortal Sin could be killed, now all of a sudden we may be looking at the apocalypse." Alysia nods and smiles sweetly at me as Mitch and Jake remain quiet.

"You have seen many lifetimes, and I am sure that you are not easily fooled," she says. "But things are changing and unfortunately for you, no matter how much you want to ignore it, things do involve you, Alexis." My breathing hitches as she says that name. No one has spoken that name to me in thousands of years.

"Alexis?" Mitch asks as he tries to cut through the tension and understand what is being said.

"That is your name, isn't it?" Alysia asks me gently. "Alexis Morningstar?" I get a chill run through me as all I can do is nod in reply and she again signals for me to take a seat. There is no way she would have know that name, it has never been uttered in the human world, it was never mentioned again after I left my fathers home, and I have never ever told anyone my name was anything other than Rosa Moon. "Please, sit down." I swallow hard before reluctantly nodding then I take a seat. The room is deadly silent as she takes a deep breath before speaking again. "Before I begin, I say to all of those who visit me that I cannot give you all the answers that you seek, I can only open the doors to enable you to find them yourself. And I am sure you do not want me to do the whole theatrical, over the top fortune teller act." I shake my head, I would rather her drop the act that she gives the humans that come in here and just give it to me straight. "As I said previously, the sin Greed is not the first." I inhale sharply as this strange feeling hits me again and I don't know what it is. "9 days ago, a man was pulled out of the river, no ID was on him at the time and the authorities have said it was an accident, possibly he fell in the water and drowned... but he was murdered and his body dumped."

"Who was the man?" Mitch asks, but I get the feeling like I already know.

"Rosa would know him by the birth name of Wrath," she says gently and I just nod, not being able to comprehend the words, as though none of what is currently going on around me is real. "Greeds death is being highly publicised and is all over the news this morning, unfortunately, he was also not the only one lost last night bringing the total already to three." The room falls silent and I can see everyone staring at me to see how I react or what I will do.

"Who was it?" I force out as I can feel myself becoming more uncomfortable with the situation, almost as though I don't want to know the truth and my entire body wants me to get up and leave right now.

"In this world they were know as Siena Driver," she replies and I let out a weird strangled noise, half laugh, half disbelief. Part of me still thinks what she says is a load of crap and the rest of me is struggling with the fact that she would even know these names, and I know categorically that she is not telling me lies.

"Siena Driver as in the big Instagram star?" Jake asks. "She has 100 million followers, is a socialite, absolutely gorgeous... people pay her to be seen with their products and she doesn't even have to lift a finger to do it. Millions would kill for her life, she has everything so easy, does fuck all and gets paid for it. Surely that is not the same..."

"Is she Sloth?" Mitch interrupts him and I just nod in response. I don't know what to do. How can three of them be dead already and no one noticed? "How did it happen? If she is as famous as Jake says then people would know, right? It would have made the news as well this morning."

"Her body hasn't been found yet, but when it is, it will look like a drug overdose," Alysia tells him. "The person responsible for these deaths is being careful not to make them all look the same so it doesn't attract any unwanted attention." Out of all of my siblings, Sloth wasn't so bad, she was just fake as fuck and always living for the attention of others, or having every one else run around after her so she did not have to do anything. Sort of too laid back to care about me and my feelings at all. But no matter how bad any of them were, they did not deserve these kinds of deaths, the kind where no one would even know who they truly were in this world.

"Who is killing the Sins?" Mitch enquires as I remain silent, running through a million different thoughts in my head.

"That is something that I cannot see. Sometimes things don't reveal themselves in the way you want. But the real question that you should be asking is why the Sins are being killed," Alysia replies to him.

"I know exactly why the Sins are being targeted. It is because someone needs to destroy the bloodline to get the current ruler to break and give up the throne," I say as my voice shakes and I just stare at the table in front of me as I think. "One point that is always missed out from the stories is that when the rising happens and the Veil falls, not only will it bring Hell on earth, but the only way to then restore balance and save the human world is for the current ruler of Hell to say so. If Lucifer was to either die or step down to allow a new king, it would give the opportunity for rebirth. That way, if so desired the new ruler could restore the Veil, on the other hand the new ruler could start the apocalypse, there is no other way of restoring the Veil except during this change of power. If Lucifer's bloodline was non-existent then there would be less resistance or claim for the throne. He would be more likely to relinquish power, killing his children will make him more inclined to bend to the will of this mother fucker who is responsible."

"I don't understand," Mitch says quietly.

"Basically, if Lucifer relinquishes power, if all his children are dead and the Veil falls," I try to explain. "Then there will be nothing to stop the new ruler of Hell from destroying life as we know it. That is the aim of the rising, to bring Hell on earth completely. So the Veil is the last hope that this world has and must be protected."

"It can still be stopped," Alysia says calmly. "But it will not be easy. Only the last star of the morning can end the rising, now that it has already begun."

"I'm sorry to interrupt," Jake says cautiously. "You said "last" star just now, you didn't say that part to me before."

"Things have changed, events have already been set in motion now," she replies. "Very soon, you will have few options left."

"So, you mean the last, as in the last one born?" Mitch asks and the massive sinking feeling in my stomach tells me that his deduction is wrong. "That is who we need?"

"No," I say quietly with the realisation of just how much shit I have landed myself in. "She means last, as in, soon the rest of Lucifer's children will all be dead and that will only leave me left... excuse me," I stand up abruptly, forcing my chair back then quickly leave the shop to go outside. I feel like I can't breathe, my lungs are on fire and my entire body is shaking. I spend a moment to myself, trying to come to terms with the fact that she is saying three of my siblings are already dead and there was nothing I could do to stop it. Why do I even care so much though? I walked away from my family so long ago, that they probably don't even remember I exist any more, so why should I give a fuck if they did go and get themselves killed?

"You alright?" Mitch says cautiously as I eventually turn around to head back inside. He is stood in the doorway, just watching me so I hide all of the shit I now have in my head and force a tight smile so he can't see the turmoil now rising inside of me.

"Yeah, I am great," I lie to him. "I just needed some fresh air, that's all. The place is full of incense and shit, tickles my nose." Crossing my arms to hide my discomfort, I slowly walk back towards him.

"It is OK to grieve, you know. They were still your family," he says gently but I shake my head and almost laugh at him.

"It is a long time since they have been anything that could resemble my family. Plus, why do you care?" I ask sarcastically. "After all, it was only last night you said that they should have all been wiped out a long time ago. You said that you wished they were all dead." I push past him and head back inside towards where Jake and Alysia are still sat at the table before Mitch has a chance to respond to my comment. Alysia and Jake are both silent as I retake my seat, I pause briefly to regain my composure then clear my throat. "So... what we know already is that someone, but we don't know who yet, is killing the Sins to enable them to dethrone Lucifer and take over Hell," I say calmly. "Whilst doing that, they are searching for the key, as they need to use it to bring down the Veil and create Hell on earth. Making it a free for all, for every demon and supernatural arsehole around to pretty much run amuck and do whatever the fuck they want." Mitch listens from the side of the room as he leans against the wall, he doesn't say anything at all as I speak. "As much as I should enjoy that prospect, with being who I am, I quite like this world and if the humans get wiped out, then I suppose both Heaven and Hell will be worthless and then cease to exist. No human souls means no afterlife, which means we are all royally screwed."

"What is this key to destroying the Veil?" Jake asks seriously, trying to understand everything as I ignore his question. It is not my job to tell him, I was not the one who took his abilities, made him mortal and lied to him his whole life.

"Erm, how about we have a word, you and me, in private," Mitch says to him as he looks around the room. He can clearly tell that everyone else knows something that he doesn't. Eventually, he just nods then gets up from the table and follows Mitch outside, leaving me and Alysia alone.

"So, what happens next?" I ask her as the room is silent.

"That entirely depends on you," she replies. "Three of the Sins are already lost, and I am afraid that it will not stop there. Soon it will be too late."

"Why me?" I sigh. "Why I am meant to be the one who stops it?" Alysia closes her eyes for a moment and breathes deeply, trying to get the answers that I seek.

"I think you are connected somehow, but I can't see fully, it is more of a feeling that I am getting. As though if you were to walk away right now, we would all be doomed," she says gently as I listen. "You need to reconnect with your past, rediscover who it is that you really are and embrace it fully. You are of no help to anyone when you spend your time pretending to just be a human waitress in a coffee shop. You are more powerful than even you know, and we face a threat that this world has never seen... and now this world needs Alexis Morningstar." She pauses and I sigh deeply before speaking again. I have never believed in destiny but I do believe that what she says is correct. If someone is capable of killing the Sins then it can only mean disaster if it is left unchecked.

"Who is the next Sin that will be targeted?" I ask. "Maybe if I can warn them, try and stop this thing before whoever is responsible reaches the Veil then..."

"It is already too late," Alysia interrupts me. "Even if you left now, by the time you reached the next target..."

"Who is it?" I ask firmly as I stand up from my chair. "I refuse to just let it happen. Who is the next target?" Alysia debates for a moment about telling me, before finally nodding.

"They are close, actually I feel that they are only a few streets away. There is a dating agency and couples therapy business, it has won many awards for matchmaking and bringing together life partners plus reaffirming marriages and helping couples of all ages," she informs me. "The Director of the company is visiting the offshoot branch in this city for a few days, which will leave them vulnerable... but like I said, you will be too late."

"Lust?" I ask, but she doesn't reply. "Alysia, tell me, please, is it Lust? Is she the Director of the company?" Alysia reluctantly nods again then sighs deeply.

"A few streets over, you can't miss the sign," she tells me and I don't wait to hear any more before I turn and exit out of the shop as quickly as I can.

"Don't fucking dare try to justify this," I hear Jake shout at Mitch as soon as I get outside. "My whole fucking life has been a lie, how do you expect me to react to that."

"It was for your own safety," Mitch tries to explain.

"I should have been given that choice," Jake snaps back. There are multiple people standing watching the growing commotion outside the little fortune-telling shop, but I don't wait to hear any more, I have more important matters, so I just run. It takes me about 10 minutes to get to what I think is the right place. Up ahead I see a large bright red shop front with blacked-out windows and a sign that says "who needs true love when you can have a bit of lust".

I bolt through the front door and enter directly into a large open plan reception and waiting area. There are a few doors leading to small rooms to one side and a corridor at the other. The entire interior is white and immaculately clean, with large ornate mirrors on the walls, expensive artwork and the room is dripping in crystal decorations. At the far side of the room, behind the several white leather sofas with people sitting on them, is a desk with a smartly dressed young man, he has a wireless headphone in one ear and he talks away whilst typing on the computer in front of him. I take a second to regain control of my breathing, so that I do not look like a complete mad woman then approach the desk.

"Hi, I am here to see..." The young man holds his finger up to stop me speaking and I am quite taken aback by it, so I just stand for a moment in shock. Did he seriously just shush me?

"So, I told him, Sugar, if you ain't going to put a ring on my finger, then you know where the door is," he continues his conversation with the person on the other end of the phone as though I do not exist. "And do you know what he did?... No, that mother fucker packed his Gucci bag and walked straight out that door... I know right, he..." I casually lean over and push the button on the phone in front of him to end the call, cutting him off and he instantly looks up, staring daggers at me. "What the actual fuck do you think you are doing?" He snaps at me, trying to remain professional as a few waiting clients turn to see what is going on.

"Your boss, I want to see her," I say firmly, not taking any of his shit.

"Then you can make an appointment, like everyone else and wait your turn. You are nothing special, a lot of people want to see her," he replies sarcastically. The door opens behind me then out the corner of my eye I see Jake, looking a little lost. He must have seen me run off and followed me just to try and get away from Mitch and his truths about who he really is. I take a deep breath to try to make myself remain calm but it doesn't work, so I swiftly reach out and grab the young man by his shirt then yank him forward until he is leaning over his desk. Several of the contents on the top are knocked over including his cup of tea which spills on the keyboard.

"Listen here, you little shit," I try to say quietly through gritted teeth as to not attract too much attention from the watching eyes behind me. "What room is the big boss lady in?" I push, persuading him to tell me the answer.

"Down the corridor, end door. But she is in a meeting," he says as his voice shakes. Jake approaches me slowly from behind and watches what I do.

"In a meeting with who?" I ask firmly.

"I erm... I actually don't know," he says, clearly confused as to why he can not remember as he is meant to know the meeting schedule, coordinating who comes and goes. "Miss Lux came in early, about 9 am and went straight to her office. I know she is meant to be in a meeting but... I can't remember anyone going in." I drop the young man and he just stands trying to think, as though he has missing memories that he now cannot recall. It is almost 12 noon according to the large clock on the wall behind the desk, she has been in that office for 3 hours and if he can't remember who went in, and no one has come back out... then I could already be too late. I bolt from the reception and run down the corridor, not stopping till I get to the end where there is only one door with a nameplate that reads "Miss Felicia Lux" then knock. I am a bit impatient so after only a few seconds I knock again.

"I am sorry," the young guy says from behind me as his voice quivers with fear. "But if you don't have an appointment then I will have to call security, I will..."

"It's OK," Jake says to him as he follows us. "No need to inform security, I am a cop." There is no answer from knocking so I try the handle but the door is locked. I take a brief moment to calm my breathing as I suddenly feel sick to my stomach, my heart is pounding and I know everyone is watching me. I need to get in, I can't wait any longer so I take a step back then kick my boot into the door, the door frame snaps and the door itself crashes into the office wall on the other side, sending wooden splinters and bits of plaster scattering everywhere.

"You will have to pay for that, that is criminal damage. You will be prosecuted and.." the young guy falls silent as I slowly walk into the large office. There is glitter and diamonds everywhere, the very girly and bold decorating choices of pink, black and red, smack you in the face as soon as you enter. Several large sofas dot around the room with a large black glass desk at the far side. Behind it, sitting in the very expensive red leather chair is Lust. She has a gun in her left hand that now hangs loosely and rests on the arm of the chair, her other arm dangles lifelessly at the side. Up the wall behind her is an unimaginable amount of blood splatter, chunks of brain and random fragments of skull. As I cautiously approached her, I can see that the entirety of the back of her head is missing, blown to pieces, leaving a gaping hole in her from the exit wound of the bullet, that looks as though has been fired whilst the barrel was inside her mouth as blood drips down her chin. The crimson liquid coats the back of her chair as I take it all in, then all I can hear is the young guy from reception start to scream.

I can't do anything but stare at her. Her beautiful long wavy blond hair matted with chunks of flesh still attached to bone that now lay on the floor, her pristine white suit stained and her eyes... her eyes have a look of shock or fear, they are not the eyes of someone who was at peace with themselves enough to end their own life.

"Go back to your reception and call the police," Jake instructs the young guy and tries to calm him down. "Get everyone to stay seated as they may have seen someone or heard something that could be useful."

"She erm... why would she do that?" the young guy says as he tries not to sob with shock. Jake ushers him out as I just stand, silently looking around her office, trying to see if anything seems out of place or unusual. I know categorically that Lust would not have killed herself, for starters it would take more than a bullet to the brain to do that, plus she loved life. I mean, she really loved life, every single bit about it. The only way that she could have been killed, is if she was not who she was meant to be, but what I am seeing is not possible, this is not something that can possibly happen. Thinking about the other Sins, the way that they have died, if it was all done by the same person then it wasn't a specific weapon that did this, all of the deaths are different. Wrath drowned, Greed was cut into pieces, Pride was a drug overdose and Lust has a bullet through her skull. This doesn't add up, something isn't right... How could they die?

"Hey," Jake says gently behind me as he comes back into the room. "Is she a Sin?"

"Yeah," I sigh. "She was Lust... I just don't understand."

"It looks like suicide," he says carefully. "You just never know what is going on in someone's head and..."

"I know what it looks like," I snap back, interrupting him harshly. I didn't mean to, it just slipped out. "But it is not suicide, this is murder. I don't know who is responsible, but she is now the 4th Sin to be lost and I don't know how to stop it from happening again."

"You guys are immortal, aren't you?" Jake asks and I just nod in response to his question. "Then how do you die, if you are meant to live forever?" I think on that for a moment before answering. The thoughts in my head all lead me back to one explanation but I do not know how it could be possible, it is too far fetched.

"There are very few ways to kill someone who is immortal," I say, thinking out loud. "But all these deaths, the ways in which they have died, points to only one answer. As unbelievable as it is, as I have no idea how it could be possible and I don't even know how it could be done, but... someone stripped them of their immortality first so that they could easily murder them as though they were nothing more than human."

93

Chapter Seven

"Is there anything I can help you with?" Mitch says quietly to Jake as I sit in the waiting area alone. The whole place is swarmed with people, cops, forensics, paramedics... Even news reporters are hovering outside to try to find out what is going on. All of the people who were here for various appointments have been interviewed and let leave, the receptionist has had several melt downs and was taken to sit in a police car so he could be looked after, and everything just feels so surreal. Mitch must have followed Jake after I ran off and found this sight, not something any of us expected to have to deal with today.

"I think you have done enough, don't you," Jake snaps back at almost a whisper at Mitch, still angry that their friendship was all based on lies. "And I am not the one who needs the help right now." I know they both keep glancing over at me, but I have just been sat with my head down, lost in my own thoughts as everyone carries on around me. All these humans have no idea how significant this is. All they see is a business woman who took her own life, whereas I see a sign that the end of the world is near.

"Hey," Mitch says gently as he approaches me but I don't look up, I feel too lost, too out of control and I do not like it. "We should all talk, properly about what we need to do."

"We do not need to do anything together," I say offhandedly without even looking up. "We don't need to talk, I am not your friend, I do not want to work with you and I certainly do not want to be involved one bit," I scoff then stand up, Mitch stays silent and just watches me. "After all of this, the rising seems like it is pretty imminent. So my advice to you would be to get Jake somewhere safe, hide him if you have to and then forget about me. The last thing you need, is to be associated with a Morningstar. Angels and demons are not a good combination." My voice shakes, which surprises me. I have all of these strange feelings inside of me that I have never experienced before. Maybe I have lived in the human world too long, their weakness is rubbing off on me. I take a moment to breathe and find my inner strength again, before heading towards the door to leave.

"Rosa, wait," Mitch encourages me to stop and I do, just to see what he wants. "I know things are unusual, but you are now in a position where you could do the right thing and help us to stop this."

"The right thing?" I snap and turn to finally look at him. "You lot didn't do the right thing when you stripped a half-ling of their immortality. You didn't do the right thing when your actions left him vulnerable. And you sure as hell did not do the right thing by bringing me in to this... I was perfectly happy living in ignorance, and I will be again when you guys all leave me the fuck alone."

"Rosa, you are the one who is meant to save everybody, your actions will protect the humans," Mitch says with a strange tone, I am not quite sure what it is though... Pity? Denial? "You need to stay and help us."

"I am the daughter of Lucifer," I say firmly as I get in his face and stare him straight in the eye. "I don't give a shit what happens to the humans, let them all perish then see what your God has to say about it, because I do not take orders from Angels, and I do not take orders from you." We both stand in silence, I can see it in his eyes that he is angry with me, that I am showing blatant disregard for what is going on around me but I don't care. "You arseholes are always just thinking about yourselves, believing that everyone worships you and has to follow your word. But what about what I want? What about the beliefs I have?"

"We are talking about the potential end of the world," Mitch says quietly so that no one else hears.

"So?" I say back. "Your God is infallible. Your God is almighty. If you think he is so great then go to him for help. If he is such an amazingly strong creator, then he could stop this, he could fix everything in a blink of the eye... If he could do all that, but doesn't, then to me it seems like he won't want to. So why should I bother my arse to fight when your creator sits back and waits for the world to burn?" Mitch doesn't answer me so I turn on the spot and leave. Jake looks confused as to where I am going but just as he tries to come after me, he is approached by a police officer so stops to speak instead.

I don't know where I am going, I just walk. From the moment I was born, I was told that God created life on earth, that his angels watched over his creations with love, and those who did not fall in line or do as they were ordered, were cast out, my father being the first. He used to be Gods favourite son, he was beautiful, intelligent and powerful, but his potential was stifled. God wanted to rule alone, he didn't want anyone to be able to threaten his position, so when my father wanted more, when he wanted to be as great as God, he was punished for it. God punished his son for wanting to be just like him, he cut off his wings and threw him out of Heaven, disregarding him like trash and forcing him to rule Hell instead, where he would spend the rest of days as he would never be given the grace of God again.

At first I admired my father. He showed traits of a true leader, powerful beyond words and he enjoyed playing with Gods creations who God loved more than his own Angels. If my father had treated me as he treated my brothers and sisters, I probably would never have left, however, my love for my own father quickly started to fade the longer I stayed in his home. I felt outcast by him, the same way he was with God, and because of it, I no longer admired him, instead I started to hate him. I tried, I really did, to be who he wanted me to be. I worshipped my father, I did as he commanded but yet I became forgotten about. The more I tried to please him, the more he pushed me away, until one day I finally left and never looked back. I wanted to forget I was even related to him, I hated the Sins, I envied his love for them and the longer I was away, the happier I became.

But now I am being told that because of who my father is, makes me a target for some mother fucker who wants to destroy all of creation. Maybe I should let them, in my youth I often dreamed about being able to harm and maim the Sins, but that is all it was, dreams, because over all my time alive, I have never come across something that can make a demon like any of the Sins, turn mortal. They had to be practically human to be killed, and I have never come across any sort of magic or being who is capable of doing such a thing... Unless, it is God doing this. If he is so all powerful to be able to create everything around me now then I am sure he would be able to make someone lose their immortality... But if that was the case then why would Mitch be trying to stop it? If he is the Archangel Michael that I have heard about in all of the stories, then there is no way he would go against God's word. It was even said that Michael led God's armies against my father during the great war of Heaven, which ultimately led to my fathers defeat and his banishment to Hell. He was meant to have exceptional strength and courage, he fought for good to prevail over evil and he protects and defends those people who love God. So why the fuck would he want to work with me? It is his duty to kill me, in his God's name, he should fight to protect the humans and banish evil. And that is what I am, evil. I always have been. You don't go through life being the daughter of Lucifer by being good and nice. You do it by showing everyone around you how powerful you are, even if my father didn't give a shit what I did. All of this is not my problem, let the big "I am's" deal with it, it does not involve me one bit.

"Rosa?" I am snapped out of my thoughts as I hear my name being spoken. I wasn't even watching where I was going so I now find myself in the middle of the high street, the paths bustling with people still trying to get gifts for their Christmas shopping and even though it is still freeing cold, I hardly noticed the temperature with being so lost in thought. "Hi, we never thought we would bump in to you again, it is good to see you," a young woman says to me as she holds on to the hand of what I assume to be a husband or boyfriend. They both smile as I look at them, both wrapped up warm in winter coats, hats and scarves.

"Erm... Hi," I reply, I think they look familiar but I cannot recall where I know them from. Maybe they came in the coffee shop once or I saw them somewhere.

"Bella and Conner, we met a couple of years ago in a bar in town." Bella says as she can probably see the confused look on my face. "Erm... you sent drinks over to our table then invited us to your apartment to..." she goes bright red then nervously looks to her husband for support.

"As you know it was the first time we had done anything like that," Conner says a bit shy as I listen. "But the money you gave us after... we used it to get married."

"Oh, that Bella and Conner," I smile as I finally remember them. "How are you both?" I nod and act civil. I forget sometimes that humans form strange connections to people and like to be sociable, and I usually forget most of them that I meet.

"We are good, thank you. Actually we had hoped to run in to you again, sometime, we always looked out for you but we never saw you in that bar again," Bella says nervously. "We erm... after trying to settle down properly we struggled with buying a house and saving for a deposit has been a nightmare, not that we are begging or anything..."

"We know it is unusual but if you did want us again, sometime to..." Conner takes over as they ramble on. "We are very open minded after you showed us and..."

"You need money and you are wondering if I will gift it to you, just as I did last time after we all fucked?" I ask quite casually. I always like to compensate for the time of the people I sleep with especially when some of them are not exactly voluntary, a little push can make humans do things against their will but only if deep down they desire to do so first. It wasn't hard to charm these two in to my bed. I was casually drinking at the bar, and I saw a beautiful raven haired woman walk out of the toilets and sit with a very handsome man. Both young and full of life, energy overflowing and they appealed to me. I sent them a bottle of champagne and they invited me to talk, after a while and a couple of nudges they ended up back at my apartment and they were both very willing to please. The small gift of cash was also an added incentive for the newly engaged couple who dreamed of a fairytale wedding.

"It is not exactly how I would have put it," Bella says, going bright red in the face again. "We just thought that maybe... seen as though you said last time that you would like to again and..."

"I have nothing else to do today," I interrupt her. "Plus I could really use the distraction," I smile and glance at them both, a little group play may be fun, then I can forgot about everything else and carry on with my life until the end of days.

It doesn't take us long to get back to my little home over the closed coffee shop, and as I lead them in to the sitting room area I can almost feel how nervous they both are. It makes my mind flash back to when I last had them in my bed, they were so naive, never even contemplated anything like this before.

"You two should relax," I push them a little and they bend to my words. "The more you relax and let go, the more fun we will have together... The more fun we have, the more money you will receive." Bella smiles at me as I see a calm instantly wash over them both. Humans are like puppets, so easy to influence and manipulate, over the years it became easier each time I did it, and now I hardly even need to try with them. "Why don't you both go in to my bedroom, get comfortable and begin whilst I get myself a drink," I say and they both nod before holding hands and heading for my bedroom without me. I take a moment to myself, trying to push all of the shit out of my head, the shit that does not concern me at all. I don't care if we have one day or one year left before everything explodes around us, at least I will spend what remaining time I have left having fun and being me.

There is not much vodka left in the bottle as I pour the rest of it in to a tumbler and take a sip, I must have drank more of it than I thought last night when I was talking to Mitch... but that doesn't matter, soon I won't even remember who he is, because Bella and Conner will take my mind off everything. I casually wander to the bedroom, drink in hand, then head straight for the chair that is pushed up against the far wall that faces the bottom of the bed. Bella and Conner are already half naked, their clothes dumped on the carpet, and as I enter they don't even notice me so I sit down to watch whilst I drink, contemplating the little life I have left.

I have to admit, Bella is very nice to look at. Her long legs, her large breasts, she could have easily been an underwear model with her figure but I remember she told me that she was a school teacher and it makes me smile to think that the young boys in her class would probably think they had hit the jackpot getting to look at her every day. Conner is athletic, a little shy but that is what first appealed to me, his gentle nature was so innocent and it was unusual because he was very handsome, as though he should have been the much loved jock in school. However, instead he was the little geeky kid who wore braces until his late teens, then went in to nursing, so he could look after other people. I take another sip, enjoying the harshness of the burn from the cheap vodka as I watch Bella wriggle out of her tight denim jeans, leaving her only in her black lace panties and bra. Conner is only in his boxers as he climbs towards her and they kiss passionately, his hands trailing the curve of her body before working its way down between her thighs and gently stroking against her mound through the lacy material. I can tell just by watching them that they share a great love, it is not just about sex with them, it is something deeper, something which has always eluded me. I always thought that having any sort of human emotion, including love was a weakness, but watching them as they explore each others bodies, makes me feel kind of alone, because I have never had a true connection to any one I have ever met.

Conner sits back slightly and gazes down at his wife as he slowly pulls off her panties before dropping them to the floor, she watches him contently as he leans down and spreads her thighs in front of him then smiles before moving his mouth to her clit. Bella gasps as it connects with her, the intimacy getting my attention straight away as they make eye contact with each other whilst he plays with her. Her hand runs through his mousy brown hair whilst she moans deeply, his tongue swirling around her clit, making her relax more as she watches him.

"Oh, shit," Bella moans loudly as Conner slides two fingers inside her pussy, giving her a much needed new sensation, slowly he moves them, taking his time and allowing her to build in pleasure. I smile slightly as I find myself getting wet, becoming turned on with their intimacy, the moans piercing my loins and sending shivers of anticipation right through me. I want to watch her cum, to be overcome with that intensity whist she writhes on my bed. I take another sip of my drink whilst enjoying the show, Conner begins to fuck Bella with his fingers, delving deeper as the sounds emanating from her increase and I know as well as he does that she is close to climax. His mouth working as one with his hand, both simultaneously stimulating her, giving her exactly what she craves just like Mitch did for me last night... why did I think of that? The last person I want to be thinking about right now is that arsehole of an angel. I shake my head to clear my thoughts and focus on Bella again as she grips on to the sheets below her, her head falls back and I find myself almost begging her to cum, to cum so hard she screams in pleasure. I can't help but nibble my bottom lip, adding a welcome dart of pain as my core starts to burn and I think about the last time I played with them both, we played for hours and I would happily do it again... but what if we don't have hours left? What if the rising was happening right now? Jake is exposed, out in the open and right next to where a Sin has just been killed. Which means that whoever is doing it is close by. They could have demons patrolling looking for him, by now, they would have figured out that the previous men they took were not the key and it doesn't take a genius to figure out that if an angel was spotted on the streets then he must be here for a reason. Right now, seeing the Archangel Michael wondering around a crime scene of a dead Sin is just asking for trouble.

Bella cries out as she finally reaches climax, cumming hard as her sounds echo around the tiny room, getting my attention again as I glance towards them. Her legs shake as her back arches off the bed, her orgasm consuming her before her body relaxes again and welcomes that wave of satisfaction. Conner sits back as Bella moves to kneel in front of him so that they can kiss again, their tongues playing wildly, passion clear between them both that seems to emanate from inside their very souls. Conner moves closer, his hands wrapping around her back then unhooking her bra, allowing her supple assets to be free, her nipples already hard and begging to me touched.

"Are you joining us, Rosa?" Bella says confidently as I look up to meet her gaze, she is kneeling fully naked on my bed and she smiles at me as Conner begins to kiss her neck, caressing her skin as his hands play with her breasts, gently squeezing them, teasing the curve as his fingers stroke across her nipples. I look down at my now empty glass, knowing that I have nothing else in the apartment as I have done no shopping for days, and even though the prospect of sex is extremely appealing, I need something stronger to block out the thoughts in my head which are creeping back in. I need to get blind drunk and I can not do that here. I stand and approach the bed as Bella smiles more with each step I take before I lean down and gently kiss her lips. I can taste her own juices on her mouth that have been transferred from Conner after he played with her, and it makes me smile more.

"As much as I would love nothing more than to play right now," I sigh as she gazes longingly at me. "I need a drink and to clear my head. I am sorry, it is not your fault, you are blissfully unaware of what is about to happen," I gently stroke her cheek as she listens. "Today you are going to spend time together, love each other, fuck hard if you need to and have the best day of your lives... as it could be your last. I will leave some cash in an envelope on the bench, there is no hurry for you to go home so take your time, I won't be coming back here again." She smiles as I gently kiss her forehead then she turns her attention back to Conner and I watch for a moment as they kiss each other again, lost in the euphoria as I told them to be.

After I leave the bedroom, I empty what money I have left in the safe in the kitchen into an envelope and seal it, before placing it on the bench for Bella and Conner when they are done. There is nothing else I need here, no sentimental items or anything of worth, so I grab my jacket and leave without looking back. Even the coffee shop downstairs will be a distant memory soon, I guess Lily will get a shock tomorrow morning when she comes in for her next shift, I suppose I should have told her what had happened by now but the less I involve other people in my life, the better it will be for everyone. I walked around for a bit, sat for an hour or so on a park bench then walked some more. I suppose I have lived long enough anyway, if Hell comes to the human world, at least I know that I can have a little fun fighting and fucking before everything eventually implodes in on itself. Finally, my father will be knocked down a peg or two, then him and God will be overthrown and made to look like fools, I guess that is the perfect outcome really, it all has to end someday.

It is just starting to get dark as I head up the steps in to the Bunny Hole, it is strangely quiet, not too many people around but I don't mind. I just want a drink. As I enter, there are a couple of girls dancing on the stage, I watch them for a moment, so vulnerable that just the slightest injury could mean death to them. Why did God think it was a good idea to create something so utterly weak, even if they do offer endless amusement. I sigh heavily then turn towards the bar but stop dead in my tracks as I see Jake sitting on a stool, drinking a pint alone. A deep groan of frustration escapes me at seeing him, knowing the possibility that Mitch will not be too far away so I turn to leave, I will find somewhere else to drink tonight.

"Rosa?" I hear Jake call to me across the club, making me stop. "Rosa, please. I could really do with someone to talk to right now," he almost pleads which makes me sigh.

"Talk to Mitch," I shout over as I look back around. "You don't want to associate yourself with the likes of me." Jake watches me, clearly thinking of something else to say.

"I don't want to talk to Mitch," he replies with anger still in his voice. "He lied to me, I thought he was a friend when all along my life was just a job for him. Now what do I have? Nothing, my entire life, everything I knew was not real." Jake seems deflated as he picks up his pint and takes a large drink before just sitting staring at the bar, becoming lost in his own thoughts again. I should walk away, this does not concern me and the further distance I put between myself and the key to destroying the Veil then the safer I will be. But instead I find myself reluctantly walking towards the bar and taking a seat next to him. Gary is on shift again so he comes straight over, pours my usual tequila and leaves the bottle without saying a word, knowing that things seem a little tense with the man sat next to me.

"Here drink this," I say to Jake as I hand him a shot of the neat liquor, he swiftly downs it before I refill the small glass from the bottle and he drinks that one as well. "What did Mitch tell you?" I ask as I pick up my own glass.

"That I was some kind of key thing," Jake says as he stares at the counter. "That all my life I thought I was normal when in fact my parents were immortal and my blood could destroy the whole world, or something like that." I nod along then fill up the glasses again.

"Yeah," I sigh. "Sounds pretty shitty when you put it like that."

"Tell me," Jake says cautiously. "What will happen if the Veil does fall and the rising actually happens." I am reluctant to tell him, what I say would not be good but he deserves to know. He is more involved in this than I am and if he is the key then he has the right to know what will happen if he is used.

"The Veil acts sort of like a barrier," I start. "Protected by magic that was created at the dawn of time to separate the humans from everything else. When Lucifer claimed his place in Hell, he grew an army, one with unimaginable power, some of whom still try to this day to get in to the mortal world. On occasions beings do slip through, even in this world there are forces that you will never understand... but if the Veil is broken completely, if that protection is no more, then every demon, beast or monster will have nothing to stop them taking over this land. And they will, in the thousands. The horde will initially break through at the single point where the blood of the Key is spilt, making that the Hell mouth then the more the Veil crumbles the harder it will be to contain it until eventually the thing that separated Hell from the humans will be no more, sort of like bringing a plague that will eventually enslave humankind. Once a new ruler sits on the throne, they can get rid of the Veil forever and ensure every human then belongs to them, thus destroying every soul and eliminating the need for a true Heaven or Hell, which in turn would destroy everything we know around us."

"And you would happily walk away and let that happen?" Jake asks as he glances across at me. The question catches me a little unaware, but I need to answer with something.

"I am a demon, why wouldn't I want to revile in the enslavement of human kind," I say then take another shot as Jake laughs at me.

"I don't think that is true at all," he smirks then drinks again, he already seems as though he is a little intoxicated, clearly he has been here for a while before I showed up. "I know probably nothing about all of this, all that Heaven and Hell bollocks, but I do know that a demon wouldn't have helped a human in the first place if they didn't care for humanity." I laugh at his statement and shake my head.

"You do remember who I am, don't you?" I say sarcastically. "The daughter of Lucifer, the Devil himself, the furthest possibly thing you could get from someone who cares for humanity."

"Then why did you help me?" he asks straight back and I struggle to reply. Why did I help him? I knew from the get go that he was involved in the rising, I heard him mention Monroe and yet I could have walked away then, but I didn't. "You had plenty of chances to turn your back on us and leave, even after you knew who Mitch was you still stayed... personally I think it is because you are scared."

"Shut the fuck up," I scoff at his remark.

"Protest all you want, but when you found your sister, Lust, dead. I saw the fear in your eyes, even if you will never admit it," Jake speaks and I fall silent. "It was at that point that you knew everything was actually really real, and it scares you to think that someone is wiping out your entire family, and you don't know how to stop it." I listen to his words and don't answer him back, I have never been scared of anything in my life. All the battles I have fought, the beings I have killed. What he says cannot be true... can it? Jake keeps glancing at me for the next two hours whilst we continue to work our way through the bottle of tequila, me trying to ignore everything that is going on and him drinking away his problems. "I wish I was in your position, you know," Jake says to himself as he sighs. "You could just fuck off, go where ever you want and not have to worry. Whereas I could potentially have an army of demons searching for me right now. Him there, he could be a demon," he slurs slightly and points to Gary. "Or her," he says turning in his seat slightly and randomly gesturing to the whole club which makes me smirk. "I am going to get killed... Dead, that is what I will be soon. So it won't even matter who or what my parents were or what I did with my life because I am just a stupid fucking mortal human who will be killed for my blood... at least I won't have to live with the guilt of destroying the world for too long." I sigh heavily and try to think of something to say to calm his mind but nothing comes in to my head so we go back to silence. I did at one point think about pushing him to forget, make him not remember who he really is but I didn't think that would be very fair on him, no matter how much it hurts him to know the truth. A couple hours later and Jake is so drunk that he can hardly sit on his stool without wobbling and for the past 40 minutes he has been telling me his life story, not that I have actually listened much, I just came for the alcohol. Jake is now just my unnecessary and unwanted distraction.

"Not to piss on the party," I say as I stand up from the stool, I still feel fine, alcohol doesn't have the same effect on me as it does with humans so I need at least 4 times what I have drank tonight to get me intoxicated to the same level as Jake currently is. "But I think you have had enough to drink, go home and sleep it off." I grab my jacket and put it on whilst Jake forces himself to stand, swaying on the spot before turning around to look at me whilst I speak. "I will call you a taxi, if you tell me where you are staying and..." Jake places his hand on my shoulder to steady himself before leaning in to kiss me. I was not expecting it or even gave him any impression that I liked him so I just stand for a moment until I realise what is going on and gently push him away.

"Sorry," Jake apologises. "I have had too much to drink, haven't I?" he slurs and I just smile sweetly at him.

"Yeah, just a little," I reply.

"I didn't mean to kiss you, it is just..." Jake says then stops as he looks genuinely hurt by what he has done.

"Forget about it, it is fine," I reply then take his arm to lead him outside.

"No, it is not fine," he protests. "I am sorry, I don't know what has come over me." I don't blame the guy, this is him going through an existential crisis.

"I will make sure you get home, where do you need to go?" I ask but he instantly shakes his head.

"I can't go back there, I had a hotel room because I got kicked out of my apartment, so shared it with Mitch and I really do not want to see him right now," Jake says. "I will be fine, I will find somewhere else." He starts to walk off towards the door, stumbling slightly, and against my better judgement I go after him.

"I have a place nearby," I say as I take hold of his arm to steady him. "We will get a taxi and you can sleep this off." He nods gratefully as I lead him outside and stand him up against the wall for support as I call a cab.

A little while later and Jake is fast asleep in my bed, he passed out pretty much as soon as his head hit the pillow so I removed his shoes and covered him with a blanket before I left him alone and went to search my kitchen for alcohol. He was quite surprised when the taxi brought us here instead of the little apartment above the coffee shop, I haven't been to this property in quite a while, but the elderly doorman downstairs recognised me straight away and opened the lift for me. This is one of the more expensive properties that I own. It is a large and very spacious four bedroomed penthouse at the top of a block of exclusive homes for the incredibly wealthy. The view is amazing from the open plan black and silver marble kitchen-come-dining area that filters into a luxurious living space with what looks like a cinema screen on the wall. Everything is very modern and sleek, the epitome of money. I take a couple of bottles of expensive wine from the rack then just sit on my huge leather sofa and watch the world go by as I drink. I don't think that I could sleep anyway. The word "scared" won't leave my mind after Jake said it, but I don't know what I have to be scared of, it is not like I care about any of these people and I couldn't give a shit about what happened to the Sins... yet at the same time just thinking about there being someone out there who is murdering them with the goal of bringing the end of days has my stomach in knots. Is that honestly what I want to happen? No, I don't think I do. But I have no idea where to even start by looking for who ever is behind this. And then of course, if I do find them, how do I stop them? How do I ensure I keep them away from Jake and save the entirety of humanity?

Four bottles of wine later and I am finally starting to relax, maybe if I shut my eyes right now I will be able to rest. But one minute later, and just as I am starting to doze off the intercom buzzes near the door. If I ignore it then it might stop, but 30 within seconds it buzzes again so I pull my arse off the sofa and wander over to press the button.

"Yeah?" I ask, half asleep and feeling a little worse for wear.

"Apologies, Miss Moon," the voice of the old doorman says. "But there is a man here, claim's to have followed some sort of tracking device on a phone and is looking for the young lad that you came home with a couple of hours ago." I groan loudly before reluctantly replying.

"Let him up," I sigh then unlock the door and leave it open slightly before heading over to the kitchen bench to grab another drink, if Mitch is coming in then I need something to get me through this.

"Hello?" I hear Mitch say cautiously as I turn around, drink in hand and lean up against the breakfast bar as he enters. "You are with the kid?" Mitch asks me as he sees me standing but I don't reply. I have nothing to say to him. "Is he alright?" he asks more and I take a deep breath before answering.

"He is alive if that is what you mean," I reply offhandedly. "He is in my bed, asleep."

"Did you fuck him as well?" Mitch asks with a tone of anger and I nearly spit my drink out at the statement. "I went by the coffee shop, found two naked humans in your bed, then I finally tracked down Jake and find him here with you." He stares at me but I don't reply. "Is this all a joke to you? The whole fucking world

104

could end and you don't give a crap about anyone but yourself. All you demons are the same, so self-obsessed... what do you plan to do? Sleep with as many people as you can before everyone dies, get a few last flings in?" I drink my wine as I try to remain calm, but the more Mitch speaks the more annoyed he is becoming. "You do realise that you are the one who could end this, right? Not God, not me or the kid, but you. And yet you are happy to just turn your back on everything. The way you are acting, for all I know, you are the one causing all of this, I bet you have thought about overthrowing your own father for centuries, just like he did. Like father, like fucking daughter, both as delusional and egotistical as each other." I slowly place my wine down on the bench and take a deep breath. I understand he is frustrated, but I can not be arsed to deal with all of this shit right now.

"What's wrong Mitch?" I ask sarcastically. "Do you not like it when things don't go your way? Well, boo bloody hoo. You think you have all the answers, but you know fuck all about me or what I am thinking at all," I say as my voice begins to shake. As much as I do not want to admit it, everyone else is right. I do need to step up, if I don't my entire family will be wiped out then humankind could cease to exist... and maybe I am a little scared. Maybe I am scared that I will end up just being another murdered child of Lucifer, or what if I do try to help but I just make things worse.

"You are selfish," Mitch spits. "Only thinking about yourself, your needs and wants, your life... and you are willing to risk everyone else to ensure you are happy."

"I am leaving," I snap before grabbing my jacket and heading for the door, storming past Mitch and pushing him out of the way.

"Yeah, that's right," Mitch calls after me as I walk along the small landing towards the lift doors. "Walk away, I wouldn't expect anything else from a filthy fucking demon." I hold my tongue as I get in the lift and press the button for the ground floor. I could have told him exactly what I was thinking, told him where I planned to go, but things are easier this way. Me walking away like this means they won't come after me, and as long as they are both far away from where I plan to go next, then Jake might just be safe. I did not spend years of my life protecting the Veil to just turn my back now, the key needs protecting at all costs. The doorman nods as I enter the lobby then hurries towards me.

"Miss moon? Would you like a car?" I stop as he asks and nod gratefully.

"Yes, I would," I smile back. "I need to get to Khemory Prison. It is about time I pay my brother a visit, looks like we have some family business to discuss."

Chapter Eight

"Hi, I am here for visitation," I smile at the prison guard in reception as I stand in the small line of family members waiting to see their loved ones for their designated one hour a month.

"Prisoners name?" he asks me back in a gruff voice, not paying any attention to me as he stares at the computer screen, his customer service skills are highly lacking but I just continue to smile.

"Curtis Invidia," I say and the guard instantly looks up, which makes me struggle to hide my smirk as it is clear that he recognises the name.

"Inmate Invidia doesn't have anyone registered to visit," he replies cautiously. "To gain entry you will need to file a request and then if the prisoner accepts your..."

"Shhh," I say quietly giving the guard a little push. "The paperwork was done months ago, Invidia approved, and he is waiting to see me." The man sits captivated by my words as I speak. "You will have one of your guards escort him from his cell and in to the visitors area like any normal prisoner would be."

"Yeah," the guard says a little unsure. "My mistake, the paperwork has all been done, everything is good. If you make your way through to the next room, one of my colleges will search you before you are escorted to the visitors area." I nod in understanding and go where he directed me to go. A quick search to make sure I am not carrying weapons or contraband, then the group of visitors are escorted in to the building and herded in to a large concrete room with no windows and only two doors. One where we came from that runs back along the lengthy corridor

106

towards the guards station and one door that leads in to the prison, through thick metal bars and steel entry ways that all require keys. I find a seat at a small table, roughly in the middle, facing the steel door and wait. After about 30 minutes the guards bring in the prisoners, they all look happy to see their loved ones and go straight to them. After they have all come in and everyone is sat down, I am still waiting alone.

"I am telling you, there has been a mistake," we all hear a man shout out in the corridor. "I don't fucking get visitors."

"You do today," a male guard replies. I look over and smirk as I young man, late 20's looking, gets forced in to the doorway, he is shackled and cuffed, unlike the rest of the inmates who are free of bindings whilst visiting occurs. The prisoner is dressed in the usual khaki coloured outfit, his hair a little messy as it covers half of his face, but his tattoos are very visible, especially the snake that wraps around his chest and goes up the side of his neck.

"This is just a waste of my fucking time," he shouts back at the guard. "I don't get..." I stand up slowly and catch his eye, stopping him mid sentence as he sees me. His gaze roams my face, taking in my features, hardly believing that I am standing in front of him now.

"Are you going to sit down, or what?" the guard pushes him forward and Curtis nods before heading towards me, the sounds of his chains filling the room as everyone around us watches him after the slight commotion. He stops in front of the table and just stares at me before I sit back down and he does the same, then everyone around us goes back to their conversations.

"Alexis?" he says in disbelief and I quickly shake my head.

"I haven't been known by that name for quite some time," I reply. "The name is Rosa now, Rosa Moon." He nods in understanding before we both sit in silence for a couple of minutes. I am not really sure what to say. "Have you seen the news?" I ask and he nods.

"Yeah, I saw yesterday about Smith. Then I heard a rumour about a woman committing suicide but they didn't give a name," he says cautiously as he keeps looking around to make sure no one hears our conversation. "I wasn't sure if it was connected or not but..."

"It was," I interrupt him. "We have already lost four, Wrath was found drowned, Sloth was a drug overdose, Greed was mutilation and Lust was found with a bullet through her brain."

"How is all of that even possible?" he asks. "Was it you? Did you kill them?"

"Why does everyone keep asking me that?" I scoff.

"Oh, I don't know," Curtis replies sarcastically. "Maybe because I haven't seen you in nearly 2000 years and then when you do wander back in to my life, it is when my brothers and sisters are starting to die... You always were jealous of us all, couldn't handle the fact that father loved us more." I roll my eyes at him as he speaks, this is what I get for trying to help. "What I can't figure out though is how. How did Greed end up in little pieces? Was it a weapon? Magic of some kind?"

"I don't know," I sigh then fall silent as a prison guard approaches the table.

"You hit on lucky today, Invidia," the guard says casually as he places two paper cups down on the table and pours a dark red wine in each one from a plastic bottle. "It is the prisons 100th birthday so every visitor and inmate are getting a little something to help celebrate." Once he is done he goes to the next table and repeats the process, going around the room as we talk. Curtis looks at the cups in front of us then picks them both up, examining them carefully before switching them around so he takes the one that was given to me. Typical really, my cup had a tiny bit more wine than his so he wanted what I had instead. Envy by name, envy by nature. That is why he ended up in here, couldn't resist wanting what other people had, even if that meant steeling it, he has done it for years, only this time he got caught. Even though I hadn't seen or interacted with them for years, I still kept tabs on a few of the Sins, watched what they did with the privileged life they were handed.

"Someone is trying to take down our father, they want to bring about the rising," I continue after our interruption. "I went to try to warn Lust yesterday after an Oracle told me that she would be targeted next, but I was too late. I was the one who found her," I say quietly as he picks up the wine and drinks it. "I am as clueless as you, but whoever it is, they are strong. They are looking for the key to bring down the Veil." Curtis watches me carefully, I can tell he doesn't want to believe me but all the evidence is there, no matter how ridiculous it all sounds.

"How do I know you are telling the truth, that you are not the one behind this?" he asks me seriously and I sigh.

"Because if it was me, you would be dead by now," I reply honestly. "I wouldn't bother to explain first." I pick up my paper cup and take a drink of the wine, it tastes like shit, the cheapest crap ever made but I force it down, anything is better than nothing right now.

"OK, so what does this have to do with me?" he asks and for a moment I am not sure how to answer his question.

"I don't know, I just thought I needed to come here," I explain. "You guys might not have been in my life for a long time, but you are still my family. Seeing Lust yesterday after I found her with... it hit home, you know. Made me think that life isn't everlasting after all." Curtis nods and sits in silence as the guards keep walking up and down the aisles, checking on the inmates. "I feel like I need to do something, but I don't know what. I don't know who is doing it or why."

"Have you spoke to father?" he asks and I shake my head. "If what you say is true about four of my siblings already being dead, then I am sure he will know as well. If someone is trying to overthrow him then he will be getting ready for a war, won't he? He will fight."

"Not if he is backed in to a corner," I say. "He cared about you guys, a lot, and if he is faced with losing all of his children it could make him weak, his line being destroyed could end him... plus I am aware that it seems some of his trusted followers are going against him and helping whoever is..." my words stop suddenly as a loud bang echoes around the small visitor room then the sounds of screaming fill the air. I cautiously turn my head to the side to see the guard that had been walking past our table, crumple to the ground, his head looks as though it has exploded and I can feel his blood splattered up the side of my face and in my hair. I look back at Curtis who doesn't know how to react as everyone around us starts to panic.

"Oh fuck," a man says loudly from behind me as he begins to laugh hysterically. "His head just popped like a grape." A surge of visitors and inmates try to run towards the steel door heading in to the prison as I turn around and see a group of 5 people standing at the entrance door, one holds a shot gun which he just used to shoot the guard. A second man, who looks a little mousy with a green shirt on steps forward and shouts in to the room.

"Everyone remain calm," he says as he smiles, clearly entertained by all of the faces of panic. "We will get around to killing you all in good time." The rest of the party who are with him laugh. There are two women and three men, but one of the women doesn't seem as entertained by all the commotion as the rest of them as she stands back slightly, just observing. The guy with the shot gun walks forward a couple of paces before raising the gun and shooting again, aiming for the group now banging on the door, I didn't even see it get locked, as the last I noticed there was a guard standing there. More screaming rings out as a couple of the humans fall to the ground, then the rest all freeze or try to find cover under the tables, some huddled in the corner scared for their lives. No one really knows what to so for the best, they are just petrified they will be next to be shot at. Eventually everything starts to quieten down through fear, the humans too afraid to even speak until it gets deadly silent, that is when the woman who had been standing back finally steps forward. She is unarmed, doesn't look scared or unsure of herself in any way, in fact she looks a little bored at the moment. Dressed in a long flowing red dress, her hair long and dark as it falls in waves around her shoulders, and she has a clear air of confidence about her as she looks around the room, slowly taking in the scene before her.

"If you all co-operate with us, then this will all be over very fast," the unknown woman speaks. She sounds old, but her looks are as youthful as mine, and extremely beautiful. "You humans are all so pathetic, constantly living in fear of death... Even after all this time, I pity you all," she says as she smiles sweetly. I can smell that the group are not human, as though the scent of the pits or death itself

109

lingers on their skin from spending all of their time in the other world, but I don't recognise any of them, I have never laid eyes on them in my life. I spent the good part of 2000 years seeing everything that Hell had to offer, so whoever these people are, were well hidden maybe. "So which one of you lot of parasitic worms is known by the real name of Envy?" I freeze on the spot, not even wanting to look back around to Curtis in case it gives something away. I am now faced with the prospect of finding out who killed my siblings, but all I can think of is finding a way to get out. "No one? Not a single one of you will admit who you are? Oh, I had hoped that you would hide from me, makes the game more fun," she laughs at herself. "I know you are in here, in this room, internally thinking of a way to escape me... But I can sense a Sin is close by, just like I did with the others, you can not hide from me in the human world, your stench is so strong and I will kill every single person in this room if I have to just to get my hands on you," she says as the rest of her group head in to the room and start grabbing random humans and forcing them forward so that the woman in red can look at them, luckily they didn't come to us first, if they had, I am not too sure what I would have done just yet. Each of the demons hold a different human in place, almost in a line at the front whilst everyone else remains too terrified to move in case they are killed. The woman approaches the first human, a man in inmate coveralls, the demon holding him is smaller than him, dressed in black, but clearly more powerful as the inmate struggles to move from his grip. The woman spends a moment looking at him, she reaches out and gently strokes the humans cheek then looks along the line of men, all being held in place, all scared to death in her presence. "Kill them all," she says suddenly before screams fill the air again and we can't do anything but watch as the demons snap necks or slit throats with pocket knives, creating pure carnage. Blood splatters everywhere as they are killed for fun, making a spectacle and glorifying what they are doing. The room is very tense and it is clear that there is no escape as I can tell the doors are specially reinforced to stop prison breaks and there are no other exits to be seen. I haven't properly used my power since I came to the mortal world but it shouldn't be that difficult to get Curtis out of here alive if I need to, after all, I was the Guardian of the Veil, I did not get that job title for no reason. I slowly try to stand up so that I can back away, if I can get to the door then I should be able to force it open and get out, otherwise I will have to fight my way out, then my only option will be to kill them all myself... not that 5 demons stand much of a chance against me, this could actually be fun, relieve some of the pent up aggression and tension I have been carrying lately.

 "We need to go," Curtis says quietly to me as everyone else is distracted by the humans being slaughtered. He slowly stands, trying to make sure to not draw any attention to himself and starts to follow me towards the wall when he is grabbed from behind. I act quick, trying to get to him to get him free but a hand wraps around my throat and hoists me off the ground, leaving my legs to just dangle below me helplessly. I grab at the demons wrist who is now holding me, to force myself free from his grip... but nothing happens, I can't get him off me. He squeezes my neck tighter and cuts off my breathing making me instantly panic, there is something wrong, there is no way he is this strong compared to me, he has no idea who the fuck I am. "Rosa!" Curtis shouts as he sees me in trouble, he stands for a moment, clearly knowing that if we are to get out of this then he needs to stop acting like a normal human, and instead being that powerful son of Lucifer that he has always been. He pulls his wrists apart to snap his chains, to get free from his human bindings so that he can fight but his face quickly drops as they don't come off, not even a slight bend. I don't understand what is happening, those are mortal bindings, he should be able to get free of them without any issue.

"Well, what do we have here," the demon who originally had the gun says as he sees Curtis trying to get to me with a mix of panic and pure confusion on his face then laughs before punching him in the face hard, sending him across the room and smashing in to several tables whilst the rest of the group laugh along. How did that hit affect Curtis so much? He is Envy, one of the strongest of the sins, even against another demon, he should be able to withstand that blow.

"Those two are interesting... Bring them both to me," the woman in red says calmly as I am placed back on my feet then pushed towards her, I fall on to my knees and gasp for air now that the hand no longer restricts my breathing, a million thoughts are racing through my head. My feet slide on the blood that now covers the ground off the several dead humans as I try to stand up again, then Curtis is roughly manoeuvred to my side, being held up by shot gun guy, his face a bloody mess off receiving just one punch. The unknown woman steps forward so that she can look at us both properly then she slowly raises her hand to touch my cheek, I instinctively recoil and take a step back but the demon in green who had hold of my throat is right behind me, so he grabs my arm, twists it and forces it up my back, making me cry out as pain rips through my shoulder.

"Let her go!" Curtis shouts but the woman ignores him completely as she looks me up and down, taking in all of my features then taking a moment to inhale my scent.

"You smell unusual," she says as she watches me closely. "You smell like the humans do, the aroma is so overpowering but it is mixed with strength and something more, you are not from this world, are you?" she stares in to my eyes as Curtis fights to get free, desperately trying to get out of the grip of the demon holding him. I don't reply to the woman's questions so she moves from me and goes to stand in front of him instead, she smiles as he struggles more as it amuses her. "Ah, there you are," she says to him. "I knew I would find you, Envy, at least in here you have less chance of escape unlike the rest of your siblings did."

"Fuck you," he spits at her but she just smiles more. "My father will never let you take his throne you psychotic bitch."

"Your father will not have a choice," she replies casually. "Once I kill all seven of his children, I will then bring down the Veil and he will kneel at my feet."

"That will never happen," Curtis snaps then lunges forward but he hardly moves under the grip of the demon behind him. There is no way these demons should be stronger than us, we are children of Lucifer himself, unless they have been enhanced somehow, a magic that could give them more power. I can see Curtis doesn't understand why he can't break free either, but we are not the only ones, the woman also sees this and laughs at his helplessness.

"Strange, isn't it," she smiles. "How quickly you can lose your confidence when you feel overpowered. The fear that starts to creep in when you feel useless... almost human, wouldn't you say?" The group all laugh as the spare two demons, play with the rest of the humans behind us, keeping themselves occupied as the woman in red speaks to Curtis. They don't care who they kill as long as they are having fun. I can hear the screams of desperation behind me, then blood being shed but I can't see what is going on at all. "Before I get to the good part, why don't you tell me where I can find the last two Sins? They seem to be a little more hidden than the rest of you, possibly they realised they were being hunted so went in to hiding, I feel like they have left the mortal world for protection."

"I will never tell you fuck all," Curtis replies. "Do your worst, you can't kill me bitch, I am a Sin and I..." the woman is quickly handed a knife from the other female demon and before Curtis is even finished speaking, she drives the blade in to his shoulder. He cries out in pain and falls to his knees as she twists the knife in his flesh making blood cascade down his chest, causing him to scream in agony even more.

"You were saying?" she smiles then removes the blade before slowly licking the blood off the metal. "Hmm, it tastes human to me."

"That... that is not... possible," Curtis forces out through the pain. A Sin can't be injured like this. What the fuck is going on? "The knife... is it... magic?"

"No, my sweet child," she replies softly then smiles. "Did you enjoy the wine?" She asks and his face drops. "You see, you clearly don't know who I am, if you did then you would know that you cannot win against me, for I am the first, the mother, and the only one capable of reversing creation. For God is not infallible, he is ignorant and deserves to be punished for what he has done, and I will be the one to do it when I take your fathers throne."

"Who are you?" Curtis asks as his voice shakes now that he fully understands that he can actually be killed, the blood is a dead giveaway as Sins do not usually bleed, just like our father. The concept of bleeding is a human thing, one of the many things I inherited that my siblings did not.

"Who am I? I am the one who will rule the land," she says gently. "I am the one who will ultimately overthrow your father and claim what is rightfully mine," she moves forward and grabs his chin roughly, forcing him to look her in the eye. "And I am the one who will slaughter you, just to send your father a message... Don't look so shocked, it is not magic, it is all about the blood. Just a few drops of my blood in the wine you drank was enough to strip away your immortality. Although, it will only last a day or two, you will be long dead before you can even return to normal... now tell me where I can find the other Sins." I can see Curtis shake under her grip as he processes everything that has just been said. She can't do this, I can't just stand by and let her kill him. I struggle against the grip of the guy holding me, but the more I pull away the firmer his grasp gets and the more pain I feel as he almost rips my shoulder from its socket.

"Rosa!" Curtis cries, he pulls his chin from the woman's grip then tries to help me but we are both too weak... then it hits me, I drank the wine as well.

I am mortal?....

"Who is she to you?" the woman asks him but he ignores her and continues to try to get free. "A girlfriend? A lover, maybe? If you won't tell me where the other Sins are, then maybe she will."

"No!" Curtis shouts but the woman focuses on me instead as she slowly wanders back in my direction and stops, before smiling at me sweetly.

"Did you know that that man was a Sin?" she asks me gently. "One who is the son of Lucifer, the son of the man who does not deserve his seat in Hell." I don't answer her so the guy behind me wraps his free hand around my throat from behind and squeezes, cutting off my breathing again and making me panic instantly as I now know I can be killed. "I do love that look, the look of desperation when a worthless human knows that they are so close to the end, when they have nothing left in their life and they know that they are about to die." Tears start to fall from my eyes as my chest burns. I desperately try to concentrate, I am surrounded by human souls and if I can harness their power then I can get free, but I don't sense anything, not a single flicker of energy, I can't breathe and I am utterly powerless. "You will tell me where the Sins are Envy, or I will kill this girl." The woman doesn't take her eyes off mine, captivated by the life slipping from them. My body starts to go weak against my will and my eyes roll as I instinctively buck against the demon holding me, my entire being struggling to survive.

"Stop, I will tell you what you want to know," Curtis shouts over. "Just let her go, she has nothing to do with this." The woman glances to the demon behind me and nods to give an order before he releases his grip on my throat, making me splutter and cough now that I can breathe again, then the demon lets go of my arm and I fall to the ground in a useless heap. How can this be possible though? How the fuck can I be mortal, just from drinking wine. She said her blood had the power to take our immortality... who the fuck is she?

"The Sins," she reiterates her original question. "Where can I find the other two?" Curtis glances at me, knowing that if I can escape then maybe I can warn them, maybe I can stop this and get to father for help before it is too late. But he also knows that we are now both mortal and no matter how much we try to fight, we are too weak against demons, this will only end with us both being killed.

"Tell me who you are?" Curtis tries to say with confidence but I can see he is shaking. "You are not someone I have met before, I know all of my fathers followers."

"I have not been one of your fathers followers for a very long time," she says as she smiles wildly. "All you men are the same, so demanding, thinking you are better than me. I was once so naive, so willing to please my God. But he didn't want me to be my husbands equal, he wanted me to be his whore. He created us both from the same earth and I deserved everything that was originally given to me, but my husband demanded that he be superior, that he was made in the likeness of our Lord God and that made him better than me. Just like all men now think. So when I stood up for myself, when I fought for my rights to be seen as an equal, I was punished for it, cast out from the garden of Eden and banished just because I didn't want to be my husbands slave. Then I was replaced, Eve took my role and what I got in return was a life of fire and torment, I would be forever cursed to watch my children die and all because a man wanted to be on top," she snaps at the last part and backhands Curtis hard across the face, almost making him black out from the blow, but the demon holding him up keeps him on his feet. The woman pauses for a moment to regain her composure then takes a long slow breath before speaking again. "So now I will take back everything that I deserve, starting with your fathers throne." Then it clicks in my head, this woman, the one standing before us now has been long presumed gone. No one has set eyes on her in so long I almost forgot her name.

"L... Lilith?" I force out as I look up at her from the ground. Anyone who has a direct link to the creator could sit in the throne, I thought that meant only my father as he was one of Gods angels, but Lilith was literally created by his hands, moulded in to flesh and blood by God himself... a direct link. She looks down at me and smiles gently.

"I see you have heard of me, child," her voice is soft as she speaks to me now. "Stand up and show me that you are not scared," she asks of me but all I can think of is that word. She said the word scared, just like Jake did, and deep down inside I am scared. I am terrified of facing her because I know what she is capable off. When she fled the garden, she hid from the angels who tried to kill her on Gods orders, instead they found her baring Adams children so they killed the babies instead to punish her. Wanting revenge she went back to the garden but found she had already been replaced by Eve, so she forced herself on Adam whilst he slept and stole his seed. She wanted to show God that she was not a weak woman any more, that she wanted to be better than he ever could be. She tried to have children, just as Adam and Eve did, but many of her offspring were born deformed, cursed to die within a day of life. Those that did survive became some of the most notorious demons who ever lived... Lilith was the first, the mother of demons and creator of monsters. She is so powerful that her flesh was said to have the remnants of Gods touch, which is why her blood can give or take life, or in our case, strip us completely of our immortality.

I slowly force myself to stand in front of her, my breathing shaking against my will as she waits patiently for me, knowing that she has the upper hand as there is no way I can fight her right now. My mind is racing, trying to think of a way out of this but if I am practically human then I can't beat them, I can't warn the others and I can't stop her from killing Envy. Lilith gently places one of her hands on my shoulder and turns me around so that I am facing my brother, directly in front of him. The demon holding him is joined by the second woman who stands behind him and for a moment all I can think about is the fact that I am about to die.

"Now," Lilith says softly as she stands close, wrapping one arm across my chest and gently stroking the skin on my cheek as her other hand, the one that holds the knife trails to my hip. "Tell me where the last two Sins are, or I will kill her." Just as she says that, we all hear alarms go off around the prison, warning everyone of a disturbance. Lilith sighs at the disruption then speaks to her men. "Close off the entrance and begin the next phase," Lilith instructs the shot gun demon. "I want this place to look like a war zone, so that everyone thinks a prison riot broke out and everyone was killed in such tragic circumstances." He nods at his commands then disappears towards the entrance doors. Lilith remains silent until sounds of explosions ring out close by, making the whole room around us shake. "Make sure the rest of the humans are all dead, I want no survivors," she tells the demon in blue who instantly goes back to slaughtering anyone who moves. The screams mix with the sirens as me and Curtis just stare at each other, knowing that this is the end. "Where were we? Ah, yes. The Sins?" I can see Curtis debating what to do, if he tells her, possibly she may spare his life, but I doubt it.

"Don't you dare," I force out as my voice shakes just in case he does something stupid. "If you tell her, you will condemn your own father." Curtis nods and remains strong then we are hit with a blast that explodes near the entrance door itself, creating large cracks in the wall and starting to make the ceiling above us collapse in.

"Well, that is unfortunate then," Lilith says almost in my ear as she leans in close. "Guess I will just have to keep looking all by myself," she begins to laugh, then moves quickly, an immense pain rips through my spine as she drives her knife deep in to the bottom of my back, I want to scream in agony but I can't catch my breath as my legs go weak beneath me.

"Rosa? No!" Curtis cries then steps forward to help me but he is instantly tugged back as a noose is swiftly draped over his head and tightened around his neck from behind. He struggles against the rope as the two demons behind him secure it over a metal light fitting above us then hoist Curtis off the ground. Lilith holds me up and forces me to watch as Curtis kicks his legs to try to get free, but the more he struggles, the tighter the noose becomes around his neck. Tears escape my eyes as I watch on helplessly as he is strangled, the ligature cutting off his breathing and all I can see is panic in his eyes. Lilith removes the knife from my back and I almost collapse as I can hardly feel my legs, but she grabs my throat and turns me around to look at her face as more noise erupts around me and the room shakes with chunks of concrete falling to the ground.

"I am sorry that you had to be part of this," she says gently, with sadness in her eyes as I fight to stay calm through the pain. "But I can't risk any one getting out. I suppose I have more work to do now though so I can not stay and watch all the fun," she smiles then forcefully tosses me away. Before I know what is happening, my body smashes in to the wall that is already fractured due to the explosions around us. The stone almost explodes when I hit it, sending me in to the corridor and the whole supporting wall crashes down on top of me. All I can hear is more explosions and screams, the sounds filling my ears until eventually the air goes silent and I think I lose consciousness.

I can't move. The amount of rubble pinning me down, stopping me from getting up is frightening and I feel as though I am lying on jagged chunks of concrete and steel. I have what feels like a block of metal across my chest, crushing me and stopping me from being able to breathe fully. My spine and ribs could be broken by the amount of pain I am in, but I can't even move my legs to check, in fact, I don't even think I can feel them at all. Blood pours from my head, the liquid matting my hair and covering my face, it is in my eyes, making them sting as I try to force them open, plus the stab wound in my back is still bleeding as I can feel it pool on the stone beneath me. My mouth is filled with dust, making my throat so dry that I can't even swallow. The only thing I seem to be able to do is move my left hand, which is in the open and free from the debris, and a small gap through the rock above enables me to see my surroundings, but the roof is totally gone so all I can see is the night sky. I can't hear anything near me, no cries for help or anyone still alive. Just the faint shouts of inmates as the rest of the prison is in lock down. If the amount of damage in here is any indication of what happened around us, then I can only imagine that it could take hours or even days to sort through the rubble and find all of the bodies, by that time I know that I will be dead.

Time seems to pass slowly as I drift in and out of unconsciousness, my body becoming weaker by the hour and the chances of anyone coming to my rescue before I slip away is near to none. When I next open my eyes everything is dark, through the little gap in the stone I can just make out the glow of the moon up above, the night sky clear but ice cold as I shiver uncontrollably with the drop in temperature. I guess this is the point in time that I need to make peace with myself, and I start to think about my family and if it was the right thing for me to do when I left them behind. What if I believed Mitch and Jake sooner? Would I have gotten to Lust in time, could I have stopped her being killed? A sudden shadow seems to fill my vision, obstructing my view of the sky, maybe I am seeing things, but it looked unusual. There it is again, but it is not a shadow I don't think, the moon light is glinting off something. I blink a few times to try to focus to see what it is, a bird possibly? It has wings, bright white feathers that fill the space above me and seems to be getting closer as though something is flying down to land. Maybe I have lost so much blood that I am hallucinating, after all I have never experienced a true death before so I am not sure what will happen. Soon the shape gets to the large open hole in the roof, it is far too big to be a bird, easily the size of a man, but with wings? My eyes roll in to the back of my head and I seem to lose time again, a dark emptiness filling my mind then I hear rocks being thrown which seems to bring me back, the sounds echo around the quiet room then I hear footsteps on the dirt below.

"I am going to assume you are Envy?" the quiet voice of a man says to himself from nearby. "May your soul rest in peace," he says with genuine feeling in his voice but I can't focus properly and my head pounds as I struggle to keep my eyes open. There are more sounds of things moving, scraping metal as though someone is searching for something then I hear the man's voice speak again, louder this time. "Rosa?" he shouts in to the room, but I drift off as everything around me feels like a dream, as though the world around me is no longer real and soon I will be gone. "Rosa!" he says with desperation this time and I think I may recognise the voice. "Rosa, I need you to be alive in here, come on, tell me where you are," he shouts and then I hear more rubble being moved.

"M... Mit..." I try to say but my voice croaks and because of the pressure on my chest, I feel like I am being suffocated.

"Rosa?" he shouts again as he searches.

"M... Mitch?" I manage to say fully that time, then everything falls silent. Did I imagine him?

"I can hear you," Mitch says with clear relief in his voice. "I need you to tell me where you are."

"Mitch... p... please," I struggle to say it loud enough so he can hear me and for a moment I think I might have dreamt him as the whole place is silent again, the only thing I can hear is my own waining heartbeat and the rattled breaths that I am struggling to take. Then suddenly I feel a hand take mine as it lies outstretched from below the rocks, it grips tightly to let me know he is there and I don't want him to leave go, because I feel like if he does, I will surly die.

"I am going to get you out," Mitch says as he begins to remove the rubble and steel from on top of me, then he lifts the concrete that is pinning down my chest, he groans as he uses his strength then tosses it to one side as though it was almost weightless before standing over me. Everything seems to go still as I see him properly. His torso naked and firm, covered in dirt from the stone he has been moving, his face kind and gentle as he looks down at me and the wings... large glorious white feather wings that arch from the top of his back and drape effortlessly as he stands, cascading down until the tips almost touch the floor. I have never seen anything as magnificent before in my life and I just stare at him in awe, not believing my own eyes. "Rosa?" Mitch says with panic as he kneels by my side and places his hand on my head to check the injuries. "You need to heal these wounds, there are bound to be souls nearby, you can..." I try to shake my head and he stops then notices the pool of blood I am lying in. He carefully places his hand under my back and I cry out in agony as his fingers connect with the wound. "Rosa?" Mitch says confused as he looks at the blood covering the skin on his hands. "What happened? Why are you not..."

"M... mor... mortal," I force out as my breathing rattles in my chest, making me cough slightly and sending pain ripping through my chest.

"You can't be," he says in disbelief as he looks across my body, all broken and almost lifeless, covered in my own blood and dirt. "The Oracle said you were the one to stop this, she said..."

"T... tem... tempo..." I struggle and cough more instead, blood starting to fill my lungs.

"Temporary? This is temporary? Is that what you are trying to say?" Mitch asks and I nod as best I can as tears fall from my eyes. I know I am in a very bad way, and if I am mortal like the other Sins then I can't heal, I will die like they did.

"P... please," I say as I begin to sob, which is new for me, I don't cry, emotions are not something I have experienced much before but right now I have no control over them. "I... I don't... don't want... to die." My head rolls again as I struggle to stay awake but Mitch quickly places his palm on my cheek and moves my face to look at him.

"Rosa, open your eyes," he says frantically. "Rosa?" I force my eyes open, they sting and it is taking all of my energy not to give in to the sleep. "I promise you, I will not let you die," he says as he stares in to my eyes. "I swear on my own life, OK?" I nod, then he carefully tries to pick me up off the ground, but I groan loudly in pain as it consumes me, forcing me to almost gulp for oxygen as he pulls me in close and cradles me in his arms. "Just hang in there," he says gently then I feel a rush of air past my face as it feels like I am swept upwards, and all I see is the flash of white feathers as he flies us to safety.

Chapter Nine

I can't seem to catch my breath. My ribs and spine are in agony, my body is shaking and my chest rattles as I begin to stir. I don't know where I am, what time or what day it is, or even why I am in so much pain, I have never in all of my long life experienced anything like this before. Of course I have been injured and even killed through the many fights I have been in over the years, but never like this, never have I felt so useless and weak... so utterly human.

"She is waking up," I hear who I think is Jake call to someone else as I try to force my eyes open, but they are so heavy and I am so very tired. A hand is placed on my brow and the slight touch makes me feel sick as pain darts through my skull. I instinctively try to push the hand away, to get it to stop hurting me but quickly my arms are grasped and moved away from my face. I moan as I try to fight them but I have no strength at all. "Rosa, it is OK, it is me, Jake, don't touch your head." My eyes flicker open and for a moment I can just see shapes and lights, nothing solid as my vision is blurred. "Rosa, can you look at me?" Jake asks and I try my best, but the more I focus, the more my skull pounds. "You are safe, OK, just try to relax." Jake leaves lose of my wrists as I lie on a bed, I should feel comfortable as the mattress below me is soft but everything hurts, right down to my bones.

I am lying on my side slightly, with pillows behind my back to stop me rolling and some under my head to keep me propped up. As I focus more I see that I am in my penthouse, the bedroom is lush and expensive, my large bed covered in the finest white cotton sheets that money can buy and the walls are all white and silver, stunningly decorated with splashes of crystal. I am extremely groggy, I feel sick and every little movement hurts.

"Rosa, I will be back soon, you need to stay still," Jake says gently as he readjusts the blanket that is covering me as I am shivering. "I am going to go and see if the pharmacy around the corner has anything that can help with the pain," he smiles slightly then leaves my view. There is nothing else to look at as I am facing the wall, away from the door, a white chest of drawers is all I can see so after a minute and me being impatient, I force myself to move. If I can sit up then I won't feel as bad, I am not weak, I am the daughter of Lucifer and... I stop half way and cry out as my back is consumed with pain, so much so that I can't breathe and I just freeze in place as the agony rips through me.

"Jake told you not to move," a firm voice scolds me as I look towards the doorway and see Mitch. Tears flow uncontrollably down my face and I start to sweat with the pain of it all, my muscles spasm by themselves and I can't do anything to stop it. Mitch sighs at the sight of me then comes straight over to help, he gently puts his hand on the top of my back and helps me to reposition myself so that I am comfortable again, placing me back down on the bed and moving another pillow to behind my neck to keep me still. My entire body is shaking as I try to slow my breathing and relax. Mitch takes a bowl of water and a cloth from on top of the drawers and sits on the side next to me before gently dabbing my face as I seem to be having a weird cold sweat. He doesn't say anything for a while, just sitting, trying to help me feel better as I force my eyes to stay open, even though they sting like mad. My mouth is so dry, so I go to swallow to relieve the harsh burn in my throat but cough instead, sending pain ripping through me again so I tense up and groan loudly. "Easy, try and take it slow," Mitch says then quickly grabs a glass of water from the bedside cabinet. "Here, let me help you," his voice is kind as he places his hand under the back of my neck to support me so he can sit me up slightly, just enough to be able to drink. I sip the cold water, the refreshing liquid just slides down my throat, coating it in a much needed moistness before he helps me lie back down.

"Thank you," I force out faintly. This is not good. If this is what being a human feels like then I don't want it. When I am immortal it is easy to distance myself from human emotions, pain, death... but now it is all I can think about. I came so close to losing my life that I didn't give any thought to living. All these years, I just focused on making myself better, doing what I wanted and catering to my own needs, but now I can't get the thought of my siblings being killed out of my head. They went through this, Lilith made them mortal then slaughtered them just to prove a point to my father, she nearly did it to me without knowing who I actually was. If Envy had let slip that I was also Lucifer's child then she would have made sure to snap by neck, her only goal to teach all the men who ever wronged her a lesson. Not that I disagree with her to some extent, if I was treated as she was I would be pissed off as well, but after living in the human world, interacting with them and actually growing to like a few of them, I see things differently. And I didn't realise how much so until I was faced with death. I like this world, even though it has many flaws and some of the population are vermin, it is a wonder to behold. To see the kindness in those who have nothing, the strength in those who push to carry on, the love in the eyes of a couple who live for the moment and do not give a thought to what could happen tomorrow. If this world is destroyed then there will be nothing, and my life would suck. "Is Envy dead?" I ask Mitch to confirm for me. "I never saw his body."

"Yeah," he sighs as he watches me. "I'm sorry," his voice is filled with kindness and I don't know why, I don't deserve his kindness. Tears threaten my eyes again but this time I can't hold them back, I am not strong enough to do so. The prospect of losing everything is overwhelming and I feel guilty that I couldn't save my brother regardless of how our relationship was, he was still my blood and I should have been able to stop it from happening. I worked my entire life to be strong and powerful, but yet in one moment, everything was stripped away from me. "And I am also sorry for what I said to you before you left," he says carefully. "I was out of order... I spoke to Jake and he told me what you guys talked about in the bar and that nothing happened between you two, not that it is any of my business if it did," he pauses and sighs deeply. "I was just frustrated. I have been trying to protect Jake for years whilst looking for some way to stop the rising, then we found you, finally we had some form of hope or something to help us, and yet you didn't want to know. I let my hatred for demons cloud my judgement, and it was only when we went to leave the next day after Jake woke up that the doorman downstairs told us where you went after you stormed out. It was at that moment that I realised what you were doing, that you went off on your own. Then we heard news reports about a prison riot and how there was multiple dead, that the place was on lock down and there were explosions..." Mitch falls quiet as he thinks of what else to say, I remain quiet, I am a little pissed off and upset by what he said, plus my head is not in the right frame of mind right now to be dealing with this. "Just know that I am sorry, OK?" I nod my head as he watches me carefully, waiting to see if I say anything back but I am too lost in my own thoughts. "How long until you are back to normal?" he asks me, changing the subject.

"A day or two, maybe," I reply quietly as I just lie, trying to remain still as each time I move I get in more pain.

"I erm... I stitched you up as best I could, it has been quite a while since I last did it so I was a bit rusty," he laughs at himself slightly which makes me smile. "I am no expert but you were in quite a bad way, I think you broke a few bones and the gash on your head was quite nasty... In the prison, when Envy was killed, did you get any information as to how or what was going on?"

"Yeah," I say, and he waits for me to say more. "The mortality thing is to do with blood... ingesting it maybe, we didn't realise what had happened until it was too late."

"Blood? What kind of blood?" Mitch asks and I know this is not going to be good.

"The blood of the first," I force out as just thinking about her makes my voice shake. Damn these human feelings. "Created by your God, her flesh holds his touch and she is now on a rampage, seeking revenge to undo Gods creation." Mitch just stares at me for a full minute whilst he thinks about what I have told him then eventually, he slowly shakes his head.

"No," Mitch scoffs at my remarks. "That is impossible, you are talking about Lilith and she has not been seen in thousands of years. She was presumed dead long ago and..."

"Well, she didn't look very dead to me," I interrupt him and he stops before slowly getting up from the bed, he stands just debating to himself about saying more until the front door can be heard slamming shut.

"Hey, I'm back," Jake calls through from the living area before appearing at the door. "I said you needed to let her rest," he scolds Mitch as he comes straight over and begins to fuss with the pillows around me. "You need to be on your side a little more, to take the pressure off your back," I just nod and he helps me to move whilst I stifle my moans of pain then he takes a couple of boxes of pills out of the bag he brought in and starts to take a few out. "Take these, they are probably not ideal but it was all I could get. If they curb the pain a little then it might help you relax so you can heal." Jake helps me take the pills and holds the glass of water for me so I can wash them down before ushering Mitch out of the room. "We need to leave her to get some sleep... and we need to seriously have a talk." Mitch glances at me and forces a smile before nodding at Jake then they both leave me alone. It takes me quite a bit of time to get comfortable enough to sleep but when I do, I sleep deeply, I don't even dream.

I feel like I could literally sleep for a week. My muscles ache and I am stiff, but I am so thirsty and hot that I have no choice but to try to move. Rolling over, I kick the blankets off me as I am sweating and force myself to sit up. There is pain, but no where near the amount I felt before I went to sleep. I shuffle to the edge of the large bed, my head is banging still but it is now bearable and as I place my feet down on the floor, I see I am still pretty much fully dressed in my jeans and t shirt so no wonder I was so warm with all the blankets as well. The only things that looks as though have been removed is the jacket I was wearing and my boots. My clothes are covered in blood and dirt and when I turn around to look back at my crisp white sheets, you can blatantly see the marks of where I have been lying in the bed. It seems dark outside as I wander out of the bedroom and along the passage towards the large open area of the rest of the apartment. The skyline is hardly noticeable through the high glass windows that overlook the city as thick clouds cover the sky and it is snowing heavily. The only light in the space is from the small runner lights that sit dotted around the breakfast bar over by the kitchen so I head over that way to get a drink as the penthouse remains silent. I grab a glass from the cupboard then get some fresh water out of the fridge.

"Hey," I hear someone say behind me which makes me jump, almost dropping the glass I turn around and see Mitch sitting in the dark on the sofa just watching it snow.

"You scared the shit out of me," I say as I laugh at myself.

"Sorry, I saw you get up but you seemed in a world of your own," Mitch replies as he stands then walks over towards the kitchen.

"I needed a drink," I smile then devour the water as I am so thirsty. "Where's Jake?"

"Sleeping, he took one of your other bedrooms, hope you don't mind," he sighs and stands watching me as I shake my head in response. "How are you feeling? You have pretty much slept for 16 hours."

"Groggy, my head is killing but I am alive," I look down at the floor, unsure of what to say. "Thanks, by the way. For coming to get me."

"It's fine," Mitch brushes it off. "Forget it, I only did it because we kind of need you and..."

"Thank you," I say genuinely, cutting off his words and making him smile at me. "I have never had to rely on others for help or needed anyone, but the last few days, then the whole mortal thing... erm, showed me that maybe trying to do things by myself is not going to work this time. I guess that I need you guys as much as you need me." I place the now empty glass in the sink then groan as I turn as my back is stiff.

"Well, seen as you say you need us," Mitch smirks as he comes around the counter towards me. "Maybe you will let me see how your back is healing." I hesitate for a moment, he notices that I am thinking about it in my head so he pauses then laughs slightly as he gentle places his hands on my shoulders and turns me around, making me stand with my palms on the bench before carefully pulling up the back of my t-shirt. As soon as his fingers touches my skin I wince in pain and stiffen up. "Sorry, I will be gentle." He slowly removes what feels like gauze over the top of my knife wound to look at the damage. "Do you want the good news or the bad news." I smile again and shake my head, his words and demeanour are surprisingly nice and playful. "Well, the bad news is, I seem to have been more rusty than I thought with the stitches, looks like a Frankenstein monster there," I laugh at his words. "But the good news is that you probably won't have to deal with it for long as it looks like your body is starting to heal nicely. A few more hours and you should be back to your usual immortal demon self." He pulls my t-shirt down to cover my back then I turn around to face him, he is rather close as he just stands and looks down at me then slowly raises his fingers and tucks my hair behind my ear, so it is out of my eyes before skimming over the large gash that

123

was on my head. "This looks a lot better as well," he says softly as he gazes down at me then steps closer, he places his hand cautiously on my hip and for a moment I just freeze, unsure as to what he is doing. "I was so close to losing you," he smiles at me then leans down to kiss me, as soon as his lips connect with mine I feel this strange panic like thing in my chest, almost as though my heart can't regulate the beat and the closer his body gets to mine as he moves towards me and slides his hand around to my back, the more out of control of my own actions I feel. My mouth instantly opens to his, allowing him to gently play and for some strange reason my body relaxes in his arms but my heart almost pounds out of my ribs. I quickly place my hands on to Mitch's chest and gently push him away before looking down at the floor, purposefully trying to avoid his gaze.

"Erm... I should get some more rest," I force out then Mitch removes his hand from my back and takes a step away. "If I can get a good sleep in then my body can heal quicker."

"OK," Mitch nods as he watches me carefully. "You do what you need to do." I can tell by his voice that he is slightly hurt by my rejection of him, but I have too much on my mind to be dealing with his advances right now. He is a fucking angel for Christ sake, I can't get involved with that, it is wrong on a million different levels. Last time I was swept up in the moment, I am not saying that it was a mistake but I don't think it was a smart thing for me to do. Plus I don't even like him that much, he is an arsehole... well, I don't think I like him, do I? Mitch just stands silent, waiting for me to leave and head back to the bedroom but I don't move. The way he looks at me sends shivers down my spine in a good sort of way, my stomach feels unsettled but not as though I feel sick, it is more for excitement, he makes my pulse race and my soul feels so happy being close to him. My very limited experience of angels makes me unsure of what I am actually feeling, is it just his energy that is drawing me in, his divine power? Maybe it is because I am not fully back to normal and he was the one who saved me, I possibly hate him less because of that. "Rosa? Are you OK? You are just standing there, in a world of your own." Mitch asks and I pause before replying, I said I was going to sleep more but I don't think my body wants to let me leave.

"Yeah, I am fine," I reply as I just stare in to his eyes. My head is telling me to just walk away, he is bad for me and now with what is going on I can not get sidetracked... but everything else is begging me to kiss him again.

"As long as you are feeling better, that is all that matters," Mitch smiles gently then sighs as he breaks eye contact and looks down at the floor. "Go and lay down, you need good rest, hopefully you will be all patched up soon and..." I don't know fully what comes over me, but I step forward, place my hand around his neck and pull him down to kiss me, cutting off his words as he is speaking. There is a brief moment where I am as shocked as he is with what I am doing, our lips touching but neither of us moving and I don't think I am even breathing. After a very awkward few seconds of not knowing what is happening, our lips part and I cautiously look up at him, his eyes meet mine and he smiles. "I thought you said you needed to go lay down?"

"I guess I changed my mind," I reply then nervously nibble my bottom lip, I don't even know why I do feel nervous, it is not like I have never kissed or fucked anyone before, it is just something about him makes me feels so strange. He carefully reaches up and runs his fingertips across my cheek as we stare at each other, I can feel the pure magic like energy flowing from his skin and my soul is begging me to find out more.

"I really like you, Rosa," he says softly. "Regardless of your name of who your father is, I see the real you, I see your amazing beautiful soul." My cheeks flush at his words, no one has ever said anything like that to me before. "I know I said some choice things to you, but please know I would never mean it, I felt so bad after you left and..."

"Shut up and kiss me," I interrupt him and smile before he leans down, his lips softly brush mine, the total opposite of how he kissed me in my other apartment when he pinned me up against the wall. There is no urgency this time, he kisses me slowly, tasting my lips as his hands gently start to roam my body, following the curve of my hips then brushing over my ass. The more we kiss, the more I relax in his arms, almost as though all the shit that is currently surrounding me no longer exists and I feel completely safe.

My hands find their way under his T-shirt, his abs are rock hard and warm as my palms explore his skin, Mitch removes his shirt and drops it on the floor as we continue to kiss sensually then he unbuttons my jeans and slides them down the top of my thighs. I wriggle them off awkwardly as we both giggle slightly at my actions then kick them to one side whilst Mitch removes his belt and kicks off his shoes. My mind is not thinking clearly any more, I am just letting my body do what it wants, and right now it really wants to feel Mitch's touch very intimately, just like last time.

Mitch's hands glide over my hips, slowly tracing the curves before taking hold of me and lifting my feet off the ground then carefully sitting me down on the kitchen bench. There is a slight twinge of pain in my back but nothing that would distract me from this moment. The white marble counter top is cold under my ass cheeks but it just masks me smile as Mitch moves closer to stand between my thighs and turns his attention to kissing my neck. My head falls back and I moan as his lips tease my skin, gently working it, making my breathing quiver more the slower he moves, painfully slow which makes me almost want to beg him to just take me, fuck me hard like he did last time. Mitch pulls back slightly so that he can look at me whilst he removes my blood covered shirt, leaving me sat on the bench in my bra and panties, he drops it on the tiles at his feet then leans back in to explore my body with his mouth. He trails kisses across my chest as his hands gently skim my thighs and I can not help but run my hands across the curves of the muscles on his arms, just feeling him so close to me and knowing that I am completely safe with him. As he continues to sensually kiss my body, I undo his jeans and slide my hand inside to feel that he is already rock hard and wanting of me. He does not seem in any hurry, however, almost as though he is holding himself back, letting the passion between us build so we enjoy it more, but personally, I am already starting to get restless, I want it now. I can feel my own wetness already between my legs as my mind flashes back to when we last had sex, how primal it felt, how rough and sexy as fuck it was, how hard I orgasmed and all I can think about is how much I want that again. I have never been the kind of person who is known for her patience, so if I want to be fucked right now, then I will make sure I am.

Pushing down his boxers slightly to free his cock, I pull him closer towards me to allow him to fuck me here on the bench but he does not take the massive hint that I am giving him, continuing to kiss my neck and ignoring the fact that I am becoming a little impatient with waiting for it. What he is doing does feel nice, but I am so used to getting what I want, and I know completely how to get it. If Mitch does not want to fuck me then I will just have to make myself cum on my own, not like I have not done that before either, so I shuffle my bum to the edge of the worktop, and move my free hand between my legs so I can play beneath my own panties as my other hand works his shaft. I let out a deep satisfying moan as I start to twirl my fingers around my own clit, I am already soaking and they just glide effortlessly over my bud which tingles the more pressure I apply. Closing my eyes I just let myself get lost in the moment, the soft caresses from Mitch mixes with my own playing and I soon find myself wanting to cum hard, needing to feel that release as though it is my drug of choice and it is now all I can think about. My moans get louder as I pleasure myself, Mitch groaning occasionally as my left hand continues to stimulate his cock and I know I am going to make myself orgasm very soon as I smile to myself. The feeling builds deep inside, my breathing falters slightly as I get ready to welcome the sensation then just as I am about to cum, Mitch grabs my wrist and moves my fingers, holding it in place on the counter next to me. I go to pull away so I can continue to play as I was so close but he stops kissing my neck and takes hold of my chin with his free hand so he can tilt my head to look at him, giving him my full attention.

"What is your hurry," he smirks slightly as I gaze in to his eyes, he knows I was about to cum and he stopped me. My face probably looks a little pissed off by his actions which is currently why he is smiling more as my chest heaves off being so aroused.

"Well, we are nearing the end of the world so time is not really on our side," I say sarcastically back at him but he just grunts in response, not letting me move which makes me a little unsure of things, maybe I misread the situation. "If you don't want to then that's fine, it is not like I am going to force you to fuck me or anything," I fake smile at him but inside I do feel a little hurt, I thought he wanted this, I read what he was doing as sexual advances but now I am really confused.

"I didn't say I did not want to," he says gently as he leans in close to me again, allowing me to inhale his scent. "But something tells me that you don't often relinquish control and just let things happen naturally, you always have to be the dominant one, so demanding in everything that you do and just wanting to get fucked and cum... Is that right?" His words are playful but I do not reply to his question. "Whereas right now, I do not want to just randomly fuck you. I want to take my time, explore your body and experience the real you fully, I want to guide you to pure ecstasy not just give you an orgasm, I want to make you forget about the end of the fucking world and just let go completely... I want you so lost in my arms that I become the only thing you focus on and the only thing you feel." For a moment I am unsure how to reply. I loved how forceful he was last time, how he took control and gave me exactly what I wanted, but this is a different kind of control, still dominant but caring at the same time, one that I am definitely not used to and not too sure how to handle.

"Well, what kind of thing did you have in mind," I ask him, my voice unusually quiet as I feel a mix of excitement and intrigue, I feel shy and nervous and I don't think I have ever felt like this before.

"Stop asking questions," he responds then gently kisses my lips, just for a second and as he pulls away again it leaves me wanting more. "Just go with it and let yourself be free." The only way I can think of responding is just to nod my head, and when I do he smiles and kisses me deeply, his tongue exploring my mouth and playing with my own before effortlessly lifting me off the bench, making me wrap my legs around him for support and walking over to the sofa so he can sit down with me in his lap. I try to push out everything I am thinking about and just feel him instead, his cock already hard as it rubs through his boxers below me, the thin fabric of my panties already moist with wanting him. His movements are deliberate, slowly gliding his hands over my skin before unhooking my bra and carefully removing it. I don't do anything, instead allowing him to control what happens next, and deep down I kind of like it, not having to worry about pleasing him or myself as he cherishes the moment.

Mitch slowly teases each of my nipples in turn with his tongue, occasionally sucking them to make them hard, and all the while turning me on more than I thought possible as I watch his mouth taste my skin. I can not help but moan in frustration as he continues to make me wait for any sort of intimate touch, I was already on the edge of orgasm so now every slight movement from straddling him sends my pulse racing. As much as I have pretty much done every single sexual practice there is during my time of being alive, the one I never really enjoyed much was edging. When I have sex I like to cum, a few times if I can, so when I am forced to not cum, get right to that point of ecstasy and have to stop, it doesn't make any sense to me.

"Mitch?" I moan as he goes back to kissing my neck as his finger tips trail up and down my spine. "Please, I want to cum so bad. I can't take the teasing." He moans against my skin in response then gently moves his right hand from my back, skims over my thigh then places it between us where his fingers instantly make me buck as they connect with my pussy through the panties. "Oh fuck," it just slips out as he finally touches me intimately, teasingly playing through the thin fabric.

"I can already feel how wet you are," Mitch breathes in to my ear before moving the fabric out of the way to one side and sliding between my moist lips, connecting directly with my clit which makes me moan deeply. "Mmm is that what you wanted?" he asks me playfully which makes me smile wildly before I wrap my arms around his neck and kiss him deeply again, letting my body surrender to his playing as though it is the only thing I ever wanted in the whole world. Shivers dance across my skin and I find myself quickly consumed again with the need to cum, still already sensitive from playing with myself it takes only a minute to get me straight back to the heights of euphoria. I struggle to breath properly as I continue to kiss Mitch so I move my head back and moan loudly, Mitch smiles as he watches me, staring in to my eyes as he enjoys what he is doing.

"Fuck that feels so good," I say through deep breaths.

"How much do you want to cum right now?" Mitch asks and I have to bite my lip to stop me from begging for it. He can see that I am so close, so he purposefully slows and lightens his touch on me, edging me and keeping me waiting. "Well?" he asks again as he can tell that I am trying so hard to hold back, but I do have to admit, this strong but playful man in front of me right now is turning me on beyond words. All those preconceived ideas I had about angels told me that I never wanted to be anywhere near one, but now I am I straddling a very good looking one who is extremely talented with his fingers.

"I want to cum so fucking much," I finally give in and tell him.

"Good, because I loved hearing you cum last time," he smiles. "But try not to get too loud, we don't want to wake Jake. That could really ruin the mood if he was to walk in right now." A giggle slips out at his comment but quickly catches in my throat as Mitch quickens his movements, my body bucks against his hand as I grab on to his shoulder, almost digging my nails in to his flesh as the pleasurable sensations hit me hard.

"Oh, shit!" I say loudly then quickly try to shush myself by biting my lip hard, any more and I will draw blood.

"You know, the longer you wait, the better it will feel," Mitch smirks as I breath deeply, trying to concentrate on remaining silent but failing miserably as I cry out loudly, the sounds of pleasure echoing around the apartment and mixing with Mitch's slight chuckles of amusement. "You are so fucking beautiful," he groans as he moves his other hand between my thighs and readjusts himself slightly, I know he is rock hard and throbbing, clearly no hiding the fact that he is as turned on as I am even though he is trying to go slow.

"I want to feel you deep inside of me," I moan and he nods in reply before shuffling slightly under me. He pauses momentarily from stimulating my clit to allow me to move, the head of his cock just slides straight towards my pussy as I am dripping wet. I slowly settle down on him, letting him fill my hot hole, the penetration instantly sparking all of my nerve endings and making me almost gush all over his lap.

"Mmm, take it slow," Mitch groans as he goes back to stimulating my clit as I begin to slowly rock back and forth on his cock now that I am comfortable and enjoying the feeling of fullness. Closing my eyes, I just let go completely, pushing out everything else I had in my head and try to just focus on Mitch and the amazing sensations that are threatening to explode between my legs. "Oh fuck, Rosa... I want you cum all over my cock," I look at him and smile, already knowing how close I am to orgasm, I have been for a while and I am not sure I could hold it back any longer even if I wanted to... and I really do not just want to, I need to cum so badly. After saying that Mitch focuses all of his attention on playing with my clit as I quicken my movements, riding him and allowing him to get deeper inside me every time I thrust my hips forward. Everything feels like pure magic, his cock is large and fills me to complete satisfaction, his fingers work my clit as though a pianist playing the perfect renditions of a Beethoven classic, his arm wrapped around the bottom of my back to support me reminding me that I am safe and everything together makes my mind go blank. The energy that builds between us is so pure that I want it to last forever, almost blissful as it gets to a point where I feel like I am floating and cum hard. The skin all over my body is sensitive to the touch, my hands grab on to Mitch's arms for dear life as I let myself get lost, letting go of all my thoughts, fears and emotions and just feel him, so close and deep inside of me.

"Fuck," I moan deeply as I can hardly breathe, then open my eyes again to look down at Mitch as he smiles at me.

"That was so hot, you drive me crazy," he says then carefully moves me, turning me slightly so that he can lie me down gently on the sofa, flat on my back being very careful not to hurt me. "Are you going to cum for me again?" he asks me, but before I reply he kisses me passionately, fucking me slowly whilst he rests on top of me, one hand supporting him, the other teasingly playing with my breasts. His cock feels so fucking good that I know I could probably cum again for him just by him telling me to. He continues to kiss me through loud moans, penetrating me slowly but deep as he takes me completely, enjoying being inside of me and getting as lost in the moment as I am. My hands roam up and down his back as he lies so close to me, feeling his skin which is warm and inviting. I am right on the edge of orgasm again but this time I don't want to rush him, I want to just enjoy it with him, both of us locked in our own little world, one where there is no worry or stress, just us, happy and lost in pleasure. He pulls back and stares deep in to my eyes as his hips continue to thrust forward, each time they do we both breath deeply, matching each other and feeling like one. "I want you to cum with me," he says and I just nod. I am so captivated by him that I don't even think I could speak anyway. His thrusts get deeper and he quickens his pace as we just stare in to each others eyes, letting the heat build until we both are almost gasping for breath and he then nods at me.

"Yes," I reply knowing that he is ready for me. He fucks me harder and instantly we both cry out in pleasure, all that built up energy exploding between us as we both cum together, connected as one as he stares down at me, watching me and knowing that he has my full undivided attention. We both cum so hard that when he does stop we just spend a full minute holding each other, blissfully lost in each others eyes. I can still feel his cock throbbing inside of me as I smile up at him, my cheeks blushing as he looks at me like no one ever has before, so full of passion and adoration.

"Hi," he says gently after a while of silence.

"Hi," I reply and smile uncontrollably. "That was nice."

"Yeah, it was," he smiles back. "You need solid rest. We need you on top form, and I need you feeling better." He helps me up then escorts me to the bedroom, makes sure I am comfortable and leaves me to rest, but as soon as he shuts the door I can not help but beaming so much, he makes me feel so special, I think I do like him a little bit.

I feel like I slept the day away, so when I next wake up I just lie staring up at the ceiling for a little while whilst my mind runs through all of the things that have happened over the last few days. It almost doesn't seem real, how quickly my life changed. All the pain I was feeling is gone, the only thing that is uncomfortable is the stitches that are still in my skin to hold together the wounds I had, so I get up and head to the bathroom so that I can see myself in the mirror as I try to remove them. They tear my skin as I take them out, adding new little cuts to my body but a couple of minutes later and a quick shower to get rid of all of the dirt and blood, makes me feel better and the tiny marks start to disappear again. I throw on some clean clothes, nothing special just a pair of jeans, my converse and a vest top then head to the main apartment to get something to eat now that I am feeling more like the real me.

"Hi," Jake says eagerly as he sees me, he stands up from the sofa and smiles. The look on his face is that of relief so I am guessing that things are still a little awkward between him and Mitch, who just sits silently watching the TV from the sofa with a serious deadpan expression. "Are you, you again?" he asks me and it makes me smile.

"Yeah, I think so," I reply then head to the kitchen to grab a snack.

"I was thinking... maybe if you are not too busy... and of course I am not forcing you at all but, erm... that you might be able to help me," Jake continues a little nervously as I stuff meat and cheese in my mouth that I get from the fridge, suddenly feeling rather starving, I can not even remember when I last ate with everything that has been going on. Even though I do not come here often, I still have staff who ensure the place is clean and stocked if ever I do stop by, and thinking about it, I must waste so much food if I am never here to use it.

"Help you with what?" I say offhandedly as Mitch remains silent, but his face looks nervous at the coming question.

"With me not being me any more," Jake says cautiously. "I have a super powerful demon person hunting for me and if she finds me, I will die. Even you struggled against her and with me being human, I don't stand a chance." I pause from what I am doing and listen to him. "I wasn't born this way, I guess I had some sort of power or just not mortal, maybe. So, I was thinking that if you could help me become who I was meant to be then I might not be so vulnerable and then it might stop the rising." I glance over to Mitch who forces a small smile but doesn't speak.

"Why can't you do it?" I ask Mitch but he looks down at the ground and does not respond.

"He said that because my immortality was stripped away by angels that they could not return it as it would be breaking some holy law or something," Jake explains. It sounds like bullshit but I nod to show him that I am listening. "And you are a demon, right? So you must know how to unlock my potential maybe? To help me not be so... human?" he looks at me pleadingly as he waits for an answer.

"Well," I think hard, it is not something I have come across before. "To be honest, the only way I would know of being able to stop the rising and make sure your blood was not spilt at the Veil and create a Hell mouth, would probably be to kill you now." I shrug. "If you were already dead, then there would be no key, no threat and Lilith wouldn't be able to use you to bring down the Veil or take my fathers seat... Yeah, so if I murder you, we will all be fine." Jake goes pale as he takes in my words, but I struggle to hold back my smirk then after only a few seconds I begin to laugh. "I am kidding," I smile more. "I'm sorry, it was a silly joke. It is one possible solution but I seem to have grown fond of you, however the whole making you immortal thing would not be easy... But I suppose brimstone might help."

"How will brimstone help?" Mitch finally speaks.

"In Hell, Gods wrath was personified to such a level that it formed the start of torment. Just because my father was cast out and made to rule Hell, does not mean he created it," I explain. "So, technically because brimstone was made to burn for eternity and can, in essence, cleanse a sinful soul of any remaining traces of purity, plus the damaging properties it holds against immortal beings, it could strip Jake of the protection you guys put on him and return him to his former half demon, half angel self." Mitch smiles wildly at my words.

"That is amazing," he says laughing at himself. "I have been racking my brains for years to figure out some way of reversing it if it was needed, and you do it in literally seconds."

"Well, I am not just a pretty face," I smirk back then unintentionally blush at the way Mitch is looking at me, the way he gazed at me last night when we were intimate and all the feelings I had then come flooding back. "Although, it is far easier said than done," I say quickly to divert any attention away from how I am feeling. "Jake cannot just go to Hell unless he is dead and sinful, his soul will not be able to cross the Veil, I think, and brimstone is not found in the mortal world because if it fell into the wrong hands it could cause trouble. So I guess it would mean having to go there then bringing some back here to use."

"Then we can get it together," Mitch says happily as he stands from the sofa and prepares to leave.

"That is not an option," I stop him quickly. "You may be immortal, and you have very good intentions but if you set foot in Hell you will be stripped of your faith and lose your wings. As much as many of my kind would enjoy seeing an angel fall spectacularly in my fathers kingdom, you would be worthless to anyone, that is if you survive at all. So that is not an option." That last line catches me off guard as I say it, almost as though I actually care about him deeply and do not want to see him hurt or die. "I need to work out a plan, figure out how I can get what we need without being seen," I pause and take a deep breath as they both watch me, both eagerly awaiting my solution to everything but I cant think properly with them looking at me like that, so hopeful that I will suddenly be able to fix everything. "I need to clear my head so I am going to go for a walk, no offence to you both, but I will think better if I am alone."

I get multiple objections from both Jake and Mitch, apparently they think I need protecting after the last time I went off alone but I assured them that I am a big girl and will not lose my immortality. That was a mistake on my part, one that I will not make again. After they finally accept things, I grab a warm jacket and leave. It is dark and lightly snowing still but I don't mind, it makes the streets quiet and calm which helps me to relax and think about what I need to do. Getting down to Hell will not be an issue, I have travelled there and back many times before, I know I haven't been home in a while but I still know my way around. Although things have changed, and I will have to keep a low profile if I go, just because I kept to myself does not mean that some who dwell down there do not know the very legendary name of Moon. I did have quite a reputation so me suddenly just strolling in the Lucifer's kingdom may raise a few brows, plus getting the brimstone out once I have it won't be easy. Hell has many guards, and because no one knows that I am Lucifer's daughter, getting close to my fathers home and to the brimstone without anyone asking questions may be tricky, then if I do succeed they will never let me just walk out with it.

I find myself walking along the high-street, everything is dead as no stores are open and there is no one around but as I head past a locked up newsagents something catches my eye. Just through the window I can see the papers from yesterday and the front page of one of them gets my attention, I stop and read it as best I can from this distance. From what I can gather the man that was pulled out of the river has still not been named but he has been laid to rest in an unmarked grave in the local city cemetery. That means Wrath has already been buried and not a single person attended his funeral, he was utterly alone and no one from this world even knew who he really was. The city cemetery the article mentions is not too far away and with it now being quite late the place should be empty, especially tonight. With everything that has been going on, I totally lost track of my days and it is now Christmas Eve already.

It only takes me about 20 minutes to get to where I need to go, it is almost 11pm and it has stopped snowing but there is a very cold chill in the air so I wrap my coat tightly around me and slip through the small side gate and head on inside. This is not the first time I have been in this cemetery over the last 150 odd years. I have travelled the globe and seen all the wonders but this city is where I made my home, and also where I made many human acquaintances. That is the one massive downside of being an immortal in the human world, you lose a lot of people you know but I just thought that was part of my life. I didn't really mourn their loss, I just accepted that that is what happens. Humans die, some old, some not, they all end their lives the same way, that is why I always made sure I never got too close or attached. But now as I make my way to the back of the large open area, I can't help but think of them all and subsequently think of my siblings and how they are now lost. The moon is just peeking out from behind the clouds and can be seen through the branches above that dot amongst the graves, and as I get close I wander under the small cluster of old trees then stop dead in my tracks as I see a man standing in silence at the foot of a freshly dug grave. He has his back to me slightly, standing in an expensive black suit, his blond hair slicked back meticulously and he just remains still whilst lost in his own thoughts. I try to stay silent as I move to hide behind the cover of the trees so that I am not seen, I thought I could just come here and pay my respects to Wrath, but the last thing I wanted to do was run in to my father.

I am a safe enough distance from him that he will not know I am here, he is too preoccupied anyway with mourning the loss of one of his precious children and it makes me wonder if it was me buried in the dirt, if he would even care that I was gone. I do think about just turning around and leaving, just walking away and acting like I never came here in the first place, but I feel the need to stay just to honour Wrath's memory, his lose, just like the rest of my siblings have affected me in a way I never expected them to. Like the rest of my family, me and Wrath never really got along, but his body is now lifeless and cold in a wooden box right there in the ground. For who he was and what he represented as a Sin, this is not what he deserved. After about 10 minutes and just watching my father thinking about the loss of his son, I decide to take my leave, head back home and figure out how to stop any more of my family from being killed so I give him one last look and turn to walk away.

"Fancy running in to you here," the voice of a woman rings out through the silent night air. I pause and turn back as curiosity grips me, to see Lilith approach my father, flanked by the demons from the prison. She stops at the head of Wrath's grave and smirks as my father takes a long deep breath and looks up at her to meet her gaze.

"What do want, Lilith?" he asks her as I take cover again and see what happens. "Is it not enough for you to kill my children, but you have to come here and torment me with it as well." Lilith laughs as she crosses her arms and looks down at the lose dirt at her feet.

"He was one of the easiest to kill, you know," she smiles as she speaks. "Although not the most fun, he hardly even put up a fight, whereas Greed he was blast... You could stop all this Lucifer, step down and hand me your throne and you can just walk away."

"That will never happen," he replies quickly. "If you were to control the throne, you would destroy everything."

"Destroying everything is the point," she smiles wildly back. "This whole existence thing is a joke, creation is based on lies and it all needs to end, that is the only way." There is a moment of silence whilst everyone waits to see what happens next, my father thinking of a response that will not result in her getting more pissed off.

"There was a time when you believed in more, when you actually loved the life you were given and lived as though you did not care what God did, when you did not want the revenge any more," my father says quietly and I have to struggle to listen fully from this distance.

"That was a long time ago, Lucifer," she says with pain in her voice at the memory. "A different time altogether when I actually thought I loved you. You were my life fully, you created a fire in my soul and made me desire more... but then just when I thought my life could not be any more perfect, when I was surrounded finally with happiness, the curse that was bestowed on me by my creator, ripped out my heart and it made me despise you." I don't know what they are talking about but my father seems a little uneasy with the subject. "Do you know what day it is tomorrow?"

"I do," my father replies cautiously and for a moment he looks as though he is deliberating whether or not to say any more before he speaks. "It would have been her birthday."

"She was perfect, and the second she was born I knew that she was the most spectacular creation I had ever made," Lilith says with true emotion, true heartfelt love as she speaks. "Our daughter could have changed everything, she would have ruled by my side and ensured that the mortal world kneeled at our feet, she would have helped me bring an end to my suffering and show my God what true power looked like, but I lost my Alexis the same day and you just walked away as though you did not care at all." My chest suddenly hurts as I realise I am not breathing then I quickly clasp my hand over my mouth in case anyone hears me desperately try to force air in to my lungs as I listen more. I can not have just heard what I think I did, could I?

"You know I cared Lilith, I loved you like no other, you were everything to me and I was devastated by what happened," he replies kindly. "You were not the only one who lost a child that day."

"She was in your care, she was your responsibility and you let her die before I even got a chance to hold her," Lilith snaps and I swallow back the lump in my throat. I can't believe what I am hearing, maybe there is another Alexis, it may have been a common name at some point, because it can't be me they are discussing. I was always told my mother was human and mortal just like the other Sins, plus they are saying that their baby died and the last time I looked, I am very much alive.

"I know you blame me for what happened," my father says gently. "And I will always be sorry for that. But you knew when we found out that we were having a child together, that there was an overwhelming chance that the curse would take her."

"I don't blame the curse, I blame you," Lilith says with anger in her voice. "It is your fault that she died, and it is your fault that you did not stand by me when I wanted to get my revenge against my God. You abandoned me, turned your back and told me to my fucking face that I was crazy. The only thing I have ever been crazy for was caring too much about the people that I loved. I was crazy in love with you, then I was driven crazy with everything I lost... Your children are now dying, your throne is threatened and I will bring down the Veil and create Hell on earth because you all think I am crazy. My creator took too many of my children from me, so now I am taking yours then I will destroy everything. Only when it is all gone, will I be content and happy." They both stand staring at each other for a few minutes before Lilith and her demon back up turn around and leave my father alone with Wrath's grave once more. After a tense moment of me trying to stay so still that no one would even hear my heart beat, and when Lilith is fully gone, I try to understand what I just heard.

"You can come out now," my father says loud enough for me to hear him clearly but I don't move. It can't be me he is talking to, I am very good at hiding and making sure I am not seen. He sighs deeply then turns to look over towards where I am standing behind the trees and smiles gently at me. "Hello Alexis. This is not how I intended for you to find out, but I think now is the time to tell you the truth about who you really are and why you are the most important person I have ever know."

Chapter Ten

I don't move, in fact I don't even blink as I just stare at my father who waits patiently for me to do or say something instead of looking like a really out of place statue. I haven't properly spoken to him for hundreds of years and now I have all this new information that I do not understand, and it seems a lot of my life may have been a lie. It cannot be possibly true, can it? Lilith cannot be my mother.

"Alexis, I think I should start by apologising," he says gently as he watches me but I can not even comprehend that he is actually speaking to me. "Things between the two of us has never been very good, from your point of view I believe the Sins had my attention and love, you tried so hard to better yourself and prove that you were strong but I never acknowledged it." I cautiously step out from behind the trees as I listen to what he has to say. "But the truth is, and what I am so very sorry for, is that I purposefully pushed you away, I forced you in to leaving your home and there has not been a day that has gone by that I didn't regret what I did to you, but I had my reasons."

"What possible reasons could you have to show such dislike for your own daughter," I ask as my voice shakes, anger quickly coursing through my blood.

"I knew that one day, the survival of creation would hang in the balance," he explains. "And I knew that only the most powerful creature would decide the fate of human kind. I did what I had to do because I couldn't risk you being on the wrong side."

"What the fuck are you talking about?" I ask confused as he slowly walks towards me then stops a few feet in front before casually putting his hands in his trousers pockets. Even after all this time and his now relaxed nature, his demeanour is strong and unyielding. I wanted to be just like him when I was younger, so dominant, so fearless... but he just made me hate him.

"The day you were born was amazing, having a child is such a gift, one that I was always thankful of, but I knew that I had a decision to make," he says carefully. "As much as I loved your mother at the time, I knew that if you were to grow up by her side, you would be the one to bring down the Veil and ultimately make everything we knew, cease to exist. So I did the unthinkable, I told her you were dead, that you were just another of her children who were killed because of God's vengeance for her disobedience. And then to make sure she never found out that you were alive, I pushed you away, I made you leave and change your name, and I made you never want to come back home... But I watched you, I watched you every day, you grew in strength and worked harder than anyone I had seen before you, and I am immensely proud of the person you became. You may not understand but I did what I thought was best." I look up at him, the same man I remember from all those years ago, the man who I fought to be seen by, who allowed the Sins to tease and bully me because he didn't love me like he loved them, the same man who didn't even notice when I left... or so I thought.

"You lied to me," I force myself to say as my voice shakes more, it is not through fear or nerves, it is through sheer frustration and anger towards him. "When I was only 10 years old, I asked you about my mother, you told me she was mortal, that she lived in the human world and that she had sacrificed her soul to her Dark Lord to grant life and gave you a child. You looked in to my fucking eyes and lied to me like the arsehole you always were. You never loved me, you hardly even acknowledged my existence, so how can you possibly stand here now and tell me that everything you did was for the best." Lucifer sighs deeply as I race through everything in my head. "Lilith is my mother? That fucking bitch who murdered my siblings in cold blood, is my actual real life mom?" My breathing shakes as I try to remain calm but I am really struggling, none of this can be true, I do not even believe that those words are coming out of my own mouth.

"You were destined to stop her," he says gently as he can see how overwhelmed I am with this very unexpected revelation. "She is so focused on destroying everything. The one who controls the crown, controls the throne and that is all she now wants, she will do anything to take it... But you, you my darling Alexis, can be the one who saves us all and..."

"What if I don't want to save you all," I snap and interrupt him talking, my voice getting uncontrollably louder. I know he is my father and I should respect him for who he is as the Devil himself, but he lost my respect a very long time ago. "What if I am so pissed off with my own flesh and blood that I just walk away and let you all fight it out between yourselves. What if I don't give a flying fuck what happens to you, to the Sins, or to God, or the humans or anyone else who thinks they can tell me what to do or how to live my fucking life," I shout at him and I can see he is getting angry with my words. Not even the Sins would have dared speak to him in such a way.

"Watch your tone with me, Alexis," he says trying to remain calm but I know from past experience he hates being disrespected. "You may not have lived under my roof for many years but I am still your father." I can't help but scoff at his words.

"You stopped being my father a long time ago," I retort, much to his distaste. "You are an absolute joke, you made me believe I was worthless and you drove me away... Go to Hell... and this time, stay there for good," I turn on the spot and walk away, I can't breathe, I can't sort out all of the things in my head and I don't know who it is that I am any more.

"Alexis?" my father shouts after me as I walk through the cemetery. "Alexis, I did love you, more than life itself, I had to do what I did, to protect you... This is where your life has been leading, now is the time to step up and take your true place in the world. You can not walk away from this."

"Fucking watch me," I yell back without even looking over my shoulder. I didn't think I could hate him any more than I already did. But now I am fuming, he twisted my feelings, he manipulated my life and he lied about everything. My father would never do one single thing unless it was of benefit to him, even when playing with the lives of some of his mindless followers in the human world, he would not bother unless he gained something. I can't even process what he has just said to me, how he knew from the moment I was born what exactly my life would hold and that I would grow up to destroy everything. I spent my life protecting this world, when I guarded the Veil to stop whatever was in Hell being released on this earth, I did the complete opposite to what he is saying would have happened if I had known my mother. Obviously, I know full well who I am, that I am Lucifer's daughter and part of Hells royal family, but I cannot imagine wanting to undo creation. If I set out to do that, I would be condemning myself and every single speck of life that exists now, no matter how much demon blood runs through my veins, I would not want to destroy everything.

I can't think straight, I have a million different thoughts battling to win my attention but I can not decipher them and seem to zone out, so end up just walking and seeing where my feet take me. Eventually it starts to snow again and the freezing air fills my lungs as I am consumed with an emptiness that I fear will now never go away. I always wondered what my mother was like, what kind of life she led within the human world and if she even thought about me at all after I was born. Once the first 100 years of my life were over, I eventually accepted that if my mother was mortal that she would more than likely be dead and long gone, and I hoped that she had had a good life and was happy. I never once questioned my father after he told me about her, I never doubted his words because I had no reason to. At that still young age, I would never have considered that my father would lie about something like that. But yet now, I find myself second guessing every little thing he has ever said to me, I don't know what was truth and what were just more lies that came out of his mouth. I never thought I would be able to hate him any more than I already did, but tonight proved to me just how wrong I was because now I am starting to hate myself for not standing up to him sooner, for letting him push me away.

The sound of the distant singing of a choir catches my attention and I finally stop walking to see where I am. The street itself is quiet, quite open with a small park surrounded by trees that sits opposite a large church with steps leading up to the front doors. From inside, I can hear the people joining in with hymns, the warmth that shines through the cracks in the partially open doors appeals to me, and before I know it, I find myself climbing the steps towards the entrance. I pause briefly at the top, thinking that me being here will be noticed and that the big God almighty that everyone looks up to will strike me down just for thinking about entering his house of worship, but I slip inside without anyone noticing me, and carefully make my way to the side of the aisles as the choir and standing congregation continue to sing. But it is not the the atmosphere that is attracting me to this house of God right now, it is the need for answers. I need to know why me? Why out of every soul that has ever lived or graced this earth, did it have to be me that everything is now imploding around. I tried to be the best version of myself I could be, most of my years I kept my head down and made myself stronger. Sure, there are a lot of people who hear the name Moon and know who the fuck I am, in the sense that they know I am a very powerful demon who doesn't give a shit and loves to have fun. But the name Alexis Morningstar, the weight that comes with just accepting that as the true me, terrifies me. I have never been Alexis, I never felt like the daughter of Lucifer, I just felt like an outsider and someone who had to bury the old her to be able to live her life.

At the far side of the grand church, I see a young man come out of a small wooden confession booth so I head on over as curiosity gets the better of me. I have so many thoughts, doubts, questions in my head that I feel the need to vent. I have never been in a church before, let alone spoke to a priest but I guess now is as good a time as any to try new things. As I go inside there is a small seat that faces a hatched wooden screen so I sit down and think silently, letting all those questions flood my thoughts. I know there is someone in the next booth, probably waiting to hear me confess my sins and cleanse my soul, but I am not sure how to start.

"May God, who has enlightened every heart, help you to know your sins and trust in his mercy," the kind voice of an older man says through the small gaps in the screen between us, then falls quiet as he waits for me to speak.

"I suppose this is the part where they usually ask for forgiveness and confess their sins to you," I say, almost thinking out loud. "Those humans who show remorse for all the bad things they have done so you can absolve them of it and save their soul," I laugh at myself slightly at the thought of it. "If only you truly knew that no soul will ever be safe."

"Is this your first time at confession, my child?" the old man replies without judgement.

"Yes," I answer honestly. "Although, I didn't really come here to confess my sins... During my life I have done many things that your God would class as sinful, but I do not regret any single one of them and I do not come here now seeking absolution."

"Then why are you here?" he asks gently. "If you admit you have led a sinful life but yet you do not show remorse for your actions, why are you here in the house of our Lord God, seeking confession?"

"Because I need to understand," I reply. "I need to know why this is all happening. Why I am who I am, and why your God doesn't do something to stop it."

"Stop what?" he asks and I pause for a moment to think.

"The end of days," I say. "It seems inevitable that very soon creation will cease to exit, once she finds what she is looking for there will be nothing to stop her from bringing Hell on earth and undoing everything that your God laid out," I stop to take a deep breath and sigh deeply. "I am sure that there have been many a human through these doors who have issues with their parents, it is one of the commandments isn't it, that you should honour your mother and father? Well, my mother and father are pure evil, and no matter how much distance I have tried to put between us, they seem to be about to ruin my entire life."

"There are many a person who thinks that an evil spirit lies within a parent," he replies. "Not everyone can control the environment they are brought up in, but they can control who they become and who they want to be. Who is it that you want to be?" he asks me and for a moment I an unsure of how to respond.

"I don't know any more," I sigh. "I thought I did, I thought that I had everything I wanted from life and that I didn't need anything or anyone else. But things are changing around me and I no longer feel like I can control it... May I ask you a question?"

"Of course," he says carefully.

"Why did God create humans in the first place?" I inquire. "Were his angels not enough for him? Did he not receive the unconditional love and worship that he craved from his already divine creatures, instead wanting more? Because if that is the case and he created humans just to get gratification for his actions then how can he be pure and without sin? How can God be the good guy and Satan be the one who is evil when God himself has done more harm to the human world than any sin or demon could ever do... And why did he allow someone like me to be born?"

"Our Lord God has a plan for all things, we are here to trust in his decisions," the old priest says. "If you were put on this earth, then God has a plan for you as well. Just as he does with all of his children. He has so much love to give that he created us so we would know how love feels, he wanted to share the joy of life and watch us flourish in to amazing humans that could do extraordinary things. He did not create us for selfish reasons, he gave us the ultimate gift of life, just as he also did with you."

"God didn't create me, Lucifer did," I sigh heavily as I think about my father more, and everything he has done. "He got inside my head and made me believe that I was not worthy of love, that even though I have done many incredible and sometimes terrible things in my life, I will never amount to anything and I will forever live in the shadow of my brothers and sisters. He made me feel weak."

"The Devil tries to temp us all, to make us believe that we are not worthy of Gods love," he explains to me as I sit silently and listen. "But he can only succeed if we let him, because of our inner weakness. Our Lord God gives us inner strength by His Holy Spirit to resist temptation. We, ourselves, do not have the strength to live the way we should, and when we try to fight the Devil on our own, we often do fail. But Christ is stronger than Satan, if you open your heart to Him, He will guide you back to the light. The Bible reminds us that "the reason the Son of God appeared was to destroy the Devil's work". Once you admit your past sins and allow Him to take your hand, you will see that you are loved and you are more than you ever thought you could be."

"You don't have any idea who I am, or what I am truly capable of... But now I am not sure what I should be doing or where I belong. And I feel so lost," I shake my head and look down at the ground. The small box is dark and I as we sit for a moment I can still hear the humans singing in unison for their Lord.

"You are right, I do not know who you are," he agrees with me. "But I do know that you are here now and you have made the first step in your quest for answers. Answers that will help you to understand your place in this life and ultimately lead you to find who you truly are."

"Who I truly am?" I ask out loud as I take in his words. "Who I truly am has been buried deep inside of me for so long that she doesn't even exist any more." All this time of trying to forget where I was born and the blood I came from, and now everything around me is forcing me back to it. I can't accept any of this, I never wanted to be that person. I just can't do it.

"Embrace it, allow that inner strength to shine through, follow your heart and be the person you were born to be," the priest says as I shake my head not wanting to follow any of his advice. He doesn't know what he is talking about, just another human blindly following the words of an invisible God. I try to respond a couple of times, I want to tell him how wrong he is, that God is playing with the lives of the humans and in seconds I could kill everyone inside this church just to prove that I am not a mindless follower of his unlike them, but instead my chest tightens and struggle to breath. "God's plan for you, my child, is only just beginning. The sooner you walk in to the light of the Lord, the sooner you can accept the life you have been given and become the great soul that you were destined to be."

"I erm... you just don't understand... I am not..." I struggle with my words as my hands begin to shake. "I never wanted this, I was happy not knowing but now..." What the fuck is wrong with me? I know exactly who I am and I should not have come here. "You are wrong. You don't know shit. If God had a plan for me then it would have included me not being born, because he told me I could have been the one to end everything. Your God is a selfish bastard and he should step in and do something instead of letting all this fucking crap happen." Swiftly, I stand from the small wooden bench, swing open the door and almost collapse out of the confessional booth. I desperately need some fresh air, I can't breathe and everything feels like it is spinning uncontrollably around me. I don't know what I hoped to achieve by going in to a fucking church, I know I said I was looking for answers but those are very clear, I just don't want to accept them. I stumble past a few humans who are waiting in line to confess after me and head for the back doors but as I do I catch something out of the corner of my eye which makes me stop. Mitch and Jake are stood over the other side, Mitch listening to the words now being spoken from the alter at the front and as he casually glances to the side to speak to Jake he meets my gaze and smiles sweetly as though he is pleasantly surprised to see me. In return I shake my head at him and run. I barge past people on my way out, knocking a young couple over as I go and start to hurry down the steps as soon as I am outside.

"Rosa? Hey wait up," Mitch calls from behind me but I don't stop. I can't figure out my own thoughts and feelings without also having to deal with an angel and the half-ling that could destroy the world. As I get to the bottom, I slip slightly on the frozen ground, almost loosing my footing and falling to my knees but keep on going. Everything that has happened over the last week doesn't feel real and now I am so fucking confused. How could my father do that to me? What gave him the right to decide to stop me knowing who my real mother was? I understand what might have happened if he hadn't told her I was dead, I really do because I am not stupid, but I should have had the option to decide what I did with my own life, not him. If I grew up by her side then maybe we would have all been a family and everything would have been different but instead no one seemed to give a shit about my feelings. And my father knew who was behind this whole thing all along and he never even bothered his arse to warn his own children that they were at risk, he knew she was going to try for the throne and he knew they were a target. He did nothing, he obviously didn't care at all. "Rosa?" Mitch calls again as him and Jake hurry after me.

"You guys need to leave me alone," I shout back without stopping and head away down the middle of the street. Now that I know how I am fully linked to Lilith, having Mitch and Jake around me puts them at great risk. If she can sense the Sins in the human world, then what if she can sense me? If she gets the slightest clue to who I really am she will find me, and if that happens we are all doomed.

"What do you mean? Leave you alone," I hear Jake say as he tries to keep up. "I thought you were going to help me, I can't remain human and in danger, you said that..."

"I know what I said," I snap at him then stop and turn to look at them both as they slow now that I am not running away. "You guys need to get as far away from me as you possibly can, if she finds out the truth then no one will be safe. Just get in a car and drive as far in the opposite direction to me. Please, it is the only way to make sure you guys are safe."

"What's going on?" Mitch asks confused as he slowly approaches me. "Has something happened? Rosa, we agreed to help each other. We know what is going on now and we can stop it if we all work together on this."

"I can't stop her, I don't even want to get close to her in case she finds out the truth," I say as my voice shakes. "I thought she was pissed before, but this..." I try to take a deep breath but it quivers in my chest and I can feel my entire body shaking. "This is not what I wanted, I had put all of that behind me, I changed and blocked out all of my fucking early years but no matter how much I run from my past, it is now all coming back to bite me in the ass."

"Rosa? I don't understand what you are talking about," Mitch says as he slowly steps forward, a look of great concern all over his face.

"Please, you need to back up and leave," I try to say firmly but I am panicking. Lilith is pissed at my father because I supposedly died at birth, I can only imagine the fall out when she finds out I have been alive for 2000 years and she never knew. "If she finds me she will destroy everything and I do not know how to face her. What would I even say? Do I tell her the truth or do I fight, I just don't know."

"Rosa what are you saying?" Mitch asks as he steps forward and goes to take hold of my hand. "You are shaking, just take some deep breaths and try to calm down. Whatever has happened, I am sure we can figure it out."

"No," I say and pull my hand away. He just stands staring in to my eyes as I struggle to breathe. "You need to get away from me. I cannot be associated with an angel... you and the human are nothing to me," I lie, but this is the only thing I can think of to make sure they are safe. "You were too stupid to see that I was just playing with you, I was just having a bit of fun... Lilith wants the key and if you do not fuck off out of my face right now, I will happily hand it over and watch the entire world burn at my feet. This world has too many humans in it who think they are better than us demons because they inherit the earth, but soon they will bow at our feet and I will celebrate as they all meet their demise. You angels are not worthy to breathe the same air as anyone from Hell's royal family, in fact, you should kneel and pray to Lucifer to set you free. You are no one to me, you are pathetic and weak, and most of all," I swallow hard then step forward, getting right up close to Mitch's face to try to assert my dominance even though I feel like a I breaking apart inside. "Most of all, when you fucked me I faked the whole thing."

You were nothing compared to the demons I have fucked over the years, it was hardly even worth my time, I felt nothing. I just slept with you because I felt sorry for you. If I ever see your face or hear your name mentioned again in this life, it will be too soon." We both stare at each other in silence as I wait for Mitch to retaliate, to shout at me and get angry so it becomes easier for me to push him away, but after a few very long moments, Mitch forces a tight smile and sighs.

"Something has clearly happened to you since you left your apartment a little while ago," he says gently. "And your go to thing is to get defensive, to push us away and then probably do something stupid, just like last time." I quickly shake my head and find myself fighting back some very strong and overwhelming emotions that are threatening to explode inside of me. "I don't know what has gone on in the last hour or so, but I am not leaving your side. We both know that Jake is at his safest with you, you are the last star of the morning and you are the saviour of the human race."

"You are wrong," I force out as tears fall down my cheeks. "I am pure evil. My blood was destined to destroy the earth and I swear that if you guys don't leave right now, I will kill you both myself and hand your dead bodies over to Lilith."

"No you won't," he replies carefully. "If you were truly evil you would have tried to kill us long before now." I glance around trying desperately to think of another plan seen as though he is clearly not believing a word that I say. If someone so much as sniffs a demon and an angel working together, it will be a massive red flag and I know for a fact that it will bring Lilith's men straight after Jake. If I stand any chance of stopping the rising, then he needs to be hidden and safe.

"Stop being so god damn nice to me and just fuck off," I croak but it just makes Mitch smile even more.

"Never," he replies sweetly. "We are in this together and I am not going anywhere."

"Please," I beg. "Please just take Jake and leave. You can't be close to me, you don't know who I am."

"I think I have a very good idea by now of who you are, Rosa," he smiles.

"My name is not Rosa," I reply as my entire body shakes. "I was never really her, it was all just an act, me trying to escape the truth but she will find me... and when she does..." I gasp for air as my chest tightens again just thinking about what will happen when she learns of the truth. "She is going to destroy everything and I don't know if I can protect Jake, so please, just leave. Take Jake somewhere safe, please." I feel like I am going to pass out as my head pounds and the longer Mitch tries to help, the more I can feel my blood boil, as though there is this thing inside of me that is begging to be released and it terrifies me, because I know the blood that runs through my veins is pure evil... which means I am pure evil and I do not know if I can contain it. I have never felt more out of control, I have always been so strategic, I knew who I was and what I could do but now I don't know anything. My entire life I tried to be Rosa Moon, but Alexis was born to Lilith and Lucifer and she can not be anything but evil, nothing else makes sense.

"Who are you talking about?" Mitch asks as he watches me closely. "Do you mean Lilith?" Just the sound of her name makes my breath catch. "Rosa talk to me, please."

"You don't understand, please you need to leave," I try to say firmly but the more I panic the more my skin feels like it is burning off my flesh.

"I am not going anywhere, I promise you," Mitch says then gently takes hold of my hand. "Whatever has happened, I will help you Rosa." As soon as he says my fake name, something inside of me just snaps and I feel all of the heat and emotions just bubble over.

"My name... is not Rosa!" I yell, and force Mitch away from my hand... or I thought that is what I was doing. Because within seconds a loud explosion emanates from next to us, several of the stationary cars along the street are thrown through the air away from us and smash in to the railings around the park. Flames engulf the surrounding vegetation, the tall trees that line the street consumed with burning bright fire. Mitch is on the ground a good 10 foot in front of me, desperately trying to extinguish the now burning leather of his jacket which seems to be melting with the heat. I just stand, in complete shock then realise my palms feel strangely hot so I slowly look down. My hands look unusual, across the skin tiny flickers of fire dance but it doesn't burn, instead it feels normal, as though it was always inside of me but I never let it out before. I know my father is associated with the fiery depths of Hell and at times he has been known to control the flames but this is very new to me and I am not sure how to process it. I look up and catch Mitch's gaze, for a moment no one speaks, he just stares at me clearly as shocked as I am then screaming starts to fill the street around us. I quickly take in my surroundings, scanning the area to make sure I didn't hurt anyone. Apart from Mitch's jacket, a few cars and the tree line no one else seems hurt, just extremely scared of what I can only assume looked like a fireball, that has just ripped through the night. "I'm sorry," I force out as I watch Mitch get to his feet, and Jake just stands frozen to the spot by his side. "I don't know what that was... I'm sorry, I am so fucking sorry." Before I wait for a response, I turn around and run.

I feel like I do not know who I am any more, and I have never lost control like that ever. What did my father say? He thought I would be the most powerful creature that existed? I have never felt that way, I know I am strong but never to the extent that I would dream about challenging the highest of Hells trinity to test my abilities. I have never had to, I always assumed I reached my full potential when I was guarding the Veil, I haven't even used my actual true power since I came to the human world.

"Rosa?" Mitch shouts after me. I know he is chasing me down but I can't stop, I don't want to hurt anyone and if I lose control again, I could kill Jake and that is the last thing I want to happen right now. In the last week, since I have met them both, my mind and heart have been so conflicted, I have never felt so many different ranges of emotions before, because I have always ensured I kept my distance from people. I don't love, I don't cry, I have never even felt proper fear before this week and now it is all too much to handle. I get intense pain that spreads through my chest as I approach the end of the street where the road curves and leads to a small dock near the waterfront of the river bank. The pain spreads and causes me to stop, almost doubling over as I gasp for air, I know this is pure anxiety, everything is crashing down around me and I can't cope, I can't take the pressure. I drop to my knees and just give in as tears cascade down my face, and my entire body shakes. "Rosa!" Mitch shouts then drops to my side and quickly wraps his arms around me, holding me so tight that I cannot move at all as I just sob in to his chest, giving in completely. It takes me a good few minutes to calm down enough to actually be able to breathe normally, when I do I can already hear sirens a couple of streets away attending to the fire. Mitch gently wipes the tears from my face as I finally look up at him, Jake standing at our side full of worry and both of them not knowing what is going on.

"I'm sorry," I say quietly as I start to feel embarrassed by being so emotional.

"It's OK, just let us help you," Mitch replies gently. "Whatever it is, we can all face it together."

"It is just so unexpected," I explain quietly. "Never did I imagine that this would happen. But he lied to me and now I don't even know who I am. It scares me, all these feeling and emotions, I can't control them and I am so unsure of everything. If she finds out, I am not sure what she will do."

"Just tell me, it is all going to be alright," he smiles and I nod, knowing that I need to tell him because despite everything, I don't think I could face this alone.

"Lilith," I start. "She is... he told me tonight. Lilith is my..."

"It was you?" We hear the voice of a woman say from near by, and instantly I freeze. Mitch and Jake both look in the direction of the voice as I sit on the frozen ground, almost holding my breath as though if I do not even breathe then she will not be able to see me. "There was me thinking I felt the raw power of another Sin close by, something old and strong that is not usually seen in this world just popped up out of nowhere, so I came to find it," Lilith says with great interest. "But instead I find the girl who I thought I killed in the prison with Envy." Finally, I turn to look behind me. Lilith is standing casually in a pair of red leather trousers and a long black coat, her usual back up demons at either side and she just stares at us in wonderment. "Rosa? Wasn't that what he called you?" She smiles then looks at Mitch. "And I never thought I would lay my eyes on the great protector that is the Archangel Michael again."

"Hello Lilith," Mitch says as he cautiously stands up, trying to position himself in front of Jake but she notices what he is trying to do straight away. "Me either, I did hope you were dead."

"Mmmm," she smiles. "Now this is interesting. Not at all the boring kind of night I did have planned... An Archangel and what I feel to be a very powerful demon both together, looking as though they are protecting an unknown human male." Lilith looks at Jake fully, not taking her eyes off him for a second. Even from here I can see her mind working overtime, piecing everything together and my heart almost beats out of my chest through fear. "That means you must be my key... I have waited so long to find you."

Chapter Eleven

"Your key? What is that? I do not know what you are talking about," Mitch quickly responds as I force myself to stand up, my legs are shaking and for the first time in my life, I do not know what to say or do at all. I quickly glance at Jake and he meets my gaze, I am begging him to keep his mouth shut and after only a second he gives me the slightest nod as though he knows what I am thinking.

"Don't lie to me Michael, it is not very angelic of you to do so," Lilith smiles then looks around to the other demons with her. There are 5 of them, all of who are different to the ones I saw in the prison, from this distance I cannot tell if any of them are armed but I will hazard a guess that they are concealed somewhere. "Why don't we put our past behind us and move forward, Michael. We can start when you hand over the human?"

"I don't think that is going to happen," Mitch responds and for a moment I am actually surprised with how strong he seems in front of her. "I am not going to be forced in to doing anything by you, especially when you ally yourself with demons." Lilith laughs at his words.

"You are one to talk," she says then glances at me again. But I can't do anything but shake, no words leave my mouth and in this very moment I know I have never felt so unsure of myself. "Who are you, sweet girl?" Lilith asks me and for a second I do consider just blurting it out, telling her that I am her daughter but if I do that, then I will be jeopardising the life of Jake and as much as I hate my father,

149

he is still my blood, and I guess he did try to protect the human world. Holy fuck, I am so confused by everything, I don't know what to do for the best. "You are someone who I feel is very powerful, I don't know who you are and I wonder how I ever let someone like you pass me by. I know that you know who I am, you told me so in the prison, you know I could offer you a very substantial reward if you hand over the human to me and join my army. There is not a soul that exists that could stand against me, so make the right choice and maybe you won't die." My breathing shakes as I take in her words, then I go to reply but nothing leaves my mouth, I have never experienced these feelings of paralysing fear or being so utterly lost before, so after a few seconds of her waiting for my response, I just shake my head and refuse to accept her proposal. Am I afraid? Am I terrified that she will actually kill me? All these feelings are so new that my head can't make sense of everything and my heart hurts because I do not know who I am supposed to be. I feel torn between wanting to know my mother, and knowing my father told her I died to protect everything.

"Leave now Lilith," Mitch says firmly. "You have no power here and not one single human will ever bow to you." Lilith smiles at his words then glances to the demons at either side of her.

"Bring me my key," she casually says to them. "Dead or alive, all that matters is that I get him." Instantly the demons nod at their orders and run towards us. Mitch grabs Jake to make sure he is protected as 3 of the 5 demons all head straight for him. The other 2 come in my direction, one is tall, well built, has dark hair and wears a plain black shirt, the other a little shorter but stocky, in a crisp baby blue shirt, actually quite smart considering how seedy his face looks. The guy in black smirks at me as he takes a large knife from a holster attached to the back of his trousers, I thought they would be armed but as he comes towards me, threatening to kill me to get to the key, I just stand, totally still, not even attempting to defend myself or get out of the way, and I am not sure as to why.

He hits me with force, and the next thing I know I am on the ground, the back of my skull aching as it was slammed in to the concrete. I am so lost in my own thoughts that I can't even comprehend what is going on around me any more. The guy in black pins one of my arms down by my head as his other hand rams the blade of his knife deep in to my shoulder without any resistance. The pain hits me instantly and I cry out, but my sounds of anguish are quickly interrupted as he moves his hands to my neck and cuts off my breathing, I claw at his wrists trying to get him to let me go but I don't have it in me to fight, my entire body is overcome with fear and I don't know what to do to protect myself. I know I could fight these guys easily, I could literally rip them apart but it is as though my body doesn't want to. Is this it? Have I actually given up? I know I am immortal but right now my heart is not even in the right place to want to survive, it feels shattered with all the lies and how much my life was crafted for my fathers wishes, however my head is racing as all it is consumed with is the fact I can no longer breathe. My chest burns the more he squeezes my neck but he just laughs in my face, seeing the fear and confusion in my eyes, before holding me in place with one hand and teasingly running the tip of his knife along my jaw line with the other.

"You know, you would look pretty if you smiled more," he sneers down at me as he stares in to my eyes, then laughs as his blade digs deep in to my face and he slices it open from just under my left eye, down my cheek and through my top lip, playing with me like a piece of meat, carving my skin for his own amusement. I want to scream as the pain consumes me but no sound comes out except strangled moans of desperation. I need to get him off me so I quickly try to focus on right now and forget everything else, there is far too much shit in my head that I need to push away. I drive my knee in to his groin and he instantly tumbles to the side, allowing me to take a moment to breathe, gulping in the oxygen and filling my lungs then I glance to my side as the guy in black is already getting back to his feet quickly. He smiles wildly at me as he reaffirms his grip on the blade then out of nowhere a hand grabs a fist full of my hair and drags me off the ground. The blue shirt demon holds me up as the black shirt guys comes at me again, I watch him, knowing that he will kill me if he gets the chance but I still don't react, I don't know what is wrong with me, all my mind keeps going back to is the last time I faced Lilith, how I felt so human and she killed my bother with ease right in front of my eyes. Now I feel the same, just seeing her has me feeling weak and worthless, should I even be fighting back? She is my mother, she might not know it but she is still my blood. If I just tell her who I am then maybe she will understand that I don't want to end the world, I don't want to watch all of the humans die. But at the same time I can't help remember what my father said, that she would use me to destroy everything as I was supposed to be such a powerful creature, not that I feel like it at all. Do I stand by her and potentially watch everything burn or do I stand by my father and try to save them?

"The way our Mistress Lilith was talking, I thought you would have put up more of a fight," the guy in the black shirt says whilst he stands directly in front of me before driving the knife deep in to my gut, he stands inches from my face just watching me as pain rips through my body and I want to collapse as my legs give out beneath me, but the man behind holds me up, stopping me from moving away. He slowly pulls the blade from my flesh, allowing the warm fresh blood to freely flow from the wound. My head is banging and so not in the game, I haven't even thought about healing myself, its something that I took for granted, my body being able to heal was a natural part of who I was as a powerful soul reaper and child of Lucifer, but because I feel so lost, so now does my body and if I do just give up, I could potentially die. Which I probably will as the latest injury I have sustained is deep and even if I did try to heal, it might already be too late, just like when Mitch stabbed me, but this time I don't feel strong enough, I am no longer me, I don't know who I am any more. My face is in agony, the feelings from the knife wounds are tearing through me but all I can think about is that my mother is standing right there, watching these men try to kill her daughter and she is probably enjoying it.

He stares at me as I begin to struggle to breathe, my blood is pounding through my veins trying to compensate for the amount I am now losing and I my head is going dizzy. He slowly smells the blood that coats the knife, enjoying being in control and playing with his kill then raises the tip to my throat. I know I need to do something, anything to stop them because if this guy kills me right now I won't be able to control myself and just like when Mitch stabbed me, my instincts could kick in and I don't know what souls I would take, I can't even control my own body right now so this could be disastrous. As a reaper I know the strongest souls are human and the closest human is Jake, if I take his soul to live then I may as well just hand him over to Lilith now. My mind races to find a plan but I can't focus on anything apart from the pain, not the physical pain, that I can handle, but the deep empty pain that I feel because of who I am and what I now know about myself.

Suddenly I am on the ground, I am not sure what's going on or how I got here but I am struggling to move, my body feels weak and my breathing rattles in my chest. A hand grabs my shoulder and turns me on to my back to look at me then I connect with his eyes.

"Rosa, what is wrong with you?" Mitch shouts at me as he frantically looks at all the blood that covers me, he places his hand on my stomach to try to stop some of the bleeding as I feel it start to pool beneath me. "Heal yourself. Rosa, now is not the time to sit back". Glancing to the side and ignoring Mitch I see several of the demons scattered on the ground, one looks as though he has had his face smashed in, his black blood oozing all over the white snow that covers the stone beneath him. The two who were dealing with me are slowly getting back up again after Mitch tackled them off me. "This is the moment when you have a choice to make," he says firmly as he places his hand on my face and forces me to look back to him, regaining my attention. "You either get up and fight, be that strong ass woman I know you are inside, or stay lying in the dirt and watch everyone around you die." He stares into my eyes as I finally take in his words, making me focus my thoughts on him alone. "Do you want to watch us all die?" he asks me seriously and I shake my head in response. I don't want to watch them die, as much as I do not want to admit it, I do like Mitch, I like him a lot, and I like the kid. I am just so terrified of myself, from where I truly come from and the evil that I know lies deep inside of me. "If you don't want to watch us die then get up, stop focusing on who you need to be and just be you, be the person who is in your heart... Do you understa..." Before Mitch can finish his sentence a man in red dives at him and hits him in the chest, sending both of them rolling away from me before two more demons swoop in on him. Mitch is their main focus as he is what currently stands between Lilith and Jake, just one angel trying to protect the whole human world alone.

I hear Jake shout for help so turn my head in his direction to see him pinned to the ground on his front, the man in blue is now mounting him and all I do is watch. He pulls out a gun and roughly shoves the barrel into the back of Jakes head as

Jake desperately tries to get free. I can see that Mitch is starting to get a little overwhelmed by the other 3 demons, all of them throwing punches and solely focusing on trying to kill each other then I hear Lilith laugh as she watches the sight in front of her. This is not me, this is the exact opposite of who I fought to be all of my life. I force myself over on to my front then up on to my knees as best I can. My hands are shaking and I pause for a moment to catch my breath and clutch the wound in my stomach as the pain hits me again, the only other time I have felt like this is when I knew I was mortal and there was a great possibility that I was about to die.

When I finally look up in front of me, Lilith catches my eye and smirks wildly, knowing she has the upper hand. It would be clear to anyone watching that, even though Mitch is an Archangel, her demons are giving him a good fight and leaving Jake vulnerable in the process. Mitch cannot win against those arseholes and protect Jake at the same time when her group of over powered demon scum are hell bent on fulfilling her orders. The more Lilith smiles at me, the more I become aware of that thing deep inside of me again, the feeling is new to me, I didn't even realise it was inside of me but it seems as though it has existed since the dawn of time. The pure evil that was formed at the moment of creation lies within me because of who my parents both were, I always thought at least I had a slight link to humanity as I was told my mother was mortal but now that I know the truth, I can't ignore that fire and now I need to decide how I use it. In my heart I am hurting because Lilith is my mother, she clearly loved me when I was born and she wants to destroy everything to get revenge because her child was taken away from her, but in my head she is a sadistic fucking egotistical bitch and I will not allow her to hurt my friends or rip apart the life I have fought so fucking hard to build for myself.

"I have to admit," she says to me over the shouting and fighting that continues behind me. "I did think you guys would put up a bit more of a fight. After what I felt and what brought me here tonight, I expected more, but just like the rest of the people who have tried to stand in my way, you are all so pathetic and weak just like the human scum that plagues this earth." I exhale sharply as her words hit me square in the chest. I am a lot of things, but pathetic and weak are defiantly not some of them. Clutching my abdomen that is still bleeding, I force myself to my feet to face her properly. It is time for me to face the woman who killed my siblings, who ordered the abduction of boys that led to Jakes brother being taken, and the women who is currently laughing as demons try to kill my friends. "The weakness you show me now is the same as the Sins as I killed them, they were afraid, and living among the filth that God created makes you become just like them. You develop empathy for them, human emotions which make you vulnerable, a demon willing to die to save a human. I expect it of the angel, they are brainwashed to believe Gods bullshit but if you came from Hell you would know the truth, you would know completely who you were." I force myself not to smile at her last comment. I know what she is trying to say, that as a demon I should hate everything that the angels stand for, that we were all condemned to Hell when Lucifer was cast out of heaven by his own father and that now I should know who my loyalties lie with. However the only bullshit I have heard over the past few days have all come from my own parents. I am the daughter of two of the most powerful beings that reside in the depths of Hell, I think I am finally starting to accept who it is I actually am and know completely who I need to be. They might both be associated with evil, but after seeing everything this world has to offer and learning that the humans are not the problem, I am not entirely evil, I do have some good in me. I wince in pain as I step forward slightly, the wound in my abdomen is so deep that it feels as though it has hit an artery with the amount of bleeding that is occurring and I feel too weak to just fix it like I normally could. I need to act now, if I just embrace who I am then I can heal myself and save everyone. I need to let go and be me.

"You will soon learn," I say back to her as my voice shakes slightly, but this time it is not through fear, it is through determination. "Learn that I am far from pathetic or weak." She stares at me as her smile slowly disappears and is replaced with anger at my response for my defiance. I suppose most demons just hear her name and automatically bow at her feet... But I have never been like most demons.

"Well so far, all I have seen is a scared little girl who is too weak to put up a fight," Lilith retorts. "You were no help to Envy when I slaughtered him in the prison and from what I see in front of me now, you are no help in protecting my key. You even bleed like the humans do, you are so underwhelming, I will watch you die like they do, slowly bleeding to death and begging for mercy then my men will bring me what is mine." Her eye line flickers to the left slightly as though watching someone else and in a split second I hear a gun shot cut through the cold night air then Jake scream in agony. My eyes go wide, everything catches up and hits me as I instantly kick in to gear, adrenalin taking control and I don't even think about Lilith being here any more, Jakes life is more important than my bitter feelings towards my father or the uncertainty for my mother, the key needs to be protected, and I categorically know that I am the only one who can do it.

Ignoring the pain from my wounds I dart towards Jake who is now on his back tussling with the guy who has just shot him in the shoulder, he is quickly overpowered and the demon aims the gun towards his face to get a kill shot. Just as he goes to squeeze the trigger I grab the back of the cheap looking leather jacket he is wearing and pull him off Jake, I am actually sick of spending my life in the human world tying to hide my full power, acting like the humans do, covering my tracks and pretending to be someone I am not, so I let it all out for the first time in years. The demon is yanked up with such force from me that he is launched through the air and hits a lamppost around 30 yards away, the thick metal holding up the light bends on impact and the sound of the demons back snapping fills the night. That alone won't kill it, the human body that the demon inhabits won't die but at least he is disabled for now and out of my way.

"Thanks," Jake says gratefully as he grabs his shoulder and tries to roll over to get up, he is out of breath from the fight and seems in pain so I grab his arm and help him to stand.

"Find cover and stay safe," I say firmly then turn my attention towards Mitch but as I do the guy I was being held by earlier with the baby blue shirt sees me, he breaks away from the others and runs in my direction. He is currently not holding a weapon, and right now I probably do look a little weak still covered in my own blood but as he gets closer I smirk and finally just let go, pushing all that animosity I hold towards my father away and just focus on me.

He lunges forward to grab me but I act faster than him and take hold of his outstretched arm, twisting it to force him off balance then place my other hand firmly in the centre of his chest and take a knee, forcing him to lean back over my now bent supporting leg. He looks as though he is thinking of something to say to me, probably some smart mouth comment or tell me how much he hates the humans or some shit like most demons do then he grabs my wrist to try to move my hand from his chest to allow him to get up. However he looks a little surprised when he finds he cannot move, which makes me smile a little, my strength used to be legendary when I guarded the Veil so these crappy little demons are no match for the real me. As he struggles more I let go of his arm and allow him a moment to use both his hands to try to get me off him but the more he fights against my grip the more I start to remember how it felt to see the fear in the eyes of a being who thinks they are invincible. He opens his mouth to beg for his freedom but before he has a chance to say anything I shove the fingers of my free hand in to his open mouth and hook them behind the teeth on his upper jaw. His eyes go wide as thought knowing what is about to happen before I forcefully pull his head back. He tries to scream, to yell and thrash against me as the skin across his cheeks starts to rip, blood filling his mouth then the pop of his jaw fills my ears as his skull disconnects and his spinal column snaps. After a second his body goes limp as his cold black blood spurts all over me, splashing up the side of my face and mixing with my own blood as the top of his head separates from the rest of him, leaving his gaping jaw behind. It has been so many years since I did anything like that, I am actually surprised how easy that felt, almost no effort at all. As I stand back up, his body rolls off my knee and I pause for a moment and look down at his head in my hand, then I look up and smirk as I see Lilith's face, filled with both confusion and intrigue over what she just saw me do.

There are two demons left, one of them is the guy in the black shirt that stabbed me, the other is built like a brick shit house and could give Mitch a run for his money with how big he is. My hand is covered in thick black goo, one of the things I hate most about the inferior demons that posses human hosts, the evil that is within their souls oxidises the blood, making it impure. Just another reason that proves most demons are vermin, although some humans are no better, that doesn't justify wiping them all off the face of the earth. The guy with the knife sees that I am up then notices the body of his friend now lying at my feet, missing his skull, after a second of just staring at the corpse he snaps and runs at me. It only takes him a second but just as he gets close I grab his left wrist to stop him using the knife on me, drop the bloody skull I was holding then wrap my hand around his throat and lift him up a couple of inches so the tip of his boots are just say scraping on the floor. He quickly tries to pull away from my grasp to lunge forward, but he doesn't move much under my hold. Out of the corner of my eye, I see Mitch making easy work of the last remaining demon as he now only has to deal with one of them, so I smile and take a deep breath, getting a slight twinge in my face as the cut that is still open hurts then stare in to this demons eyes. I can feel what is left of his soul from here, it is different to a humans, black and old but its in there, hiding and pulsating with life. Its not the only thing I can feel, I can feel my own power, something which I have never properly experienced whilst being in this world as I always pushed it away, kept it hidden so people didn't find out who I truly was.

"Drop the knife," I say calmly, then watch as he stops struggling against me, he blinks a couple of times with confusion but doesn't do as I requested. I know that I always said that my persuasion mostly only works on humans but I feel strangely more in control of myself than I ever have before, now that I know my origins and I have something worth living for. Maybe I was getting soft by letting those human emotions in, or maybe I was becoming who I always wanted to be and actually started caring about someone other than myself. "Drop... the... knife," I push forcefully and instantly he releases his grip, letting it fall to the ground, the sound of metal on stone is the only thing that can be heard around us. "That's better," I smile at him and take in his features a bit more. He is nicely built, rugged kind of masculine face, his eyes are hazel and in any other circumstances I might be slightly attracted to him.

His eyes, no matter how handsome they currently are, tell me he has no idea why he voluntarily dropped his weapon, but I don't let his gaze drop, hypnotically holding him in place, just like my father can do with any creature that serves below him. The pain in my body is becoming more intense and I have passed the point now of healing myself quickly enough before the wound in my stomach makes me bleed out. To those now watching me with great interest, I look calm and strong, but my heart is pounding and I am struggling to take a full breath as my body starts to shut down with the blood loss.

"You know, you are kind of cute," my voice shakes as I speak as I use every ounce of energy that I have to stay up on my feet. "Let's see what your soul tastes like." He smiles at my words as I pull him towards me and gently kiss his lips. They are surprisingly soft, the leftover taste of fried food lingers as I move closer when he kisses me back, his tongue lightly playing with mine, my hand is still around his neck to keep him in place so I close my eyes and enjoy the feeling. I do love kissing, the intimacy of it, the closeness you feel when connecting with someone for the first time.

I inhale deeply as I let go and give control over to the thing inside of me, within seconds he starts to struggle, his arms flail and try to push me away but I hold my grip firm, ensuring he remains in contact with me as I take what I need from him. It's like a calm warmth, spreading to every inch of my body, the same sort of feeling after an amazing orgasm that makes you relax and be fully content. The skin on my face tingles pleasantly where the knife slashed open my flesh and I no longer feel the pain from the wounds in my stomach or shoulder. It doesn't take long before the demon goes still and lifeless so I open my eyes and look into the empty pools of blackness that are now sunken into his features where his cute hazel eyes used to be.

"You are not a bad kisser," I smirk then drop him and watch him crumple to the ground, dead and cold. It has been a while since I last took a soul to heal in that way, although I do admit the kissing part was all for show, and the incident with Mitch was unintentional and technically I was dead so didn't get to enjoy the full feeling of pleasure the energy I take from a soul in this way gives me. Mitch is stood staring at me, I can see from how he is looking at my face that he is transfixed on the wound that is now fading and almost fully healed so I give him a small smile as I notice the other demon is also dead then turn my attention back to Lilith who has yet to move from her spot. It is always the same when you get the big bad guys who think they are too good to get their hands dirty, surrounded by grunts who do the work for them. I faced my fair share in the past, but Lilith is something else, something different and terrifying. "Allow me to apologise," I say calmly as I pick up the dropped knife and casually clean my own blood off the blade by wiping it on the back of the dead demons black shirt. "I wasn't quite myself when you first found us this evening. I admit I have a lot on my mind, found out some old family secrets which very much got in my head and I let it impact my judgement... But I am fixed up now."

"What you just did," Lilith asks me, intrigued by what she just witnessed. "There are not many demons who can do that... use persuasion. You are no vampire, I am certain of that... and did you just take his life force? That is not possible, only..." she pauses for a moment to think and then smiles to herself. "Hmm now then, what is a soul reaper doing in the human world trying to protect one instead of leading one through death?" She stares at me and I can tell her mind is working in overdrive, trying to work out what is going on and what I would possibly have to do with protecting the key to bringing down the Veil. "Who are you?"

"Who I am doesn't matter right now, what does matter is I am currently faced with the woman who is trying to kill my friends," I reply feeling quite confident with myself now that I know she is alone and her backup demons have been disabled. "And unfortunately, no matter what feelings of attachment I may have to my old family, I can't let that happen." Lilith scoffs at me as Mitch comes to stand by my side. I know Jake is still close, he is undeniably stubborn and even though I

157

told him to get to safety, he probably doesn't want to leave in case there is some way in which he can help. I suppose I would do the same.

"Then it seems I made a mistake," Lilith smiles at herself, I know that kind of smile, that one that you give when you are trying to play it cool but you have a plan up your sleeve, and for a moment it throws me a little. "After so long of dealing with lower-level demons, I seem to have underestimated whatever you are... I promise that I will not make that mistake again," she smiles more and I get a very bad feeling. Almost instantly the air around us changes, thickening so much that I hear Jake cough from close by as a strange heat is emanating from below our feet.

"Jake?" Mitch calls over to him then goes to help him as the scent of sulphur fills my nose then the sounds of the water from the river at the side of us starting to boil and bubble gets louder, drowning out the usual sounds of the city at night. Mitch comes back to my side with Jake, his human lungs spluttering against the burning hot air that no one would be used to unless they had spent any prolonged period of time in the depths of Hell, then Lilith starts to laugh.

"If I want my key then maybe my General can get it for me," she continues to laugh as my heart sinks and the ground beneath our feet starts to shake.

"Mitch?" I say as my voice quivers but he doesn't reply, he just stands silently confused as to what is going on around him, so I turn to face him and the only thing I think of to say is, "Run!" There is a moment when both him and Jake don't quite understand what is happening then like a bulb illuminating his brain, it clicks, and as one we all start to run. I have never wanted my feet to move faster in my life because I have a very bad feeling that I know exactly what is to come. From behind me I hear what sounds like an explosion in the river, the force shooting boiling water high into the air as something bursts from under the surface. I am slightly in front of Mitch and Jake but I soon realise we are not fast enough as a large object hits the ground in front of us making us skid to a halt. It hits the concrete so hard that everything shakes on impact, the stone cracking and sending small chunks flying off in all directions.

"You know what to do," Lilith shouts at the beast that now blocks our escape as he slowly begins to stand up and uncurl himself from the crouched ball he was in when he landed. I am not usually intimidated under normal conditions but I actually know what the fuck he is and this is not someone I want to be facing.

"Oh fuck," I say under my breath. My gaze follows him as he starts to tower above us, his recognisable scent burning my nose, his charred flesh steaming with heat making the water on his skin evaporate. He rises up, standing at nearly 9 foot tall, he stretches out his tattered and war torn wings, the charred flesh looking as though it is crackling from here giving the illusion of dragon scales, the deep red and black skin noticeable and the smell of the pits linger in the air around him. His body is pure muscle, humanoid in the rough shape but his feet are animalistic, almost like a lizard with talons. His eyes are completely black, void of any life or emotion, his face filled with the snarl of sharp teeth from his twisted mouth then the curled black horns that protrude from the sides of his head tangled with the long black hair that falls down his back, and the large intimidating snake slithering around his arm, make him look like a true horror. I can tell that both Mitch and Jake are frozen in front of him, Jake focusing on the all too familiar face of the beast he has seen before, the beast that took his brother.

    I never though I would see the Great Duke of Hell again after I left my fathers domain, and never in this capacity when he is now what currently stands between me and saving Jake. The first hierarchy consists of the evil trinity, my father at the top who rules the throne, Beelzebub who fell from grace following my father and this mother fucker who rules over the legions of warriors, legions which are obviously now under Lilith's control. In all my life I never thought I would have to fight one of the most powerful creatures of Hell, but now I have no choice, I guess the only way to save Jake and protect the Veil from falling is to kill Astaroth.

Chapter Twelve

"Is that..."

"Yes," I interrupt Mitch before he even gets a chance to ask. I am not quite sure what to do, Astaroth is the Duke of Hell for a reason and his strength is legendary... but it does make me wonder what Lilith offered him to turn against my father, whatever it was, it must have been big. "I don't suppose you have one of those snazzy demon killing angel weapons that I heard about in so many stories whilst growing up, do you?" I ask as I nervously laugh at the situation. "One of those flaming swords or something?" I glance at Mitch but he doesn't take his eyes off Astaroth as he slowly shakes his head.

"No," he says quietly as though his words will anger the beast before us if it hears him. "I must have left my sword in my other jeans." His response is so dry that it takes me a second to understand the slight joke before I smile. "What's the plan?" There is a question that I do not have a firm answer for at all right now. Astaroth is just getting his bearings, he cricks his neck and starts to unfurl his wings then looks down to the three of us who now stand before him. Even I know he doesn't come to the mortal world very often so it really did surprise me when Jake described him as the one who took his brother, a small part of me had hoped I was wrong but now seeing him standing there confirms everything, and lets me know that things are now very real.

"Make sure Jake is protected at all costs," I say very seriously as I try to think of a plan. "If Lilith gets her hands on him then the Veil will fall, and I have absolutely no idea how to rectify that." That is something I do not even want to think about. If the rising happens it will bring Hell on earth, then no one will be safe and I do not think there is anyone who can save the mortal realm then.

"And what are you going to do?" Mitch asks me as I swallow hard then finally make eye contact with Astaroth. For a moment no one moves, everything is silent as he stares back at me with his black lifeless eyes then he tilts his head to the side slightly as though he recognises me, and my heart sinks. The last thing I need is for Lilith to find out who I am and get inside my head, so the less chances he has to speak in front of her, the better things will be for everyone.

"I am going to try to not get killed," I laugh slightly. There is no turning back now, I made my choice, I chose my side... I just really hope it is the right one. Who would have thought it, the daughter of Lucifer himself trying to save human kind?

"You..." Astaroth says, his deep gravelly voice cuts through the air and instantly I feel Jake cower beside us in fear. Although I suppose any human would, after all they are looking at an actual demon, in true form, not one of those wannabe ones that inhabit a human meat suit. "You look... familiar."

"I really suggest you two leave now," I say to Mitch and Jake then go to step forward to confront Astaroth but Mitch grabs my arm, pulls me back slightly then quickly he places his free hand behind my neck and kisses me deeply. For a moment I just let it happen, as though my soul wants it but I am not sure why. My lips part for him instantly, bending to this weird feeling of being protected by him again but yet free at the same time, and just as I give in completely, letting his mouth consume mine the whole world around me seems to slip away. The feeling that I had in my apartment the last time Mitch kissed me swiftly returns, almost like butterflies in my stomach but I am not scared of it, it feels so right. Mitch moves back and stares deep in to my eyes, both of us not speaking for a moment, although right now I am not sure what to say after that.

"I am glad you are back with us," he smiles sweetly as his thumb brushes over my cheek. "I was getting a little worried that we had lost you. Now be who you are meant to be and kill this mother fucker so we can save the world." I nod in response then quickly hand Mitch the knife that I am still holding. As soon as I do he shakes his head and tries to give it back. "You need that, you..."

"No, I don't need it. If we split up Lilith will have more back up to come, and I need you to protect Jake," I reply then sigh deeply. "I am a bit rusty, I really know that I am, and I don't even know if I can do what I hope to do in the mortal world... but I have to try at least. That little knife won't stop Astaroth, I need something else."

"I don't know what you mean," Mitch says confused as he clings on to my arm, not wanting to let me go.

"Trust me," I say then pull away from him. He stands for a couple of seconds, debating on saying more, before nodding in response then grabbing Jake by the arm so that they can get away. Astaroth watches them closely, he knows as well as

I do that there will be more demons on the way to serve their Mistress and get her what she wants, so at the moment he is not too worried about losing them. Now that he knows what Jake looks and smells like, he will hunt him down in minutes if he needs to. "So..." I smile nervously at the beast in front of me as he steps forward, clearly I have his full attention now, probably wondering why he was called from Hell to have to deal with this insignificant woman in front of him. "How have you been, Hell treating you well?" I ask as I try to possibly delay him for a few moments so that I can concentrate. Like I said to Mitch, I am very rusty and I have not used my true power in this world at all in all of the years I have been here. Sure, I have used my persuasion, strength and fighting skills to make a good life and build a killer reputation for myself, but nothing else. It took a lot more than strength and a few pushes to guard the Veil. I don't even know if I can use it now, I honed it whilst I worked as a soul reaper then it grew exponentially when I guarded the Veil, but as soon as I left that world behind I never really needed that power so never tested its ability here. The human world was not meant to hold true power, that is why if the rising succeeds, this world will fall and it will be disastrous.

"Tell me girl..." Astaroth growls as he continues to come towards me. "How do I know you?" He doesn't have any weapons, but him being who he is, he will not need them. I have seen him crush a man's skull without even trying, and wipe out armies of demons and angles who have dared to try to fight my father in the past. He is pretty much unstoppable and I don't actually know if he can be killed at all. This could get very interesting or I could get very dead. Either way, I guess I am about to find out.

"You don't know me, I assure you," I lie. He was close to my father back in the day, when I was young, stupid and still thought the sun shined out of my fathers ass. He met me plenty of times as a kid, hard not to meet this young girl who lived with Hells royal family, who craved attention from Lucifer. Although thinking about it, I am not sure if my name was ever mentioned in company. The Sins used to call me "Runt" or some other derogatory term, and when ever my father wanted my attention he would just call me "Girl". After the things I have learned tonight, I do now wonder if that was his way of keeping my identity secret to those outside of our family, even from the people around him who he was closest to and who he was meant to trust. If that is true, then Astaroth will not know my name after all... This could work to my advantage.

"Just before you kill me," I say trying to sound confident in my own actions. "Can I ask you a question?" He pauses for a moment and glances to Lilith before looking back to me. I assume the people he normally fights just go straight in all guns blazing and don't generally try to strike up a conversation first. "Obviously I know who you are, your reputation is legendary and your strength unmatched. You have fought wars, killed and maimed more souls than I could count and held one of the highest positions there was in Hell... So what happened? Were you no longer happy being Lucifer's little lap dog?" He snarls at my off handed question which just makes me smile.

"I am the Grand Duke of Hell," Astaroth replies with anger in his voice. "I have never been Lucifer's "lap dog" Girl." His words make me smile wildly because I know the more I keep him talking the further away from trouble Mitch and Jake might get.

"OK, my apologies," I smirk. "You were not Lucifer's lap dog... but you are now Lilith's little bitch, correct?" There is a second of total silence as Astaroth absorbs my words then he snaps, and bolts towards me. I should have expected his reaction really, it was a little cheeky, what I don't expect though is how fast he is for such a big guy. He swoops on me in a blink of the eye, his massive hand literally covers my entire face as he grabs me and for that moment the thought of him instantly crushing my skull in his hand does cross my mind. I have never had my skull crushed before so I am not sure how the whole healing myself thing would work with that one but before I get a chance to try to stop that from happening, he tosses me to the side as though I am nothing compared to him and weight no more than a new born baby. I am launched through the air with such force that I don't even see the solid brick wall that comes towards me until I am smashing through it. The stone cracks with the pressure of my body hitting it, forming a nice me sized hole in to the building then the rest of the rubble and brick falls on top of me as I land inside someone's office. I groan loudly as the pain hits me but thankfully, unlike the last time I was thrown through a wall, I am immortal and although I can feel blood down the back of my head, I do not seem to be injured much and I know the slight wound will heal very quickly now that I am feeling like the real me again. I might bleed, but I don't break easily. Rolling over, I push myself from below the debris and get back to my feet, someone is going to be really pissed when they come back after their Christmas vacation and find their office in this state. The desk is covered in dust and bricks, I must have hit the computer as I landed as that is smashed and whatever items were on the top of the wooden table are now scattering the floor. As I look back through the hole, I can see Astaroth is now heading off in the opposite direction to me, he just wanted me out of the way so that he could focus on getting Jake.

"Hey, Bitch Boy!" I shout as I stumble out of the building, knocking the bricks out of the way as I walk back in to the street. Astaroth stops in his tracks, his back is still to me but I can see by the way he has tensed up that he is not happy that I am alive. "Is that really all you have got? Quite disappointed actually, I did expect much more of a fight, and to be honest I thought you might have at least killed me a little bit." Astaroth slowly turns around to face me again at the same time that shouting can be heard in the distance. I am going to assume that Mitch and Jake have run in to some more of Lilith's minions but as I look around slightly, I can't see my bitch of a mother anywhere. It is not ideal but at least this way Jake stands a better chance of survival with Mitch protecting him, if Astaroth gets near, it will be game over.

"Do you want to die?" he asks me as I brush off the dust that is covering my top and shake it from my hair.

"Ideally, no!" I reply sarcastically. "But if taking the piss out of you for a few minutes means my friends are safer, then I am pretty happy to make that sacrifice." Astaroth growls then starts towards me again. If faced with just brute strength, there is no way I can over power him so my only option is a weapon, and the kind that I need has never before been seen in this world. Plus it is not like a physical thing that you store in the trunk of your car, it is pure energy and needs to be summoned, only problem is, I don't know if I can do that.

Astaroth is on me straight away, he swings his fist towards my face, I duck and roll just in time to see his hand make the stone above my head explode, surrounding us both with a thick cloud of brick dusk. I know I should be fully focused on him, but my mind instantly wanders to Mitch, hoping that he doesn't become overwhelmed, there is no knowing how many demons are after them and if Lilith actually decides to get her hands dirty then I have no idea what she is fully capable of when in a fight. After all, she didn't accrue the following of the Duke of Hell and all of his armies just because of her name. If I want to make absolutely sure that Jake is protected then I need to get Astaroth out of the way fast. Not that I don't trust Mitch but I do not know what he is fully capable of either, apart from being strong and having wings, and being unbelievably good in bed, plus he has this presence about him that makes me just want to run my hands all over his naked body and... Holy shit! No, that cannot be the reason, surely? I want to protect the key, don't I? Or am I actually starting to really really like an angel and want to protect him?

Astaroth grabs the back of my jacket whilst I am lost in my own thoughts then quickly pulls me in to him and holds me in a bear hug. His massive muscular arms wrap around my back as the serpent that always accompanies him slithers around my neck and begins to restrict my breathing. I never understood the snake thing, I always wondered if they were just friends or if it was an actual part of him, never really cared enough though to find out. His face is inches from mine, my arms pinned to my sides as I try to thrash my legs to get lose but the more I try the tighter he squeezes until I am no longer able to even fill my lungs to attempt to take a breath. He is stronger than I gave him credit for, and even using all my energy, I cannot seem to budge his grip a tiny bit. I can hear the serpent hiss in my ear as my lungs start to burn with lack of oxygen, for a lower level demon, their soul would be exposed enough for me to drain it, using the energy inside for myself and killing them in the process like I did with that guy when I kissed him a few minutes ago, but Astaroth is as far from a lower level demon as one could possibly get, so that is not an option. The only thing I can do is close my eyes and concentrate. If he continues to suffocate me, I will be dead in less than two minutes, then as before when Mitch killed me, my ability will kick in and just take an exposed soul to revive me... then I will have to fight Astaroth all over again so I will be back to square one.

My current weakness is that I have lived in the human world for so long that I almost forgot how it feels to truly give in to the demon inside of me and let the blood than pumps through my veins fuel my real power. I know it is in there, it will never have left me, I just buried it deep inside so that I could hide who I was and forget about my past. But now I don't want to hide, I need to embrace who I truly am, become the daughter of Lucifer himself that I always knew I was and take back my own identity. I need to finally show the world that I do exist and stop denying where it is that I come from. I close my eyes as my head falls back, my entire body goes limp in Astaroth's arms, giving in to the feeling of being crushed to death, but instead of worrying about that, I focus on my own soul and just give in. For a moment I am able to block everything out, the pain I am feeling from my rib cage snapping, the burning in my chest as it craves air, the thoughts of what may happen if I fail and die, and instead accept the tranquil calm. I did think that it would be a lot harder to tap in to my power as I hadn't done it in centuries, but instantly it is as though an unmeasurable about of adrenaline hits me and consumes every single one of my senses. My eyes dart open as I feel my entire essence burst from deep within me, then Astaroth suddenly lets out a deep gut retching cry, his arms unwrap from around me, the serpent drops from my neck and I fall to the ground. I land on one knee and take a moment to centre myself and breathe as Astaroth staggers backwards, thick black blood gushing from the top of both his thighs, spilling out of large wounds that are deep in his flesh.

"Something that I may have forgot to mention," I say smugly as I look down at my hands, oh how I have missed the feeling of wielding my blades. The pure unbridled power that connects to my core and enables me to summon the weapons which become an extension of myself. When I first became a soul reaper and unlocked this ability, I thought the scythe was a little cliché and I actually had difficulty summoning it for some reason, plus it was a bit cumbersome at times when I like to get up close and personal to my enemies. So I opted for the sickle, or I should say two of them. Before I met Lucious Monroe and was shown the ropes of reaping, I just thought you had to wield the standard weapon like all reapers did, guess I was just special, and they stuck with me when I progressed to guard the Veil. My skin tingles up my arms with the energy that flows off them as I hold them in my hands, the short intricately carved black metal handle is cold against my skin but feels as though I have never left go of them. The curve of the blades shining an opalescent blue in the dark night are reflecting the rays of the nearby street lamp, and I smile to myself because I know if Astaroth can bleed, then he can actually die. "I am not just another average demon," I say as I slowly stand up and face Astaroth again now that he has regained his composure. He looks so angry with me, but it just makes me smile more. I haven't felt this free with my power for such a long time, and I forgot how intoxicating it was.

"I will take great pleasure in killing you," Astaroth growls as he steps towards me, limping slightly with his thigh wounds, his wings pinned back ready for a fight and his fists clenched with frustration.

"I have heard that line before, many times in fact... Not to sound cocky or anything," I laugh at myself. "But the more I start to feel like the real me, the more certain I am that I am going to kill you in the next 60 seconds." Astaroth roars with laughter at my statement as the large serpent slithers around his arm, retaking its place. He inhales deeply and takes a moment to look at me fully, studying my features, trying to understand who the fuck I think I am compared to him.

"I have faced many opponents in my lifetime, and every single one of them has perished at my hands," Astaroth says. "Just to think that you could kill me is foolish on your part." He pauses for a moment then holds his arm in front of him and looks down at the snake. I have no idea what he is doing so I just watch as it begins to move, slowly gliding through the palm of his outstretched hand and becoming ridged, its scales seem to harden, the body morphing in to a new shape, one that I recognise but didn't even contemplate when I first saw him again. "I guess you are not the only one with a party trick and flamboyance for soul charge weaponry." That does throw me slightly, I though I had the upper hand seen as though he was unarmed, or so I thought. I guess that is what the snake is for, it's not just a serpent or symbol, its a link to his soul which becomes a physical weapon when called upon. I didn't know he could do that but it is very impressive to watch as a long red blade, one which seems to reflect the fire like look of his own flesh forms in front of my eyes. It curves at the end and once it has completed its transition, it is easily 4 foot in length and very intimidating to look at as he leers above me, I have never been a small woman but he makes me feel like it right now.

"I don't care if he dies, just make sure he doesn't get away!" We hear Lilith shout from close by then the pound of footsteps running, echo through the street.

"Jake run!" Mitch shouts then almost immediately Jake comes back in to sight and starts to make his way swiftly in the other direction to the one he left in, following the edge of the river. He is covered in a little more blood and some of it is black which makes me think they have been putting up a good fight, but if Mitch is telling him to run then he might be getting overwhelmed and need help. Astaroth glances to Jake, knowing he is currently exposed and vulnerable by being by himself, then smirks before lunging forward and swinging his sword directly at my head. Luckily I see it coming just in time and manage to stop the blade inches from my temple with the edge of my sickle. He nearly got off a good swing there, he pushes me back a couple of paces to try to force his weapon to connect with me but I resist, I actually feel noticeably stronger now that I have tapped in to my power again and I can tell Astaroth notices it also.

"You are going to have to try harder than that," I laugh then push him back instead, which catches him off guard as he stumbles and almost falls, but it does

166

create distance between us again, which I am thankful of. Astaroth pauses for a moment to think about what just happened, I know that look, the look of someone who thought they were far more superior than me and I just did something that they were not expecting at all. It might just have been a little resistance, but he understands I am stronger than he gave me credit for and I will not go down easy.

"Tell me who you are," Astaroth growls at me as a group of 3 men emerge from around the corner and run after Jake, when they catch up to him he will not be able to hold them off, and there is no knowing what Lilith has planned for him.

"Where would be the fun in that," I retort quickly then panic slightly as the group of demons pounce on Jake and tackle him to the ground. Mitch is no where to be seen and I know Lilith is close by as I heard her shouting. "I am sorry, I am going to have to make this quick as I have other things that I need to do," I say and lunge forward to attack. My left blade connects with his sword as he blocks me straight away, but even though he is forcing his weapon forward, I am holding it at bay so it gives me some room to ram my shoulder in to his abdomen now that he is partially exposed. I hit him with so much force that I actually surprise myself, driving him back a good couple of feet before he loses his balance and smashes in to the side of the building near us. The earth beneath us shakes with the impact but I don't wait to see what he does next, I take the opportunity to turn and run towards Jake. There is one demon mounting him, the other two have hold of his wrists to keep him in place, but as I get closer I catch sight of Lilith out of the corner of my eye and I know if she gets close to Jake it is all over. Just as I am about to formulate a plan to get him away, Lilith catches my gaze and for a moment I can't remember what I was doing, her eyes are piercing and I get consumed with the thoughts that she is my mother, that the person who stands before her is the child she has mourned for two thousand years. If I was to tell her who I was right now would she back off? Would she stop trying to get revenge and instead embrace me and show me how it is meant to feel to finally hug the woman who gave birth to me?

"If she gets close, kill him!" Lilith shouts towards her men, giving them her orders. As much as I seriously have a lot of issues to work through right now, protecting the Veil is far more important and that means protecting Jake. I manage to reach them before they realise what is happening, and without pausing I aim the blade of my right Sickle direct for the neck of the demon who has Jake pinned down. It connects with no resistance and slices straight through, the other two men have no idea what happened as they just watch the head of their comrade fly through the air before thudding on to a patch of snow, staining it black. Jake freezes as the black goo from the exposed neck of the carcase above him freely flows over his body so I quickly kick it to one side as the other two demons regain their composure and attack me. They don't even have to be fully on their feet when I know that these two arseholes are not the only ones I have to deal with as a hand grabs the back of my jacket and yanks me backwards, but I quickly manage to slip from the grip and turn around in time to see the edge of Astaroth's sword coming direct for my face. Instinctively, I duck then hear the all too familiar sound of blood splatter behind me then the warm trail down the back of my hair as it drips after it has coated me. I glance around quickly to see one of the two remaining demons now lying in two pieces, his torso sliced in half, his insides swiftly becoming his outsides as his internal organs spill out on the ground because of the blade that missed me and hit him instead.

"Jake move," I shout over my shoulder as I turn back to face Astaroth. The weapon he has slows him down a slight bit, it is bulky and large so just to readjust to swing at me again gives me enough time to get the first strike in. I dive forward and fall to my knees, I know that if I go low he will not expect the blow as I skid on the snow towards his legs that are in a readied attack stance. The way I am holding my weapons means that the blades run down the side of each of my wrists forming a nice crescent shape on the exterior of my forearms so it is extremely easy for me to ram my arms apart and drive the blades into the inside of his legs as I move, hitting just above each knee and going deep, almost connecting to the bone. I have to quickly roll out of the way as Astaroth collapses to his knees and drops his weapon, it clatters on the ground but the noise is quickly replaced with the sound of more footsteps pounding towards us. Another movement close behind me makes me tense up so I turn on the spot whilst still being on the ground and prepare to attack, but just as I am about to connect to the groin of the man standing over me, I stop and freeze.

"Wooh!" Mitch nervously laughs as he looks down at the edge of my blade which is literally millimetres from his balls. "Watch the goods." I laugh as a smile crosses his face then he steps back to enable him to help Jake who is currently still frozen on his back, covered in demon blood. The third demon who had been holding Jake is dead, I presume at the hands of Mitch but we don't get much of a chance to have our touching reunion as we are quickly swarmed by more of Lilith's minions. I try my best to hold them off long enough for Mitch to get Jake off the ground and push him away, forcing him to run from the now mayhem that surrounds me.

Myself and Mitch are stood back to back trying to fend them all off, but as soon as we manage to kill one, two more appear and swiftly there seems to be no way through the growing number of bodies. It also doesn't help that out of the corner of my eye, I can see Astaroth forcing himself back to his feet. Fuck this shit, I need them all out of my way and fast so I concentrate on taking as many of them down as I possibly can. I don't even look at who is around me, men or women, if they are working for Lilith then they are my enemy and my only goal right now is to kill them all. After a couple of minutes I am drenched in black blood, the large number of demons are down to a more manageable 8 possibly 9 of them, but I know we are not out of the woods yet because I can sense Lilith close by, which means if we are distracted with the fight, Jake is left vulnerable.

"Mitch can you handle these," I call over my shoulder as he crushes a man's skull against the concrete, his boot making light work of the bone, I am actually quite impressed, he is stronger than I gave him credit for. He looks around then shrugs.

"Maybe, I am not the one with the cool weapons though," he points out. That is very true, right now he is fighting with his bare hands, not that he is doing a bad job, but he would get through them quicker if he had something with a pointy end.

"Give me a minute and I will get you one," I say then dart away from the group, leaving him alone as I hurtle towards Astaroth. He sees me coming instantly and reaches down to grab his sword but I dive forward, putting both of my sickles in my left hand and grab the hilt of his weapon with my right before sweeping it up from the floor and swinging it in his direction. Astaroth tries to move out of the way but the injuries on his legs slow him down considerably and he can't do much else as his own weapon slices straight through one of his wings, detaching it completely and making him unexpectedly howl in agony. It is really heavy and very cumbersome, just holding it with one hand is extremely difficult and quickly I have to drop it back to the ground, it seems easier to drag. At least Astaroth is out of my way at the moment so I take the opportunity to head back to Mitch who is struggling to hold back the multiple demons as more rush him, they are coming from all directions, stepping over their dead demon buddies and only focusing on keeping us out of the way.

"Here!" I shout to get Mitch's attention as I toss the large sword in his direction and watch as it clatters on the ground at his feet. He swings a punch and hits a guy in green square in the jaw, sending him backwards in to another 3 demons, making then crumple in a heap before Mitch looks down at the sword then picks it up. I can tell as soon as he holds it in his hand that he knows how heavy it is. Against Astaroth the thing looked big, and even though Mitch is a lot bigger than me, the sword drowns him.

"What am I meant to do with this?" he asks sarcastically as he grips the handle with both hands and readjusts his stance as the multiple demons form a circle around him.

"Well, you aim the pointy end towards those dick heads and play the stabby stabby game with them... see how many points you can score," I reply and laugh as he shakes his head at me. "What? You wanted a weapon, didn't you?"

"Yeah," Mitch says unsure of himself as he swings the sword with all his might, fatally injuring three of the group with one movement. "A weapon, like a normal sized one, not one meant for a giant."

"I am sure you will manage just fine with it," I say and look around. At the moment the bulk of the demon scum are focused on Mitch, probably because they know he is an angel and they will hate any holy angelic being because they have been told to all their lives. "Do you have eyes on Jake?" I ask, but Mitch is too busy concentrating on fighting to hear me speak to him now. A weird deep panic fills me as I frantically search the surrounding space for Jake, I know he ran past before but if me and Mitch have been fighting there is no one to protect him. Finally I see movement out of the corner of my eye and whip around on the spot, but what I see makes my heart sink. Near the railings that run along the side of the river, not far from a Christmas nativity set up and small Christmas tree decorated all in white ornaments, I spot Jake on the ground, desperately trying to back away from Lilith who is currently stood over him. There are a couple more demons flanking Lilith, one man and one woman, I recognise the woman to be the one from the prison when Envy was killed.

"Please," Jakes voice shakes as fear consumes him. "Please, I don't know what you want with me," he goes to push himself up off the ground but the two demons with Lilith grab him and pull him to his feet then hold him in place, he tries his best to get free from their grip but doesn't move. I can already see that he has been fighting others away, he had blood dripping down the side of his head, his nose is bust, the bullet hole in his shoulder is still quite obvious and the way he tried to get up from the ground looks as though he has hurt his leg in some way. A quick glance back around to Mitch to see if he is still alive tells me that he is managing quite well with his new toy so I forget about him for now and start to run towards Jake.

"I have waited centuries to find you," Lilith smiles as she steps forward and gently strokes her finger tips down Jakes cheek, he tries to pull his head back but it just makes her smirk more.

"Are you going to kill me?" he asks as I get closer and my heart almost feels like it is going to beat out of my chest with panic. The key to bringing down the Veil is literally at Lilith's fingertips and my feet are not moving fast enough for my liking .

"Mortals are so funny," she smiles at Jakes question. "Always so scared of death when it is the only thing that is inevitable in your short lives." Lilith holds out her hand to the side as she stares at Jakes eyes, revelling in the fact that she can see how terrified he is of her already. The woman who is with them removes a flick knife from her pocket and places it in Lilith's palm, she quickly opens it then playfully runs the blade down the side of his neck.

"Don't fucking touch him," I shout towards them, and Lilith glances to the side and smiles at me. I ready my weapons as I am only a few meters away, one good aimed strike and I will at least get her to back off. If I cannot kill her then I will make sure she knows who the fuck I am and that I am not to be taken for granted.

"I don't think so," Lilith laughs slightly at me as something grabs my hair and yanks me backwards, I have no idea what is happening until I swiftly feel the concrete hit me full force in the back as I land on the freezing ground. Momentarily I can't catch my breath, my blades slip from my grip as I lose focus and they scatter away from me then the massive foot of Astaroth stamps down on my chest. Instantly my ribs threaten to snap as he applies his weight to hold me in place. I quickly move my hands and try desperately to alleviate some of the pressure by forcing him off me but he just scowls down, clearly very pissed off with me for cutting off his wing and taking his weapon.

"If you hurt... him..." I try to say to Lilith as I struggle to fill my lungs. "I will kill... you." Astaroth pushes down harder and I let out a strangled cry which makes Lilith laugh as she can see that I have no way of stopping her right now, before turning her attention back to Jake.

"Kill the girl," Lilith says off handedly as she stares in to Jakes eyes. "I would appreciate no more interruptions." As soon as she says that, I cry out in agony as Astaroth forces his foot down, a little bit more and he will crush my chest fully.

"You... know," I force out as I wrap my fingers around his foot and push back against his ever growing weight. "Any other time... I would probably... find this quite kinky." The pain spreading through my chest is increasing by the second and I can already feel my ribs bending, threatening to fracture if I do not do something quickly.

"Please," I hear Jake beg again as he trembles in fear. "Please, I don't want to die."

"I don't need to kill you," Lilith replies sweetly. "I already have everything I need." Out of the corner of my eye, I see Lilith run her fingers through Jakes hair, covering her hand in his blood that is freely flowing from a head injury.

"M... Mitch!" I try to say to get his attention. If I can't move then someone needs to help Jake and quickly, but I get no response, all I hear is fighting and right now I am not even sure if he would hear my almost inaudible pleas. One of my blades is only a foot or so away from me, so I reposition my hand under Astaroth's foot to hold him at bay whilst I desperately try to reach out for my weapon. My finger tip literally brushes the handle as it lies on the ground, it is right there but I can't quite reach it, just another inch would do.

"If you are not going to kill me, then what is the knife for?" Jake asks Lilith as the two demons continue to hold him in place. Lilith giggles slightly, it is almost playful compared to the current situation.

"My dear boy, the knife is for me," Lilith replies casually. I need to get Astaroth off me right now, I cannot force him up so I need him to move willingly... Think, I have got to think!

"For such a big guy," I force out and look back up to Astaroth, I catch his eye instantly and already I can tell he is struggling to crush me, even though he is using all his strength, I am managing to hod him back slightly. "I thought you would have killed me already, I guess... size isn't everything." I say as I flash him a cheeky grin, which makes him lose his temper. But I was hoping for this reaction.

171

He lifts his foot up from me in order to stamp down and finish me with one good blow but as soon as he moves I roll, grab my weapon and turn, driving the blade deep in to the back of his calf, covering myself in his blood as I do then swiftly get out of the way as he drops to his knees once more as the injury in his leg can no longer hold his own weight. I take a second to catch my breath and stretch my shoulder, which cracks as I do, the pain will quickly fade as he didn't manage to do too much damage to me then I get up, trying to shake the dizzy feeling off the sudden rush of blood back to my brain, then grab my other sickle and glance towards Jake.

"You do not need to be dead for me to get your blood," Lilith says. "This is your life force," she tells him as she holds up her hand and watches Jakes blood run down her own palm, transferred to her skin from the wound in his head. "And soon it will unlock the only thing standing between this world and the realm of Hell."

"No, no you can't do that," Jake says, panic clearly in his voice as I regain my composure and step towards them, to stop Lilith from doing whatever it is she has planned but as soon as I do a hand grabs my ankle and swiftly I find myself heading back to the ground, only this time it is face first. The side of my head smashes in to the concrete and for a moment all I see is stars, a lot of them, whizzing past my eyes before the feeling of my own warm blood covers my skin. I don't wait, I push myself up on my knees and kick away the hand that is holding me. My eyes are a little blurry with the sudden impact so when I look up and see Lilith slicing a large wound in to her own palm with the flick knife, I am slightly confused, I don't know why she would do that.

"I am done with him," she says to her followers then without waiting she turns her back to them and closes her eyes as they swiftly move Jake away towards the railing of the river and before I even process what is happening they toss him over in to the freezing water.

"Jake!" I shout as I hear the splash as he connects with the river, it is freezing cold so the temperature alone could easily kill him. I force myself up to stand and stumble slightly as I lose focus again then I see Mitch dart past me, ignoring everything else that is going on before diving over the railing then disappearing from view. "No, no what have you done?" I ask as I go towards Lilith but she ignores me completely as she starts talking to herself, sort of chanting, I can't quite make out what she is saying as it is so quiet then I hear Astaroth behind me once more. I turn on the spot but in doing so feel sick to my stomach, the injury I just sustained when I hit my head must be worse than I thought as I kind of see two of him and everything is wobbly. He stumbles towards me and I just look up at him a little dazed as he raises his arm and back hands me so hard it is almost like he is swatting a fly. My feet leave the ground as he hits me, everything goes black and when I next open my eyes I see Jesus... He is a little smaller than what I remember him to be when I met him a while ago, wrapped in a white blanket and currently he is laying in some hay... this isn't right. Looking around as I moan in pain, I see multiple faces staring back at me, a woman in blue, a couple of shepherds and some weird looking men in crowns... it takes me a few moments to realise that they are very realistic looking statues.

"Oh, for fucks sake," I groan as I see Astaroth heading towards me as I peer over the top of the small wooden cradle that sits in the centre of the Christmas nativity scene that I think I have just half smashed as I landed on a sheep. I cling on to the nearest wise man and pull myself up then pick one of my Sickles up from the ground, I can not take much more of being thrown around like a rag doll, Astaroth is far too strong so I have to take a different approach. I hold my weapon firm then steady myself by placing my other hand on the shoulder of the Joseph statue to stop myself wobbling then try to get my aim right before I throw my blade with all my might. It moves fast and silently through the night air, Astaroth hardly even has a chance to react before the blade connects with his forehead and buries in, slicing straight through his skull and lodging itself in deep. He freezes and just blankly stares at me as blood starts to trickle down over his face and he loses all focus in his eyes, the look of life slipping away, then as if in slow motion his entire body falls forwards and he smashes to the ground. I am going to presume he is dead but as he is the Duke of Hell I can not be quite sure of anything any more.

"You are too late," I hear Lilith shout across and I look up to see her smiling at me. She has blood smeared down her face now which I think belongs to Jake and stands with her injured hand outstretched in front of her. "This is just the beginning," she tells me then kneels on the ground. She gives me a last look and my heart stops because I know it is already done. She gently places her blood covered hand, palm down on the earth in front of her, and as she does everything around us falls eerily silent, there is not a sound that can be heard, not even the river as it flows or my own heartbeat. For a second I actually consider that I might have gone deaf but a low rumble sound fills the void then the ground beneath us starts to shake. Lilith laughs hysterically as I slowly stumble my way out of the Christmas nativity scene and notice Mitch haul Jake up on to the river bank and out of the water, he coughs and splutters as the freezing water purges itself from his lungs but I feel so lost, I don't know what else to do apart from just stare at Lilith.

"How could you do that?" I ask her as I feel tears fill my eyes and the deep sinking feeling almost consumes me, all that time protecting the Veil from falling and within minutes it was all for nothing. I can feel the entirety of it being ripped apart as though it is within my own soul and it is unimaginably painful. "You will destroy everything."

"My sweet child," Lilith says gently as she stands back up and smiles at me. The water that runs alongside us starts to thrash, forming large waves that seem to boil and bubble in the cold air then the concrete under my feet shakes so much that it cracks and I quickly move out of the way as the earth opens up and an ominous

173

red glow can be seen from below, it moves through the earth like a snake, spreading out in all directions like ink running through a network of veins. The whole world around me suddenly feels different, no longer protected by the shroud that hides the truth, it will now know forces so dark that they have never even been imagined before in the worst kind of nightmares. Its all over, nothing can stop it now, we are all doomed, the Hell mouth has been opened and the Veil is no more. "Destroying everything is entirely the point. I have waited my whole life for this moment, to show everyone the reality of the world that they live in, how it was fabricated for Gods amusement and now his followers will lose faith because not even he can stop me... It will not be long before my armies take control of this world now that there is nothing holding them back, they will rise from the depths of Hell and claim this land as my own. No one can stop it now, the rising has begun and the only thing left for me to do, is find my throne."

Chapter Thirteen

I honestly cannot think of a single thing to say. And it is not like me to be lost for words, I usually have some sort of sarcastic or witty remark to make, but the severity of what I have just witnessed is still sinking in and right at this very moment in time, I am not sure what I am supposed to do. Do I panic? Run around like a loony and cry for the end of days? Do I revile in the moment and embrace the darkness, have fun whilst I still can and fuck the humans... both literally and figuratively. Or do I use this opportunity to say to Lilith the things that are really in my head, tell her that she is my mother and after all this time she finally has me back in her life, only for her to destroy the world with her daughter in it.

"It is going to be glorious," she smiles wildly as she looks around to all the dead bodies that surround us then glances to Astaroth, still with my weapon embedded in his skull. "They were all worth the sacrifice to enable me to get to this moment. I had been searching for so long that I never thought a chance encounter would lead me straight to my key. I must thank you for that, without you none of this could have been possible."

"You have no idea what you have done," I force myself to say as I try my best to fight back any sort of emotion. "Literally everything will cease to exist, including me and..."

"I know exactly what I have done," Lilith interrupts me with a hint of anger in her voice. "I have spent far too long being told what I can and cannot do, having to watch my children die, listening to the pathetic humans in this world treat their so called God with respect when they do not realise the truth. Now they will know, and I will be the one to show them." Mitch slowly stands up whilst Jake sits slumped against the railings and just stares towards me, unsure of what we need to do as the ground continues to shake, as though an earth quake now rumbles beneath the whole city. Lilith looks over her shoulder and smiles slightly at Mitch, looking him up and down in a condescending manner. "I think now is the time for you to make peace with you God, Michael. Go and ask him why he sat back and let all of this happen... maybe it is guilt for the terrible things he knows that he has done... Maybe he really does not give a shit about any of us and this is his way of ending it all without having to get his hands dirty," she says to him then turns back to me. Lilith takes a moment to herself then inhales deeply, calming her thoughts and preparing for her next step. "I would love to stay and watch, but I have more important things to take care of. When I find the throne and get Lucifer to relinquish power, it will bring Hell on earth, and it will be so beautiful." Lilith turns her back on me and starts to walk away, as she does she begins to laugh then in a blink of an eye, she is gone from sight, disappearing in to thin air, leaving as quickly as she arrived in this world. My chest is heaving as I just stand still, silently trying to comprehend what has just happened. Right now, billions of humans are blissfully unaware of the impending dangers, they have no idea what is to come, what lurks beneath the earth right now. But soon they will, because not only will every demon, ghoul or creature of nightmare be able to freely roam in to this world, there is now also no one to stop them from killing and devouring the population. This is the beginning of the end, and as soon as Lilith takes the throne, this world will be buried in flames and torment until every last thing ceases to exist.

"I failed," the words just slip from my mouth as Mitch slowly walks towards me. "I failed and now because of me everything is going to end."

"No," Mitch says gently then shakes his head as tears start to stream uncontrollably down my face and I struggle to catch my breath. "Don't you dare blame yourself. We tried... there were just too many of them and there was just the two of us. We..."

"I let this happen," I interrupt him as I begin to sob. Mitch steps forward and wraps his arms around me as I cry in to his chest, giving in to all of those horribly inconvenient emotions inside of me. My whole body shakes as he holds me, his strength trying to calm my soul and protect me from my own demons but it all feels just too much.

Over the last few days, several people have told me that I was to be the one to save everyone, and each time I denied what they were saying and acted like I didn't give a shit what happened. Alysia, the Oracle told us right at the beginning that the last star of the morning was the only thing that could stop the rising from happening, and instead of accepting what I had to do, I ran away. I honestly do not even know why I did it. For all those years guarding the Veil, I knew categorically that I was the protector, I knew that in me doing that I was stopping the low life scum that inhabits Hell from reaching this world and I was fully aware that my power made me one of the very few beings in the entirety of existence that was actually capable of doing so. Was it the pressure? Was I that much of a selfish arsehole that I was willing to step aside, knowing full well what would happen if I did nothing? As all of these thoughts run through my head, there is now only one thing I am absolutely sure of, it has now happened and there is no taking it back. I hold Mitch tightly as I try to relax but I quickly get a very unsettling feeling so I pull away from him and almost hold my breath so that I can concentrate on my surroundings without the unwanted noise of me needing oxygen.

"What is it?" Mitch asks quietly as he can see that there is something not quite right with me.

"Do you feel that?" I say at a whisper. The night air that surrounds us is no longer cold, it is warm and thick, it almost reminds me of the smell of the pits that I worked in when I first left my fathers home. Then there is the scent of something else, something that makes my skin crawl and I know that it is pure evil. "Oh, shit!"

"Feel what?" Mitch asks and almost immediately the ground beneath us caves in, opening up to reveal large chasms of nothingness and making us both dive off in opposite directions to stop ourselves from falling down in the fiery depths that are rising up, consuming the earth all around us. I land on the hard ground and roll to a stop, I do try to stand straight back up but everything is trembling so fiercely that I cannot get my balance. As I sit on the ground looking across the now 10 foot wide hole towards Mitch who is on the opposite side, I know that this looks extremely bad already, but it is only the start of the horror that is to come. The whole world seems to shake as massive holes begin to appear everywhere around us, over the coming days each one will eventually grow to be big enough to engulf an entire building as the earth crumbles apart. Now that the rising has begun, the human world will quickly be over run with terror, if God really did give a damn then wouldn't he at least try to save his creations, send more than just one Archangel to protect the entirety of mankind?

In the distance explosions fill the air as the cracks start to spread and emerge elsewhere, turning the quiet Christmas night around us in to the start of an apocalyptic war zone in a matter of minutes. The carnage and destruction that the earth quakes are causing will still be nothing in comparison to the devastation caused when the undead souls and demons claw their grubby little hands out of pits and in to this world. Screams can be heard through the rumbling of earth as those humans in their nearby homes are woken with flames instead of Christmas gifts, the plans to celebrate with family will be no more and happiness will soon be a distant memory of the old times when they were oblivious to the real truth that surrounds them.

"There is going to be a first tester wave," I shout across at Mitch then force myself to stand back up, I shake quite a bit but hold my balance as I step forward to peer over the side of the chasm in front of us. I can already see the fire and flames working their way up the walls towards the surface, but heat is not the only thing they will bring. Backing away, my heart starts to pound. I know that the inevitable has already begun, but do I step aside and watch everything go to shit, or do I continue to fight until my last dying breath?

"A first wave of what?" Mitch asks back as he watches me, then he seems to notice something in front of me and glances down to the side of the broken earth, where a skeletal black hand emerges and claws at the dirt to pull itself up. Quickly more hands appear along the ridge, the first wave of undead souls escaping the pits... just like the stories foretold. I heard the tale of the rising so many times as a child that it is branded in to my memory. It starts when the Veil falls, the earth will crumble and the lowest level scum from the depths will appear first, because they are the most connected to the human world, they still have souls and human form, they are the ones who have been in Hell for the least amount of time. Most of them will have been human at one point in their existence, living as though unaware of the torment that would await them when they died. Now they are an army of brain dead monsters, that will kill and devour anything in their path for a sniff of freedom from the fire below. "Rosa?" Mitch says, trying to get my attention. I glance up at him and stare into his eyes as I continue to move back, allowing space in front of me for the multiple bodies to surface and see the human world around them again.

"Are the humans really worth fighting for?" I ask loudly as more of the undead emerge and block off any way I have of seeing Mitch fully.

"What?" He shouts back, clearly not understanding why I would ask that right now.

"The humans," I reiterate. "Tell me, are they worth fighting for? As God's creations, do they deserve a chance to live or is Lilith correct and they were only put on this earth as entertainment?" Another rumble of earth and I almost lose my footing as I stand facing a small army of around 50 souls, all of which look as though they have been in a fire, their charred flesh black and scorched of the pits, the smell of burning hair and torment clings to their skin. Every single one of them stays still, silently staring at me. Right now, I am the only thing that stands between them and the streets behind me.

"Life is a gift," Mitch explains to me over the surrounding noise. "No matter the journey someone takes through it, it is to be cherished and honoured. No one, not even God himself has the right to take that away. So yes, every single human, whether they have done good or bad things with their lives, deserves the chance to live and will always be worth fighting for." I spend a moment in silence as I take in his words. All my life, I saw angels and demons to be the conflicting forces of good and evil. I was taught to hate anything that was deemed as righteous, I viewed the humans as slaves to God, created as play things and nothing more than weak mortal beings who wasted the very short lives that they had been given. Then I came here myself, and I saw first hand the true nature of humanity. Although it has its flaws, the few bad eggs in the middle of the billions that now populate the earth, I have seen kindness, the part of humanity that is taken for granted and ignored by those that are immortal. The people I have met deserve a chance to live, they do not deserve to be tortured and maimed for pleasure whilst the world around them burns then ultimately slowly fades away in to oblivion. They need someone to fight for them... They need me.

"Mitch?" I shout across the sea of bodies in front of me. I cannot see him but I know he is still there, I can feel his presence. "I need you to find cover, get to a safe distance and pray to your God that we survive."

"What are you talking about?" I hear him shout back. "Rosa I need you to be safe as well, I need you to..." Before Mitch can finish his sentence the horde of undead charge towards me as one, their tormented screams drown him out as I open my arms wide, close my eyes and breathe deeply, allowing me to concentrate fully on my surroundings. If I am now the only thing that stands between them and the humans, then I will show every last mother fucking one of them exactly who they are now faced with. I am the daughter of both Lucifer and Lilith, two of the most powerful beings that have ever existed, so it is about time I accept that fully, stop acting like a brat with parent issue and instead start acting like the real Alexis Morningstar that I know deep down inside that I am.

I open my eyes again just in time to see the mass of burned faces sweep in on me, in seconds I am on the ground, the weight of bodies that are now piling on top of me, clawing at my skin, trying to tear me apart is overwhelming. The pain is excruciating as I feel teeth and nails dig deep in to my flesh, gouging out chunks of me and I cannot help but scream. But this is a good thing, because I know I have their full attention, the group is solely focused on me right now, working as one to take down the enemy that is before them like a swarm of locusts. My limbs are being pulled in several different directions, my shoulder pops and dislocates from the socket with a sickening crack and I know categorically that very soon they will succeed in ripping me apart. I know I could heal if I had some way to escape, give myself a couple of minutes to recoup. Or I could take the odd soul from those that surround me and stop myself being killed because if I do die now, they will leave my body behind and head in to the streets to find their next victim, meaning the city behind me will become their playground.

"Rosa!!" I can hear Mitch screaming my name over the growls and screeching of the undead. I expressly told him to find cover, why does he have to be so stubborn? "Rosa, I'm coming." By the time he makes it around the massive hole in the ground and fights his way though these beasts to get to me, I would be dead, so I do not know what kind of help he thinks he can offer me, his attempts are useless. He should be able to see quite clearly that I have everything fully under my control. It is all part of my plan, even if I do currently sound like I am being ripped limb from limb... which I suppose I am as my screams echo through the night and I feel myself go light-headed as I lose blood from multiple wounds, bites and tears that cover my body.

I can already feel my body preparing for when I die as the injuries I now have sustained have no way of healing in time before my heart stops, my power searching for nearby souls to take in order to restore my life when I lose mine. But I do not want to wait that long, and my plan did not entail only taking the one life to survive. What I have up my sleeve is something I have never tried before, but I know I can do it, I can feel it, after all, the blood that runs through my veins was descended from those that were forged at the hand of God, so anything they could do, I know I can do better. The undead have not even noticed that I did not try to fight back, maybe they think after their Mistress brought down the Veil that anyone who wanted to stop her would just roll over and die, let them run free in the human world and devour anyone that they wanted. They obviously underestimate me.

I force my eyes closed and pull my arms in to my body to stop them being ripped off completely, I scream like hell, the pain consuming every inch of me and making my mind fog with the agony that I am in. But I don't need to think, what I am about to do is all about feel... and right now, I can feel every single one of their souls. They are still fresh in comparison to those that fully lose their humanity and turn in to demons over the thousands of years that they endure torture, so their souls are fully exposed, burning bright inside of them, just begging to be released in to the universe. Even though I have my eyes closed, each one of them is like a bright light, a beacon of life calling out to me, making it quite easy for me to lock on to it and take everything they have left inside of them.

All of a sudden everything goes still, nothing around me moves, no sounds can be heard and perfect clarity washes over me. I feel calm, almost enlightened as my soul feels at one with the world around me, every one of my senses is heightened and I can even smell the humanity that used to run through their undead veins. There is a rush of heat that passes through me then my skin starts to tingle, just slight at first in the tips of my fingers, but swiftly moving up my arms and across my chest until the entirety of my body feels as though is it vibrating uncontrollably. A burst of energy and I am dropped to the ground, I land face first on my front, smashing my mouth on the floor, causing more blood to gush from me then the air around me gets so hot that I can actually hear the sizzle of skin from the heat. Rolling on to my back, I am instantly set upon again, they are relentless in wanting destruction, but when I look at the man who mounts me I can't help but smirk as his flesh starts to melt from his bones as Hell fire engulfs us all. It is beautiful and I can not help but take a moment to watch the bright light dance around us. The further it spreads from me the more alive I feel, I reap their lost souls as they all begin to die fully, taking them in to myself and destroying them all in one go. The skeletal remains of the man on top of me falls to the side as a tornado of flames circle me, cremating anything that stands in its way but leaving me at the centre unaffected by it.

I sit upright and enjoy the feeling of consuming the life forces of those around me, taking them all by force is far too easy but I am surprised by the flames. When I came out of the the church and accidentally nearly blew up Mitch, the power of Hell fire caught me off guard. I never knew I possessed that, I know my father was capable of manipulating the flames but I was not aware it was one of the skills I had inherited until the moment I lost control. Although spending most of my life suppressing my link to the royal family and Lucifer himself, probably made me suppress some of the abilities that I got from him, and now I wonder if I inherited anything from my mother. If she is as powerful as I think she is, then what can she do that I have yet to discover?

Eventually the heat around me starts to subside and I can finally see my surroundings again without looking at them through fire. Dozens of charred bones, flesh and ash lie scattered around me as I sit quietly in the middle of a few remaining small piles of embers, feeling my essence absorb their souls, leaving them nothing more than a distant memory of the army that they could have been and now allowing me to heal again.

"Rosa?" I look up as Mitch cautiously approaches me, stepping over burning remains as the Hell fire still consumes some of the bodies, continuing to burn as the air returns to normal and a chill runs through me. "Are you OK?" he asks me as he looks around at the sight surrounding me.

"Yeah," I force out then try to get up from the ground, I am still healing so find it difficult and wobble, instantly Mitch steps forward and takes my arm to help me. "That was only a small portion of the army that will emerge over the next 48 hours. Kind of like they are sending in cannon fodder to test the waters before the full invasion begins," I moan slightly as I stretch my arm, making my shoulder pop back in to place. "At least taking them out buys us a little time before more arrive, although the way the earth is opening up throughout the city, there could be multiple raid parties breaking through as we speak, I can't stop them all." Mitch just stares at me blankly as I talk, then when I stop he doesn't respond. "What? What are you staring at?"

"What the fuck did you just do?" he asks me very confused. Honestly though I do not even know how to explain it, I didn't even fully know that was going to happen. "And what the actual fuck has been going on with you tonight?"

"Erm..." I need to think of something to say. "Well, when I went for a walk I bumped in to my father and learned something about me that I found extremely difficult to process. It got in my head, clouded my judgement and for a moment there I thought I was going to give up and die... I guess once I accepted it, I found it easier to embrace what was inside of me." He listens to me as he looks around to the multiple still burning piles of bones. "Oh and those, I reaped their souls and burned their flesh in Hell fire. I have never reaped on that scale before but it was surprisingly easy once I let my power be free and..."

"Hell fire?" Mitch interrupts me, not even believing he is saying those words. "You are powerful enough to control Hell fire?" I know what he is hinting at, there is only one other being that has ever had that capability before and he controls the throne.

"Yes," I reply shyly. "I didn't know it was something I could do until outside the church when I blew up a tree... Does it make you see me differently? Does it make me evil and you hate me now?" I ask. Usually I wouldn't really give a shit what anyone thought of me but Mitch is different. The way he is staring in to my eyes, the concern, the fear, the caring nature of his hand on mine right now is all so conflicting and I do not know how he feels at all.

"The Oracle was right about you," he eventually responds. "She said you would be the one to save us all."

"Well, as you can see I haven't really done a good job of that," just as I say those words another loud explosion rings through the night from close by making us both jump slightly then a secondary rumble makes everything shake before sirens can be heard. The humans will scramble, trying to understand what is going on and putting it down to earthquakes or some "act of God" type natural disaster, but there is nothing natural about what is going to swarm the city, soon they will know the truth when the things of nightmares invade their real lives. "Is Jake alright?" I ask him and he glances over to where he left him by the railings at the river side, but his face drops and quickly he begins to look around, panicking as he does not currently have eyes on him. "Where is he?" I ask him as I turn on the spot, my voice shaking as I speak. The whole point of that fight was us trying to keep him safe and now he is gone.

"I'm here," we hear Jake moan loudly. Mitch looks over towards the voice and instantly readies for a fight.

"Get off him," he shouts towards Jake and a second man who is currently holding Jake up to stand as he doesn't seem to be able to put any weight on his leg so he is clutching on to the mystery man for dear life. The unknown man is dressed in all black leather and seems to blend in with the dark night, as though he is used to hiding in the shadows, his face is shrouded with a hood and all I can see from this distance is the glint of a blade in the street light that is strapped to his thigh. "Jake it's OK," Mitch says then turns his attention to the stranger. "I swear I will kill you if you don't..."

"Calm yourself, angel," the unknown man replies quite casually in a deep gravely voice, one that I recognise straight away which makes me instantly smile. He heads towards us whilst Jake hobbles along by his side.

"It's OK Mitch, he helped me, he's one of the good guys," Jake informs him as I cross my arms and stare at the stranger as he approaches us then he lowers his hood. He has never changed, he still sports the same rugged salt and pepper stubble and shoulder length hair, his strong jawline making his features as hansom as ever, looking around mid 30's even though he is much older than me. His striking emerald green eyes are looking slightly deeper than what I remember but apart from that, I assume he is the same unyielding, emotionless reaper that I worked alongside for decades. I know that when I first heard his name again, it was attached to what they believed to be an older man, wise and secretive, but he was always good at changing his appearance to blend in with normal folk.

"Hello, Monroe," I nod towards him as Mitch helps Jake to step away, he stands firm and looks across all the blood that is on me, the holes and rips in my clothing, the remnants of injuries and the absolute state I probably am in right now as I am covered head to toe in black goo. "You look well, considering I have not seen you in a while."

"I wish I could say the same," he replies with a slight smirk. That is about the most emotion I have seen from him in a long time. Always like ice, no showing how he felt and a man of very few words, unless he had had a drink then you could not stop the sarcasm, but one hell of a fighter and loyalty that could never be matched.

"I am going to assume you felt the Veil fall?" he nods in reply to my question then glances over to Astaroth who has still not moved yet so I think now it is safe to say he is in fact dead. "If you felt it then I guess everyone in Hell will know it's gone and be planning their move."

"Maybe," he sighs. "Although there is a rumour that Lilith is making a move on the throne, so some are waiting to see who they serve first before they rebel," he watches me closely to see what I have to say on the matter then after a few moments grunts to himself as though knowing that his suspicions have now been confirmed by my silence and everything he heard is truth.

"Sorry," Mitch interrupts our conversation. "You are Monroe? You are the one who sent us to find Rosa? You look a little different to what I thought you would." I can tell that Mitch is confused by the appearance of him now, and also the fact that he is now here in front of us, but Monroe ignores his question and instead looks towards Jake.

"The human is hurt," Monroe states the obvious.

"Yeah, he is," I agree. "Mitch I think you should get Jake patched up, he needs medical assistance. Not that it will matter too much when the city starts to burn but at least make sure you guys are safe."

"This would not have happened if the angels hadn't made me mortal," Jake snaps slightly then seems to regret saying it so bluntly in front of Mitch who is only trying to help him.

"What's done is done," I say to him. "Mitch cannot take back what the angels did to you, no more than I can take back allowing the Veil to fall," I pause for a moment to gather my thoughts and rub my brow in frustration. "But I did say I would help you, and I do not go back on my word. So I will still try to get you brimstone to restore what was taken from you. I will arrange for someone to get it to you, even if it is the last thing I do. Maybe you can experience your true self for the short time we may have left."

"Thank you," Jake says a little embarrassed. "And I know it doesn't mean much probably coming from me, but as a human right now and as I grew up in the human word, I think I have a pretty good grasp of human things... What I am trying to say is, on behalf of the humans, thank you. You tried to do what no one else did, or no one else wanted to, you tried to save us." I don't quite know how to respond. Maybe I am a little guilty that I didn't actually do anything but lead Lilith to Jake in the first place, if I had not let my own feelings cloud my judgement then I wouldn't have had my meltdown and revealed myself in this world.

"Well, I didn't really save anything," I reply and look down at the ground before thinking of my next move. "I don't know how you guys want to spend your last days on earth, if you have anyone you care about then go and hug them tight. If you want to go fuck or get off your tits on drugs then go have a blast. Once Lilith takes the throne it will be all over, so you may as well do whatever the fuck you want to in the little time you have left." Mitch catches my eye and smiles sweetly which makes my cheeks blush, after all these years of being alive, it is just my luck that I find myself actually really liking someone right when the world is about to end. And who would have thought that that someone would be an angel. "It was really nice to meet you guys," I say to both Jake and Mitch. "You guys literally changed my life... not that I am sure it was for the better," I laugh slightly but I can tell by the look on Mitch's face that he is a little deflated, as though knowing that I will not be spending my remaining days with them.

"What are you going to do now?" Jake asks me and I have to take a deep breath, making sure I am doing the right thing before I tell them.

"You are going to do something really stupid aren't you?" Mitch says as he watches me but I can't help but smile at his statement.

"Probably," I reply. "I am going to spend my time doing what I do best, although fucking for the next few days does sound tempting, it is not what I have in mind."

"Who are planning to kill?" Monroe asks bluntly, only he would know that the thing I am best at was killing people. Some things truly never change.

"I think it is time that I hunt down and kill my mother," I smirk. If I am going to die anyway I may as well do it by getting my revenge for the murder of my siblings, the destruction of the mortal world and the pain caused to my new friends.

"Your mother?" Mitch seems even more confused now. "Who is your mother?" I glance to the faces watching me, I found it hard enough admitting who my father was never mind this, and once I say it out loud it makes it true, and there will be no turning my back on it after that.

"Lilith is my mother," I tell them and they all just stare blankly at me, not one of them moving or saying a single word as they digest the information I have just given them. It was hard for me to hear it from my fathers lips, so to tell an Archangel the woman he fucked is the daughter of the king of Hell and the first woman created by God's hands must be a lot to comprehend. "And she is currently on her way to try to claim my fathers throne, I would rather die trying to stop her than watch her destroy everything." Monroe seems as though he is piecing things together in his mind, all the years working alongside him, even he was unaware of who I truly was.

"You're a Princess?" Monroe smirks slightly as everything clicks in to place.

"Don't you fucking dare call me that," I laugh back at him. "I am as far from a Princess as anyone would ever get and if you say that again I will kill you." I break away from the group and head over to the lifeless corpse of Astaroth before yanking my blade from his skull, the brain and blood ooze from the wound with a sickening squelch.

"Well then, I guess this means you are going on a trip to Hell," Monroe says as he watches me.

"I can come with you," Mitch says straight away. "You will need help and..."

"No," I stop him. "No offence but the last thing I need is an angel following me around down there, I want to stay under the radar and get in to do what I need to do without any more distractions or unnecessary conflict. Plus you would be no help to anyone as you would be powerless down there, and I cannot be worrying about you and Jake when I have bigger things to deal with. If I was you I would be questioning my creator right about now, or at the very least trying to get more angels on your side to help the humans. They need someone to protect them in this world and I guess they need faith that things may get better, otherwise they will lose their minds as well as their lives." Mitch nods then sighs deeply.

"So, this is it then? We may not see you again," Mitch says with sadness in his voice, for a moment it makes my heart actually hurt and it totally catches me off guard. All these feelings are so new to me, but I need to look at the bigger picture and focus on killing Lilith, and maybe if I am lucky, find some way of stopping her taking the throne.

"I'm sorry," I reply sincerely. "But thank you for showing me that not all angels are arseholes," Mitch smiles at my comment then nods in understanding, but I can still see the sadness in his eyes. "Maybe if a miracle happens and things are different then you can buy me a drink sometime."

"Yeah, yeah I will," he says then everyone goes quiet, unsure of what else to say. The air around us is thick and even though the sounds of the city behind us fill the night, I know my place is not here. I can't do anything if I stay in the mortal world, it would just be damage control, instead I need to face the source of all of this head on, and then destroy it.

"Looks like we are leaving then," Monroe's voice cuts through the silence before walking a few meters past me and taking the knife from the holder on his thigh. Mitch and Jake both watch him slice the blade across his palm then draw a circle in mid-air before tracing the symbol I used to use far too often to open the doorway between the mortal realm and what I knew as home. As reapers we had the ability to cross worlds, far easier than trying to claw your way out of the pits.

"You are going with him?" Mitch asks me as Jake hobbles to his side, I can tell that Mitch is unsure of Monroe and he doesn't want to let me leave with someone he does not know anything about, but I trust Monroe with my life.

"Its been a while, so having a guide through the wastelands is a smart thing for me right now," I explain. "It's not like I can just walk straight in to my fathers home without being questioned, no one down there knows my origins and the longer I can keep that a secret, the better my chance of survival." As I say that a bright light flashes from behind me where Monroe has opened the door. I try to contain my smile at Jake who stares in wonderment at the now large circular portal that has opened in the nothingness of the night just in front of us. I suppose it is a wonder to behold, almost like a mortal seeing true magic for the first time as the edges of the circle burn like blue flames that lead in to another world.

"The portal won't hold long," Monroe says over his shoulder before stepping through it and disappearing from sight without waiting for a response.

"Rosa?" Mitch says gently just as I turn to follow Monroe which makes me stop. "I just want you to know..." he tries to think of the words but nothing else comes out of his mouth.

"It's OK," I smile back. "I am not great with goodbyes either." I breathe deeply, force a smile and take one last look at my new friends before turning and stepping in to the portal. I am not sure what to do when I get back to Hell, but one thing I know is that I will not go down without a fight and now that the end of the world is pretty much imminent, I don't have to worry too much about making sure no one stands in my way of being the real me. There is a 99.9% chance that I am going to die in he next few days once the world ends, so it is not like I now have anything left to lose.

Chapter Fourteen

I have not missed that smell. It hits me as soon as I step in to my fathers realm, the burn of sulphur that lingers in the air, which is surprising how warm it is compared to the cold barren landscape that it currently occupies. Looking around I see Monroe waiting patiently as I step away from the portal and let is close behind me, it is weird to be here again, especially knowing that I will be heading back to the one place I vowed I would never return to.

"You look like shit," Monroe says calmly with a raised eyebrow, his arms are crossed and even though I want to protest, I just sigh and nod in agreement. "If you are aiming to take down Lilith then you need to get rest, and get changed, you look like an outsider that has just crawled out of a demons arsehole."

"I am an outsider," I sigh deeply. "Did you have to portal us in so far away from the city?" All I can see for miles is dark earth, frozen underfoot but cracked on the surface with the heat of the stale air. We are on the outskirts to my fathers realm, far away from any sort of life that would be considered civil and I know beneath the ground we walk on now, that the souls of the damned are forever being caged, tortured and used for the pleasure of demented demons who get off on inflicting pain and suffering. And I know this because I used to be one of them, growing up here I was taught that those souls deserved everything they got and you were not a true demon unless you reviled in their pain, but since I left here to go to the human world I truly see things differently. I do not feel guilty for the things I have done in my past, even when working in the pits and inflicting immense suffering on souls for centuries, it was all just part of the job. I don't feel guilty for the thousands of beings I have hunted and killed, again it was the job and I knew I was what was standing in the way of them getting the devastation they wanted. What I do feel guilty about right now, standing here and contemplating everything I have done in my life, is taking the soul of that old man before his time when Mitch stabbed me in the street, I feel guilty about not being able to stop Lilith sooner because I know that multiple humans will have already lost their lives since the Veil fell, and most of all I am guilty of not telling Mitch that I did like him, instead just leaving him behind in a new unknown world that will soon be overrun by monsters. More than how bad I look or the human clothes I am wearing, what will probably make me an outsider is the way I feel inside, the pain and hurt I have for the things I have left behind. Hell was my home for such a long time, but now it all feels so distant and unfamiliar, the human world is where my soul belongs and I didn't realise it until right at this very moment.

We walk for what feels like hours, Monroe leading the way as I follow along silently lost in my own thoughts behind him. At least I am safe in the knowledge that I still have time. Lilith may have been close to my father at one point, obviously enough to have me but she won't know the city or my fathers home like I do. I spent years roaming the hallways alone, discovering all the little hidden passages and rooms filled with wonder. I doubt even the Sins know that place as well as I do, they were always surrounded by my fathers minions and owning the limelight, whereas I stayed in the shadows and learned everything I could about where I lived. I understood from a very young age to know your surroundings, never get caught out, and always know the difference between who to trust and who to kill. Probably the main reason why I do not have many close friends, or any friends for that matter, I always kept my distance and never got close enough to anyone where my emotions would be compromised. So why now, after all this time are my thoughts consumed with that bloody angel, the only person I had ever told my true identity to, who saw me for who I truly was, and who is now breaking my heart knowing that I will never see him again.

"We will rest here for the night," Monroe's words snap me out of my thoughts and I look up to see where we are, I had not been paying any attention to where were were heading but as I soon as I see the large but very old building in the middle of nowhere, I can not help but smile slightly. We had spent far too many nights here in the good old days when I was more care free and didn't really give two shits about the mortal world, even less cares were given to if I made more enemies than I could count. This decrepit ruin of a bar is the last stop from the city before you enter the barren wasteland where we have just come from, even though it was none eventful on our short journey here, the wastelands are full of nightmares and terrors that can catch even the most resilient of fighter off guard. I guess with the rising in process, the beasts out there had better things to do with their time than try to rob us of any food or supplies we might have been carrying. I take a moment to pause briefly before I walk through the large wooden doors that have paint peeling off and think about the last time I was in here. It wasn't long before I stopped working with Monroe and started guarding the Veil, it was not a particularly good day either, I seem to recall a lost soul giving us the slip, I was a little pissed off so took it out on several of the local demons that decided that was the perfect opportunity to start a fight, things did not quite go their way, and I walked out of this bar on bad terms with the owner.

"I told you that you were not welcome in here until you pay your bar tab," the very large and very well built barman says loudly in a thick gruff voice from behind the counter. I will hang back by the door and let Monroe work this out by himself in case we have to leave quickly, as the outsider now I am probably not up to date with the locals and their barbaric politics.

"That is no way to say hello to an old friend," Monroe states casually as he sits down on a old rickety bar stool. Just glancing around I can see that the place is quite full of people, all currently quiet and watching what is going on with great interest. They all know who Monroe is, over the years down here in Hell you build up a reputation and I was no different, although I learnt to keep a slightly lower profile than him, it was my name that people knew rather than my face. "Now how about a drink to start, of course some food then we will take the room," he says off handedly as he takes a brass key out of his inside jacket pocket and places it down on the bar. The whole space is silently watching now, the barman is stunned and debates what to say as he glances around at the multiple staring faces. There is easily 50, possibly 60 people in the large bar, most sat around small tables in groups, a couple of older men huddled next to the large open fire at one side, small private booths line the far wall and the whole place is dark and dingy with a large staircase heading upstairs to the unsavoury rooms that I spent many a night residing in... a perfect place to lay low when trying to sneak in to the city, but of course, in a matter of hours everyone around will know Monroe is back here, news spreads faster than Hell fire.

"I am sorry Monroe," the barman says cautiously. "But I told you last time, if you cannot pay, then you are not welcome." Monroe inhales loudly and exhales very slowly, clearly slightly frustrated that he is not being served then without warning he stands up and the barman jumps back, expecting conflict. "Take it easy Monroe, I don't want any trouble."

"Hmmm," Monroe huffs. "Do you know what it feel like to have your soul reaped?" he says as he stares deep in to the barman's eyes, but it doesn't quite have the affect Monroe hoped for as his question is returned with a smirk.

"Is that a threat?" the barman asks as he clenches his fists. The tension in the bar could be cut with a knife, not exactly the warm welcome I was preying for, or the secret return of Rosa Moon.

"Not a threat, more of a promise of things to come," Monroe says dryly then goes to say something else but I interrupt him.

189

"Lucious!" I say firmly making him stop, he has clearly lost what little manners he had whilst he has been working alone, I guess his own company became hard on him. We made quite the pair, and we always knew how to have each others back, even if that meant fighting or defusing a situation. I didn't come here to get involved in a bar fight, rest sounds quite nice when faced with what I have to do next so I need him to play nice. At this point I know everyone in the bar has turned to see who spoke his name and who would dare get involved with the famed reaper, so I suck it up and casually walk over to the counter as Monroe continues to stare at the barman, right now, my footsteps are the only sound that can be heard. "Please accept my apologies on behalf of my friend here," I say calmly to the barman. "He seems to have developed a lack of manners over the last few hundred years that have affected his capacity to treat other people with respect." Monroe sighs and glances sideways at me then shakes his head before calmly retaking his seat, backing down and letting me resolve things. "Now then," I clear my throat as I think of something to say, after all, I have not been part of this world for a very long time and I look like a bag of shit in my human clothes covered in blood and demon remains. "I seem to recall this fine establishment was managed by Gill, we go way back and I am sure if I could speak to him then I can sort all of this mess out." The barman finally looks at me instead of Monroe, he does not look happy but at least he is listening to me.

"Gill is dead," he says bluntly. "Has been for 140 years... This arsehole killed him. And if you are are looking for anyone else, they are probably dead too, I run this bar now."

"Oh," I was really not expecting that. Monroe randomly glances around the bar, clearly trying to avoid the subject. "Well I am sure that you can help instead and..."

"Why don't you stop talking whore, take this cunt and leave my fucking bar before I kill you both," the barman interrupts me and leans across the counter trying to intimidate me in to leaving. "I am not scared of this reaper piece of shit, he lost all my respect when he started acting like he owned the place."

"I do own the place," Monroe grumbles under his breath as he ignores the growing tension. At least that part is true, he won the bar in a very tense game of bones centuries ago, but didn't really care too much for the business side of things so allowed the current owner at the time, Wesley, a nice old man who never had a bad word to say about anyone, to do all the work, or should I say, drink all the profits as it was his daughter that did the work behind the scenes and left the bar management to the late Gill.

"Then show me where your name is on the deeds," the barman spits back. "We don't have no one called Monroe paying taxes to the crown so you mean fuck all around here. All I am interested in is how much money you owe, until you pay, you are cut off. So take this bitch and your sorry broke ass far away from my bar," they both stare at each other, waiting for the other to back down but I know for a fact it will not be Monroe that yields first.

"I do not know you, and you very clearly do not know me at all," I say trying to stay relatively calm, after all he did call me a whore and a bitch, I have killed people in the past for less of a reason than that which proves that I am definitely going soft after being in the human world. "I was being nice, but I admit, I did forget being nice gets you nowhere down here." As I speak, a few of the near by patrons move out of the way as though they know things are about to go down hill very fast, but Monroe still does not move, defiantly claiming his space on that rickety old wooden stool.

"I suggest you butt out or you get out before I kill you both," the barman stares at me then slowly leans across the counter to get in my face, but I can not help but smile. I do love when men try to intimidate me when they have no idea who I really am. Even in Hell, the men think they rule the world.

"Why don't you give it your best shot," I say back, slowly placing my hands on the bar top then leaning in until my nose is just an inch from his, and I can feel his soul. A demons soul runs deeper than a humans but it would be so easy to take it, he wouldn't even know what happened as he would be dead before his body hit the floor.

"Rosa?" the sweet voice of a young woman catches me off guard and I momentarily forget what I was doing. "Rosa Moon? Do my eyes deceive me or have you truly returned?" Everything around me is deadly silent as I slowly turn my head to the side to see Esmera standing on the landing at the top of the staircase that overlooks the bar below. Her amber eyes watch me as I stand up, forgetting about everyone else in the bar and just focus on her, dressed in a floor length gown of deep red satin, the corset hugging her curves as though it was perfectly made to measure and her long wavy raven hair falls effortlessly around her shoulders, the vision of beauty that she always was.

I was still quite young when I met Esmera, as much as I was not one for having friends, I guess she would be the closest I ever had down here. We met way before I even knew Monroe, I would spend long hours working in the pits, earning my own way then come out here, far away from anyone who may know me to relax and acquire a taste for a bit of normality. Her father Wesley owned this place for as long as I could remember, he was the kindest man I ever met and I had heard rumours a long time ago that he had passed away, leaving the place to his daughter. This run down bar was a breath of fresh air after growing up in my fathers castle, constantly feeling like an outcast or being worthless, in here I felt like I belonged and ultimately me being settled here made me want to go to the human world... I just did not say good bye when I left.

"I thought you were dead," Esmera says with a tone of sadness in her voice. As much as everyone else in the bar is quiet I begin to hear the whispered conversations between them, all looking for clarification that they did in fact hear my name correctly. The name Moon is legendary in our world, it was associated with one of the most powerful of soul reapers, someone who fought in the wars that protected the Veil and became a name that could easily strike fear in to the heart of even the toughest of demon. Luckily for me not many people associated that name with a woman, so it was easy to go unseen most of the time, and even now I can tell by the way the barman is staring at me open mouthed that he doesn't even believe it.

"I think now is a very good time for a drink," Monroe says very quietly to the barman who just glances at him and nods his head before taking an old spirit bottle off the back shelf. He places a couple of clean glasses down and pours two drinks, one for himself as he seems to be slightly in shock, after all he did almost start a fight with the infamous and mysterious reaper know only as Moon.

"Is she really..."

"Hmm mmm," Monroe answers the barman before he has a chance to ask then casually takes the glass from the counter so he can drink.

"You just disappeared," Esmera says as she starts to descend the staircase and the people around the bar go back to their normal conversations now that the tensions have settled. When she reaches the bottom she pauses to look at me, I do try to think of something to say, an apology maybe after how I left things, sorry for the state of the bar floor soaked in demon blood and bodies everywhere because they caught me on a bad day, but nothing comes out of my mouth. "And you look like shit."

"I told you so," Monroe says under his breath so I playfully punch his arm to get him to shut up. I know I look like shit, I do not need people to keep telling me.

"Grab the key, your room is just as you left it," she tries to hide her smile at the state of me then turns and heads back upstairs, so I grab the rusty brass key from the counter and follow her, leaving Monroe behind to drink.

The upstairs of the old run down bar seems bigger than I remember, a lot of doors, some leading to private rooms that the regular drinkers downstairs can rent by the hour with a girl thrown in to please them. Some rooms of course can be rented for the night to sleep in, even on the outskirts of Hell you still get the odd person passing through, although they are usually being hunted or trying to escape the pits, no judgement in here. And then right at the end of the long landing that follows the curve of the rooms around the edge of the building and overlooks the bar below, is room number 17. The only room that is privately owned by someone other than Esmera and one that no one dare to enter without having the key, the same key that I hold in my hand now and nervously play with as Esmera silently waits for me to unlock the door.

"Let me," she says softly as she takes the key out of my hands and unlocks the door, I just stand for a moment as she opens it and heads inside. I was a fool to not consider that she would be here, she was always here, waiting for me dropping by and then spending the nights talking and... "I can't remember you ever being this quiet." I glance up and clear my throat, forcing a small smile before following her in to the room. "I am sure you left some of your old clothes in the trunk and there is hot water available so I can run you a bath," she continues as she starts to potter around the room, taking clothes out of an old trunk that sits in the far corner and turning the taps on in the deep cast iron tub. The room is very large, contains two decent sized beds but not much else apart from a very distinct lack of any sort of decorating style. We just used to crash here when we were not working, it had everything we needed, even the local company was good at occupying our free time... there were plenty of nights where things got very wild and intimate in here, in Hell there isn't much else to do, I suppose that is where I found my love of sex and where I found Esmera.

"You don't have to do that," I say quietly but she doesn't even look up as she continues to fill the tub with boiling hot water and carefully lays some old clothes of mine out on the bed closest to the door.

"It doesn't take a reaper to know you smell human, and you look as though you spent the last week being dragged around the pits," Esmera says off handedly then stops, sighs deeply and finally looks up at me. "I thought about the night you left every single day since. You just walked out, didn't even care about what you left behind."

"I know, I lost my temper and I guess I didn't have to kill those guys, it was just easier to..."

"It was me that you left behind," she interrupts me and for a second I get a hollow pain in my chest, as though her words pierce my heart. "No goodbye, no nothing from you. Although I should have expected it, you never were one to put down roots or care deeply for anyone but yourself." She stops speaking, almost ashamed of the words she has just said then goes back to sorting the bath and acting like we no longer know each other. A few hundred years ago I would have laughed at what she had just said, knowing it was true and not giving a shit about it at all, but now those words actually hurt, I am not the person I used to be.

"Esmera, stop, please?" I say with strength in my voice and she stops, turns off the taps and just stands silently staring at the floor. "I agree with you," I speak honestly. "I was a self absorbed arsehole. Didn't care about hurting anyone else's feelings... the night I left here I did not give a second thought to you or anyone else down here, at the time I was lucky to find myself in a position where I could move on, I got a new job and left you and everything else behind. And to be perfectly honest it was easy to not give any thought to you at all. It has been... what? 400 years since I left here, stopped being just a reaper to become the Veils guardian and..."

"682," she says with a hint of sarcasm in her voice which stops me speaking.

"Wow, that long ago?" I honestly did not realise how long it had actually been since I changed positions and sort of just disappeared from this world. The whole room falls deadly silent as I think of something else to say before sighing deeply and knowing exactly what the next words out of my mouth need to be. "I'm sorry. I am sorry for just walking away and not considering your feelings. Of course I am also sorry that I left the bar a mess, covered in dead bodies and demon blood, but I am so fucking sorry to you because even though you are struggling to even look at me fully, I can see the pain and hurt in your eyes because of what I did." Esmera finally looks up and me and forces a tight smile. "I was a complete and utter ass hat, I was fully self-absorbed, I did not give a shit who I killed or who I hurt and most of all I was pretty much an ignorant cunt... but I am not that person any more. Although, I hope I am not that person because saying all that out loud sounds like I was such a horrible person."

"You were never horrible," she says quietly. "You just never shared any sort of feelings and you were always running away from something. As though you had this massive secret that you were afraid people would find out, so you never got close to anyone." Her words are so true they hurt.

"I did care, Esmera," I reply honestly. "You were the closest thing I ever had to an actual friend, and I have never said this to anyone before, but I guess I did love you, in my own way. After so long I really do not think an apology is going to fix everything I did, as I can not imagine how much I hurt you when I just walked out of your life."

"It's OK," Esmera nods but I don't feel like everything is OK, far from it in fact.

"No, no it is not," I sigh. "You are right. Everything you said, is right, and I am finally at a point in my life where I am accepting that and who I am as a person."

"Rosa you don't need to explain to me, I am just gad you are not dead and..."

"My name is not Rosa," I say and for a moment the silence that surrounds me gets a little uncomfortable and I am not sure if what I am about to do is the right thing. "All those years of coming in here, talking to you, being close to you... I was running from who I really was and I was carrying a massive secret, one that will no longer matter if the rising finalises and Hell is brought to the human world."

"I had heard rumours that Lilith had destroyed the Veil and that the rising had begun, people talk a lot down here," she says cautiously then waits for my answer, and to be perfectly honest I could really do with just being able to talk to someone that I trust, I used to trust Esmera and the look she is now giving me tells me that I still can.

"My real name is Alexis Morningstar," I begin, and saying it is surprisingly easy now that I fully accept who I really am. "My father is Lucifer Morningstar, the one true ruler of Hell and my mother is Lilith, the first, the mother of demons and the one who is currently trying to destroy creation. Yes I can confirm first hand that the Veil has fallen, I was there and regretfully failed in stopping her finding the key, but she is yet to take my fathers throne so that gives me a little time to rest before I find a way in to the city to try to face her. But I am not quite sure how to do that part, I don't know if I am strong enough or even if she can be killed at all, plus I then have to face the fact that she is my mother and after so long of not even knowing who she was, I don't know if I will be able to physically do it or... or..." my words trail off as I notice Esmera desperately trying not to laugh at me.

"Whenever you got nervous about anything, which I do admit was very rarely, you always used to talk so much that I could not keep up," she says as she smiles more. "And I can also tell by the way you are saying all of this to me now that I am but one of a handful of people who know this from you." I nod in reply and smile back as she watches me. "Your secret is safe with me, what you have told me will not leave this room, you have my word... You should get cleaned up and changed, I will sort some food and drinks for you and Monroe... I always knew you were special, even if you never said, on your darkest days your soul always shone brightly." She nods at me then goes to leave but as she walks past me I quickly stop her.

"Esmera wait," she pauses and I swiftly head over towards the large wooden trunk where she got my cloths and shove it a foot to the side, the sound of wood on wood screeching fills the room before I pop the floor board and reveal the small hidden hole that still contains a few leather pouches of coins. Not even Monroe knew about this little hide, if he did, the coin would have been cleared out years ago. Taking out the smallest bag, the coins inside jingle as I feel its weight then replace the floorboard and move the trunk back over. "This should cover Monroe's bar tab and plenty left over to cover any upkeep costs for the room and board," I say as I hand her the money.

"Thank you," she smiles then turns to leave again but I quickly grab her arm and to stop her for a second time.

"There is a very high possibility that I will die trying to stop the rising from happening," I tell her with actual real emotion and the way her face softens instantly lets me know that she can hear it, which is probably the only time other than showing anger that she has seen anything real from me. "And when I do, I am not sure how long it will be before creation collapses in on itself." She listens to me carefully as I move my hand from her arm and spend a moment gazing in to her eyes, the same eyes that lit up whenever I used to walk through the bar doors, or the eyes that smiled when we got a little intimate, or the ones that I get the strong indication cried when I left and never returned. "I may have kept many secrets and told many a tale about my origins or my past, but one thing I never did was lie to you. I did love you Esmera, I might not have realised it, or maybe back then I took you for granted and I am truly sorry that I never told you." Her eyes turn a little glassy as though fighting back tears which makes me smile as I know she fully understands what I am trying to tell her, that even though I always used to show that cold hearted hard exterior, I did genuinely care for her. We both stand silent and wait for the other to say or do something, then after a few moments I gently stroke her cheek with my fingertips then lean in to kiss her. She reciprocates straight away, slowly allowing my tongue to play with hers, memories of times gone by where we lay in each others arms and explored each others bodies come flooding back, she was the closest thing to a real connection I ever had back then and now being close to her again feels so natural. She smells like rose water and her lips have the taste of cookie dough, which is unusual considering Hell is the last place you would actually find either of those things, but the reminiscent thoughts of the human world make me smile.

"Rosa?" she says gently as our lips part and I wait to hear what she has to say. "I missed you so much."

"I'm sorry I left the way I did, you deserved better from me," I reply softy as she reaches up and wipes away the stray tears that fall from her eyes.

"Well, you cannot go and face your mother looking like that," she sniffs back the emotion and smiles as she looks at all the blood I am covered in again. "And if you are planning on saving the entirety of existence, I better make sure you have sustenance and rest. Then after you survive tomorrow, you may not be as much of a stranger again around here."

"I promise, if we all don't get destroyed by the end of days, I will visit you often," I say truthfully, now that I am at peace with who I am and where I come from, maybe it will be nice to not have to hide all the time. Maybe I can finally be me.

Chapter Fifteen

Shortly after my brief reunion with Esmera, she leaves me alone to bathe and change. I do admit that the water was relaxing and quite soothing, being back here feels like home and for a moment I wonder why it was that I never did come back. All those times I lay my head on that bed meant nothing to me after I stopped working alongside Monroe, thinking about it I was a heartless bitch, the human world has made me realise quite a lot about myself, some of it I really dislike. Hopefully though the majority is for the better but it does scare me as I seem to care more than I used to and I know that if I fail when I face my mother then all those people that I knew will be lost, my heart breaks just thinking about that prospect... emotions are very strange and although they may have made me a better person over the last few days, I hate the way they make me feel.

The outfit that Esmera got out of the trunk for me is classic hard bitch reaper Rosa Moon. It still fits perfectly, and there was me thinking I had put a little weight on after I found my love of human food, speaking of food, I would kill for a nice slice of chocolate fudge cake and a strong coffee right now, that would be acceptable as a last meal I suppose seen as though I am probably going to die at my mothers hand. As I stand and look at myself in the old cracked mirror in the bedroom I have not slept in for over 600 years, I no longer recognise the face that stares back at me. Who would have thought that I would finally find the real me after hiding her away for so long when this could be the last night I am alive, and the last chance I have to save what few friends I have left.

"Well, this is the last thing I thought I would be doing on Christmas," I laugh at myself as I finish buckling up the tight leather trousers that I am now wearing then turn to grab the sleeveless black jacket from the bed before putting it on over the top of the black cropped vest. The leather clad, bad ass woman staring back at me would look totally out of place stood behind a little coffee shop counter, but in Hell I could pass as a demon, one whose reputation precedes her and one who takes no shit. "And at least this birthday will be one to remember," I smirk at myself, take a deep breath and head for the door.

The noise that the slight heels on the boots I am wearing make on the landing floorboards as I walk towards the stairs echo around me and the sounds from the bar below become noticeably quieter as I descend the staircase. Esmera smiles from behind the bar as she sees me and swiftly gets one of the serving girls to make two grogs of ale to take them over to a table where I can see Monroe sitting by himself waiting for me. My natural instincts when being somewhere with a lot of people make me scan the area before I reach the bottom, a few more people in here than when I first arrived around an hour ago, most keeping to themselves apart from a rowdy group of men in the far corner who seem to be celebrating a good day with a lot of ale and a couple of the scantily clad working girls. Near the end of the bar counter are two men, they have their backs to me but their smell stands out amongst the rest of the demons in here, the scent of the human world lingers on their clothing which tells me that they have spent a bit of time above ground very recently. They catch my attention more when they try to keep their heads down to go unnoticed but also keep glancing across to one of the dark booths not too far from where Monroe is sitting, I know they are not looking at him because Monroe would know if they were, they are watching someone else, someone who I can not see from here.

"You look like the old you again," Esmera smiles as I walk over towards the bar.

"I feel like the old me in this outfit, not sure just yet if that is a good or bad thing," I laugh but keep my eye on the shady guys, there is something not right about them, well, I know this is Hell and I am surrounded by demons, but those two really stand out right now. "Did you mention food?"

"I did, I will get it brought over to your table," she replies then heads for the kitchen. I hover for a moment and wait for the two guys to glance around again so I can see who they are watching, but when the one of the left turns his head, I recognise him straight away as one of the demons that accompanied Lilith in the prison when they killed Envy. Which also gives me the very sinking feeling that the person they are watching, is someone special, someone who they have probably been tracking for a while and found them here. And if they are tracking someone on Lilith's orders then they must be very important to her plans.

Monroe glances up from the booth and nods to acknowledge that he has seen me as he now sits with two full mugs of ale in front of him so I nod back and start to make my way towards him at the same time the two shady demons turn and start to slowly move towards the booth behind ours. I can tell that is where they are heading and also that they are being very cautious, almost as though they are not too sure of themselves or who they are about to face, but they need to fulfil orders so they have to suck it up and do as they are told.

"Finally," Monroe states as I get close to the table. "I'm starving, so hurry up and..." I don't wait for him to finish, I grab the two full mugs of ale, swiftly turn and move to the next booth just as the two demons approach.

"Excuse me," I say loudly so that a few people turn their heads to look as I squeeze past them, doing that makes them stop in their tracks, clearly not expecting anyone else to be interested in the stranger that is sat huddled in the corner of the booth, a large hood covering their face so that their identity remains anonymous. The demons back away quickly as people are watching them now so I slide in to the bench opposite the stranger and place the two ale's down, one in front of me and one in front of the silent mystery person. In the background I hear Monroe complain loudly that I took his mug but I ignore him as I casually pick mine up and drink, it tastes as shit as I remember but gets you off your tits drunk really fast which used to be quite handy when I tried to forget who I was related to. I sit silently for a while, just drinking and out of the corner of my eye I can see the two demons return to hover at the end of the bar, occasionally glancing over to make sure their target has not escaped them and debating whether or not to approach again now that there is an extra person to add in to the mix. As soon as I finish the first ale, Esmera makes sure I have another waiting and takes the empty one away, she doesn't say anything as she does as she can tell things are a little off and could result in something big happening, so she just watches and gives me a small smile before leaving again. The stranger still hasn't moved, the drink still sat on the table as though it does not even exist and I am starting to get a little impatient with being ignored.

"You know, if you wanted to stay off the radar, I can think of much better places to hide than in a bar full of demons," I say off handedly as I slump back on the seat and get comfortable, the ales effects starting to take hold and giving me a calming feeling that is nice when the whole of existence seems to be crashing down around me. "Especially ones who would turn on you in a heartbeat and hand you over to Lilith if they thought for just one second it would save their sorry asses from death when the end of the world comes."

"I don't know what you are talking about," the voice of the man under the hood tells me, slightly distorted to try to cover how he truly sounds, as though thinking that I will back off and not know who he is.

"Oh, my mistake," I reply sarcastically. "There was me thinking that I knew you... very well in fact," I chuckle to myself but the man does not even glance up, his vision restricted by the hood.

"I heard them call you Moon," he says quietly. "I know of the name but never had the pleasure of meeting the famous reaper." I can not help but smirk at his comment, so to hide it I drink more then lean in slightly so I can speak very quietly, making sure no one else hears me, especially Lilith's cronies.

"Well, we have met, a few times actually, quite hurtful that my own big brother would forget about me so easily," I smile more as I see the twitch of interest as he tries to see my face without moving his hood. "Nobody but me and the two arseholes following you know that Lilith is currently hunting you down... I think, possibly, news does travel fast, but I do get the feeling that they won't make a move in public like this. Plus even if they do approach you right now, they can not do shit and their Mistress is currently far too busy making her move on our fathers throne. So why don't you stop hiding for a moment, drink your fucking ale and stop being such a pussy ass bitch."

"When did you grow yourself a pair of balls, Alexis?" He scoffs at me but I can tell by the way his voice is now relaxed that he is trying not to smile.

"And when did you lose your own self worth enough to hide in the shadows as though you were ashamed of who you are, Pride?" I ask back then smirk at myself as what I just said to him could be said exactly the same about me. But I am done hiding, and I will never be ashamed of who I am any more, I guess I would go as far as to say that I am proud of the woman I have become, even if I do only have a day left to live. Pride sighs deeply then carefully removes his hood, his blond hair just like fathers, very handsome and youthful, he was always the one out of us all who bared the closest family resemblance to him. I give him a moment to settle, I can tell he is nervous about being out in public, probably been shitting himself ever since he found out someone was killing the Sins.

"So," he finally says then takes a long drink from the mug before placing it back on the table and actually looking at me. "I would never have guessed in 1000 years that the name Moon that was so legendary was actually my pathetic runt of a sister," I shoot him a look that could kill which makes him stop and sigh. "Sorry, old habits and all that. After so many years I still just think of you as that scared little girl that followed father around like a lost puppy. I guess after you left, you changed, obviously for the better. Although I always did wonder what had happened to you or where you went."

"Somewhere in what you have just said was a sort of half-arsed compliment," I smile. "But I will take it, coming from you that is high praise indeed." He forces a chuckle and looks down at the table, I can never remember a time when a Sin was so quiet, I guess he is suffering inside. I know I should say something, the usual me would laugh the silence off but something else pops in to my head, something that was said to me. "Listen, I'm sorry for your loss," I say gently and he nods in reply. "I know it is hard to lose someone you are close to, and your siblings meant a lot to you deeply. I can not imagine what pain you are going through."

"They were your family as well," he cuts in quietly and for a moment I am not sure how to respond. They never really acted like my family but when I started to lose them I felt something I had never felt before.

"Yeah, I never really felt like I was part of that family at all," I reply and drink more. This conversation got heavy very fast, I would have much preferred the sarcastic bullying I normally got from the Sins, I was used to that and could deal with it a lot easier than this. "Anyway," I swifty change the subject. "The human world will probably be the safest place for you now, I know that is not ideal seen as though the other attacks happened there, but with Lilith now in Hell and heading for the throne she will be less inclined to leave to follow you. The longer you stay here the more vulnerable you make yourself."

"I am fine, right where I am," Pride says back as he glances over to the two demons still watching us. "If what you say about Lilith is correct then I am sure I am more than capable of handling those two. You do remember who I am, right? All the humans I have brought to fathers kingdom, more than any of the others, I am a Sin, the son of Lucifer himself and I am..."

"What you are is a cocky mother fucker," I smirk as I cut him off. "Always thinking you are better than everyone else, your massive self inflated ego gets in the way of all common sense. And I hate to be the barer of bad news, but there are now not two demons to deal with, you have six, things are swiftly starting to take a turn for the nasty." I stare at him as he takes in my words then quickly glances around. He was too concerned with knowing more than me that he didn't even notice the four extra men that walked through the door a minute or so ago and now stand at a safe distance exchanging looks with the original two. Anyone else would probably not see the subtleties of the way they are watching Pride, but it was what I was trained to pick up on and I saw it straight away. "Please, for once in your fucking life, take someone else's advice. Stop being so arrogant and notice that the world does not revolve around you." Pride stares back at me for a full minute, clearly not happy with what I have just said to him. He is just like father, hates when someone actually stands up to him and speaks the truth that he does not want to hear.

"Fuck you," he spits then angrily gets up from the table and pulls his hood back up to cover his face. Just before he walks away he leans over and gets close so he can speak quietly. "Just because you have yourself a name now, does not give you the right to speak to me like that. I will always be better than you, and I will always see you as my pathetic runt sister, and you will never be powerful enough to even think about earning the title of a Sin. You are a no one compared to me." I force a smile and nod as he walks away, leaving me sitting in the booth alone with my second near empty ale, and reminding me why I left in the first place. For a brief moment I stupidly thought that he was actually a normal person, someone who could be reasoned with and have an actual grown up conversation with, oh how wrong I was. The world will probably end soon so why should I care what happens to him now, we are all going to die anyway, right. From behind I hear the commotion start as Lilith's men approach Pride now that he is alone before he has a chance to reach the door. The sounds of shouting, a struggle breaking out, a few punches being thrown, smashed bottles... Pride said he could handle it, after all he is the eldest son of Lucifer and a know it all idiot.

"You just going to sit there and let him get killed?" Monroe says casually as he leans up against the edge of the booth so in reply I just shrug and drink the remaining ale in the mug. "Oh well would you look at that, some of the locals must have heard about the reward money, terrible thing rumours, I had heard someone was paying quite handsomely to ensure any Sins were restrained." I glance up at Monroe and shrug again, what do I care, they clearly never gave a shit about me.

"He will be fine," I finally speak. "He is the almighty Sin Pride, there is nothing he can not do, plus he is immortal, not like anyone in here could kill him anyway." Monroe grunts and continues to watch the unfolding scene behind me. It sounds like quite a fight has broken out, regardless of how many people are trying to take him down, they can not hurt him, and I do not care.

"Hmmm, I guess you are right, he is immortal," Monroe agrees with me as he crosses his arms and relaxes back against the booth so he can watch the scene. "But lets just say, for example and totally hypothetically, that at least one of the demons is carrying a weapon that looks as though it is ingrained with blood, red blood which doesn't come from any demon in here. And also lets just throw in the thought that it may be from someone that had the ability to kill immortal beings... what would happen then?" I stare open mouthed at Monroe as I run through what he as just said in my head then stand up.

"Fuck!" I say to myself and quickly make my way out of the booth then turn around to see what is going on. Pride is on the floor, rolling around with two guys who are trying their hardest to grab his wrists and pin him down, around him is a circle of another seven men, all focused on the testosterone fuelled tussle and totally oblivious to the destruction that they have already caused around them, then there are more men waiting in the wings, trying to get a piece of that reward money. There are smashed tables, broken chairs, a number of demons lay unconscious on the ground and the guy behind the bar looks mad as fuck because of the mess. Then I notice exactly what Monroe was talking about, the guy from the prison holds a knife in his hand, it is nothing special but I can see from here that the blade is covered in dried red blood that has been etched in to the metal, which means if that is Lilith's blood then one cut and Pride will be mortal... then Pride will be dead.

"Hold this fucker still," the greasy haired arsehole from the prison says loudly, thinking that he is in charge when his Mistress is out of sight. I hear a couple of the guys reply to his command, calling him by the name Juro, not a name I have heard before but one that is now firmly on my list of people that I would very much like to kill. I really wanted to keep my head down, get to my fathers castle without bringing any attention to myself, oh how naïve I was to think that my plan would work smoothly. Nothing else goes easy for me so why should this? I know I need to make a decision, the longer I try to make up excuses for not helping my arsehole brother the less time he will have left to live, and do I really want to be responsible for him being killed when I know I could very easily save his sorry arse right now? I glance around and Esmera catches my eye, I can see she is used to the nightly fights that happen when demons let their egos take over, but I can also see it on her face that she knows that there is something more going on and if someone does not do anything, things could be extremely bad. After a few seconds she gives me a slight nod which lets me know she is telling me to help, telling me to stop being a selfish demon cunt and do what is right for once in my life.

"And there was me thinking that when you lot killed Envy, it would be the last I saw of you," I say loudly to get the attention of the current ring leader known as Juro, who immediately stands up straight with his back still to me and readies for an attack, but I am in no hurry to kill him just yet, I want some information so I step away from the booth and stand strong, knowing that down here, right now, I am an unstoppable force.

"I recognise that voice. You are the girl from the prison?" he asks me then slowly turns around, a wild grin on his face which soon falters when he notices who actually spoke and I watch him quickly piece it all together in his head. That silly little mortal girl who was hanging around with Envy was actually the unbeatable reaper known only as Moon.

"I do admit that you guys did catch us off guard in the human world," I smirk as I slowly step towards him, the rest of the demons who are tussling with Pride fall silent and no one else in the entire bar moves. Most of the people in this bar know who I am, if not by my face, they certainly know my name and it will be no secret now that Moon is back in town. "That little trick that Lilith can do with her blood? Very clever, I would never have seen it coming, although I didn't see it coming, did I, and neither did Envy, or any of the other Sins you have murdered lately. Pretty handy when you can just carry around an immortal killing weapon in the palm of your hand." A few of the demons glance at the blade he is carrying, piecing together what I have just said about Lilith's blood and a weapon that can kill immortal beings. Although the average demon is not fully immortal anyway, they are just a soul in a meat suit, but I am guessing not a single one of them would take the chance to be made almost human and killed today.

"This does not concern you," he tries to say with strength in his voice but I can see it by the look in his eyes that just knowing my name has him spooked. "I don't know why you were at the prison, it was unfortunate that you got in the way, but Lilith will..."

"Lilith will what?" I interrupt him and for a moment he just stands glancing around at the other demons watching him and waiting for his instructions. "Hmm? Please, tell us all exactly what Lilith will do. Because I have a very strong feeling that right now she will do fuck all, she won't care what happens inside this bar right now as she is far too focused on getting Lucifer to bow before her. She left you to handle her mess and in my very humble opinion, she chose a shit demon to kill Sins in her name. Looks to me like she just wanted you out of the way and occupied elsewhere." He snorts back at me but doesn't move, even Pride is silently still, being held down on the floor, just watching and listening to what is being said. "I bet now that the Veil has fallen and she is close to getting the throne, she won't even care if the remaining Sins live or die, because after tomorrow, when she takes control, every single thing in creation will be on its last breath."

"I could kill you right now," he scoffs and reaffirms his grip on the knife he is holding whilst making sure everyone can see it, an intimidation tactic to let me know he has a weapon, whereas right now I do not, which gives him the upper hand, or so he thinks.

"Yes, I suppose you could," I agree with him. "You obviously know the knife you are carrying could kill anyone, make them mortal, it would be so easy... but at the same time I would really love to see you try to kill me with that."

"You have no weapon, you are defenceless, and you seriously underestimate me, I am not lower level," he laughs.

"I may have no weapon in my hand right now, but I assure you I am far from defenceless, no matter what level you think you are, you are no more than a piece of shit," I say then go to attack but just as I do the barman who we had a run in with on our arrival picks up a half empty glass bottle of moonshine from behind the counter and launches it as the Juro's face, clearly a bit angry that they are starting a brawl in his bar. He doesn't see it coming until it smashes across his temple, sending shards of glass and alcohol in a shower of shit all over the demons which surround him.

"Get out!" the barman says firmly as he makes his way around the counter to face Juro. "I don't give a shit what your issues are, but tonight my bar is off limits to cunts like you and..." He doesn't get a chance to finish before Juro plunges the blade he is carrying deep in to the barman's abdomen, which makes him freeze on the spot, and makes the rest of the entire bar fall silent. The greasy-haired mother fucker, Juro, rocks a little, slightly dazed with a face full of fresh demon blood off the gash caused by the glass. He blinks a couple of times, probably seeing stars from the sudden bash then smirks and reaffirms his grip on the weapon that is deep in to the barman's flesh.

"Was that the best you can do?" He sneers then glances either side of him as a couple more men move into a defensive position, but something else happens, something which they have all never seen before. The barman starts to gurgle on his own blood, and as it falls from his mouth and the fresh wound, all the demons around him surge back as they notice his blood is not black like a demons should be, it is red, just like a human. Juro pulls the blade out, and the barman instantly falls to the ground, blood gushing out of the gaping hole and pooling beneath his body, which convulses as he struggles to breath then goes still. In all of my years of being alive, I will bet all the money in the human world that a demon has never died this way in Hell before and never in front of spectators who have no idea what just happened before their eyes. The brief mention before about an immortal killing weapon has now been revealed as truth, I guess I should be a little careful when taking him down, after all, I did experience the effects of Lilith's blood first hand. "Now, where were we?" Juro says as he slowly looks back towards me now that that slight distraction is out of the way. "Ah, yes. You do not have a weapon, and defiantly not one that can counter my own," he smiles knowing how powerful the blade in his hand is. I had hoped the glass bottle to the face, however unexpected it was, would have at least knocked him to the ground, but then again, after being in the human world for so long, it is easy to forget just how hard real demons fight. And I am just now realising he is not the average lower level one like the others that Lilith had, I guess he was correct about that at least.

"I will take what just happened as a warm-up," I laugh. "He was clearly testing the waters slightly. And from what I have just observed, you are not as weak as the other minions of Lilith that I killed tonight," I see him scowl at my words, maybe those other cronies were his friends, and now he has a real reason to want to kill me, although I am not finished gloating at my own accomplishments yet. Call it re-establishing my position now that I am back in Hell. "Now, Astaroth, there was a demon worth fighting, but I still managed to take him down as well." The sudden shift of uncertainty is noticeable throughout the people in the bar. Down here, the name Astaroth is second only to my fathers, sure I might have got lucky whilst taking him down tonight, but he is still dead, and I am still very much alive.

"Astaroth can not be killed," the gruff voice of one of the guys holding Pride in place says, but I just smile in response.

"Are you entirely sure about that?" Monroe says from behind me as he casually sits on the top of the table at the booth and continues to drink. "Because I could have sworn that it was that big bastard that was lying in the dirt with a sickle embedded in his skull. Of course, I could be mistaken, but there are not many demons that look like him and smell as foul." I can't help but chuckle slightly at Monroe's comments, same old Monroe, doesn't give a shit about anything but himself and does not care who he offends. Back in the day I quite liked it, those days when I was probably the same, cold-hearted and a complete twat with as massive ego.

"Believe me or not about Astaroth, I really could not care less," I say confidently and prepare for what comes next. "Because I very much doubt any of you will be alive in the next few minutes to even contemplate the fact that Lilith's

General is now no more than a very ugly memory." There is a brief moment of total silence, all I can hear is my own heartbeat, steady and sure because I feel confident in myself right now, and I know that when I told them that they would all be dead soon, I was not lying.

It all happens in a split second, the whole bar erupts as one and the threatening shit storm begins. Juro lunges forward, the knife aimed at my chest to try to take me down quick, but I grab his wrist, twist it till I hear the snap of bone then shove his arm to the side, making his blade plunge in to the chest of one of his friends. He cries out in pain due to his newly broken arm then goes to punch me with his free hand, but I grab that wrist as well, hold both his arms down either side of him and head butt him so hard in the face that I feel his blood splatter all over my own forehead before he falls backwards to the ground. There are a lot more of them than there is of me and most of them are armed, I do not want a single one of them getting close enough to even contemplate using that blood covered blade on me so I need to make this very quick.

I smile slightly as they all swarm on me, then feel the powerful electricity darting down my arms before the all too familiar handles of my soul sickles caress my palms as they fully materialise once more. The next few moments are like a daze, there is a lot of yelling, a lot of blood and to be honest a lot of me feeling invincible as I my weapons become an extension of my very soul. To the outsider watching the deathly dance, they would probably see me swiftly swinging my weapons with such accuracy that the most experienced surgeon could not compare. The blades slice through flesh with ease, hacks off limbs like a hot knife through butter. Not a single person gets close enough to even get a hit in until I am stood surrounded by random bits of demons and dead bodies. In front of me, just getting back to his feet is Juro, his face all busted open looking pissed off as fuck and three more guys offering back up, these are the last ones left standing out of all the demons who joined in and all that stand in my way of me ensuring Pride gets out alive.

"Nice party trick," Juro scoffs as he wipes his black blood from his face. "But I don't think even those weapons will protect you from mine," he steps forward and goes to lean down to grab his blade from the chest of the the dead demon but I quickly stop him as I speak.

"I swear I will kill the rest of your goons before you even touch that handle," he pauses for a moment and looks up at me, trying to decide just how believable my words are when his hand is only inches from his knife. But eventually he scoffs, shakes his head again and goes to grab it. Before he has even moved a millimetre, I throw and flick the sickle in my right hand, everyone watches as it flies silently through the air, curving as it goes until it suddenly whips around like a boomerang, changes direction and slices straight through the necks of the three demons who are still stood behind Juro. The sickle stays its new course until it heads back in my direction and I catch it again before the guys even drop to the ground. Juro freezes with his hand on the blade and cautiously looks around to the headless bodies that now lay where his muscle stood. "That was the warning, so my advice to you would be to run away like a good little boy all the way back to Lilith." I hear him swallow hard as he debates his choices in his head then slowly stands up, leaving his weapon still embedded in the demons chest.

"Alright, you made your point," Juro nods. "But the Sin is Lilith's property, we can trade, you take the weapon, and I will take the Sin?" I nod to acknowledge his offer then he smiles before turning around and heading for Pride who is still lay on his back on the ground. I let Juro take a couple of steps before I launch my sickle again, this time directly towards him. The blade hits him square in the back, going deep, probably through his spine, deep enough to shatter a couple of ribs and bust a lung. Almost instantly he falls to his knees then his body hits the floor hard.

The whole bar is silent as I take a deep breath and look back over to Pride who is yet to move off the floor. He is covered with splashed demon blood and shards of glass, but is unharmed, yet very bewildered. There are random pieces of demon flesh covering the floor, dead bodies everywhere and a lot of destruction for such a small amount of time. My chest is heaving but it is not from being out of breath, it is because I feel so empowered, I have not fought in that way for a long time, so unyielding and uncaring about the outcome of my actions, and being in Hell, having people see how powerful you really are, is invigorating. I should now gloat in Prides face and tell him he is worthless in comparison to me even though he is a Sin, that he will never be as strong as me or have the ability to wield soul weaponry and if he truly knew what I was actually capable of he would never try to belittle me again. But instead I place my second sickle on top of the bar counter then step over Juro's corpse and hold my hand out for Pride to take, he hesitates for a second then sighs before taking the offer of help and I pull him to his feet. He spends a moment brushing the remnants of the fight from his clothing, whilst noticeably trying to avoid my gaze. This feels quite awkward actually, the deathly silence almost deafening as everyone else just watches the aftermath.

"I can not force you to take my advice," I say trying to break the growing tension and suppress the overwhelming feelings of knowing that I am better than him, that was a part of me I did hate, the ego which made me cocky as well. "You are your own person, much like the rest of the Sins you are stubborn and..."

"Thank you," Pride forces out quietly and those words catch me totally off guard. It might just be two little words from the average person, but coming from a Sin they are massive. It sounds so unusual coming out of his mouth that I am not even sure I heard him correctly.

"I'm sorry, what did you just say?" I ask and he huffs at me as though thinking I am being sarcastic in making him repeat them.

"I said, thank you," the reluctance to say those words again is very clear in his voice and I have to force myself not to smile, but I am lost for words and not quite sure what else to say now.

"OK everyone," Esmera shouts loudly for the whole bar to hear as she heads over and takes my weapon out of Juro's back, ignoring the amount of blood covering it, and places it on the bar with the other. "Anyone who helps get these arseholes cleaned out of my bar and sorts this mess, can have free drinks for the next week." Almost instantly the majority of the punters flock on the dead bodies and carnage for the incentive of potentially unlimited alcohol. Typical really, if I thought I was going to live after tomorrow I may jump in on that as well. Whilst everyone else is distracted, Pride puts his hood up to cover his face and starts to head for the door, but I quickly stop him.

"Pride wait," he stops as I speak then patiently watches me pull the knife from the chest of the demon I killed with it as he is carried past me to be disposed of before I wipe the blood off the blade. "Take this, no matter where you decide to go, a weapon that can kill an immortal will come in handy to protect yourself." He nods and takes it from me before tucking it away under his shirt then I stand awkwardly, unsure of what else to say, so I just nod back and go to walk away.

"Alexis... Sorry, Rosa?" Pride gets my attention quietly. "What you said before, about me and... you know. I guess you might be a little correct, maybe, possibly, I should listen, if you hadn't... well, I mean, I would have been able to fight them off, I was just caught at a bad time that's all, but..."

"Just be safe," I say seriously and cut off his nervous waffling which makes him sigh deeply. I know what he just said didn't really make much sense but it was also hard for him to say what he did. He was always stubborn and prideful like father, so seeing this slightly different side to him is quite nice. "Whatever has happened in the past should really stay there. Use this big impending end of the world arse fuck to finally accept that some people are different to what we thought or remember, and others, like yourself, will always be a massive twat." Pride laughs at my words, a genuine laugh that makes me smile upon hearing it and for a moment I have a memory of my childhood, being in fathers castle and hearing the joy and happiness from my brothers and sisters. Granted I was never really a part of that, but it does make me think of home. It makes me a little embarrassed so I put my head down and try not to show it.

"I am heading above ground, you are right, the further away I can get, the safer I will be. I can not stand against Lilith and her growing army. If father can be defeated by her then I do not have a chance, but maybe you do," he says to me. "You are most certainly not the runt I remember... You are in fact, now a woman that I never imagined you would ever be, and I am proud of you," I glance up at those words and feel my cheeks blush even more.

"What?" There is no way he said those words, thank you was enough, but that?

"I am proud of you, Rosa Moon. I am proud to call you... family, and thank you for not letting your understandable hatred of me hold you back from saving me. I owe you my life, and you gained my unwavering respect." I don't think I am breathing upon hearing my arsehole of a brother say that but before I can form any sort of vocal response he steps forward and hugs me. It is a little awkward so I just stand, unsure of what to do, I have never been hugged by my father or any of my siblings before. "This is the part where my little sister hugs me back," he whispers in my ear which makes me smile again before embracing him also. He holds me tight, with so much feeling that I never thought him capable of and I almost have to fight back the building emotions I feel threatening just at the thought of actually having family that care about me. I spent years only caring about myself, but now I really need him to be safe because I feel like my heart would break if I lost another sibling.

"You should go," I finally say as I step back, but smile at how great it feels to have an actual connection with him, and then quickly get a sinking feeling knowing that I have lost others and I didn't get a chance to make amends before they were killed. Maybe after all this time away from them, things would have been different, they might have accepted me the way Pride has but now I will never know.

"Are you scared?" Pride asks me which helps divert my thoughts away from the Sins.

"Of tomorrow?" I ask him and he nods. "Honestly, I am fucking terrified," I laugh. "I have never wanted to die, the fear of that absolute end is what drove me to get stronger, more powerful so that I would never have to be faced with it myself. But now the Veil is gone, people all around me are getting killed and I don't know if I can stop it, I feel like I have the entire weight of the mortal world on my shoulders and I could break at any moment."

"Well, if what I saw in that very brief few seconds of fighting is anything to go by, I think the mortal world and everyone who still shows loyalty to father is in very good hands," he smiles.

"Were you always this positive about life?" I laugh which make him smirk.

"I am extremely positive about the things I am proud of, and right now you are right at the top of that list." My cheeks blush again, I am not used to this at all.

"OK, please leave because you are really starting to freak me out with how nice you are being to me," Pride laughs more then nods as he knows he needs to get as far away from here as he can. He is still vulnerable, and will be until either the end of the world, or Lilith is dead.

"OK, I'm going, hopefully I will see you again," he gives me once last small smile and heads out the door, leaving me behind, just standing in the middle of the bar with my thoughts. What I said to him was true, I am terrified that I am going to die tomorrow, I shouldn't be, I have had a great life, a very long one, my time has to come at some point. But it is the unknowing of what will happen to me after. Do

I become just another lost soul destined to roam the pits in my fathers domain for the rest of eternity or do I just cease to exist? After being a soul reaper I know that the dammed do not have anything to look forward to in the so called after life, so I will be no different, if anything, my soul will be so black that I will be locked away in the deepest, darkest place of Hell and never see the light of day again.

"Hey, are you alright?" Esmera says gently as she places her hand on my shoulder.

"Yeah, I am fine," I lie and I can see it in her eyes that she knows that I am not telling the truth.

"How about you sit down and eat," she says cautiously but I quickly shake my head. I feel strange, lots of pent up emotions threatening to overflow, kind of like I either want to rip someone's head off, drink myself in to oblivion, or fuck someone senseless. The thought that this is my last night alive is really getting in my head and I do not like what it is doing to me.

"I am not hungry," I lie again. I am actually starving but the thought of having to put the shit stale fucking awful food that is a Hell delicacy anywhere near my mouth makes me want to vomit. "If you will excuse me, I need to go somewhere else... anywhere but right here." I don't wait to see what else she has to say, I walk off, past all the watching eyes and head straight up the stairs towards my room. The door slams behind me and I take a moment to slow my breathing, all of a sudden it feels like my lungs don't work and I might drop dead at any second. Maybe that would be a good thing, then I would not have to face my mother and the unyielding torture I will receive when I fail to stop her. I mean, she is unstoppable, if she could easily be fought then father would have done it already, he would have reclaimed his kingdom and saved his children...Or her creator would have already taken her down... So that only leaves one possibility, that she is stronger than Lucifer himself and most definitely stronger than me. My heart feels like is it going to break out of my rib cage as I close my eyes and try to slow everything down, this is how I felt outside of the church, when I lost control and almost set Mitch alight... There is that sinking feeling again, the thoughts that I just left him and Jake up there, possibly surrounded by hordes of the undead. For all I know they have already been ripped limb from limb and there is actually nothing left in the mortal world to save.

"Well, this has certainly been a very interesting night indeed," Monroe says loudly as he barges through the bedroom door.

"Don't take this the wrong way but can you kindly fuck off?" I unintentionally snap at him and I hear him take a long drawn out breath from behind me and then shut the door without leaving.

"Do you want to know why I sent the key to you when I learned about someone wanting to take down the Veil?" he asks seriously but I don't answer. "Because out of every single being I have ever known in my lifetime, I have never felt anyone to be more destined for greatness, and I knew if there was anything that could be done to protect our worlds, then it would be you who would do it." He waits for a moment to see if I respond before continuing. "Remember that time I was pinned down when trying to secure the rogue goblin from the Abyss whilst on a bounty? I was overrun, surrounded by 20 arseholes with a knife literally stuck in my back? Who was the one who came in all guns blazing and killed the lot of those mother fuckers before I had even the chance to blink?"

"Me," I sigh quietly as I know he will just keep going if I remain silent.

"And who was it that faced a basilisk in the lake of fire and cut its head off just because she was pissed off at losing a game of bones?" Monroe asks more.

"Me, but what does..."

"And tell me who in this room is the daughter of our one true ruler Lucifer and a descendant of the first being created by the hand of God? Giving her the potential for unlimited power and who will face death tomorrow and be victorious like she always is?" Monroe states. "Because it sure as fuck is not me."

"Since when did you give pep talks?" I look around at him and see him casually leaning up against the closed door, his arms crossed and a small smile on his stupidly hansom face.

"Since one of my oldest acquaintances is acting like a whiny little bitch," he smirks, which makes me smile and relax slightly. "Oh woe is me, my mommy wants to kill everyone, and my daddy never hugged me," he mocks, which makes me smile more.

"You are an utter cunt," I chuckle and sign deeply, forcing all the shit that is in my head to slip away.

"I know, and that is why you always loved working with me so much. It was my amazing personality... that and my massive cock that kept you by my side." Monroe stands up and looks at me fully, the kind of look which tells me that he has other things on his mind than just cheering me up with his magical sarcastic words.

"At least one of those attributes is true," I respond as he walks towards me then stops, I can feel his breath on my cheek as he watches me closely. "And it certainly was not your glowing personality." The comments make my mind think about the good old days, me and Monroe working together, we were a team and we quickly found ways to help each other relieve our frustration, and I can not deny that right now I am so frustrated and stressed to bits that I could snap. There is so much pent up energy inside of me that if I do not do something to relieve it soon, I could explode. "Take your pants off and get on the bed," I say suddenly, the fight had me brimming with fire and now the thought of fucking that all away is turning me on so fucking much.

"Yes Ma'am," Monroe smiles and swiftly kicks off his boots, unbuckles his pants, slides them off then lays in the middle of one of the beds. I am not going to lie, I used to love our sessions together after those long jobs, just feeling the release of an orgasm over and over whilst letting all the heat of a good battle fade away. He stuffs a pillow under his head and just lays there as I remove my own boots and trousers then straddle him without even thinking things through fully. Instinctively I cover my fingers in my own saliva and place them between my thighs to make sure I am sufficiently lubricated then reposition Monroe's already rock hard cock to enable me to ease down on it.

"Oh fuck," the words slip from my lips as I settle fully, at least he was right about one thing, he does have a very sizeable cock and right now I feel so tight around him. As I accept how full my own pussy is, it makes me want to cum and the more I think about it, the more I want to just fuck him so hard that I forget everything else. It doesn't take me long to start to enjoy the fullness, so I close my eyes and ride him, forcing my hips forward as the burning in my core burns stronger. Monroe moves beneath me to match, each thrust getting harder and deeper, making me moan loudly as I feel the want to cum grow, that overwhelming need to orgasm so hard that all my cares and frustrations vanish so I can relax in the after glow.

"Mmmmm," Monroe groans as I feel his fingers dig in to my thighs, the pain being caused by the strong grip just turning me on more. I open my eyes and look down at him, placing one hand on his torso so I can go harder, as thought something purely primal inside of me has taken over and this is the only thing that can satisfy its needs. My hand goes between us as my fingers rub my clit, it is throbbing, the sensations already so pleasurable that I am struggling to breath, but there is no way I would slow down, I want to be fucked so hard I lose my mind. The more Monroe smiles up at me, the more I am becoming agitated with him though. I don't know what it is, I am having fun, I know I am going to cum soon, but he is just laying there, not doing anything particularly strenuous and I think that is what is annoying. I grab his right hand and move it to my clit, allowing him to take over teasing it, so I can cum but after only a few seconds he moves his hand away back to my thigh, his grip pulling my hips forward more forcefully and it is at that moment that I realise what he is doing. This was not about me having pleasure, this was about him getting a release, so he is now just focused on him being able to cum. If I was not so horny now I would stop and tell him to fuck off but instead I resume my playing more, almost making this now a race to the finish line which seems to falter slightly as Monroe leaves go of my thighs and places his hands behind his head to relax back and let me do all the work. I try to forget about him and just focus on me, how my body feels, how the fire is threatening to explode and my mind wanders to my life in the human world, the sexual experiences I have had, the amazing orgasms, the passion and heat, the pure adrenaline you feel when you are with a partner who makes you feel special, makes you feel alive. The one major difference between a human and a demon, their soul shines with life and love.

"Fuck!" I moan as I feel myself about to cum, that couple of seconds before hand when you know it is about to happen and it is too late to stop so I ready myself, playing with my clit faster to make it explosive and then it happens, that sensation when all the playing accumulates in to one moment of pure pleasurable bliss. The joint orgasm from deep in my pussy and my clit take over, my legs are shaking as I try my best to keep going, to prolong the feelings I am giving myself until they slowly subside and I can slow down. My chest is heaving as I open my eyes again and look down to Monroe, just still laying there, unmoving with his dick still inside me and a smug grin on his face.

"So do you want to grab us some food and a couple drinks? I am starving," Monroe says bluntly and I just stare blankly at him. Did he seriously just do the human equivalent of a man asking a woman to go make him a sandwich after sex? "I am sure Esmera mentioned making you something special so I will have some of that as well?"

"Are you taking the fucking piss?" I snap at him, totally bewildered. "I am not now, nor have I ever been your fucking servant so if you want something you can get up off your lazy arse and get it yourself."

"Lazy? Me?" He replies confused.

"Yes you. I don't know what or who you have been dicking down in the last couple of hundred years but I certainly do not remember sex with you being compared to fucking a corpse."

"You loved taking control and using my cock for your pleasure, and I quite enjoy letting you," he grins but it just pisses me off more.

"Where was the heat? The intensity, the passion?" I ask as he sits up slightly on his elbows as he realises I am not joking.

"Passion? Who the fuck wants passion?" he scoffs back. "All that mushy love making shit has no place in Hell. We drink, fight and fuck, that is what we have always done, that is who we are."

"It is not who I am any more," the words come out truthfully. "I don't want to just drink, fight and fuck, I want to really live, to appreciate the wonders that exist." He stares at me for a moment before he speaks again.

"Hmmm... Is this to do with that angel?" he asks and I am taken aback by it. "You do know that angels are all pussy ass bitches of God, right? Bet they are all virgins and never even busted a nut before. And that one who I sent your way with the key looks like one of those lovey dovey kiss ass types, I saw the way he looked at you when we left, like a fucking love sick puppy all teary eyes and..."
Something just snaps and before I realise what I did, I punch Monroe so hard square in the face that my knuckles burn and his face has a nice outline of my fist over his right eye which will leave a bruise tomorrow. "I am going to take that as a yes then?" He beams at me which just frustrates me more so I climb off him and

swiftly get dressed as he remains laying on the bed. I can not blame him, this is who he has always been, a cocky fucker with no filter when he actually has something to say, and because I was exactly the same back in the day things between us just worked. But the more I am around demons, the more I really see, or maybe it is just the fact of being back in Hell that makes me fully realise how much I did change, quite a bit and that there is lot more in my life than just a couple of drinks and a quick fuck to fight for. I need to fight for the mortal world, I need to fight for life and not just my own.

"You need to leave," I say as I put my boots back on.

"Why? What will happen if I don't," Monroe teases which makes me stop, sigh deeply and turn around to look him in the eye.

"Because if you do not leave this room right now, I will fucking shove my fist so far up your arse I will be able to poke you in the eye," Monroe laughs at my words but moves to get up any way. He is purposefully going too slow just to wind me up more so I grab him by the arm and force him towards the door, briefly holding him in place whilst I open it then push him on to the landing and slam it in his face. Taking a deep breath to try to calm myself down I hold it for a second before a knock distracts me and again I sigh deeply.

"Can I at least have some pants?" Monroe laughs from outside. I grab his pants and boots, open the door and before he can say anything else I shove them in to his chest then slam the door for a second time. I have more important things to think about now than being scared of being killed or how much of a bunch of cunts pretty much every demon in Hell is, now I have to think about someone other than myself, and when I say someone, I mean the entire human race.

Chapter Sixteen

I tossed and turned all night, trying to plan out every scenario possible in my head to ensure I was ready to face my mother and not run in to anything unexpected. I wanted to be fully prepared, but every outcome resulted the same way. Me being alone, surrounded by unknown enemies and Lilith being far to strong to do anything to, then ultimately me dying and fading to not exist when the entirety of the universe ends.

Heading down the stairs in to the bar below, the place is noticeably quieter than last night, there are still people in here drinking and enjoying the female entertainment, even though this is a 24/7 kind of dive, this early morning start means most people are asleep or too drunk to notice me.

"Did you sleep well?" Esmera smiles as she sees me come down the stairs, I do think about lying to her again but with everything going on around me I would rather not distance myself more from the people I am finding myself caring about, and it is not like I have too many friends anyway.

"Not really, too much in my head to rest," Esmera smiles more, knowing that any other time I would have told her the opposite. "Has he been there all night?" I ask and nod towards a booth against the far wall, Monroe is asleep huddled up on the bench, the table top in front of him covered in empty ale glasses and two semi clothed working girls are snuggled in to him. I am going to assume that his night of fun and frolics did not end when I threw him out of the room after we fucked...

well, I say we. I did all the work.

"Yes, he never changes does he?" she chuckles then a look of uncertainty comes over her face. "Whatever happens today, please know that I will be praying for you. And at least if the worst does happen... we will all face that part together." I just nod, not quite knowing what to say before forcing a smile at her and heading over to Monroe. I kick his boots that are hanging over the edge of the bench which makes him stir, he mumbles something about letting him sleep under his breath, but I don't have the time or the patience for him this morning.

"It's time," I say bluntly as he opens his eyes, takes in my words then nods in understanding. It takes him a minute to wake up and get his bearings, saying his thanks to the girls which kept him company last night, then before I know it we are on the road, and heading for my fathers castle. I know for certain that Lilith will have spent the night gaining entry, pushing her way through each of the inner circles. Her growing army clashing with my fathers, resulting in many deaths and a lot of destruction. I have no doubt in my mind that she will find her way inside eventually but unlike her, I do not need to force entry or even go through the front doors. "I think this is close enough for a moment," I finally speak again after the silent walk. We are stood just at the edge of what is the bridge that leads across the river of fire that surrounds the inner kingdom like a moat. The air is thick with stale, thick smoke that rises from the river that oozes and moves like lava, incinerating anything it touches. More than a few demons have met their demise over the years from getting a little too merry then slipping in to the scorching waves below. I did think that our journey would be more eventful, especially walking through the little villages to get here, but everything is still, as though everyone knew who was coming and fled in fear.

At the other side of the bridge is the looming castle that I once called my home, stood high above the few scattered buildings and houses below, all the structures built in to the ancient jagged mountain, every piece of stone on the castle carved in intricate patterns detailing all of the different torture techniques that could be used to torment the lost souls which wrap around the walls. The bricks a deep blood red with cracks that shine as though actual flames dance through it, and the steps that lead up to the grand entrance which are usually protected by the kings guards, are covered in the lifeless corpses of the warriors that they once were, their blood now staining the ground that they gave their life to defend. In the distance you can hear the shrill cries of agony coming from the pits below the surface, the tormented souls that spend eternity here after they die just left to rot as I assume the wardens are now too busy fighting, whichever side they chose to be on. This entire area would usually be brimming with people, demons going in and out of the castle to follow orders or work, mingling in the streets to gossip or chat about their latest victory, but today is a first even for me, it is eerily deserted. Or at least it will be until Lilith calls forth the rest of her legions of soldiers.

"It looks like she has made it inside," Monroe states the obvious quietly as he takes in the scene before us. "I have never been in the throne room before, will it be easy for her to locate?"

"I hope not," I sigh whilst thinking. "I know she is my mother, but I am unsure how close they were as a couple. To get to the throne room is like navigating a maze, visitors that are summoned to stand in front of my father are usually led there by a guide, one who would never betray my father and lead his enemies to him. So at least I know it will slow her down." Monroe follows me as we cautiously head across the iron and wood bridge then approach the front entrance, on a normal day it is intimidating, the edges lined with skulls of my fathers enemies that have now become more of a decoration, so many in fact that most of the castle corridors are lined with stacks of them, to show his strength. Monroe starts up the steps, readying himself for any resistance he might face as we will probably walk straight in to Lilith's men, but he pauses as he notices that I walk straight past and make my way to the side of the structure where there is a very narrow gap in the stone. He doesn't say anything as he watches me disappear in to the small crack a couple of meters deep then hoist myself up to navigate the gagged stones above, climbing a good 20 foot of the ground then take the roughly laid out pathway that curves up further and around the back at a steep incline, far away from the normal entrance that everyone else, including my father would take.

"Hey, wait up," I hear Monroe call after me as he climbs the steep rocks that overlook the fiery depths below, plunging like a cliff edge to certain death if one was to lose their footing and slip. To an outsider this would just look like any other part of the mountain that encases my fathers castle, but to me this was my secret entrance that I made to ensure I did not have to run in to any members of my family whilst I lived here, I don't even think my father knows about it, or if he does, he never said anything or closed it off. "How far up are you taking me?" He calls again which just makes me smile as I haul my ass up and over an 8 foot tall boulder that seams to close off any further possible route.

"What's wrong? Are you getting too old for such physical exertion?" I tease then see him smile and shake his head before following me further. After a couple more minutes, the ground starts to even out and we emerge on to a solid path that runs alongside a sheer vertical drop at the very back of the castle. "It's just through here," I direct then slip between an opening in the stone, which is hardly noticeable to the naked eye, and straight in to a dimly lit corridor, the only light coming from sparsely placed lanterns and the odd candle scattering around the walls. Breathing deeply, I spend a moment to get used to the fact that I am back home for the first time in longer than I can even remember, whilst I wait for Monroe to catch up.

"The front door with all the dead bodies might have been easier than that," Monroe says, slightly out of breath as he comes to stand beside me then glances up and down the corridor. It is all exposed stone, dark and strangely calming with circular windows every so often so that you can see the view outside. Echoing through the hallways we can hear the fighting continuing as Lilith and her army move on the throne room, eliminating anyone in their path but first I have something else I need to do, and a promise to fulfil. We silently move in the shadows in the opposite direction to the noise, Monroe doesn't question where I am going, he will probably already know how much shit that will be in my head just with being back here again, so he remains silent. After a few minutes and lots of deserted twists and turns, the décor starts to change, as though we are now in a forgotten part of the castle, no lanterns to light our way, the walls bare and void of any sign of life, so I push forward in darkness, almost counting my steps as I have walked this route many times, until I come to what I know to be a small light wood door. The handle is a freezing cold metal, it may be dark but I know exactly where I am and what lies on the other side. The handle clicks as I turn it then slowly push it open, reaching to the wall on the left and pushing a stone button which emits a sizzling sound before several flaming lanterns light simultaneously all around the small room, I know I am home. After a few moments my eyes adjust and I wander inside fully, taking in the sight before me, the bed, covered in thick fluffy purple and red blankets, the small wardrobe in the far corner filled with handmade clothes, the walls bare brick covered with multiple small paintings of flowers and animals that had been seen in books over the years that I was raised here, in an attempt to brighten the room. On the right hand side is a small window, barely big enough to even see out of but from which I know overlooks the molten river below that makes the air rise up and give the sky a moody red glow, and on the windowsill, displayed as though they are precious gems are several rocks of unusual shapes that make me smile as I see them. It wasn't like I had any toys to play with like a normal child does nowadays, so I sought my own entertainment in the limited beauty and wonders I found in the world around me, and from what I read in the many books that filled the library halls, I knew there was more to see than rotting skulls and death.

"Shouldn't we be finding the throne room?" Monroe says cautiously behind me as he stands and looks around at everything but I ignore him and gently run my fingertips over the stones, remembering where I found them and what they used to mean to me when I was all alone in here with just my thoughts.

"We... are not going anywhere," I reply off handedly. "I, as in myself, am going to find the throne room, you are taking this and heading back to the mortal world to fulfil my promise." Monroe shakes his head at my words as I turn and hold out the small black rock that sparkles with red as it catches the light. "Please Monroe," I say very seriously. "Over all the years we have known each other, I have never asked you for anything as important as what I am begging you to do now." After a moment of silence he carefully takes the rock from me and inspects it in his hand.

"Is this brimstone?" he asks and I nod to confirm it. "What do you need me to do?"

"Follow the way I brought you in, once you are out and across the bridge I need you to portal back to find Mitch and Jake," he snorts as I mention them but does not interrupt me. "I made a promise to Jake that I would do everything I could to get this to him before it is too late and the world ends... Please?" Monroe sighs and nods before shoving the rock in his pocket then turning to leave, just as he gets to the door he stops and glances back over his shoulder.

"Moon?" he says with actual emotion in his voice, something that I do not recall ever hearing from him before. "If the worst happens... It was nice to call you my friend," he forces a small tight smile then disappears from the doorway and back in to the darkness, his footsteps quickly fading away leaving me alone in my bedroom. It feels very surreal, being back here, the place where I was teased, belittled and felt so much like an outsider. My bedroom was my sanctuary, my safe place, the only room in the entire kingdom where I felt I could be myself... Then like a brick to the face everything catches up with me and reminds me what I came here to do, I slam closed my bedroom door then swiftly push the small wardrobe to one side, it is surprisingly heavy but after a moment it is far enough out of my way to see the small hole in the wall behind it that has been smashed through the brick. I crawl along the little make shift passageway on my hands and knees, then after just a minute I come to what looks like a dead end in the old, bug filled tunnel, so I swing my legs around till I am on my backside then forcefully kick my feet directly in the wall that I am faced with, it takes me a couple of tries but eventually the frail stone starts to crumble away and I slip through the hole and in to the room below. I land on my feet directly behind a large cabinet that impedes my view to the rest of the area, but I know where I am, this was just one of the many secret passageways I had to enable me to get around the castle and avoid having to talk to or even see my family.

Squeezing out via the very small gap at the side of the cabinet, I finally see where I am. The room is dim but every couple of meters candles burn in holders on the walls, the floor shines and is made from pure gold, the walls a dark black marble and the room itself is quite narrow but long with what looks like a walkway straight up the middle. Thinking back, I don't even know if the Sins have ever set foot in this room, fathers closest allies have never been allowed to enter here and I only stumbled on it by accident one night after a very tough day of being hit with rocks by my so called siblings. At either side of the walkway sits piles of treasures, gold, precious stones and much more, weaponry made of brimstone which has the potential to kill the strongest of foe, and that is not seen outside of Hell. Legend has it that brimstone, when forged in the fires can create blades so powerful that it could even kill a God... which is probably bullshit, but I do know that it holds certain properties that can restrict strength and power, sort of like an immortals kryptonite. That is why is never leaves Hell, in the wrong hands it could be used against my father. Then at the far side is a marble plinth with a large old ratty ass book on top of it, my fathers pride and joy. It is closed but I have flicked through it a couple of times in the past, not something that interested me too much as it contains magic and forces that are controlled by mortals in the human world. It is at least a foot thick and two foot tall, the front cover adorned with the symbol of an inverted pentagram in silver which is almost scorched in to the old black leather. I over heard my father once call it the Dark Grimoire, one of his most prized possessions as it contains the names of his most loyal disciples who follow the dark path of witchcraft, and also has a mortal realm equivalent that sits in the church of their Dark Lord and protected by some human self proclaimed High Priestess. I always thought the book was sort of like a collection of whores and bitches who my father liked to fuck in exchange for giving them some shitty ass power to make a feather levitate, some of whom were entertainingly wiped out during the witch trials. I am not exactly fond of witches, a lot of bad blood in the past and I have never met one that I actually liked, luckily they are quite rare around where I live above ground so I have not had the displeasure in a very long time.

Above the book, hanging on the wall, secured only by two iron nails that it rests on, is a very insignificant looking crown, entwined black metal that looks quite familiar to the crown of thorns that Jesus Christ himself has been depicted wearing, but this one has tiny flicks of gold running throughout, but which I don't think has ever moved from its place on that wall in my entire life. Memories are strange things, but ones which can be distracting so I give my head a shake, shift the Grimoire, dumping it on the floor out of the way and hoist myself up on top of its plinth, the marble rocks slightly under my weight but I balance enough to be able to reach up towards the ceiling and climb in to the air duct above.

More crawling is taking its toll on my knees, making them sore even through my trousers but that slight inconvenience is not going to stop me as I approach another air duct and slip through it, before carefully and as quietly as possible lowering myself down then dropping to the floor, trying not to make a sound as I can hear voices quite close by.

"Have you found him yet?" The distinct and very recognisable voice of Lilith says with disgust. I am currently hiding from sight behind one of the many large statues that line the walls of the main area in the throne room, each one a larger than life replica of the most infamous demons that ever lived. The ceiling is high and arches above us, the room is around half the size of a football pitch with black carved walls depicting the journey of the King of Hell over the years. Dark stone that shows my fathers transition from angel of God to ruler of tormented souls, on one side you see him fall from grace, on the other you see the horned demon surrounded by his naked disciples, dancing on the broken souls of humanity below. At the far side, opposite the large double doors are a lot of steps that lead up to my fathers throne, it is overly large, far too grand for any king, living or dead, made of gold and marble. And the way it sits at the top of the flight of golden stairs as though anyone who claims it will over look all the peasants below, showing the world who is truly in charge, is very egotistical. But from my hiding spot right now behind a black marble statue of Astaroth, I can not see much, so all I can do for now is listen.

"No Ma'am," says a male voice in return to her question. "We are sweeping all the open areas now looking for him and have all the exits and entrances blocked so he can not escape." Even though I can not see much, I know that they are not the only two people in the room, but I am not sure how many.

"I need him found now," Lilith replies firmly with anger in her voice. "I can not claim my throne unless he is either dead or abdicates, and I sure did not come this far to be eluded by him now." She pauses for a moment and takes a deep breath to compose herself. "How about the last two Sins, have they been disposed of?"

"Not yet Ma'am," comes the man's reply and then Lilith sighing deeply with frustration straight after. "Although we did receive word late last night that Pride was spotted in a bar on the outskirts of the wastelands. Juro took a few men to capture him but never returned, upon an inspection of the property a little while ago, no trace of Juro was found and none of the locals were willing to talk, although there were rumours of a fight and the presence of a woman known only by the name of Moon." There is a moment of silence before anyone speaks again.

"A woman?" Lilith asks as she thinks. "The name Moon is familiar to me, I have heard of it spoken before in this land but I always thought she was man," again there is another silence then she laughs slightly. "It can not possibly be a coincidence, so now I am left to wonder if this woman known as Moon has the first name of Rosa."

"That is something I can not confirm at the moment Ma'am, but I can have some men look in to that and..."

"No," Lilith stops him. "I do not think that is necessary. If I am correct then Juro is dead, Pride has slipped away and this mystery woman will more than likely turn up here soon, so be prepared for confrontation and reinforce the front entrance... I want to focus solely on getting my throne and finding..." her words are cut short when the large double doors at the far side of the room burst open, the noise echoing around the high ceilings. "On finding him," Lilith says happily as the sounds of a major scuffle drowns everything else out, but even though I can not see, I know who she is talking about, which makes my heart sink. "Finally, my guest of honour has arrived."

"Tell your men to unhand me," my father says loudly and for a moment I wonder who has hold of him, surely he is stronger than any of the normal demons that Lilith has with her. He should be able to just kill them all on the spot if he is close enough.

"Very well," Lilith replies, and I try to move slightly to get a better view, I need to see what is happening instead of staring at the marble arse of Astaroth. "I did not think that you would run away and hide from me."

"I was not hiding from you, Lilith, your men are just really shit at finding things," Lucifer replies casually. Now that I have moved, I can make out a small

221

section of the room through the gap in the legs of the statue. My father is standing firm, not a single sign of a struggle on him in a crisp navy blue suit that he is wearing and is currently straightening the collar of the white shirt underneath, his blond hair slicked back and a very out of place smirk on his face, given the current situation. Behind him blocking the exit to the doorway is around 10 demons, all human form and all armed, plus they are strong, I can not sense their souls at all from this distance so they must be old and buried deep. Opposite my father, around 10 meters away is Lilith, dressed in a long white gown that hugs her curves perfectly and looks fit for a queen, adorned with crystals that drip across the top of the sleeves with a high collar partially hidden by the loose waves of her raven hair. Behind Lilith is a mixture of men, some I recognise to be soldiers of my father, or ex soldiers now, others are the Generals who lead a few of the 40 legions that Astaroth ruled over, at least 5 possibly 6 of them that I can see from here, most of them beasts in their own right. Astaroth had 40 legions of warriors, that means so does Lilith if she had control of him, so possibly 40 Generals somewhere close by. In total I would give a conservative guess at probably 50 people in the throne room right now, and there is only me that is currently on my fathers side. Facing Astaroth one on one was tough enough, but facing a number of his ugly ass Generals, all with very high ranked speciality skill sets whilst surrounded by soldiers may be near impossible. If I was in the mortal realm and this was a room full of humans, I could just storm them all now and reap their souls, but there is not a soul reaper alive that could touch the majority of the demons in here now, soul reaping is a predominantly human thing, which does not help me much now, when faced with enemies far more monster than anything else.

"Never mind, you are here now and right on time," Lilith smiles wildly, takes a deep breath then turns to look up at the throne, towering above her men. "You know what it is I want, I had hoped that the slaughter of your children may have hurried things along a little, encouraged you to relinquish power sooner, rather than me having to force the Veil to fall in order for you to notice me again."

"I never stopped noticing you, Lilith, you are always on my mind, consuming my thoughts with the days gone by and the pure power that ran through your veins," my father replies whilst staring at her. "I craved you for centuries, wanted nothing more than a wife to rule by my side, but instead that was not enough for you, you wanted God himself to bow at your feet, and because you could not get that, you decided to end everything." Lilith smiles at his words.

"Yes, that is correct," then she scowls slightly before she continues. "You craved me so much that you quickly replaced me with your magical human whores. You built yourself a harem of love sick witches that worship the ground you walk on in an attempt to feel what we once had. But I do not live in the past, Lucifer, I do not miss the primal passion that we shared, I live for the future, and the future is glorious nothingness." The whole room is silent, not a single person moves or speaks, but each and every one of them are ready to move or fight on

Lilith's word.

"So," my father says loudly with a chuckle. "I think that is enough talking, let us get this over with, shall we?"

"I could not agree more," Lilith encourages then waits for my father to speak again. He casually looks around the room, all the faces staring at him then smiles again.

"Alright," he laughs. "I, Lucifer Morningstar, the first and true ruler, King of the seven circles, fallen angel extraordinaire and devilishly hansom Lord of darkness, hereby renounce my claim to the throne of Hell and allow for a new Queen to take my place." As soon as my father stops speaking, Lilith laughs with joyful mania then quickly turns, the men behind her part to allow her through as she starts to ascend the steps to the throne, and with each step she takes the more my heart starts to pound. I glance to my father who just stands there, he casually crosses his arms but apart from that he does nothing. Is he not even going to attempt to stop her? He didn't even put up a fight, almost as though he wanted this to happen all along, that he wanted to step aside and let Lilith take control then destroy everything. But I did not go though all that shit to just stand by and watch the world burn now, even if I do get myself killed, at least I can die with the knowledge that I tried my best. Lilith reaches the top of the steps and takes a moment to look at the glowing gold and marble seat before her before turning around, giving one last smile to Lucifer below and goes to sit.

"STOP!" I almost scream as I leave my hiding spot and run in to the middle of the room, instantly all of the demon soldiers swarm forward as one as I stare up at Lilith.

"Wait!" she commands them and they pause as she almost hovers over the seat ready to claim her place then slowly stands back up fully and stares me dead in the eye, thinking carefully about her words before she speaks to me again. My father stands silent a couple of meters behind me, I don't even turn around to look at him, his actions disgust me, instead I focus on Lilith. "Hello again," she says politely with a distinct air of calm. "I am glad that this time that we meet, I actually know exactly who you are, Miss Rosa Moon," she smirks. "Now I finally understand why you were so adamant on trying to protect the Veil from falling, unfortunately you failed in your mission. But at least now you will have a front row seat to see exactly what your pathetic attempts to stop me, have done." She gives me a small nod then goes to sit down again before I can think of a response. Knowing that she needs to be stopped before it is too late, I try to run forward to get to her but the soldiers pounce on me in one solid wave of bodies, I don't have time to fight them off so I try to just push through but in the gap between the many arms now holding me back and clawing at my clothing to keep their grip, I can not do anything but watch Lilith take the throne. A blow to the back of my head makes my knees buckle then before I know it, I find myself pinned down on the ground, the weight of possibly 10 men piling on top of me as I try to claw my way forward, my fingers desperately trying to dig in to the solid stone floor. I need to get to her, but I can't move. I manage to twist around to free my arms enough to get in a few really good punches then squirm my way on to my back, I take a deep breath, close my eyes and let my inner demon free. If I can not reap their souls, then I will burn them all alive.

Hell fire bursts out of me, throwing the men that are on top of me away with such force that I hear their bodies smash in to the walls of the hall, those still close enough to be within touching distance of me start to scream in agony as the flames consume them, burning the flesh from their bones and allowing me the opportunity to get back to my feet before the heat eases. As I stand I see a few men try to get to me, forcing their way through the fire that burns brightly in a circle all around me on the floor for a good couple of meters. There are two of Astaroth's Generals making there way towards me with them, seemingly unaffected by the flames due to their many years of fierce battles and time spent in the wastelands, which tells me that I need a weapon instead, for them the fire is not enough. The all too familiar tingle of electric shoots across my palms and before I even wait for the full form of my sickles to take shape, I swing my arms then hear the loud clash of metal as my weapons are counteracted by theirs, thankfully the force of it sends them back a few feet so I can ready for another attack, but as I do, I glance up and watch Lilith sit fully on the throne. I am not the only one who notices as everyone else stops, no one moves, they all just watch the new Queen take her place. She closes her eyes and inhales deeply as she revels in the fact that she has finally fulfilled her life's plan, and my heart sinks, knowing that I am too late to stop her. Everyone in the room falls silent, their eyes fixated above to see what happens next as the new ruler of Hell takes control, even I forget what I was doing and just stand, helpless as my Hell fire fades, now knowing the end of the world is imminent.

After a moment of me holding my breath and assuming everything around me will implode, Lilith opens her eyes again, glances around the many faces watching her with intrigue and anticipation, then scowls back down at my father, clearly very unhappy. Although I do admit, I also thought that there would be more of a moment, fireworks or a fan fair maybe to announce the new Queen. But instead the air is deathly silent and I am now not actually sure that what I just witnessed worked at all.

"What did you do, Lucifer?" Lilith snarls through gritted teeth and just stares at him, but after a moment I hear him laugh to himself then he steps forward, gently places his hand on my shoulder as though to reassure me, then smirks as I look up at him, look up at my father and see the man I had been avoiding for most of my life seem to actually care about me.

"My dear Lilith," he says smugly. "Did you really think that it was going to be that easy?" Lilith stares daggers at him as she slowly stands up and starts to descend the steps back towards him. "That I was just going to stand by and let you destroy my legacy?"

"Tell me what you did?" she says with so much anger that I can see her hands shake from here. "Give me... my throne," she snaps and for the first time I can feel her unbridled power almost ooze from her skin. There is a very clear uneasiness amongst the men that now surround my father and me, all of them like coiled springs ready to go off and come for the kill.

"If you want the throne, then the only way I would ever willingly give it to you is when you prise it out of my cold, dead hands," my father says with such strength that it rocks even me to my core. I suddenly feel so insignificant, standing between two unimaginable forces of nature, the likes of which I have never encountered before. The king of Hell and the first woman ever created, it is intimidating to say the least, but for the first time in my life, I don't feel like the odd one out, I fell like I belong.

"If the only way for me to claim the throne is for you to be dead," Lilith snarls. "Then I am sure that I can arrange that for you." She flicks her hand and the two Generals who attacked me step forward to confront us again so I ready my stance for a fight, strengthening my grip on my weapons, but I become very confused when my father moves quickly, swooping in front of me, blocking the oncoming danger as if trying to protect me. I am clearly not the only one who notices the gesture as Lilith narrows her eyes as she thinks.

"I knew there had to be more to this little charade that you are playing," she says as she slowly approaches my father, the Generals at either side of her just waiting for the command to strike. Peering over my fathers shoulder I see Lilith stop only a foot in front of him, close enough to touch him if she wanted and definitely close enough to see the pure hatred in her eyes. "I have never seen you protect anyone but yourself, Lucifer. So I can only imagine that what I am seeing now, is something new, something you never even showed me... You care for the bitch, love her even?" She stares at my father but he does not reply. Eventually she loses her forced calm and screams at him. "ANSWER ME!" Her words echo around the room then my father sighs deeply before speaking.

"Yes, Lilith, I care deeply for the girl," he says and I just stand, unsure of what to do or say. "You could even say that at one point I made a very difficult choice, and I chose my love for her over any feelings I ever had for you." There is a moment of absolute silence, I don't even think a single person in the entire room is actually breathing, everyone knowing the impact of the words my father has just spoken to Lilith will result is a massive fall out.

I don't even see it happen, Lilith lunges forward, her hands going straight for my fathers throat, the force sends him to the ground and pushes me back as he collides with me. I stumble then fall on my arse, my sickles slipping from my hands and scattering away from me as I see Lilith mount my father, letting her anger get the better of her as they tussle on the ground, but as I look around the room I notice that her soldiers are not sure what is going on, do they fight? Do they help her? We all just watch them both having some childish play ground fight in the middle of the floor, as though all reason or common sense has abandoned them. There is hair pulling and screaming, not the sight you would expect from two of the most powerful beings that live. I slowly and very cautiously stand up, then go to reach for the sickle closest to me that was dropped when I fell, the other has skid across the floor and is a few meters away, but all at once every eye in the room moves back to me then down to the weapon that I need to arm myself with and I pause, as they now realise that I am just stood here, vulnerable, unarmed and I know that I am now in big trouble.

"Erm... hi," I say then move quickly. As soon as my hand touches the hilt, they pounce on me, sweeping me off my feet and sending me back to the ground hard, smashing the back of my skull off the stone and momentarily leaving me dazed. My ears are ringing, my eyes are blurred and all I can focus on is the pounding in my head, I feel myself take another hit, possibly a boot to the temple, then everything around me goes black.

The next thing I hear is lots of shouting, screams of agony, the clash of weaponry then hands dragging me across the floor. I force my eyes open as I am roughly sat propped up against the wall then see my father in front of me, but he is not pristine and happy like before, he is covered in soot as though from a fire, his hair messy and his face... his face is covered in blood, red blood like mine, and which I have never seen from him before. "You are bleeding," I force out as I try to shake the dizziness from that blow, I can't even concentrate on healing fast enough so I have no choice than to get used to the feeling of my own blood dripping down the back of my neck for now.

"Reinforcements arrived, some of my men are holding them back for now, but soon they will be overpowered," he says as he glances around slightly to keep an eye on what is going on behind him. We are partially shielded from the fighting now taking place, I am going guess at some point after I hit my head and blacked out, reinforcements arrived and clashed with Lilith's men. "I tried to keep her talking for as long as I could before my men made it through their barriers but the legions no longer bow to me, I have no control after Astaroth betrayed me."

"How are you bleeding?" I say confused as I reach up and touch my fathers face, the warm fresh blood coating my fingertips as I make sure that what I am seeing is actually real. "I have never seen you bleed. You should not..."

"Don't concern yourself with such things," he stops me, takes a hold of my hand and removes it from his face before laughing to himself slightly. "I should have know after I used my home made brimstone weapons on a God that it was not a good idea to keep them around when she was on her way here. If they could hurt him then it is quite obvious they could do damage to me as well, but I..."

"A God?" I ask confused. "The brimstone weapons? What are you..."

"Never mind," he stops me again, then sighs. "I will do everything I can to keep Lilith occupied, we need to ensure that she does not claim power." I nod in understanding then blink away the fading dizziness, it feels as though my head wound is healing now so my mind is clearing. "We both know fully the cost if she becomes Queen." I nod and push myself up from the floor, my father stands up and just watches me for a moment which starts to make me uncomfortable. "You need to..."

"I know what I need to do," I interrupt him and scan the area to try to find my weapons, even though I was briefly knocked unconscious, I did not recall them, so I must have dropped them instead. There are too many people in the middle of the throne room to see anything, the sound of blades clashing, the floor covered black spilt blood and the loud shouting of Lilith barking orders to her soldiers make for a noisy scene. "I will do everything in my power to protect the throne."

"No, forget the throne," my father replies and suddenly becomes deadly serious. "The throne doesn't matter, it is no more than than a glorified lump of gold."

"But I..." I try to protest but he grabs my shoulder and forces me to look at him, to make sure I am fully hearing what he has to say.

"Listen to me," he says, getting my full attention. "You do not need to protect the throne, you, my child, my beautiful Alexis... you need to protect the crown."

"I don't know what that means, is it not the same thing?" I ask and my father goes to answer but as he does a large explosion rings out, shaking the entire throne room. All the people that were occupied fighting over the far side of the hall are thrown through the air, creating carnage as large rocks fall from the ceiling as it cracks then crashes to the ground, hitting a few more men on the way down. But the amount of bodies fighting mean I can not tell who is on my fathers side or who fights for Lilith, so any sort of plan involving me trying to incinerate everyone is not going to work in case I wipe out the backup, plus the mixture of men is sending my senses in to meltdown. I can feel some souls, then others are too hidden, but I do not know who is who. My father regains his footing then speaks again.

"Do you understand what I am saying?" he asks and I nod, even though I have no clue at all. "Protect the crown, protect it with your life," just as he finishes his sentence two soldiers approach him from behind, I watch him as he swiftly turns around, delivers a devastating uppercut to the guy on the left, breaking his jaw so bad I can hear the crunch of bones from here then sending him to the floor. The second guy lunges forward with a black stone dagger, my father grabs his outstretched wrist then twists it back so far that it points in the opposite direction, the soldier cries out in agony as it dislocates then his hand is forced towards him, sending his own blade deep in to this chest. The soldier drops to the floor dead then without looking back, my father runs directly in to the action to fight alongside his men.

I stand for a moment, trying to work out what he told me to do, but all I can think about is everyone else fighting and I know that I can't just stand by any longer. Glancing out from my cover I spot one of my sickles laying on the ground, then just as I think about running out to get it, it is kicked away by one of the men fighting against my father, I watch it shoot across the stone before disappearing again in to the sea of soldiers. I know I am good at fighting, but against an army I will not get far without being armed, so I suck it up and head in to the middle of the carnage to get what I need.

Running as fast as I can, I manage to dodge a couple of oncoming attacks then fall to my knees and almost slide under the legs of one of the Generals who fails to catch me as I move beneath him. Keeping low and under any ones line of sight, I spot my sickle then watch for a second time as it is kicked away from my grasp. Whilst I am trying to locate which direction it went in, a hand grabs my hair and yanks me backwards, my feet momentarily touch the ground before being thrown through the air and smashing in to one of the statues standing at the side, soon after I hit it, it topples over and slams in to the wall, the stone crumbling beneath its weight then I drop to the ground. A couple of ribs feel broken and my thigh is burning with pain, as I look down a large gash is very apparent probably due to the fake weaponry the statue I hit was carrying slicing through my flesh as I landed on it. Clutching my side I get myself back to my feet just in time to see the 8 foot tall brute that flung me through the air run at me and tackle me to the ground. He is on top of me in seconds, he is heavy and big, not as large as Astaroth was but clearly one of his Generals with skin that is a strange light green pearlescent colour, covered in scars that are stacked on top of each other, as though thousands of blades have cut him over the years. He wears armour that suggests a warrior and a partial helmet that reveals only half of his face that is singed and cracked with burns.

"Wow, you are one ugly mother fucker," I say up at him right before I see his fist come straight towards my face. I manage to get out of the way slightly as his knuckles connect with the stone literally millimetres to the side of my head which feels like a mini earthquake from the impact. He pulls his arm back to try again just as I see one of my elusive sickles whiz towards me as it has been kicked again so I reach out and grab it then waste no time in raising my weapon and slicing through the throat of the beast above me, making his black blood spill out all over me and then collapse on top, almost crushing me with his weight. It takes some effort but I manage to push him off and get back to my feet, there is distinct pain in my ribs but I know soon that it will ease with every passing second that it heals, a few minutes and I will be as good as new. Now that I have a weapon I am starting to feel so much better, so I look back at the mass of bodies fighting then go in swinging. I take a couple of them down fast, cutting through flesh as though there was nothing in my way but air then smile over to my father as he spends a second watching me fight, an actual look of admiration in his eyes for me, the same way Pride looked at me after I saved him. He has never look at me like this before, or if he ever has I never saw, maybe what he said about hiding me away from the world really was to protect me after all. He nods to acknowledge me and I smile back.

"MOON!" I turn on the spot as I hear my name screamed over the sounds of the fighting to see Lilith staring at me then she slowly smiles. "Catch!" I hardly have time to react before I see my other sickle hurtling through the air towards me, she threw it with such force that I can not formulate a plan as I dive backwards out of the way, then feel the sting of metal as my own weapon catches my right cheek. I hit the stone floor, landing flat on my back at the same time as my weapon lodges itself between the bricks in the wall above my head and I spend a dazed moment just looking up at it, fresh blood coating the edge of the blade which is unusual as I don't feel like the cut on my face went deep enough to bleed that much. Forcing myself to sit up, I have to pause for a moment to try to blink away an overwhelming dizziness, I don't recall hitting my head but it hurts as though I did and the bash to the back of my skull from earlier is throbbing again, actually worse than before. "Surprise!" I look up to see Lilith standing in front of me, she is still a couple of meters away and she does not try to attack me just yet, instead just watching, waiting to see what I do next, which is confusing as I don't understand her remark. She smiles wildly at me then holds up her left hand, her palm pointed towards me which is cut deeply then wiggles her fingers as though to wave at me. I don't understand what she is doing, but then I hear a weird sizzling noise, like water on electrics and I look around to see my sickle flicker, the soul energy faltering then it disappears. Not like fall to the ground and get lost, but just vanish as though it no longer exists, the glowing blade fades before my eyes as though I no longer have any control over it enough to keep it charged, and then it hits me. I reach up and touch the fresh cut on my cheek, the blood warm on my fingertips with no sign of healing at all and the injuries I had previously sustained gradually becoming more painful.

"What the fuck?" I say to myself as I am hit with immense pain in my ribs and a metallic taste in my mouth as though I have taken a punch to the face but none of this should be happening, I should just heal like I always do, not get worse. Unless...

"Let's see just what Lucifer's little whore is really made of," Lilith sneers before she bends down and grabs me by the throat then hoists me off the floor with so much strength that I just dangle there, my hands going instinctively to her wrist to get her off me, but I have no energy and all I succeed in doing is making her squeeze my windpipe harder until I can no longer breathe. "Pathetic," she smiles as I desperately struggle against her, tears starting to stream down my face as she raises her left hand to her mouth and licks her own blood from her palm which starts to heal, at the same time as I realise the blood on my blade was not my own. It was hers, which now means I am... "Mortals are so easy to kill," she stares in to my eyes as I kick my legs to get free but my feeble attempts do nothing but amuse her more. My entire body is panicking, knowing that I am now seconds from death,

I just didn't think I would die a mortal, I always imagined my last moments being in the middle of a battle and going out in a blaze of glory. Being made human by my own weapon was not even on my possibilities list, that is a stupid death, I really do not want it at all. "It has been nice meeting you again, Miss Rosa Moon." My eyes start to lose focus as my hands drop to my sides, I don't have any fight left in me, this is the end. My mother is about to kill me without even knowing who I am and then soon the rest of the world will be gone.

There is a blurred movement in front of me then the next thing I know I am on the floor in a heap, gasping for air as I see my father tackle Lilith to the floor, then a swarm of his men pounce on her to keep her at bay. She dropped me in the process and I land roughly before my father scrambles back to his feet and runs to pull me up. He grabs my arm to help me stand but my legs give way underneath me and I collapse back in to the wall, I am disorientated and have no idea where I am for a moment. All I can hear is Lilith screaming as she fights off the rebels.

"Look at me," my father says as my eyes roll in to the back of my skull and my head falls back against the stone. "Look at me!" he says more forcefully then shakes me to try to get my attention. "You need to get out of here, now. There is still time."

"Time for what? I am as good as dead," I force out as I feel blood in my mouth which makes me cough and splutter. The multiple hits I had already sustained from the fight and being flung around like a rag doll must not have been fully healed so when Lilith's blood made me human, all those nice injuries have stayed with me.

"No," he says to keep me on track. "You still have work to do, remember what I told you. Get out now whist she is distracted." I don't get a chance to respond before he drags me forward then pushes me towards the open doors to the throne room. I have no idea what to do, where to go or even what he is talking about. "GO NOW!" he shouts and I just nod then head for the exit, I hear Lilith call after me from behind as she tries to fight off my fathers men but I don't look back as I know my father will try his best to keep her at bay, so as soon as I get out of the hall I just run. My feet move instinctively, occasionally loosing my footing and hitting the odd wall or two, or trampling on the skulls that line the corridors but I know I need to recoup, think everything through and come up with some sort of plan, or at least figure out what to do until I die as there is no way I can possibly stop her or offer any help at all to my father if I am mortal, I can hardly even breathe now without my entire body being racked with pain, so how am I going to stop the end of the world. Last time I was made mortal it took two days to fully get back to being me, I definitely do not have that amount of time, so whatever I decide to do, I am doing it as a human.

There is no one following me as I stumble down the long dark corridor then almost fall back through the door to my bedroom, it was the only place I knew I would be safe as I try to understand what it is I need to do. I close the door behind me then stand for a moment to catch my breath as tears continue to fall uncontrollably down my face and my chest heaves, fear is slowly slipping in just like it did before and I don't know how to deal with all of this on my own. I have no plan, no option and no hope for the entirety of mankind. I can not stop the rising and I can not stop my mother from destroying everything... It's over.

    I take a deep breath and reach up to push the stone to illuminate the room when an arm wraps tightly around my waist, capturing me and almost picking me up off the floor, then another swiftly covers my mouth as I go to scream. I was sure I wasn't followed, but now I am sure that this is where I will die. The one place I thought I would be safe will be where I take my last breath.

Chapter Seventeen

I kick my legs frantically trying to escape the vice like grip that is holding me, desperation consuming me as I know if I am pretty much a mortal and human, that I can not fight any of Lilith's soldiers off me, and especially not when I am already injured and in so much pain.

"Shhh, hey calm down," a man's voice says gently behind me as I struggle more. "Rosa, it's OK, calm down, please," the voice is familiar and strangely soothing, not the kind of demanding tone that would come from someone trying to kill me, I do as he says and stop trying to fight against him then he carefully places my feet back on the floor and removes his hand from over my mouth. His skin smells like sugar cookies and I can't help but blush before I even turn around, but when I do he just stands smiling softly down at me.

"Mitch?" I say not even believing that I am seeing him standing in front of me. "Mitch," the smile beams across my face then I almost dive towards him, he wraps his arms around me and I just stay there for a moment, my eyes closed, safe and calm in his arms, feeling his warmth and a massive relief of not being alone. The overwhelming amount of emotions inside bubble up and tears flow freely from my eyes.

"Hey, are you alright," Mitch says as he looks at me full of concern then wipes the tears from my face. "Are you in pain? Is this blood yours?" I nod my head slightly before he continues. "I am going to assume you faced your mother and things didn't end well, but it's OK, you are safe now." I smile up at him more, his eyes captivating and gentle.

"I couldn't stop her, now I'm mortal again," I say up at him as my voice trembles slightly. "And the world has gone to shit," laughter slips out as I speak, not that everything is funny but because I never imagined that at the end of my life I would be thankful to have found an angel that I actually didn't hate. "From what I witnessed in the throne room, Lilith has considerably more men than my father, she controls the legions, soon his forces will be overpowered and he will be on his knees. It's over, we are now in the end of times." His thumb gently strokes across my cheek as I feel myself get lost in his eyes, those calming eyes that have a strange effect on me, no matter how bad I feel, they make me smile then a thought suddenly pops in to my head and I step back. "Wait! How are you... you can't be here," he looks a little embarrassed as I race through everything in my head. "An angel can not step foot in Hell, without... You would be powerless, your wings would..."

"Shhhh," he tries to sooth me as panic takes hold again so he pulls me in close and just holds me, my head against his chest. "It's OK, I am fine," we stand in silence for a moment as I begin to enjoy having him so close to me again, and I smile because I actually missed him. I run my hands slowly across his back, just feeling him again and he tenses up instantly, groaning in my ear with pain. "It's nothing," he says quickly as though knowing that I will panic, but I need to know what is wrong. He watches me silently as I carefully move to lift up the back of his t-shirt to find what is causing his discomfort then freeze as my eyes see his back. On his shoulder blades, exactly where his wings would form are large deep scorch marks, the slight smell of melted flesh still lingers on them and as I run my fingertips across the skin around the blackened and bloodied marks, I can still feel the heat from the fire that burned away his faith. "Listen, I know it looks like I fucked up coming here," he says softly as he turns around to look at me again, but I just remain still, my heart hurting for what he has done to himself. "I no longer have my wings, I have tainted my soul and I don't think I have any sort of power now at all. But being an angel was something I was willing to sacrifice if it meant spending my last moments alive with the person that I have found myself caring about more than life itself." I look up at him as I take in his words, his soft smile melts me inside and in all my long life, I can categorically say that I have never felt the way I do now about anyone else before. He takes hold of my hand and holds it on his chest as he gazes down at me. "The mortal realm is a disaster, it quickly became overrun when the Veil fell, the city will soon be destroyed and I know that if I had stayed up there I would have just continued to watch everyone die without being able to stop it. I know that the end is close, I think we have all accepted that now, so I wanted to spend my last moments fighting by your side, I don't want you facing this alone." I smile back up at him as I get those strange butterfly like feelings again in the pit of my stomach, but this time I know exactly what they are and it just makes me smile more as I reach up, pacing my had behind his neck then carefully pulling his head down so that I can kiss him.

More tears escape by themselves as I slowly taste his lips again, almost like a release of emotions as I forget all my worries and just relax in his arms. My tongue plays with his as his hands begin to roam up and down my back, wanting to explore and touch me fully, my entire body calms and for a minute I don't even think about everything else that is going on around us, not the pain in my ribs, the throbbing headache or the amount of blood I am covered in, I just focus on here and now. It may be selfish, but the world could end right at this very moment and I would not care because I feel happy and safe with him, I feel at peace. His mouth moves from mine, gently starting to kiss the skin on my neck and I moan deeply as I give in to him and the burning desire that is beginning to build in my core. Then in my mind all I can think about is how much I need to have sex with Mitch, if I am really going to die, do I want my last sexual experience to be with Monroe? I want to die feeling adored, having real passion and chemistry with someone. I don't want to just fuck and cum, I want to feel that deep connection that only comes from being so intimate with someone you really like... and I really like him.

"Oh fuck, I want you so fucking bad," Mitch groans in my ear as he continues to tease my neck. We are both thinking the same thing, and when faced with certain death, we may as well get a little pleasure before we die. My hands go straight to his jeans, unbuttoning them quickly then slipping inside to feel his cock start to grow hard against my palm. He moans at my touch then stands up fully, turns me around so that I am facing away from him, then he goes back to kissing my neck as he unbuckles my belt and slides down my pants and panties together, his hands skimming the skin on my thighs then placing his hand in the middle of my back so that I bend over slightly and place my own hands on the bottom of my bed. His fingers slip between my thighs from behind, they find their way straight to my clit and he begins teasing it gently, making me moan just from feeling his touch so intimate again.

I try to stay as still as possibly as the sensations make my body buck against his hand, and with every movement my ribs ache more, sending shooting pains through my chest but I need to ignore it, so I close my eyes and just focus on Mitch. His fingertips glide over my bud as my own juices coat his skin, my pussy getting so wet for him already, but he does not seem in any hurry to fuck me just yet, he likes to play and I know he loves to hear me cum for him. His fingers move slow, letting it build and the longer he continues the deeper my breathing becomes.

"Mmmm, are you going to cum for me?" he growls in my ear and I just nod as his touch becomes firmer and faster, my moans getting louder before the deep burning gets all too much to bare and it explodes deep within me. I cry out loudly as he continues to stimulate me, my fists clinging on to the fabric of the blankets in front of me as I orgasm hard, letting the wash of euphoria consume me and make me forget the pain. "I fucking love hearing you," he moans as he removes his hand from between my thighs and replaces it with his now rock hard cock. The throbbing head teases my opening, staying shallow enough to make me squirm as I push my hips back against him so I can feel him fully. His cock slides deep in to my soaking pussy with ease, I am already so fucking wet for him that the lack of any friction makes him fit perfectly, as though we were made for each other and I had missed him for centuries before I even felt his touch.

He wraps his arm around my waist and helps me stand back up so he can hold me close as he slowly fucks me, his other arm across my chest so he can go deeper with each movement and allowing us both to just get lost in each other. He groans with pleasure as he resumes gently kissing my neck, my head falls back against his shoulder and I moan deeply, smiling as I have never felt this kind of connection with anyone and knowing that this is what people must mean when they say opposites attract, as you can not get much more opposite than an archangel and a demon.

"Oh, fuck... Mitch," the words slip out as I feel myself edging towards orgasm, my breathing is trembling as I try to stay upright, ignoring the multiple bumps and pains. I think he notices my discomfort as he repositions his arms so that they do not press on my ribs too much and instead focusing on making sure I am comfortable.

"Fuck, you feel so good," he says quietly as he goes a little harder, the penetration is so pleasing that I just moan in reply, getting gradually louder as I feel myself getting close again. He joins me, both of us enjoying the pleasure, trying to go slow to hold back, to prolong it as though neither of us want this exact moment to end. He slows more, drawing out the feelings, knowing that every second that we wait before orgasm, is another second of bliss that we get to share together before we die. I don't want to lose him, I have found myself really caring about this man and I know that when the time comes that we have to face the end, I am going to be heartbroken. Behind me, I can hear Mitch's moans get deeper as he tries his best to hold back, to make sure I am ready.

"Shit, I'm going to cum," I force myself to say through deep breaths, just to give him the go ahead, and just as I am right on the edge, Mitch picks up the pace, going harder and deeper. My pussy tightens around his shaft as I cum hard, my legs shaking as he holds me then he explodes inside of me, cumming just as hard as I do, the sounds of our shared ecstasy echo around my little bedroom until we are both almost gasping for air, I don't want him to stop, I want to stay like this, close to him and not letting go but eventually he slows down when he is sure we are both spent. We just stand still and silent for a moment, his cock still throbbing inside of me, him not wanting to let me go and me not wanting to forget what he feels like. Mitch moans with satisfaction then gently kisses my neck as I close my eyes and wish that this moment would last forever.

"Are you alright?" Mitch asks me as he carefully steps back then I moan and groan a bit whilst pulling my trousers back up and buttoning them before I buckle the belt, I am in a shit load of pain but I can not help but smile. "I tried to be gentle with you."

"I'm still alive," I giggle slightly then turn around to look at him again as he fixes his jeans and zips himself back up. "I want to thank you, not for the sex, although I do quite enjoy it," he laughs at my awkwardness which make my cheeks blush again, he has such a strange effect on me and he can clearly see it. "It may be morbid, but it feels nice to not face death alone... To die by your side, is such a heavenly way to die," I quote and he smirks at me.

"Mmmm, I did always like that song... And now it is quite ironic considering where we are," he forces a smile as he looks at me, knowing that he is probably seeing me properly for the last time, as I am with him. As soon as I walk out of that door, everything will be final and there is no escaping that. "So, what do you want to do now?"

"My father kept saying something about protecting the crown," I tell him as he listens. "I guess that means just trying to keep Lilith from taking control, maybe, delay the inevitable for as long as possible. But I don't understand why he was so adamant on me doing that, he had men fighting beside him so why me, what made him think that I could..." my words trail off as something else unexpectedly pops in to my head, it is something my father said but not what he told me today, it is what he said to me whilst we were stood at Wrath's grave.

"What are you thinking, you have that look," Mitch asks as I run through it all in my head.

"He did know," I say to myself. "He was giving me little clues all along, almost as though he knew how things would end... I know what I need to do," I smile and dart over to the small hole behind my wardrobe then get down on all fours, clutching my side and groaning as I do, but stop just before I leave. "No offence, but you may be a bit big to follow me this way," on saying that I can not help smile more at him as I look up at his muscles, knowing how they feel against me, the strong grip on my skin.

"Nope," he protests immediately then comes straight over, takes hold of my arm and pulls me back to my feet. "I have watched you run head first in to a fight by yourself, far too many times already, I am not going to sit on the sidelines now so you are not leaving my side, understand?" The commanding nature of his voice sends shivers down my spine, a million thoughts running through my head about how much I want to fuck him again or have him tie me up and spank me, tell me I am such a naughty girl, and for him to take full control.

"Mmm hmm," I manage to say as I stare up at him and nibble my bottom lip, I can tell by the glint in his eye that he knows he turns me on, and he knows exactly what I am thinking. The room is silent as I debate pulling him close to me so I can kiss him again, taste his sweet lips, feel his hands all over me, fuck all the consequences, just get lost in each others arms until we die. "Mitch I have something I need to tell you," I say seriously and he nods to let me know he is listening. If these are really the last moments we have left to live, then I need him to know how I truly feel. "Mitch, I have never met anyone like you in my very long life, you make me smile so much and I really need you to know that I that that I lov..."

"Shhh, I'm listening," we both pause as a quiet voice speaks from outside my closed bedroom door.

"Just knock," comes another in a hushed tone.

"You knock," the first voice replies. "I am not going to, I do not need that hassle." Mitch heads over to the door and opens it as I stand in the middle of the room, I cross my arms as two very embarrassed faces freeze and fall silent when they realise we heard them. "Oh, hi," Monroe says then looks around the pitch black corridor. "We were just admiring the architecture on these beautiful walls here." I smile as I see Jake standing nervously beside him, trying to avoid any sort of eye contact with us which makes me wonder what exactly they heard.

"How long have you been admiring the architecture of the dank and disgusting hallway for?" I ask them as Mitch tries not to laugh.

"We literally just got here," Monroe replies. "60 seconds, maybe."

"10 minutes," Jake replies truthfully then goes bright red with embarrassment. "You guys sounded a little busy so we didn't want to disturb you." He focuses on the floor, but I am not even bothered about them hearing me and Mitch have sex, I am just glad he is alive and safe, even if he does look a little battered and bruised. I head straight over to him and hug him, I can tell I caught him a little off guard as he just stands for a moment, unsure what to do before he hugs me back.

"Did you get it?" I glance to Monroe as I step back. "The brimstone? Did it work?"

"Yes, I got it," Jake replies and pulls the small black rock out of his pocket and holds it up for me to see that he is telling the truth and that Monroe followed through on what I asked him to do. "But no, it didn't work. I'm still human me." My deflated sigh is loud and makes everyone fall silent, I was sure it would work, all the tales I had heard about how brimstone could strip faith led me to believe it could make Jake his true self, but I guess that is just another thing I failed to do.

"So," I think quickly to try to come to terms with having other people here now, I assumed I would die alone so I wouldn't have to worry about anyone else. "I am mortal, injured and in a shit load of pain. Mitch is no longer an angel, had his wings burned off and I am assuming quite vulnerable to being killed and Jake is still human, totally normal and has not even had time to recover from nearly being sacrificed before coming to Hell."

"I'm still me," Monroe says smugly.

237

"Awesome," I sigh. "We have three of us who will be killed within seconds if we try to fight and one old ass reaper with a self inflated ego and cocky bullshit attitude to stand against Lilith and her legions of soldiers."

"Hey," Monroe groans. "I am not that old, still life in this dog yet." He smiles as I shake my head at the current situation. My plan of dying did not include having to think about the lives of other people, that is why I left Mitch and Jake behind in the mortal realm, and why I sent Monroe away. It was selfish of me, but it was easier to go alone, I didn't want to see them all get hurt. "So, what is the plan?" All three of them watch me, waiting for me to give some grand pep talk or tell them how I am going to stop the end of the world, but I wasn't really prepared for this.

"The plan is that we are all probably going to die," I shrug. "The end of the world is coming, there is no one that exists that can stop it and I have accepted my fate. But I get to die knowing that I found happiness, even if it was unexpected and very late in my life," I look at Mitch and he smiles at my words, then I glance to Jake. "I get to know that my life had purpose and the thing I was protecting ended up becoming a good friend," he nods at me to acknowledge the sentiment. "And that no matter how hard things get or how much time has passed, loyalty is something to be thankful for." Monroe forces a smile, he has been close to death many times, and like myself has taken many souls and ended many lives, we both know that it is now our turn to face the void. When I die my soul will be treated like the vilest of beings and I will end up being ripped apart endlessly and tormented in the pit, that's just on a good day, luckily though with the end of the world imminent, that part won't last too long, so I'm thankful for that at least. "So with all that in mind, I am going to face death head on. I have never been the kind to hide, so I am not going to do it now. I'm going to be an absolute arsehole and show my mother just the kind of pain she didn't know existed."

"You are going to tell her the truth?" Mitch asks me and I nod.

"Yeah, I am going to hold the one thing she wants most in the world in my hand, and tell her to kill her own daughter to get it," I reply.

"Do you think that will change her mind, make her stop?" Jake asks but it makes me laugh.

"Fuck no," I shake my head then sigh. "She is a psychopath, hell bent on destroying creation itself, I doubt she will be that bothered about killing me to get it, no matter who I am." I feel strangely calm now with the prospect of facing her, what is the worst she can do to me? Kill me? "OK, if you lot are adamant on coming with me then we need a way in to my fathers collection room," I explain more as we head in to the corridor together and I lead them to where I know the entrance to be, we see a few men roaming the halls, patrolling in groups in case Lucifer has more resistance or back up on the way. But I know this place like the back of my hand, so we manage to keep to the shadows and go unnoticed, the last thing I need is us getting killed before I even make it back to face my mother. "It is just down here," I say at a whisper as we come to a large metal door at the end of a long corridor, it is the only door here and if we can not get through it then this may as well be a dead end. "This would have been so much easier if you had let me crawl here, it's not my fault you are too big for my tiny hole," I say to myself as I inspect the door, knowing that I could have slipped inside here easy with the secret tunnel.

"That's what she said," Mitch smirks as he stands next to me and it takes me a moment to realise what he meant before it makes me laugh. "Are we just going to look at the door or open it?" he teases and I pause for a moment before giving my reply. The door itself is large, very large and pure ancient metal that is a foot thick, it has stood here longer than I have been alive. It is covered in deep carved markings, symbols and things that look familiar but I am not knowledgable on their origins, I have never entered this room through this way before, I always used my secret passage. Scanning the door, there are no noticeable places that you would use to unlock it with a key and there is not even a handle, so I place my hands on the cold metal and push, thinking it might just open somehow.

"You don't know how to open it, do you?" Monroe says from behind me and I try my hardest to ignore him.

"The room should be just around this next corner," we all turn and look up the long corridor as we hear someone speak in the distance, then multiple footsteps, Lilith must have figured out what she needed to claim the throne so sent her goons to retrieve it, which means if they turn in to this corridor, we will be sitting ducks with nowhere to hide.

"Moon, open the door," Monroe encourages me as the sounds get closer, the stone walls make every little noise echo so it won't be long until they get here. My breathing quickens as I frantically search for some way to get inside, knowing if I do not then we will be killed here, until Mitch places his hand through the back of my hair which is still mattered off the gash on the back of my skull then holds his hand up in front of my face, his fingers covered in my still lightly trickling blood.

"For the daughter of the Dark Lord, the ruler of black magic in the human world," Mitch says smirking. "I am surprised you do not recognise blood magic when you see it." The symbols that are carved in to the door, it is blood magic, I knew I recognised them but as I have a strong aversion to witchcraft it is not something I pride myself in knowing. Mitch runs his fingers down the middle of the door, smearing my blood over the central indent and I hold my breath, waiting to see what happens.

"That's the girl from before, Lilith wants her dead," we hear loudly as I turn around and see ten men, all armed with weapons and the one who spoke pointing directly at me. Monroe moves fast, stepping forward a couple of meters to block the path between Lilith's men and the rest of us, the tension builds swifty and I can see the men ready for a fight as Monroe stands with his back to us then the door behind clicks as it slowly opens by itself.

"Monroe let's go, quickly," I say as I shove Mitch and Jake through the small gap and in to the collectables room just before Lilith's men start to run towards us.

"You go," Monroe replies confidently without turning around. "I have got to try to protect the Princess somehow, right?" he chuckles to himself then readies his stance, a bright flash of blue light almost blinds me in the dimly lit hall then I see the glint of his blade, the impressive scythe that is all too synonymous with a reaper shines bright as it looms over his head. His soul charged weapon is truly beautiful, but I know I do not have time to admire it. "Moon, go!" he shouts then I dart through the gap. Mitch forces the door closed just as we all here the clash of blades from outside then silence falls as the room relocks, leaving Monroe behind. I can tell that Mitch and Jake do not know what to say to me as I just stand and stare at the door. I want to believe that Monroe will slay all the men who are fighting him, but I also know that the soldiers that Lilith has with her are not the average run of the mill demon that we usual face when reaping souls. Souls are connected to humans, and these demons are the furthest thing from human you can get, even I struggled to sense them, and if they have weapons that could hurt my father, then they have the potential to kill Monroe.

"Hey," Mitch says gently as he places his hand on my shoulder. "We need to stay focused, he would want you to." I nod in reply then try to take a deep breath to calm my growing nerves. Monroe was the only one of us who had any sort of chance in facing the soldiers, now he is no longer with us we don't have much of a survival outlook.

"It's on the far wall," I say to divert my thoughts then head down the middle of the long room. Mitch and Jake follow close behind, taking in all of my fathers treasures as we go until I get to the end where the Dark Grimoire still sits on the floor where I left it earlier then take a moment to look up at the wall. "He who wears the crown, controls the throne," I say out load, quoting what my father said to me. It has never moved off that wall in all the time I have been alive, and I have never seen my father wear it at all.

"If we managed to get Lucifer to wear his crown," Jake says cautiously as though knowing I was thinking about my father. "Would he be able to regain control and re-establish the Veil?" Mitch and myself both turn and stare at Jake, my mind running through what he just asked over and over, cross referencing it with what I know about the tales of the rising and trying to decide if what he asked is possible or not. Glancing at Mitch I can see him thinking the same, but I am not sure on the answer.

"The stories say that whoever claims the throne can decide what happens to the Veil," Mitch says, thinking out loud. "I don't think any of the versions I have heard ever mentioned that it categorically had to be someone new who took the throne, just that someone had to control it, so maybe if the crown controls the throne and Lucifer wears it, it might work. Then again, I have heard so many variations on the tale that anything could be true at this point."

"Well if my father did wear the crown, he would technically be in control. The stories say just to claim the throne, but I am not sure where the crown fits in, do you?" I ask and we both stare at each other. "Does that mean it can be stopped?"

"I am not 100% sure but it is worth a try, right? It is not like we have anything else to lose," he replies and I smile before reaching up and removing my fathers crown from its display hooks and holding it for the first time. It feels strange, the metal that it is made from is warm and almost vibrates in my hand, as though it is made of pure energy. Just touching it gives me chills as I know if this falls in to the wrong hands then it is game over. "Now we just need to find your father and..." Mitch's words are cut off when a loud bang shakes the whole room, emanating from the locked door. After a second another loud impact as though someone outside is trying to force their way in rings out, and thinking on that my heart sinks as it confirms Monroe failed in holding the men back. "The door won't hold for long, is there another way out?"

They do not argue when I inform them that to get out we need to crawl through the air ducts above our heads, then I make them two go first whilst I hook my fathers crown on to my belt, climb up on the plinth and kick it away as hard as I can to throw the men off where we went. I hang for a moment on the edge of the hole above and realise that my ribs are so painful that I am struggling to hoist my own body weight up, I can usually dead lift multiples of my own body weight so now this whole being mortal thing is getting to me and showing me just how weak humans really are, luckily I don't have to hang around too long before Mitch appears again and helps me up. It takes us a couple of minutes to work our way back through the ducts in to the throne room, then silently lower ourselves to the ground below.

"It will not be long now," we hear Lilith say confidently as we hide behind the statues at the side of the room, some of which are now nothing more than piles of rubble and stone. Through the small gaps I can see a lot of bodies, random limbs, carnage and blood everywhere, I can't even count how many dead there are, but I do see a gathering of people stood over by the far doors, Lilith in the middle with not a scratch on her from the fight, which is more than can be said for my father who is currently bound with black chains wrapped tightly around his wrists and neck, kneeling at her feet. He is covered in a mixture of his own blood and that of his enemies, I can not see a single one of his men still alive so all of the soldiers in the room now serve only Lilith. I mouth the words "stay here" to Mitch and Jake, signalling for them to keep low and hidden then try to create a little distance between myself and everyone else. As quietly as I can, I head in the direction of the steep steps that lead up to my fathers throne, knowing that if I do face Lilith again, my friends will be safer away from me, I can not bare the thought of them

241

getting hurt.

"You don't suit white, you know," my father groans through the pain as he looks up at Lilith. "You are hardly angelic or virginal," he laughs but Lilith is not amused by his words she so swiftly back hands him hard across the face, causing him to be dazed and blood to freely flow from his mouth, which he spits out on to the floor before smirking back up at her. I have never seen my father like this before, so vulnerable or even just in pain, the weapons that Lilith's men are using against him must be made from brimstone as well, I think that is what he meant by the black blades being able to hurt a God, so I assume they could also hurt him. That also means the chains that bind him are also made from the same substance, I didn't know that it could have so much of an effect on him.

"Watch your words, Lucifer," Lilith snarls down at him. "Other wise I will rip that slick tongue of yours, right out of your head." If I am going to face her then I am going to do it confidently, show her that she can not intimidate me, even if I am shitting myself on the inside, I need to be strong till my last breath, at least I might be able to make my father proud of me before I die. Whilst they are all distracted I silently climb the steps towards the throne then cautiously sit on it, I was slightly afraid that I might burst in to flames from just touching it, but if Lilith can sit here, then so can I. The doors to the throne room burst open again and everyone eagerly turns to look as several men enter. "It is about time, hand me my crown," Lilith beams but the men look uncertain of how to reply.

"We do not have it, Ma'am," one of the bigger and uglier looking ones says from the front. "There were people outside the room when we arrived and..."

"What people?" Lilith snaps and you can visibly see everyone around her cower away slightly, knowing that she will be angry with the reply.

"The woman from earlier," he informs her cautiously. "And three men, two of who I do not know, however I recognised the face of the third." As he says that two more soldiers drag Monroe in to the room, he has the same thick chains around his neck as my father, which are choking him as he can hardly breathe, multiple wounds over his body with a very noticeably large one in his gut, and blood gushing down the side of his head. He collapses to his knees as he is forced forward, then the clatter of metal on stone echoes around the room as his weapon is tossed to the ground by another of the goons. At least if his weapon is still here then I know he has not been made mortal. "His name is Monroe, he is a reaper and..."

"I know who he is," Lilith interrupts and just stares down at him, as they talk more soldiers appear and line the walls, easily 50 or so men, her forces are probably endless in numbers. "Monroe and Moon... It is nice to finally be able to put faces to the names, even if you have become insufferable and a stain on my plans."

"I wish... I could say the same," Monroe forces out as the chains restrict his breathing. "I was honestly... expecting a bit more... power." Lilith leans forward and grabs the chain, pulling Monroe high up on his knees and choking him further, making him unable to speak.

"You wanted more power?" she asks menacingly as she stares in to his eyes. "I have more power in my little finger than a reaper like you will ever contain. You play with souls after they die, I destroy lives before they even begin. Too bad that you are not in the mortal world to take advantage of all those nice juicy souls, instead you get a front row seat and will die whilst I end the world;" she pauses for a moment and takes a deep breath before speaking again. "Now, tell me where is my crown?" Monroe forces a smile but does not reply which only makes Lilith angrier. "Where is the girl?"

"The room was empty when we managed to break down the door," the soldier from earlier speaks again. "The girl and the two unknown men just vanished." I can not help but smirk as I relax back in to the throne and try my best to look confident in myself, I am actually quite surprised no one has noticed me yet. "And when we entered, the crown was not where you said it would be, we searched the room but..." Lilith drops Monroe who slumps back and gasps for breath, then she moves towards the soldier, places her hands on his head and snaps his neck within seconds before he even has the chance to protect himself. His body crumples to the ground and the whole room falls silent. I know myself how difficult it is to snap the neck of a demon and have it kill them instantly which just shows how much strength she does really have.

"Poor guy was only doing his job," I say loud enough for everyone to hear and Lilith freezes as she hears my voice. "It is not his fault he couldn't find the crown." She slowly turns around and grimaces when she sees me sitting here then she catches sight of the crown now nestled in my lap. My father watches me, but I can not read his emotions, and I suddenly feel like I have just made a massive mistake. He does not look happy with me being here. She takes a few steps forward, anger consuming her then stops as though she has just realised something.

"The other two men that were with you," she says and my heart sinks. "Do not tell me that you would be so foolish to come here... Michael?" her words are no longer directed at me as she slowly looks around the room, thinking to herself. "And I can smell the human... you brought my key along to witness what he helped create."

"All of this power trip must be going to your head because I have no idea what you are talking about," I say as my voice shakes slightly.

"Find them," Lilith commands her men and instantly they fan out around the room in search for my friends.

"Forget them, it is me you want," I say quickly then stand up to draw her attention. "And this, you are desperate to get your hands on this crown." I hold it up and she stares up at me again. "I know I can't beat you, I am mortal thanks to

243

you and it is plain to see that you have full control over the current situation." She listens to my words as I take a couple of steps down.

"What is it that you hope to achieve?" she asks me. "Coming here, all you have done is bring me what is mine." There is the sounds of a scuffle breaking out to the side of the room and several of Lilith's soldiers drag Mitch and Jake out of hiding, securely holding them in place, they both attempt to struggle, but without any power they are both helpless compared to the strong high level demons. "This is really the best you all could do? Minimal resistance and then childish games, it is just delaying the inevitable, but it is alright, there is no one in the whole of Hell who can stand against me, who could do or say anything to dull the glory that I already feel."

"Oh, I wouldn't be so sure about that," the sarcasm slips out, another trait I picked up from my father. "You see, you don't truly understand who you are looking at." She tilts her head slightly and smiles.

"I am looking at a foolish girl," she replies. "One who became a very unexpected thorn in my side when she started popping up and interfering with my plans. Rosa Moon... legendary reaper, who is now mortal and will be dead very soon." I laugh at her words, it is quite comical how much she does not know.

"I do like the name Rosa Moon," I say. "But it is not the name that was given to me at my birth. And I am not just a legendary reaper." My statement peaks her interest as she watches me. "I am one of the best reapers that ever lived, I was the keeper of the Veil and protector of the night... Although you were correct about one thing that you said earlier, I am close to Lucifer, very close in fact, but I am not just another of his whores... I am the youngest child of Lucifer himself, the child that was hidden away for centuries because I seem to have a mother who is an absolute psycho and wants to destroy creation." Lilith's face drops, confusion, anger, lots of different emotions consuming her as she tries to understand what I am saying. I know her first thought will be that I am a Sin, which will quickly get batted away as she is smarter than that.

"What is your name?" she snarls at me and I smile more, knowing that the next thing I say will change everything, for me and her.

"My name is Alexis Morningstar," I say proud of that title for the first time in my entire life. "And I would say that is was nice to finally meet you, Mother, but we both know that I would be lying." She looks around to my father then back to me, then back to my father as she tries to work out if I am speaking the truth or if this is some elaborate hoax.

"You wouldn't," she says to my father and he smirks up at her from his knees. "All this time you let me believe she was dead? Why?"

"Because this world did not need two of you," I answer for him. "A few hundred years ago I might have admired the whole bad ass bitch persona that you have going on, but after actually getting to know you a little over the past few days, I can see why my father did not want me to be anything like you." She breathes deeply to compose herself then turns back to face me.

"Alexis, my child, my daughter... give me my crown," she says forcefully but I shake my head.

"No, this crown belongs to my father, you will have to kill me first because I will never give it to you," there is a moment of silence, I see her debating in her head about what to do, before she smirks back.

"We will see," she smiles then holds out her hand to the side whilst holding eye contact with me, instantly one of her soldiers steps forward, places a knife in her palm and she wastes no time before throwing it towards the side of the room. I don't even see what is happening until the blade is embedded deep in to the centre of Jakes chest, he looks down at it as the audible noise of him attempting to breathe is muffled by the blood that flows from his mouth and fills his lungs, then the two men holding him up, leave lose and he collapses to the ground. Everyone watches his struggle to breathe for a moment until he goes still, his lifeless body just laying there, and I don't understand what I just saw. Mitch shouts and struggles against the men holding him, desperately trying to get to his friend as Lilith laughs, then she begins to walk towards him instead. He is no longer an angel and if she gets close there will be nothing to stop her hurting him as well. I throw the crown on to the seat of the throne behind me and run down the steps, I need to stop her.

"No," I shout as I realise I just watched her effortlessly kill Jake, my new friend, the key I had sworn my life to protect who is now gone. It all happened so fast that I didn't even get the chance to think about helping him and even now I don't think it has fully sank in yet that he is dead. I knew it was close to the end, but I thought we may have still had a chance, however tiny it was, I never wanted to watch my friends die. "What did you do!" I force out as tears escape my eyes and I step over the multiple dead soldiers as I try to get to her but she ignores me completely, as though I do not exist to her.

"Let him go," she orders the men holding Mitch and they step back, leaving him standing in from of her. He looks unsure of himself, knowing that in his current state he can not do much against her. "Let's see just how cocky you are without your wings, Michael." He looks devastated as he glances down to Jakes lifeless body then back to her, his eyes puffy and I know he will be trying his best to face her without fear, even though he knows what is about to happen next. "Where is your God now?" she smiles at him as I pick up a weapon from the ground as I run towards her, it is nothing flash, some kind of sword that one of the dead soldiers has dropped, then ready to attack but just as I reach her she turns, grabs me by the throat and hoists me off the floor. My legs dangle beneath me as her other hand grabs my wrist and squeezes so hard that I feel my bones splinter and I have no choice but to drop the sword.

"Rosa!" Mitch shouts then lunges forward, but is swiftly restrained again and forced to his knees.

"Nice try," Lilith smirks then throws me away before she turns her attention back to Mitch, he tries to get to me to see if I am alright as I crash in to the side of the wall, bounce of it then land on top of the remains of one of the statues. I cry out in agony as I feel my side pierced by some sort of sharp edge that tears my flesh open as the weight of my body slides down it, then hit the floor, blood covering the stone under me as I gasp for breath. Mitch manages to slip out of the grasp of the soldiers then darts towards where I land but Lilith grabs his arm just as he passes her, twisting it up his back and forces him back to his knees. Mitch shouts out in pain as his shoulder dislocates, the pop of cartilage echoes around the room then she wraps her hand around his throat and cuts off his airways. I can hear my father and Monroe desperately trying to break free from their bindings, but even if they did escape, there are 50 soldiers just waiting for the chance to fight for their future Queen.

Forcing myself to roll on to my side I groan in pain, then struggle to get up as my ribs feel like they are restricting my lungs and I can not put any pressure on my wrist to push myself up. From what I can feel, I know I have a couple of broken bones, definitely my wrist and a few ribs, my knee feels twisted, my shoulder is painful and every muscle in my body aches. I must have hit my head as I landed as well, as I can not see straight and I feel sick with dizziness, blood drips down my forehead and falls in to my eyes as I struggle to focus enough to see Mitch as the blood loss starts to make me woozy. Being human sucks.

"P... please," I force out as I manage to get on to my knees, I sway quite a bit and stumble but get up from the floor, then after a very painful moment I step towards Lilith. "Please let him go," I beg her but she just glances in my direction and smiles more as his free hand claws at her fingers, desperately trying to get her off so he can breathe.

"Mmmm I do like that you are begging," she says to me playfully as Mitch struggles more. "But if you were truly my daughter, you would not be so weak to reach the moment of having to beg." Making my way back towards them so I can help him, I can see his eyes glaze over but just at the point that he would lose consciousness, Lilith releases her grip on his neck and he gasps for breath, inhaling deeply before she looks up to one of the soldiers standing patiently behind him and gives her next command. She grabs a fist full of hair and tilts his face up so she can stare in to his eyes.

"Kill him," she says bluntly and within seconds the soldier steps forward, pulls a knife from a holster on his belt and draws the blade roughly across Mitch's throat as she holds him in place.

"NO!!!" I scream as his own blood cascades down from the now gaping wound across his neck, soaking his t-shirt. His hand drops lifelessly to his side, then just as I reach him, Lilith lets him go and he falls face first to the floor. Everyone else in the room is silent as she stands over us, just watching. I drop to my knees, my hands are shaking like mad as I can not believe what is happening. I try my best to turn him on to his back as tears stream down my cheeks but when I see his face fully I am consumed with a pain that I have never felt before. "No, Mitch, please," I sob as I check for a pulse and try to stop the bleeding, my hands becoming covered in his blood then I shake him to wake him up, he is just asleep, this is not real. "Mitch wake up... please you need to wake up," I beg him as his eyes just stare in to nothingness, void of all signs of life. "You can't leave me yet," I cry in to his chest as I hold his body then place my hands on his cheek so I can gently stroke it, smearing his blood across his soft skin. "I didn't get a chance to tell you that I loved you," I say then gently kiss his cold lips. "Please? Please don't be dead... I need you." My chest is so tight that I can hardly breathe as I collapse on top of him and sob, I have never felt this overwhelming amount of grief before, not even when I found out about my siblings, it feels like a piece of my heart has literally been ripped out and crushed.

"Moon!" Monroe tries to get my attention but I feel like I am lost, I finally found a real connection and I don't know how to live without it any more, my life is over. "Moon, snap out of it." I lay my head on his chest, praying that I can hear his heart beat but there is only silence, he is gone and I couldn't stop it.

"Alexis!!" my father shouts, making his voice echo around the room and making me look up towards him. My eyes are blurred with the amount of tears and blood that cover my face, but I do see him nod towards the throne so I glance around and see my mother casually stepping over the massacre that covers the floor then she starts to ascend the steps to collect her crown, the crown that I just left on the throne for her. Looking back down at Mitch, I just want to curl up next to him and wait to die, but something inside my soul tells me that I need to keep fighting, no matter how useless I am right now or how close to death the world is, I can not just roll over and give in. It takes me a few seconds to get back to my feet, my head is pounding and my energy levels are quickly waining with the amount of blood I am losing via the deep gash in my side, but I clutch it to try to stop some of the bleeding then head after my mother, she is not bothered about the scene behind her, instead reviling in her moment as she gets closer to her end goal. As I reach the bottom step I hear commotion behind me, the soldiers realise that maybe I might be an issue again so they move to try to stop me but I ignore them and go as fast as I can, using every ounce of strength I have left to get to her, I cannot let her destroy everything.

She reaches the top and pauses for a moment, just looking down at the seat where the crown lays which gives me a slight opportunity to push forward, I can feel men right behind me, trying to grab the back of my clothing as I barge past my mother and try to get the crown away from her grasp, but than I feel myself yanked backwards as she tries to get me away from her destiny. The force is so strong that my feet leave the ground and I am tossed backwards, almost like slow motion as I fall through the air off the top of the monument where my fathers throne sits, knowing that when I hit the ground I will be dead as I am at least 20 foot above the room below. Lilith makes eye contact with me and snarls as I am air born, then I realise I have hold of the crown tightly in my hand, taking it away from her once again which fills me with happiness, a final chance to fuck with her plans so with my free hand I defiantly flip her the bird and smile wildly before I hit the ground.

    My skull smashes off the stone, the sickening crack of bone radiates through my head as I skid across the floor and come to a stop before I feel my own blood pool beneath me and my eyes lose all focus. I can not move my limbs, pain consumes me, then I realise I am not breathing. There is shouting and sounds of a struggle that is quickly drown out by the sound of my own heart beat in my ears, gradually slowing down until it stops fully and I descend in the darkness that is death.

Chapter Eighteen

Everything around me seems so calm, as thought I am floating on air, weightless and free of all thoughts or worries. The relaxation is better than any massage or sexual release I have ever experienced before, just pure tranquillity the likes one would only dream about reaching through years of meditation. I am so comfortable that I have no desire to move one single inch and all I can think about is how blissfully happy I feel. As I breathe, the air is pleasantly warm and smells like fresh brew coffee and sweet desserts, and I can not help but smile. I love the wafting scents of my coffee shop first thing on a morning, it is my happy place and I am completely content.

"Wake up," a soothing voice of a man says, but I am far too relaxed, I want to keep enjoying the peace, I'm so comfortable.

"Get someone else to open up today," I moan in reply, after all I am the boss and I deserve a day off at some point. "Let me sleep."

"There is no time for sleep," comes the voice in a calming manner. "Open your eyes, Alexis Morningstar." Those words pique my interest straight away, no one in my coffee shop knows that name, my name is Rosa Moon, nothing else in the human world. My eyelids flicker and for a moment I struggle to actually open them, my surroundings are so dazzlingly bright that I have to squint to see anything. Using my hand to try to shield my eyes from the light, I sit up and look around, but everything is pure blinding white.

"Hello?" I say to whoever's voice I heard. "How do you know that name?"

"I know everything about you, Alexis," the voice is coming from behind me, so I quickly get myself off the ground and look to see who is speaking. Casually smiling gently at my now very confused face is a man, one who I have never seen before. Dressed in a white flowing shirt and trousers, he has dark shoulder-length hair, neatly tied back in a ribbon with a robust beard and really strange shoes. The floor below our feet seems to move on its own, almost like white wisps and there is nothing else here but us two, but unusually I don't feel scared of it all, it is actually comforting.

"Do I know you?" I ask the man, his eyes seem so kind as he looks me up and down, taking me in completely. Glancing at myself I see that I am covered in blood, rips and tears in the fabric of my clothing where wounds or injuries were sustained, for a moment I do not know why I am not at home in my shop, then suddenly I remember falling through the air and my skull sounding like it exploded, sending blood and my brain splattering all over stone. "Am I dead?" I reach up and feel the back of my head, it does not seem unusual at all and I am not in any pain. "And is this some sort of joke? Because if this is me being dead and my eternal torment is to live in a white box for the rest of days then whoever got me to torture in the pits is doing a pretty shitty job so far. I was expecting fire, hordes of flesh eating monsters or zombies maybe, just not this, this is too... clean." The man chuckles at me slightly as I try to see where I am fully, but there is nothing but endless bright light.

"Answer me a question, Alexis," he says and I just nod in response. "Why did you chose to try to stop Lilith?" Lilith? He wants to know about my mother? I try to think, apart from hitting my head I can't remember much else... there was a fight, maybe? I went home back to Hell, I saw my father and I...

"Mitch!" I remember seeing his eyes, his blood covering my hands as I desperately tried to wake him up and I suddenly feel consumed with loss, my chest is so tight I can hardly catch my breath.

"Answer my question, Alexis, please," the man encourages me gently and I try to think of an answer, so I take a deep breath to calm myself before speaking.

"I wanted to live," I say as I try not to break down and cry as my heart hurts so much. "I didn't want to watch my friends die at her hand."

"No," he replies and shakes his head. "That is not the answer that lies within your soul. Look deeper."

"In my soul?" I ask, unsure of myself and he just smiles more at me, putting me at ease. "She wants to destroy everything, to undo creation... when she succeeds, there will be billions of innocent lives lost. No matter who my parents are, I could not stand by and watch that happen... But I failed and I lost so much, everyone I love will be gone." My breathing shakes as I desperately try to come to terms with it all. "Where am I?"

"You already know where you are," he replies and I shake my head because this is not Hell, I would know if I was there as I know that is where I belong, that is where I should be, but this is not it. "You sacrificed yourself to save billions of humans that you did not know. You fought for what you knew to be right. You stood up and tried to help when no one else would despite knowing you were facing certain death... That is the true definition of a selfless act." Laughter escapes me slightly as I can not believe what he is saying.

"You are fucking with me, right?" I scoff. "No... this is a joke... The white light, weird-ass cloud floor... That would mean this is... but it can't be... this is..."

"Heaven, yes," he smiles sweetly as I let out a strangled chuckle.

"Then that would mean, you are..."

"Mmm-hmm," he nods. "I believe you said I was an old invisible man who wears sandals, so I thought that would be the look I went for today, except the invisible part. Not exactly my usual every day dress up, but I have been known on the odd occasion to partake a bit of fashion." I have no more words, nothing at all, not even a joke to lighten the mood. "Let me start over," he says as he can clearly see I have no idea what is now going on. "Your actions spoke louder than any soul before you. I knew the day that you were born that it would end this way, that the only way for you to see who you truly were was when you stared into the eyes of your mother." I try to understand his words and everything that is going on, but instead of being thankful that I am not currently burning in the fiery pits of Hell, all this just pisses me off.

"Are you saying that you knew all of this was going to happen and you just stood by and let it?" I snap and he calmly listens to me. "That city has been destroyed, countless humans have been killed... I watched Mitch and Jake be murdered in front of me and you did nothing at all to stop this... Where is Mitch anyway, is he here? He is a angel so he would have..."

"No," God interrupts me. "Michael is not here, he fell from grace when he entered your fathers realm, his soul was tarred so he is now lost." My chest tightens more as I think about him, his soul could be in Hell right now and that is not where he deserves to be.

"If you are truly God then why did you do nothing? And don't give me that, everything happens for a reason bullshit, because there is no logical reason why this had to happen." He sighs, then casually places his hands in his pockets and smiles gently.

"Just because you know me as God, does not mean that I control every single thing that happens," he says. "That would not be life, that would be control and even I have limitations, the human world has grown expectationally, from that garden of Eden, billions of lives were created, and belief in me started to become less. A God is only as strong as the people who believe in Him. And on Earth, there are many beliefs spread over the mortal coil, that have changed and adapted over time. But I still watch, hoping endlessly that my children take the right path."

"None of that makes any sense to me," I say truthfully. "All I know is, my mother wants to destroy creation and there is no one who can stop her."

"Life is about balance," he explains. "For every action, there is an opposite, the whole good vs evil thing, if you will. There is belief so that creates a saviour, a Heaven so there is also a Hell, there is a God so there is also a Devil. One is not in control of the other, nor do either have unlimited capabilities. Your father can not change what happens in my home and I can not not change what happens in his, that is why there is an eternal battle raging in the human world, sin and purity constantly at war but also coexisting at the same time. All that gives balance, and that is what life is."

"Hmm," I force a smile but my face clearly shows that I think what he just said is a load of crap. "So, if everything has an opposite, what is the opposite of my bitch of mother killing everyone? Because if it was meant to be stopped by you lot, you did a shit job and you only sent one angel... an angel I cared about more than life itself and who I lost." He smiles at my words then holds out his hand as though wanting me to take it. I am a little apprehensive, but I know no harm will come to me.

"Alexis Morningstar," his words are so calming that I just nod and wait for him to speak more as he gently holds my hand in his. "The opposite of Lilith, the mother of demons, the first human and the one who can destroy life... is you." I go to reply but no words leave my mouth. "Ever wondered why you had the power to reap souls when all other reapers are born that way, descended from death himself? You don't just become a reaper, you are made one... It is not the soul that fuels your power, it is the life, or in your experience so far with it, the death that plays a role."

"I don't understand," I say confused.

"You do not wield a Scythe because you are not a blood line reaper," he continues. "You use the sickle, a symbol of the harvest... I suppose you do harvest souls, but it is more about life than it is about death. The sickle represents prosperity, giving, it has always been used to bring new life and sustainability to humans, so think about what that means to you. Your gifts, your powers, are not random. You are exactly who you need to be."

"Even if I did understand what you have just said to me, none of that matters," I sigh. "I stood against Lilith and I failed, as soon as she takes the throne the end of days will come." God smiles brightly at my comment then nods.

"Well then," he says surprisingly happily. "You better make sure she doesn't take the throne then. You still have work to do Alexis, now is not the time for you to accept death, now is the time that you accept life and who you really are."

"What do you mean, who I really am?" I ask. "Even if I could do something, the human world has already been destroyed."

"Yes, that is partly true, at the moment the destruction caused by the undead is centred around the Hell mouth that was opened when the Veil fell and many lives have already been lost, their souls have passed over and you know that when that happens, they can not be returned... but that does not mean that the ones who survive have to remember... And always know your worth, just because someone is mortal, does not mean they do not have power, that is one thing that lies deep in the soul and can never be destroyed," he smiles more which just makes me more confused. He makes no sense at all. "So, are you ready?"

"Ready for what?" I ask straight back but as I do, he places his free hand on my head and I am consumed with a searing pain through my skull. My ears are ringing so loud that I am not sure if I am screaming with the agony and I can not help but close my eyes as it feels like my entire head is going to explode, I can not even breathe, my chest so tight that my ribs might snap and every inch of my skin is crawling, as though covered in insects. This is the worst thing I have ever had the displeasure of experiencing in my life, and it seems to last forever but eventually the pain subsides down to a dull ache and I hear voices again, distant but familiar.

"How could you do that?" the voice of my father says with anger and sadness, but my head feels like it is under water so I have to really concentrate to hear more. "She was our daughter."

"If she was truly my daughter, Lucifer," Lilith replies with strength. "She would not have been so pathetic and easily killed. Although she did put up quite a bit more of a fight than your bastard children the Sins... This, all of this is your doing." I am in a lot of pain but I can tell from how I am lying that the wounds that I did have previously are healed so that I am no longer haemorrhaging blood, but I do feel extremely weak and groggy as fuck, as though Lilith's blood still runs through my veins, keeping me mortal. "Just before you told me that my daughter had died was the last moment of my life where there was a possibility that I could have been happy. My daughter was going to stand by my side and show the world that God was fallible and his creations were nothing more than unworthy worms. I was told that I didn't deserve to live because I wanted more, and yet the humans are handed everything, but soon none of that will matter because every single one of them will be dead and existence will not even be a memory."

I moan quietly as I open my eyes and realise I am about half way down the room, a fair distance from where I started at the top of the stairs so I must have been thrown quite far. I am flat on my back, the noticeable feeling of brain and blood under the back of my hair makes me particularly revolted but I know that my skull is back in one piece and I am alive. However my head is pounding, the blood loss still prominent as I try my best to sit up. My vision is blurry as the dizziness takes hold and I have to stop myself as bile rises in my throat, I am exhausted and drained although it is strange, I do not feel totally human still but I also don't feel like the normal me. I have no idea what just happened but I am certain that I am back and I still have work to do.

"Alexis?" I hear my father say shocked so I look around and see him still restrained at the feet of my mother who tilts her head to the side and just stares at me as everyone else in the entire room falls silent. I suppose this is not what anyone was expecting to happen after she killed me.

"By the look on your face," I moan in reply as I manage to force myself off the ground and to my feet, I wobble a bit but thankfully stay upright, even if my legs do feel like jelly. "You would think someone had died," I laugh at myself slightly. The men look ready to pounce but Lilith raises her hand to stop them, clearly as confused about everything as I am, with the amount of blood and brains that I have just stood up from, it is very clear to see just how dead I was, no one would have survived that. A couple of meters to the side of me, Jake and Mitch lay motionless, their bodies still laying where they fell. I want to cry just looking at them, but I need to stay strong, I can not back down now. The rest of the room is still covered in random bodies and limbs, the kind of scene you would only find on a battle field and from what I can tell, apart from my father and a very badly injured Monroe, there is no one left here that opposes Lilith.

"How are you still alive?" Lilith says with anger and confusion. Even from here I can see her hands shaking with frustration, just when she thought everything was going her way and she finally got rid of me, here I am again to fuck things up.

"I am not exactly still alive," I say casually as I look around without giving too much away, no matter what, I still need to make sure she does not have the crown, I just can not see it right now so I must have dropped it when I hit the ground. "I did die, totally dead... dead as a dodo kind of dead." My feet slip on the still fresh blood as I step over a couple of soldiers bodies and move closer to where my friends lay. Everyone watches me carefully as I reach Jake, take a moment to not let my emotions get the better of me then pull the knife from his chest before wiping his blood off the blade on to my own trousers across my thigh. I then reposition his body so he looks more comfortable and lays next to Mitch, his eyes still staring into nothingness which is breaking my heart, but I would never show it right now. I do not want my mother to see how much her actions have hurt me.

"Choose any weapon in this room that you like," Lilith laughs at me slightly as I stand between my two friends with only the small knife for protection. "You are all alone and no matter how hard you try, you will never be a match for me." She looks around at all her men and a few of them join in laughing with her.

"You are right," I agree with her. "I am all alone and this weapon would do nothing to harm you, but something happened very recently which made me realise something."

"And what would that be?" she smirks as she watches me, clearly amused by me right now.

"That there is something inside of me that I have never let out before, something that I didn't even know was there but the more I think about it, the more I can feel it," I glance back down to Mitch and Jake, slowly thinking through what I need to do next in my head, trying to believe in what I was told by God and hoping that what I try next, actually works. He said that even a mortal can still have power deep in their soul, so no matter how shit I feel, I am hoping that mine was not fully destroyed. Lilith starts to slowly make her way towards me, I know that once she gets close enough she will kill me again, rather do it herself than let her soldiers have all the fun. The knife in my hand is nothing special, something that would be easily found in the mortal world, but right now it is exactly what I need. "Let's see if this works," I smile and see her narrow her eyes at me as though wondering what my next move is, then I run the blade of the knife across my palm before swiftly swapping hands and doing the other then dropping the knife to the ground, leaving myself with two deep cuts which are now bleeding.

"What are you doing?" she snarls then glances to some of her men, who all move forward to surround me, but I am not concerned with them right now as I hold my hands out to the sides then let my own blood drip on to the chests of my dead friends. Closing my eyes, I try to block everything out, concentrating only on my own heartbeat as I feel a strange pressure in my chest, it is not pain, more of a heat, as though something inside of me burns and the more I embrace it, the more alive I truly feel. My skin feels as though it is vibrating, pure energy dancing around me, something beyond powerful that I have never felt before, I am not even thinking any more, just feeling and letting that thing inside of me be free.

Suddenly, I am hit with such force that I am swept off my feet and slammed up against the wall, my head receives another bash to the back of my skull, but before I can even open my eyes to see what is going on, a hand is wrapped around my throat. My feet dangle helplessly beneath me as I instantly struggle to breathe and become pinned against the stone behind me, when I manage to focus enough to see, my mothers eyes are staring deep in to my own, her face twisted with a sadistic snarl.

"Whatever you plan on doing, you are already too late," she says slowly and very deliberately to me. I can tell she is holding something back, hidden emotions that she does not want anyone to see, I recognise it in her as I do the same.

"It is... never... too late," I manage to say before she squeezes my throat tighter, cutting off my ability to take a breath.

"I do have to admit, you are very beautiful," she smiles at me as she looks at my face. "You have my eyes... unfortunately for you, not my level of power. Your father was always weak when it came to his children, it is what made him vulnerable and easy to manipulate to get the information I needed all that time ago on how to overthrow him. Men are always led by what is in their pants, if you had grown up by my side, you would have been magnificent, instead you are just a disappointment to me." Tears stream down my face as I desperately claw at her hand, but I am far too weak, any energy I did have I used whilst attempting the impossible and the only thing I will succeed in doing is dying for a second time today. "Bring me my crown," she says loudly, giving a command to her men who instantly start searching for it. It will not have gone far, but as soon as she is handed it, it will all be over and everything that existed will be lost. "Now then," she focuses back on only me and breathes deeply to try to relax. "Let's end your pathetic life for real this time. You are unarmed, all alone and you have no hope."

"You are... wrong," I force out as I squirm under her hand and give myself a tiny opportunity to speak.

"Oh really?" she laughs. "And what makes you think out of everyone in the whole of existence that only you could stop me?" She loosens her grip a fraction to allow me to answer, so I smile at her, knowing she will not like my reply.

"I know I can stop you," I say happily, feeling fully confident in my actions considering the fact I am still so weak. "Because God himself told me so," the look on her face is quite amusing as she tries to work out why I would say something like that or even how or when I spoke to God, but just as she goes to reply, the very distinctive noise of two people suddenly taking a deep gulping breath at the same time fills the room and I smile more. I can not see much whilst being pinned up against the wall, but I do notice a lot of the men currently surrounding us are fixated on Mitch and Jake as they now sit in their own blood and try to regain their normal breathing. Coming back from the dead is a real shock to the system, so it will take them a moment to realise what is going on.

Lilith leaves go of my neck and I drop to the ground, my legs giving way under me and with not having enough strength in my body to support myself, I end up slumped on my knees. She turns on the spot and just stares at them both as they look around, trying to understand what is currently happening before Mitch slowly stands up from the floor and inspects the blood that is covering his shirt, he feels his neck as though remembering that his throat was slit, then finally makes eye contact with Lilith.

"How are you alive," she says shocked and in total disbelief, but Mitch smiles in reply at her.

"I feel so much more than just being alive," he says then as though I am watching one of those epic magic movie moments, he grabs the front of his blood covered t-shirt then rips it off to reveal his amazing sexy torso underneath, then bright white majestic wings bursting forth from him, easily spanning 12 feet as the feathers sparkle like diamonds amongst a see of dead. I am not even breathing as I stare up at him, in total awe of how beautiful he is and even from here I can feel his angelic power dripping from his skin. Lilith takes a step back, almost as though she is unsure of what to do when faced with the Archangel Michael in full form, even her soldiers are unsure what to do as everyone surges away, giving him space to feel his own power consume him fully again. Lilith glances down to Jake who still remains seated on the floor, shaking uncontrollably, his lips almost blue with the freezing cold that only he seems to be currently experiencing. He exhales and his breath is visible as the subzero temperature of it evaporates in the warm air around.

"Anyone else really cold?" Jake asks as he looks up to Mitch then tries to get off the ground, his breathing quivering as he does so he wraps his arms around himself to try to keep warm.

"I do not know how you are alive," Lilith says cautiously as she glances around all of her soldiers who are now surrounding us all in a sort of semi-circle. "But you will soon be dead once more." Instantly a few of the more certain of themselves soldiers rush forward, but before Mitch has the chance to turn around to fight, Jake instinctively holds up his hands in defence to try to protect himself from the oncoming onslaught and we all just watch, captivated as six of the approaching men all stop dead in their tracks. They try to move their feet but they are stuck to the ground, ice almost magically surrounding their boots then spreading swiftly up their legs as they start to realise what is happening as their flesh freezes and panic quickly consumes them. No one else moves as the affected men grab their chests as their hearts freeze then before they fully change in to meat popsicles, the ice shatters sending frozen pieces of demons scattering across the floor, leaving nothing more behind than the icy feet in the boots that remain attached to the stone. Jake looks down at his own hands as everyone stares at him, it does not take a genius to work out that what happened was caused by him, everyone saw it with their own eyes.

"Was that me?" Jake says to himself then looks around to Mitch who smiles wildly at him, then over to me, still slumped on the floor behind Lilith who stares daggers at him.

"Holy fuck balls," I laugh as I know he is no longer human, his powers released and the protection that the angels put on him when he was born has been removed. "Your father was not just a demon... he was a dragon demon." I thought they were long extinct, normal demons do not have the power I have just seen Jake use accidentally and it certainly did not come from any angel. He goes to speak again but before he has a chance the rest of Lilith soldiers take their opportunity to pounce. Jake hits the ground face first as a few men all dive on top of him to try to restrain him at the same time as Mitch starts fighting off more of them, but this time they do not seem overpowered, they are both strong and fully their true selves, they are both amazing.

"How did you do that?" I hear Lilith snarl right before I am dragged off the ground and slammed back against the wall once more. Both of her hands going straight for my neck and strangling me instantly, cutting off my breathing and making me struggle against her, but no matter how much I try I can not get her off me. I may have succeeded in reviving Mitch and Jake, and restoring their full abilities, but I still feel as weak as a mortal after using what little energy I did have to ensure my friends lived. Behind her I can just say make out the blurs of a grand fight, even the Generals are falling at the hands of an Archangel. Jake manages to break away from some of the soldiers then heads over towards where my father and Monroe still remain restrained with the chains. I can see he is unsure of himself but after a few seconds of talking with my father, Jake places his hands on the stone and freezes it, making the temperature of it plunge enough to just snap them, freeing my father from his shackles and then quickly repeating the process with Monroe. With the brimstone shackles gone there should be nothing to stop my father and Monroe fighting either, the one thing that could suppress their strength now gone. At least I know I am no longer alone, I have friends and actual family, no matter how much I probably still have issues with that part, they are here and as soon as my father reclaims his crown, this will all be over.

"There! Get it," one of the Generals shouts, Lilith glances over to see some of her men have located the crown and are now finally retrieving it for her.

"It is a shame," she says as she turns back to me and smirks, knowing that I can not breathe and the panic probably starting to show on my face. As much as I know what dying is like and I have done it a couple of times now in the past week, it is still unpleasant and I know if I do die again then there will not be another opportunity to stop her. My eyes go blurry as oxygen can no longer reach my brain and I lose any fight that I might have had left. "We could have been amazing together. We could have ruled the world, I suppose it is not entirely your fault, you did not have a mother to guide you and show you the truth. But now at least before the end, you will see exactly who your mother is, and that she everything you wished you could be." I lose focus completely, my limbs hang lifelessly and I feel myself drift towards that darkness once more... but then I hit the ground hard, my instincts take over making me gulp in the air as my lungs burn. I can hear shouting, Lilith now fighting with who I think is Monroe and she has found a new weapon, one of the black stone blades that I saw earlier, but everything is spinning and the scene before me is very blurry, although I do then see him thrown across the room and smash in to a wall so that part is not going splendidly, then I feel hands gently placed on my face, tilting my head up so I can see.

"Hey," Mitch says gently as his gorgeous face comes back in to focus and I can not help but smile at him. "Lets get you up," he takes hold of my arm and helps me stand, I am no use to anyone like this. "And nice hair by the way," he smiles then carefully runs his fingers through my hair before I notice an inch wide strip of pure white where my usual red would be, sort of like a mallen streak. "You met him didn't you? You were touched by the hand of God," I go to reply as I am still thinking about what happened to my hair, but just as I go to say something he places his hand around the back of my neck and pulls me in close, kissing me deeply with so much passion that I just stand, dazed and bewildered, ignoring the fighting going on around us and instead just feeling him completely. "You must really have liked me if you brought me back from the dead," he smirks then turns around and punches a soldier with such force that he is launched across the room and lands on a spear from one of the broken statues, impaling him atop the rubble.

"The crown," I remind Mitch as he looks back at me. "Get the crown to my father, we cannot let Lilith have it." He nods then runs off leaving me behind again, everyone else is fighting, and even though Lilith's men outnumber us 10 to 1, now that Mitch and Jake are fighting at full potential, and my father and Monroe are no longer hindered by their restraints, we are managing to hold the soldiers back. But I know Lilith is strong and she will not back down, not when she is so close to reaching her goal. Lilith notices Mitch run for the crown so she quickly goes to intercept him, you can see the power they both hold as they head towards it, and for a moment I do think Mitch will just push her out of the way, but she grabs his arm, leaving him slightly vulnerable before plunging the black stone dagger in to the muscle of his wing, instantly staining his beautiful white feathers red. He cries out in pain which only gives her a chance to strike again, this time stabbing through his shoulder and sending him to his knees. If she was using a normal human weapon, the damage would be minimal, but I have never seen brimstone used in this way before, I did not realise the full properties that it possessed until today.

I don't even think, I just run, hopping over bodies and dodging attacks to enable me to reach Mitch and attempt to offer some form of help before the next strike that he receives is directly through his heart. Lilith pulls the blade out of his shoulder, standing over him she raises her arm, and I use every ounce of strength I have to spear her, my shoulder hitting her as hard as I can in her side and sending us both to the ground. Not because I over powered her, but because she just was not expecting the blow which is quite evident by the fact that she gets straight back to her feet and glares at me. I clutch my shoulder and roll over, I took the brunt of that hit as it feels like I drove my shoulder in to a brick wall then she goes to reach down to grab me just as Jake runs towards her but he doesn't even get close as she ducks down to avoid him, grabs his legs and catapults him over the top of her head, face first back to the ground. Hopefully he won't be too injured by that, maybe quite dazed but still in one piece now that he is no longer human.

Before Lilith has a chance to get to me once more, I am dragged back off the floor by one of the soldiers fighting for her, then back handed hard across the face, sending me back to the ground. Blood fills my mouth and I try to spit it out just as the boot of the soldier hits me directly in the ribs, forcing me to hunch up and cry out in pain. Hands grab at me, pushing me on to my back then a knee is placed in the centre of my chest to hold me down. I try with all my might to get free, but being mortal makes me weak compared to any kind of demon, I can not fight at all. The soldier is heavy and already covered in blood that is not his own, dressed in grey armour that has probably seen many wars over the years, and now only has one goal, to do anything to protect his future Queen and ensuring she takes the throne. He raises his arm, weapon in hand ready to kill me but I just watch as the flash of a bright blue blade cuts straight through his outstretched arm, cutting through the bone and splattering black blood everywhere, then the body of my father dives in to him, getting him off me before the soldier is detained and has his neck snapped. I just spend a moment looking at my father as he releases his grip of the soldier's head and his body falls to the ground, then Monroe gives me a cheeky wink as he steps over me, holding his Scythe and acting like this is just a normal day at the office for him.

They don't wait around to help me up, instead continuing to fight other soldiers around us, although I am very grateful for the help. I glance around and see that Mitch has managed to grab the crown, I catch his eye and he smiles at me but he is knocked to the ground as he is tackled again by two soldiers, the crown slips from his fingers and skids across the stone, stopping at a clearing in the middle of he carnage. My father and Monroe both see it at the same time Lilith does and all three of them run towards it, Lilith moves like a bull, forcing through anyone that is in her way, even her own men stand no chance against her as she sends one of them pounding in to a wall, smashing his jaw against the brick as she goes. I feel completely useless against anyone as I try to get up off the ground and contemplate finding cover instead of fighting, I could not even hold my own against one of the weakest soldiers, never mind facing the rest of them, and there is still a lot of them to fight.

My ribs are aching as I stumble my way away from the bulk of the fighting, trying my best to not be noticed too much as I know the men who fight for Lilith will earn great pride for killing any of us right now. Monroe makes easy work at ensuring a path through some of the men is achieved, his weapon a perfect extension of his soul, effortlessly flowing through the air and hitting its target each and every time. I have not seen him fight like this in such a long time, when he truly had something to fight for, something he actually believed in. Some of the soldiers try to get out of the way of the blade, which pushes Lilith back, she stumbles slightly and trips over a couple of the bodies which sends her on her arse to the floor. As the rest of the men are pushed back, my father manages to get to the crown, he carefully picks it up of the ground and almost everything in the room falls silent again, as though a blanket of pure unbridled power can be felt flowing from him. Lilith forces herself back to her feet as Mitch and Jake head over to stand by the side of the room near me, the soldiers no longer interested in anyone but my father.

"All of this, so much death, just for this piece of metal," my father says calmly as he holds it.

"Lucifer, give me my crown!" Lilith shouts as he looks down at the twisted metal in his hand, her soldiers slowly surrounding them both, poised to strike but cautious because one wrong move will mean their Mistress will not get what she wants.

"Was all of this worth it for you?" he asks her and she takes a deep breath, trying to remain composed. "You watched our daughter die, you have brought the legions Generals to their deaths, you have destroyed parts of the human world and all with full disregard for the ramifications of your actions."

"The slaughter of millions would be worth it for me to get what is rightfully mine," she spits back.

"I can not let you take control, the Veil is vital in keeping everything in order, keeping the souls that I control in their place," he explains but she just laughs at his words.

"I don't give a shit what you or anyone else thinks," Lilith scoffs. "Or even how much utter bullshit you spout to make yourself look good. I categorically know that you wearing that crown right now will not undo the falling of the Veil and you will not stop the rising in the human world now that it has begun. All you will accomplish is being in charge when Hell takes over Earth, so either way, I still win because my soldiers will not rest till every single human is dead." Everyone is so tense as they wait to see what happens next, I hate to admit it but she is right, my father wearing his crown will not create a new ruler, it will not release the change so the Veil will still be destroyed. All of this was for nothing, even if we did hope for a miracle.

"You are wrong about one thing, Lilith," he says casually then smiles at her, ignoring the many blades pointing at him. "I will not choose what happens next, you are wrong because this crown does not belong to me, it has not been mine for a very long time,

so you are shit out of luck with everything you think." She stares at him, trying to understand what he is saying. "Michael?" he says loudly getting Mitch's attention and everyone, including me, turns to look at him, even the soldiers, wondering what the Archangel Michael has to do with Lucifer's words and with his crown. "Would you do the honers?" Instantly Mitch nods at my fathers request then smiles before he throws the crown through the air, away from Lilith, over the heads of the surrounding goons and directly towards us.

Chapter Nineteen

"NO!" Lilith screams then immediately darts towards us, forcing her way through the make shift barrier of men as Mitch catches the crown. Instantly everyone in the room surges forward and I suddenly feel really vulnerable standing here, almost a normal human, as all the soldiers with weapons come straight for us.

"Long live the Queen!" Mitch smirks at Lilith then before I even know what is happening, he places the crown on my head, the metal warm across my forehead and fitting perfectly, but I just freeze.

"What are you doing?" I ask up at him bewildered then he smiles more.

"Giving you an upgrade," Mitch says gently. I see Lilith hurtling towards me out of the corner of my eye, she looks mad as fuck and I brace myself for the impact of her running at me followed by the wave of men behind when I suddenly feel like I can not breathe and something unseen bursts from me, everyone close including Lilith and Mitch are thrown backwards through the air. I don't see them land as my vision is plunged in to darkness, I feel the entire castle shake around me then the burning heat from flames against my skin.

Flashes of light move quickly before my eyes as my body starts to feel weightless, as though I am lifted off the ground and now floating in a swirling vortex of Hell fire. I can just make out my own hands in front of my face, the flames surrounding me, blocking out all sources of light but even though the air is dry and thick, I have never felt safer. The flicker of tiny flames dance across my palms and I watch them them spread, moving up my arms and flowing across my chest, they tickle and make me smile, knowing that my flesh will not be burned as the fabric of my clothing is slowly singed away making way for an outfit that fits the crown. New majestic material forms in the flames, I am captivated as it forges an ornate armoured bodice and elaborate breast plate of black and gold, I watch it as on my left shoulder the formation of a gold pauldron with skulls carved in to the precious metal forms that sits atop part of a swooping black cape that runs from my left shoulder to my right hip and descends in to a billowing half skirt that is open at the front to reveal the black leather trousers underneath. My boots have been covered in greaves that perfectly fit my shins, the elaborate filigree swirling around my calves and creating the most beautiful armour I have ever laid my eyes on.

Another burst of energy hits me, making my breath catch as I feel such a rush of adrenaline, the most insane amount of power is flowing through my veins, consuming me and transforming me in to something I never dreamed possible. My father, no matter how pissed off I was with him, was always my true King of Hell. It never crossed my mind that anyone but him would sit in his throne, but now there is no turning back, the crown is now mine and with it comes the power, I will finally stop my mother once and for all.

Eventually the flames surrounding me start to subside and I am lowered back to the ground, as my feet touch the stone below I am able to see the room again, a massive empty circle around me where the Hell fire incinerated every single thing it touched, then a lot of unsure faces. Lilith is on the ground, still sat in the middle of some of the dead from where she fell when she was thrown away from me. There are still soldiers all surrounding my father to one side, not as many as before but still at last 20 or so who have survived this long against my fathers forces. Behind me I can feel Mitch, Jake and Monroe, their energy strong as I don't even have to look around to see them all watching me. I am no longer covered in blood, my hair falls perfectly around my shoulders as I stand wearing the crown proudly and embrace the look of a Queen. The entire room is silent, no one wanting to make the first move or say anything as a new ruler of Hell has never been seen before. Slowly Lilith gets to her feet, her once pristine white dress now covered in dirt and black blood off the fighting around her, her hair dishevelled and her face is consumed with anger and what I think to be a slight hint of fear.

"That crown belongs to me," she says as she desperately tries to hold back her emotions, I can tell she is furious that I am now wearing the crown, like a petulant child who throws a fit when they do not get their own way. But unlike her, right now I feel extremely calm. "How dare you think that you can do this to me? I have worked my whole life to get to this moment and you steal my lime light."

"I'm sorry," I say to her then smile slightly. "But I do not recall me stealing anything, I can not steal something that does not belong to you."

"It is mine!" she snaps back as she struggles to breathe through shear frustration. "I deserve it, I..."

"You don't deserve anything," I interrupt her and in doing so just add fuel to her anger. "You are unworthy to wear the crown." She stares at me for a moment, debating what to say next until she breaks and charges at me, heading straight for me. She lunges forward, trying to snatch the crown from my head but I grab her wrist and twist it, forcing her to her knees as she tries to alleviate the pressure I am putting on her bones. After a moment of desperately pushing back against my strength she cries out in pain and I feel her wrist snap beneath my grip, then I let her go, thinking that she will back down, but instead she gets straight back to her feet and slaps me hard across the face with her other hand. The force would usually have rocked even the toughest of opponents, it stings like a bitch and I will probably have a hand mark across my cheek but I stand firm before slowly reaching up to rub the burning skin.

"It is so cute that you still think you have a chance to win against me," I say calmly and hold her gaze as she now stands cradling her wrist, it will probably heal soon but I am sure she will take it as more than a warning about how powerful I am compared to her now. I take a step towards her and she jumps back away from me, but she trips over one of the many dead bodies, sending her to the ground where she scrambles to move away to create distance between us. She can say anything she wants, fight back with all the strength she has, but in her eyes I see the fear, I see the true vulnerability that she hides from the world.

"Alexis, my daughter," Lilith says cautiously as she forces herself back to her feet then steps over a few bodies, being careful not to fall again and slowly makes her way back away from me more till she approaches the bottom of the steps that lead up to the throne. I don't know if this is her way of trying to block me from taking my seat or if she has other plans to work through before she gives in. "There is still time for you to stand beside me. We could be amazing together," as she speaks her soldiers move to protect her, creating a wall of bodies and blades between me and her, whilst she now climbs up a few steps to make sure she can still see me in case I make any sudden moves, but I am not in any hurry to attack. "Just think about it, haven't you always wanted more from life, hated the men who tried to hold you down... look at what your own father did to you. He lied to you for centuries, made you feel weak and worthless, he told you your mother was dead and he never loved you." She climbs a few more steps, creating more distance between us but making sure she never turns her back on me. "I love you, Alexis, my daughter. I loved you from the moment you were born, and I mourned you, I thought about you every single day... all of this, everything I have done was all for you, he drove me to this, he made me do all of this because I thought I had lost you." The entire room is deadly silent as I step forward and approach the soldiers, they keep glancing at each other, clearly unsure of what they should do when faced with a new ruler of Hell but they do not back down, standing firm for their Mistress.

"I always thought that my father was the worst person that ever existed," I say casually as I look up at her. "That he did not know the meaning of love and that I was outcast because he was cruel and heartless. But then I met you, and I realised that my father did the right thing in protecting me from the truth. Because if I had been allowed to grow up by your side, I would have ended up being a narcissistic bitch just like you."

"You may now think you are a Queen, but you still are not powerful enough to stop me," she snaps back and I just smile at her. "I still have control of the legions, I have thousands of men who bow to me and who have denounced Lucifer as their ruler. You cannot control them, even if the Veil is re-established, the soldiers will keep pushing forward and the humans will keep being killed, all in my name." At least she is right about that, her soldiers will keep fighting so there is only one thing to do. Glancing at the men in front of me, I can see they are all staring at me, watching my every move, waiting to see what I am going to do or if I try to attack them, but I know I don't have to fight, I just need to be who I was born to be. Looking along the line I find the biggest brute that stands here and point towards him.

"You there," I say to him confidently and he almost snarls at the fact I dared to single him out. He is easily bigger built than Mitch, possibly a General and looking at the line up of men right now, he could most likely over power any of the soldiers. "Face me," I tell him and he smiles before stepping out of the line, he grips his large sword tightly as he approaches and everyone else watches him.

"Kill her if you must," Lilith orders him from the steps but I focus on the man in front of me rather than her right now. He pauses a few feet in front of me and smirks before looking me up and down.

"It is hardly a fair fight, when you do not hold a blade," he says to me in a gruff voice.

"Tell me, who do you serve? Who is your true ruler?" I ask him and he laughs at me as though I told a joke before glancing at my mother then back to me.

"I serve Lilith, the true ruler, not a pathetic powerless false Morningstar," he spits at me and I smile. Slowly he watches me step forward then I gently place my hand in the centre of his chest, he is not human, but I can feel his essence, his soul still calling to me.

"Any who oppose the crown, will die," I say very gently and smile. He goes to laugh at my words but his face changes almost immediately as he drops his sword then grabs his chest as I use my inner power to reap his soul, which I know will kill him in the process as it is absorbed in to me and I take all of his life force. Within seconds his eyes go black and he drops dead at my feet. There are audible gasps from the soldiers before I turn back to face Lilith and breath deeply. "All of you men who follow Lilith, hear me," I say loudly then feel my power deep inside. I have used this many times before on humans, but now I am the Queen of Hell, I should be unstoppable. "All of you... Kneel!" I order them, pushing hard with my persuasion, more than I ever thought I could, and instantly every single one of Lilith's men take a knee in front of me and lower their weapons. "You were foolish to turn your back on the Morningstar bloodline, you killed and murdered in a false rulers name, and you committed treason against the crown." No one says a word, just listening to the new Queen speak. "I am not weak, I am not pathetic and I do not need a weapon to slaughter you all. That is clear by what you have just witnessed. You should all fear the crown, as you have been led astray by a psychopath... You are all very lucky that I am nothing like my mother, you should all be killed for what you have all done, but you are not to blame, you fought for glory and instead found defeat," even though they all kneel before me I can feel how scared for their lives they are, no matter how strong they are or how well they fight, they know at the moment that they can not move against my orders and I could kill them without any effort. "Leave here, tell anyone you meet that Lilith is outcast and no longer has any strength in Hell. Tell them that the true ruler is who you serve, and if we ever see your face in this castle again, make sure you know who you bow to, that the Morningstar bloodline is the true power down here," the men all seem uncertain of my words, wondering if they do move if they will be killed, so I encourage them more. "Leave now, or die." The men all stand and quickly leave the throne room as one, so I wait patiently until they are gone before looking back up to my mother who is hovering on the steps alone with no one left to support her.

"Wait," she says quickly as I start to climb the stairs and inch closer to her which makes her try to get further away until she reaches the top, standing in front of the throne with nowhere left to go. "Alexis don't do this, think about what you are doing," she says as her calm exterior slips away and I see actual real fear from her. "We can talk, properly, as a family, come to some arrangement where we all get what we want... Lucifer tell her, tell her that I am her mother and should be respected... Lucifer?" She pleads with him as I can feel him behind me, watching me from the bottom of the steps and waiting to see what I do.

"You lost any sort of respect Lilith, when you murdered her siblings and vowed to kill anyone she loved," he replies with a hint of a smile in his voice. "I may have kept my distance from her, I may have lied to protect her, but I never betrayed her trust or hurt her that deeply in any way." Lilith shakes her head as though not wanting to accept what he is saying to her then looks back at me as I reach the top step and stand in front of her, only a meter away, so close I can see her shake under my gaze as we both know that the power that now lies inside me as I wear the crown is unparalleled.

"No matter how strong you are," she says directly to me. "You will never be rid of me, you can not kill me, my flesh will not bleed like yours, you cannot wound me, I am immortal, I cannot be cast aside like some worthless human or slay me as those demons, I am the first woman created, I was touched by the hand of God himself and I am more powerful than any living being."

"But at one point in your extremely lengthy life you were once human," I reply gently. "It may have been a very long time ago, but at one point you were the very thing you now despise. And do you know what is special about humans? About the demons or beasts that came from a human, even if they spent centuries in Hell... Every single one of them, started as that glint of energy and was given a soul, an individual source of life which was unique."

"A soul?" she laughs slightly. "After all that build up, you go back to spouting crap about being a reaper? That stupid little party trick you did to my General will not work on me. There is nothing left in me that is human, I am the furthest thing you could possibly get and any trace of a soul that I may have had, was lost long before you were even born." She watches me nervously as I step closer, so close I can smell the perfume that lingers on her skin, the scent of blood from both her soldiers and my fathers men stain her clothing, and her essence is so strong that it is intoxicating. At one point in my life, she would have been someone I aspired to be, but then I entered the human world and realised what true life looked like. She may be the most powerful person I have ever faced, but right now, her words are all she has left.

"Something else that you are very mistaken about, Mother," I smile as I stare deep in to her eyes. For years I dreamed of meeting the woman that gave birth to me, the one who gave me life, but now standing in front of her I am glad that I never met her when I was a child, as I would have been just like her, and I would have hated myself, "You may not accept it, but you do have a soul, one that is very deep and hidden, but it is there. The worst souls are tortured for all of eternity in the fiery depths, but yours is blacker than any I have seen before you and I have seen more than my fair share. Someone like you would deserve to rot in Hell for what you have done to mankind."

"Please, Alexis," she says as her voice shakes. "You are my daughter."

"No," I shake my head, I step forward then gently run my fingertips across her cheek and down the side of her neck. Her skin is as smooth as marble and warm to the touch. "I am not your daughter... I am your worst fucking nightmare." Before she has a chance to reply I plunge my fist deep in to her chest, I have heard many stories about my father doing this to retrieve a stubborn soul in the past, but never seen it with my own eyes, and certainly never felt the power or had the ability to be able to do it for myself. It feels strange, not blood and bone as you would feel normally when your hand is inside another person, but more like a void filled with energy. Purely magical in origin as I am pulled towards what little soul she has left, imagining what it might look like as it forms in to solid matter and I hold it in my fist. It vibrates, sending little darts of electric up my arm, I have reaped many souls over the years from humans, but never forcefully taken one like this. Lilith gasps for breath as I pull her soul out of her chest, leaving no signs behind that I physically harmed her, but she falls to her knees in pain, a void now left behind that is empty, tears streaming from her eyes as she looks up at me, still defiant in her actions as though she still has a deluded hope that she will win.

"What are you going to do?" she asks me with anger. "Lock me away for all eternity, put my soul in a cage and leave me to rot? You may control my actions if you control my soul, but you can not change what is in my head, the fight I have in my heart and the hatred I have for all life will never disappear." I hold her soul up to look at it, it is like a ball of black energy, quietly crackling as it rests in my palm. The thing that makes life great and can so easily be blackened with evil. "No matter what you do to me or where you put me, there will still be men who follow me, people who want to destroy the mortal world and wish to see humans gone. It doesn't matter if it takes centuries, I will never stop fighting, I will have my revenge." Smiling gently, I look back down at her and gaze in to her eyes as she remains on her knees.

"Life is a gift," I say to her. "It was given to you, and should have been cherished, you should have fought to protect it, but instead you were so overcome with rage that you did not see how lucky you were." Her eyes are indeed like mine, she was right about that, and I am thankful that I did have a chance to finally know my mother, no matter how much of a monster she was. "And life is about balance. Where there is good, there is evil. Where there is right, there is wrong... and where there is life... there is death," I pause briefly to take a deep breath, then give her one last smile. "Goodbye Mother, I would say rest in peace, but that requires a clean soul to accomplish it, however don't worry, you won't be having a tormented stay in Hell either," she looks confused for a moment until her eyes go wide and she finally realises what I mean.

"No, Alexis please," she begs. "You can't do this, you can't..." her words become strangled as I squeeze the black orb that rests in my hand, crushing her soul until it solidifies, turning to stone then cracks before disintegrating in to black sand which freely falls from my hand and on to the ground below, then Lilith collapses in a heap at my feet. I spend a moment to myself, looking down at her lifeless body, knowing that she is now lost to the void, her soul no longer existing and now bringing hope that humanity may have a chance to survive another day. Although there is sadness in my heart, no matter how much of a monster she was and all the despicable things she has done, she was still my mother, and I will never forget who she was.

"Alexis?" my father says quietly from behind me so I turn around and look towards him. Jake, Mitch and Monroe all wait at the bottom of the steps, my father beside them, as I stand in front of the throne and in front of my mothers dead body. "Are you alright?" he asks and I nod, even though inside I feel strange. Lilith was still my mother, at one point she cared for me, but I ultimately did what I had to do, even though it does feel like I killed a small part of myself in the process.

"How do I replace the Veil?" I ask him as I know that is now my only priority. "It needs to be safe." My father nods and smiles in reply.

"Sit on the throne," he says to me. "Take your place as the ruler of Hell, become our Queen officially and your hearts desire will protect the Veil and close the Hell mouth." Glancing back around to the throne, I am filled with so much anxiety, I never wanted to rule anyone or have the responsibilities that comes with being in charge of Hell. There are so many souls that need organising, demons that need to be kept in line, what if there is another uprising, what if next time I can not hold them back... "Alexis? It is OK, sit," he encourages me and I just nod then step forward, take a deep breath and turn to sit. I know I have already sat here to mock Lilith earlier, but this time it really means something. As I finally take my seat I try to be strong, focusing on what good can now come of me being here, the Veil will be stronger than ever, the shroud between this world and the mortal world will be in tact and now Lilith is gone, her soldiers have no orders to follow. It is strange to think that the daughter of Lucifer wants nothing more than peace on Earth, but that is what we need, it is what everyone needs so that life can flourish. After a moment of sitting, I look down to the faces watching me, all waiting to see what happens.

"Erm... is that it?" I ask and my father smiles.

"What did you expect?" he asks me as I stand back up again then head down the steps, and back towards my friends.

"I don't know," I laugh slightly then stand a little awkward, I am not sure what to do now.

"Well, I guess someone has to speak first," Jake says in the silence. "Thank you. I have no idea what I can do, where I fully come from or even if I still have a life in the human world, but you helped me be the real me. Even if I am freezing cold," he laughs and I can not help but smile more.

"You will get used to it, once you understand your powers you should be able to control it," I advise. "And if you are who I think you are, a dragon demon and angel being your parents, then I suppose you might have the same ability of flight as Mitch."

"Wings?" Jake says excitedly. "I get mother fucking wings?"

"That's all the world needs," Monroe jokes. "Another powerful arsehole with wings." Monroe and Jake make me smile and distract me slightly from the uncomfortable stares of Mitch as he watches me, standing next to my father which in itself must be awkward for those two, the history they share goes back centuries.

"So... Michael," I hear my father say quietly thinking no one else can hear as Jake and Monroe talk amongst themselves.

"Lucifer," he replies to acknowledge him.

"It has been a while," my father mutters awkwardly.

"Indeed it has," Mitch replies, looking around the room so that he doesn't show how uncomfortable he is. "Last time we faced each other was on the battlefield."

"Yes, it was," my father nods slowly. "No hard feelings about that, right?"

"Well, you did form an army of angles to stage an uprising, try to overthrow God and take control of Heaven," Mitch reminds him. "Many lives were lost, good angels that were killed in the battle, some of those were our friends."

"Hmmm," he ponders a reply and for a moment I am certain that they are going to snap and try to kill each other. "Yes that was all very unfortunate... So, you are sleeping with my daughter? I am not sure I fully agree with her taste in men, the new Queen of Hell can do so much better than an archangel. And at least wear a shirt or something, no one wants to see that." They both smirk at the teasing comments but what he just said makes me step in.

"About that," I say loudly and they both look at me. "The whole me being the Queen of Hell," I carefully remove the crown and look at it in my hand. "I don't want it, it is too much responsibility and power for me, and there is no Hell without Lucifer Morningstar." I hold the crown out towards my father and he nods in understanding before taking it from my hand. "And I am still retired, I don't want to be a reaper or the Veils Guardian, I don't want to rule the underworld or fight with the Legions, I just want to go home and enjoy the gift of life."

It has been a couple of weeks since I walked away from my fathers castle again, this time however everything is different. I feel like I now have a family connection, granted it is still quite rocky and now that everyone in Hell knows that the reaper known as Rosa Moon is really Alexis Morningstar and the daughter of Lucifer and the late Lilith, keeping a low profile down there was not a possibility, so I had to leave for my own sanity.

Monroe earned my fathers trust and seen as though he was in need of a new General to help rebuild his armies, Monroe accepted a new position by my fathers side. Some day he may earn the title of the new Grand Duke of Hell. His combat skills proved to be legendary and my father appreciated the loyalty. At least it should keep him out of trouble for a while, and give him plenty of opportunity to continue doing what he loves best... killing people.

Mitch left shortly after the fight with Lilith, he went back to where he belonged and rallied the angels of Heaven to help sort things out on Earth. Although the destruction and deaths caused by the undead were devastating, the humans do not remember what truly happened. When the Veil returned so did the blissful ignorance, those innocent humans are protected from all of the evil things that still want to haunt them, only now most are in hiding, at least for a little while or until they find a new psychopath to follow.

I returned home, back to my little coffee shop and my normal life as Rosa Moon. The humans do not know who I really am and they do not know how close they came to the end of days, which is nice. It took a couple of days to redo the shop, get rid of all the signs of demons being killed in here and the rest of the community has been rebuilding the places that were destroyed when the Veil fell and mourning the loss that incurred. The angels have been working hard behind the scenes, creating little miracles to make sure life returns to normal as fast as possible. Thankfully not everything was overrun, the undead did not get far and the cracks of earth that occurred under the city itself were concentrated around the Hell mouth, mostly office buildings that were empty due to the holidays and all of which can be replaced.

Then there is Jake. He didn't know where he belonged now that he was no longer mortal. He had no home in Heaven or Hell, so he also came back to Earth. I have been keeping an eye on him from a distance, and helping him hide who he now is, a little persuasion goes a long way when the humans believe everything I say. He was invited back to his Detective position, his Captain was pushed multiple times until I got him eating out of Jakes hand. And now Jake is a national hero.

The humans labelled Christmas as a natural disaster. An earthquake epicentre happened under the city, which blew out gas lines, causing massive explosions and loss of life. It is known that Jakes efforts in the rescue attempts afterwards, saved so many people and for that it has earned him a medal of valour from the police Chef commissioner. One that he is collecting today, and I could not be prouder to have been a part of his journey. As I watch Jake take to the small stage outside of city hall, standing right at the back of the large crowd who have gathered to show their appreciation for his efforts, I am reminded just how lucky I am in this world. I have friends who I care about, I have a business that I enjoy and I have a life here that I would not swap for the world. All these humans might not know what really happened but I do, and I feel good knowing that I was able to help them all.

"So how come the kid gets all the glory?" I smile as I hear the voice speak next to me and look to the side to see Mitch, standing casually with his hands in his pockets, watching Jake, dressed in a pair tight black jeans and leather biker jacket, and trying to hide any sort of emotion.

"He deserves it," I reply and look back towards the stage. "He will do good things in this world, he is a good person and his soul shines... Plus I don't think any of us willingly would have went in to all that just for the credit."

"The hidden heroes are always forgotten from the stories," he smiles. "The humans don't know we even exist in their world, but one good thing did come from all of this."

"Really? And what is this good thing," I ask and see him smile.

"How about I show you," he smirks. "I recall I promised you a drink, and I know this really cute place that I think you will like, lots of naked women there dancing around on poles and they serve tequila on tap for someone like you, Rosa Moon." Turning properly to look at him, I can not help but smile, this man makes my heart happy.

"Are you asking me out on a date, Archangel Michael?" I tease him.

"What if I am, former brief Queen of Hell, Alexis Morningstar?" He looks at me fully, his eyes captivating as I nibble my bottom lip slightly thinking how much I missed his touch over the past few weeks.

"Hmmm, I am not sure if a demon and an angel should be seen together, just imagine what people will think," I shrug playfully before he steps forward, his hands wrapping around my back and pulling me in close to him. My palms rest on his arms, all strong and safe, pressed up against this chest I just look up at him and smile.

"I don't really care what people think, now that I've found you, I am never letting you go," he says gently then leans down to kiss me, that familiar and intoxicating sweetness from his lips makes me relax instantly. Who knows what might happen, an angel and a demon is not a new thing, Jake is proof of that.

In this world, the world full of magic and mystery, light and dark, all those secrets and truths, the certainty of life and death, and the continuing war between sin and purity... an angel and a demon finding love is not necessarily a bad thing, it is just different, opposites do attract, and after all, life in the human world is all about balance.

THE END